VANILLA

2

L. O. RED

Passenger Pigeon Publishing

VANILLA

Contents

I

VANILLA

It had been thirteen hours and approximately forty-seven minutes since Leroy and I had fallen into the pool and done a terrible job of recalling the need for oxygen even above water. I blame the idiot, as I always do, who appeared to have eliminated breathing from his list of necessities in life and replaced it with any word representative of 'lip-locking'. The moment resembled some sort of break in his religious fasting, in which Leroy had experienced a life-long hunger and starved himself to the ends of the earth until the, um... well, the thing.

Naturally, I'd never had the time or proper mind to be fantasizing about any sort of first kiss—let alone my own—and still, should some fortuneteller have decided to warn me of something that long or intense of a festival, I would have politely dubbed them insane.

Either way, I had been mildly disappointed.

Leroy's hand-bound recipe book had fallen to the side of the pool during the entire fiasco; back cover thoroughly soaked beyond recognition but fortunately sacrificing itself for the rest of the inner content. Thank goodness I'd come up in time to save the rest of it and mind you, that was after I'd experienced nearly five full minutes of a certain someone pulling me back into his arms for yet another one of his attacks every time I tried to reach for the side of the pool.

"So you guys kissed fourteen times in total," Si Yin was back to exaggerating the very next day only because I hadn't the sanity to keep this inside and stay calm like Leroy obviously could. He'd acted so normal afterwards that I was pretty sure no one else could tell what we'd been doing moments before while they were away. Si Yin, who'd spent so much time with myself, was the only one who noticed my flushed cheeks.

"That is not—! There was no calculation of... I couldn't possibly count the number of times he'd, well I... goodness, I can't think." I stared down at the textbook on my desk and registered the buzzing chatter of our classmates before homeroom. "You don't think romance could have multiple side effects on one's mindfulness?"

Si Yin opted for a reassuring pat on my shoulder. "I'm pretty sure it does. Are you feeling stupid already?"

"More by the minute, yes."

"That's the way," she slapped this right across my back and I positively froze. "Is this a secret, by the way? I'm so bad at keeping secrets but I'll try. I'm having lunch with Nabila and Rosi so this is going to be harder than that product knowledge test by Marseille. Do you want to come and keep me in check?"

I told her that it wasn't all that big of a deal but inside, I was practically quaking. "That is quite alright. You have my complete trust and faith. Also, I've made arrangements for lunch with Leroy. Well, we never really established if it was public in any manner but that's probably because we never got to establish if it was a thing at all. Him and I are dating, a-and... and, um... i-it doesn't... there isn't a... u-um... dear god there it is again. Contagious stupidity!"

My best friend was quick to point out the clear tendencies I'd seemed to have developed all of a sudden: nerves absolutely fried whenever it came to speaking about Leroy and our current relationship. Not a single moment of clarity was involved in a conversation with his name in it.

"Back to your seats." Chef Palmer made her entrance seconds after the bell, meeting my gaze briefly as she crossed the room towards the instructor's desk. "I've got an announcement to make."

The shuffling of feet and dragging of chairs across the floor had begun pretty much before Chef Palmer's words and Si Yin, who'd only just gotten herself comfortable on the edge of my desk, was obliged to return to her seat. Granted, I hadn't the best gut feeling about this sudden 'announcement' that likely involved my sorry self, deduced from the look of reluctant expectation Palmer had given me as she made her way to the front of the class and cleared her throat.

"Thanksgiving is a couple of weeks away and we all know that the school's yearly food market festival's always held the day before. Registration has started and in order to submit our class's participation form, I have chosen a temporary class representative for the overseeing of this event." Her gaze swept the class before meeting my own. "White. Come up."

The consensus was a trepid silence, or so someone as socially inept as myself could tell without looking around to know that all heads were turned and all eyes, fixed upon the epitome of plain and boring. In an attempt to remain as inconspicuous as possible, I'd stood carefully and as quietly as possible before gingerly making my way up front.

Si Yin was clapping; that much, I could register. Other background noises included a slow, unimpressed echoing of palms coming together and an occasional, non-committal snort.

"For the next couple of weeks, you guys will be reporting to White, especially anything event-related. After we decide on the theme of our booth, preferably by today, we'll move on to assigning roles for finance and logistics." Chef Palmer handed me a piece of chalk and a clipboard with a to-do list attached to it, gesturing to the blackboard behind me. "I'll let you lead the discussion."

Fed to the wolves right off the bat! I'd thought nearly at once, swallowing upon the observation of cold, hard expressions coming primarily from the back of the class. They appeared openly offended and were the perfect description of everything my godfather's husband encompassed whenever they were apart from one another. Others remained visibly neutral or indifferent to Chef Palmer's announcement, as though it was really none of their business and not worth that bit of their attention.

I gave the list a quick scan. "So um, I would like to think we're all familiar with what a food market is, so I'll skip the general description of that and move on to the possible ideas we can, um, hopefully come up with by the end of class..." Silence never did bode very well for class presentations. It reminded me of the time I was passionately breaking down the science of mushroom-caramelizing in front of thirty-odd seniors five years older than myself.

No one was listening.

"According to the suggestions by the school, street food stalls are a safe and popular pick. They get relatively easy approval by sponsors as long as it is sufficiently endorsed by one of the non-profit organizations on the list and, judging by the list here, I'd say we'd have a good time choosing Southeast Asian cuisine since most of the recently-sourced organizations support cultural promotion of countries in that area.

"That aside, previous committees have approved of themed cafés and pop-up restaurants, depending on feasibility, budget, and quality of the proposed idea. Artisanal products like jams, self-brewed beer or any form of alcohol are subject to strict policies.

"So, um," I looked up hopefully, scanning the class for raised hands or lightbulb faces. "Would someone like to start off with a suggestion...?"

The long pause that ensued was one that I had no doubt expected to receive. In fact, I had been bracing myself for a moment like this and preparing several suggestions to start the ball rolling. "Alright then, I suppose I could—oh. Si Yin?"

Her hand was raised. "I vote butler café," she said at once and those around her laughed good-naturedly. Ariq was one of them. Several at the back were rolling their eyes.

I scratched this down as our first option on the blackboard before turning back to the class. Thankfully, several hands were up.

"Butler *and* maid café." "Halloween café. Haunted mansion theme." "Riverdale!" "Ew, Riverdale?" "Korean cuisine café where we can blast K-pop all day." "That Japanese lazy egg character. We can make it an egg café or something." "That would have copyright issues."

Naturally, I was doing my best to pen every suggestion down and keep up with wave after wave of café ideas whilst trying to evaluate the feasibility of every single one of them in my head. Oddly enough, everyone seemed invested in the idea of setting up a themed café. As soon as we hit the mark of twenty suggestions, all in hopes of some kind of café, I decided to offer my opinion on this.

On hindsight, this probably wasn't the best idea.

"Um," I'd raised my hand in front of the class. "If I may... there have been rumors about the class next door, 1A, doing a café as well. There might be unnecessary competition, if we'd like to be avoiding that. Our ideas may overlap, and we may be accused of copying someone else's original work... just, um, a word of caution."

"Oh yeah isn't Violet in 1A?" At the back, Li was frowning and turning to the one beside him, Meyers, with a laugh. "We'll just lose if we go up against them, especially if she's representing their class while we're stuck with him."

Oh. The great, fearful pause that trembled in the air had seized the rest of my nerves for a moment of dawning and the light, soft and dusty, had crept inside to settle there. I hadn't anticipated such words. Although now, they seemed almost humiliatingly obvious.

There had been no name to the 'him' in her sentence, or any sure tone of hostility or purpose in such a claim but it was precisely such a nature that revealed the truth of her feelings and perhaps a reflection of what several others in class were thinking as well. Everyone was oddly silent.

"Why's he leading the discussion in the first place?" Li directed this to Chef Palmer, who'd looked up from her laptop at the silence. "It's boring and we're literally not getting anywhere with this."

"What! Hello, we have twenty ideas up on the board can't you see?" Si Yin turned around to say and if I'd felt like sinking into the ground earlier on, this would have been my cue to retreat further into myself and disappear.

Chef Palmer rose form her seat and slammed her fist against the blackboard, jolting the class into paying her their full attention.

"Is it so hard to keep your mouths shut for ten minutes?" She narrowed in on Li, Meyers, Si Yin and the girl seated behind her. "Are you eight-year-olds in high school or is this actually kindergarten, huh? Why can't any of you be cooperative for once and listen to your representative when he has something to say because I'm not going to repeat this again: you, report, to him."

Our class instructor returned to her laptop screen after giving the entire class a sweeping glare, daring someone to speak up against her. It was then—when she was distracted by movement and going back to work that someone seated at the front row all the way on the other end of the class had whispered the words I'd oddly come to fear. I think it was elementary school when I first heard of the term.

"Teacher's pet."

LEROY

It was homeroom after lunch and I'd been watching *'Braised Chicken Rum Raisin is typing...'* for the past ten minutes. He ended up settling on "Good afternoon everyone." It was hard not to laugh.

He mentioned something about obtaining the report of Chen's cross-year team only after everyone sent him question marks. Then I suggested we analyze that for a bit after school. They agreed on Cayenne Lodge at six, since most of us had club activities till then.

It was by complete coincidence that he was doing a feature on the equestrian team. Si Yin was there with the rest of the new members learning how to groom their horses and there he was beside them taking pictures and asking questions. I was at the track, just cantering.

"Hey." Lee Jungwoo.

I nodded. He slowed to a trot and signaled for me to do the same. We changed lanes.

"In the kitchen the other day. You said you were busy flirting with someone, and I honestly can't tell if you're being serious or not but I'm dying to know."

"You slowed me down for *this*?" I stared.

He laughed. "Cox, I don't appreciate cliffhangers. If you're spilling half of it, I need you to spill everything. Is it someone I know?"

"Yeah the whole school does."

He looked genuinely surprised. "Didn't know you were the type to go for those kind of people. I mean you're pretty well-known yourself, so."

I ended the conversation by easing into a canter and then, galloping away. Lee was not happy, but he had vice-captain duties to attend to and wasn't going to come after me so I managed to refrain from speaking to anyone till the end of our session. Si Yin had made a couple of friends on the team and had joined them on their way to the locker room for a shower. I spotted him seated on packed straw, staring at one of the horses. I dismounted and led Caspian over.

"That is a very handsome horse," was the first thing he said, watching. "The color of its coat! Aren't black horses terribly uncommon?"

"You can touch him." I led him closer but Caspian had a track record of being more interested in straw than human beings. He lowered his neck and nudged the stack.

"He must be a non-fading since he'd been with you out in the sun rather often and yet his coat has yet to lose that rich black character," he said before gingerly stroking Caspian's neck and then petting his side. "And very obedient as well! How extremely soft he feels... a handsome stallion indeed."

Green.

"You give more compliments to a horse in a minute than an entire month with your boyfriend."

Immediately, he was all dusted in pink and protests. I watched him struggle to piece sentences together since that itself was very amusing. He also retracted his hand from Caspian after I casually added that he'd never touched me like that either.

"Leroy. You can't possibly be—be *suggesting* I pet you like I pet a horse, can you?" He said after a while. "A-also. I should remind you that... that compliments aimed at human beings are a rare phenomenon in my case. Especially if, well, if said human being is of... of high importance to me."

I led Caspian to his booth, where he was distracted by more hay. Everyone else on the team had headed for the showers.

"Yeah, but that was before," I went further, testing the waters. Just to see his reaction. "People say sweet things to their partner."

His first reaction had been to panic, scrambling for words in an area of knowledge he clearly wasn't familiar with. "O-oh! Oh, that—well, I... I'm sorry." It didn't cross his mind that I was merely playing. "I wasn't aware. That must have been a mistake on my part. Do they really? Say only sweet things to one another? I mean... now that you mention it, my godfather's husband practically showers him with compliments and flattering words. Aunt Giselle's boyfriend does the same and it would be awkward to pay Uncle Al too much attention, so I don't quite know about that one but... I, I suppose I could try to adopt another manner of speech."

I was amused. But he was making me decide between borderline unnatural dishonesty and cute facial expressions. A momentary version of the former for a lifelong memory of the latter wasn't too bad.

"Okay," I stood facing him, at arm's length. "Compliment me."

He'd paused for a good long moment before blinking rapidly and, as though coming to his senses, cleared his throat. "You are certainly, quite, infuriatingly attractive," he had his fingers laced together and was trying not to stare at them out of embarrassment. "It is awfully disarming at times."

It caught me off-guard. I hadn't exactly been expecting him to go all out and attack me with cute shit like that. He had his gaze alternating between mine and the hay strewn across the floor, seemingly nervous. I know I was the one who called for compliments but I'd made the mistake of underestimating his abilities. Should have known; he always had a way with piecing things together regardless of the situation. The words were effective—I was turned on.

"I hope you aren't laughing at me," he played with his fingers. Part of his habit whenever he felt troubled. "I can't tell if that's a smile or if you're just smirking to yourself."

"It's called being aroused." Laying this out wasn't the hard part. "But I was kidding about the compliments. Don't force yourself. Stick to the truth."

He looked like he was about to collapse. "A-aroused! What a...
that is... w-well," he readjusted the frames on the bridge of his nose.
"That *was* the truth, Leroy."

Could have had him there and then but someone else walked in
with their horse in tow and glasses nearly jumped a feet into the air
before subtly leaving some distance between us. It was weird being
private. I kept the question at the back of my mind till we were
heading for Cayenne, having waited fifteen minutes for Si Yin before she ended up telling us to head back first. Her best friend even
said something about her liking long showers, but I felt she had
other things to look at in the locker room. Had my sources.

"So we keeping this to ourselves...?" I glanced at him sideways.
The look on his face told me he'd somehow anticipated this conversation.

"I'll be honest—I've long narrated the entire incident to Si Yin,"
he admitted in a single breath. Then, after meeting my gaze, went on
to say that he hadn't told anyone else apart from her. "She conveyed
her blessings and all but I hope you're not too concerned about me
confiding in someone else about this. We could still keep it rather
private. I'm sure she wouldn't go around announcing it to the rest of
the world."

"Was banking on her doing that," I told him honestly and he
blinked in confusion. I'd snorted, reaching over to flick his forehead
but he dodged that so I caught his arm instead and pulled him
closer, resting my hand on his waist.

"Leroy!" His first instinct was to jump in my arms, craning his
neck to look over his shoulder. "It's broad daylight. Any form of
physical proximity would cause quite the uproar, which, in case you
may have forgotten, you as the school's number three cannot possible risk. An instructor could walk by any minute and banish us to
detention for inappropriate behavior."

"Doesn't matter," I took his hand instead and felt his freezing fingers. Stuffed them in the pocket of my coat. "You free this weekend?"

"This weekend," he repeated, looking surprised. "Are we about to make plans for it?"

I laughed. "We're telling someone."

He got my subtext and whatever I was referring to pretty quickly. It was easy to tell from his ears and how the general air would quieten to a simmer around him.

"I see. Um, who is it?"

"Annie." I told him.

We'd arrived at the doorstep of Cayenne and I was pulling out my key fob somewhere in the middle of the conversation when the hand I was holding onto in my pocket squeezed. I looked up and saw his eyes. Waves; worried. Slightly dark.

"Your mother? But, are you sure? There have been studies proposing the presence of consciousness in the minds of comatose beings even if they don't seem to display any signs of brain activity. I appreciate the symbolic gesture but... but what if she hears us?"

I unlocked the door and gave him a look. "That's the whole point, dumbass."

He paused, as though registering. "Oh. O-oh, you mean to say..." His feet shuffled past the entrance and before he could finish whatever it was he wanted to say in the shy, formally polite manner I anticipated and was hoping to hear, half the lodge idiots had to be roosting in the living room in front of the tv and in the kitchen.

They went straight for him.

"*Another* playdate? Didn't you guys have one just yesterday?"

"Hello, hi," very cute. "Apologies for the intrusion. I have the report with me, and the discussion wouldn't take any longer than fifteen minutes." He very quietly slipped his hand out of my pocket and returned it to his side.

Raul didn't notice. "Hey no I'm not saying that. Rosi's on dinner duty today so it's great you can come over and tell her how bad her food is."

Over in the kitchen, some hollering we couldn't make out. The two started conversing so I took his bag and headed for the dining table first, placing it on one of the chairs and then dropping mine next to it. Bank was already seated with his texts laid out on the table, making notes for a test. Rosi was a speck in the kitchen. Nabila on the couch with three others.

"You let him touch your horse," Bank looked up and this was the first thing he said to me. "You never let anyone touch your horse."

I raised a brow. "You saw?"

"Why do you keep forgetting we are in the same horse club?" He hit my wrist with his pen and I gave that a thought. He went back to his notebook. Meanwhile, the people on the couch were loud enough to wake hell and call for demons. It shocked Vanilla for a bit when he neared the living room with Raul, who made for the couch and swapped controllers with one of the guys.

"That's a gaming console," glasses came over to say, practically sizzling. "You love those. I wasn't aware the school provided such means of entertainment. You must have been ecstatic when you found out."

"It's Raul's," I told him. The guy had had it shipped over the day we moved in. "Technically, he's breaking the rules."

"Oh," his excitement remained visible. "Well, we've all had our moments of rule-breaking. This reminds me of our childhood, and the many days we'd spent picking up mystery boxes on Peach Beach." He didn't reveal the rest of the story. The one where he'd tried to work part-time at his godfather's bakery to buy a console of his own just so he could have reason to invite me over. He was four and a half.

I told him we could go to a real beach next time. That we could do other things that wasn't picking up mystery boxes and racing on mini karts.

"A, a real beach?" His eyes were different now. They were curious. "I've only ever been to one in Indonesia. It was beautiful, clear waters all around and just pristine sand granules. We didn't build sandcastles though. My uncle wasn't very keen. I've always wanted to build sandcastles, or go around collecting seashells, which we could do together i-if we were ever... to go to a, you know. A beach."

I moved to block him from the living, leaning in for a quick refill. "Promise."

"Leroy!" His first reaction was to look over my shoulder. He had his glasses askew and eyes nearly as wide as its rims. "You can't just—that wasn't. Doing that in front of everyone else, I... w-what were you thinking?"

I rolled my eyes and led him into the kitchen where Rosi was prepping for dinner. His ears were still red. She made some kind of off-handed remark about it but he was skilled enough to redirect the conversation somewhere else since lying wasn't a word in his professional dictionary. I pulled out a carton of milk and some chilled bananas for a milkshake.

"So what did the report say? Bet they loved the concept we came up with."

I let him answer Rosi's question, since he was the first person I'd forwarded the soft copy of the cross-year report to. Either way, he was better at analyzing stuff like that.

"Admittedly they did. Although perhaps one or two of the judges weren't all that keen on sharing their food. Technically, the individual dishes far exceeded their expectations as well. We fell short on timing and heat, which I'd anticipated since, well, we were practically struggling to survive in the forest back there. Apart from that, um... nothing specific really stood out. Chen was generous enough to offer us a look at his team's report but no one's heard from Tenner or Violet. The last I heard, a fellow journalist of mine has been trying to reach out to the latter."

He had my attention—like he always did—but this thing was in my chest and it wasn't the color I was used to feeling. Adding a couple of blueberries into the mix, I cranked up the blending speed.

"Hey," Rosi was shouting over the whir, mincing garlic. "Who else is on dinner duty today?"

Nabila came into the kitchen at a good timing since I wasn't going to check the roster for Rosi. A waste of time and energy. Even better, she'd memorized the entire thing so neither of us had to check.

"Mikaela, wasn't it?" She offered us a bag of truffle seaweed chips. Some new flavor. I watched him nibble on one and make a face. "But she's representing her class for the school festival and I'm pretty sure I heard they have some meeting with the other third-year representatives today."

"Oh yes." He was doing that thing again. Pushing up his glasses to hide whatever emotion it wasn't he couldn't conceal. Like I said; lying wasn't in his dictionary. "Chen did mention something of that nature."

There it was again, that color. I stopped blending and transferred the mixture into two separate glasses, handing him one. It was weird trying to hold back. It was weird having something to hold back on.

He received the drink with both hands and a short bow of his head. You could tell his manners were by the book, but his uncle was the one who actually chose the texts for him to read so that he would have it ingrained. To others, his politeness was stifling. I think it's sexy.

"When?"

He looked up from a sip of his milkshake. "Oh. Just an hour ago, perhaps. I can't remember the exact details but I recall receiving a response the moment I'd had all the details of the horse grooming article written out."

I stared at the top button of his shirt. All done up. "You guys text?"

"Sometimes, yes. He's very friendly, asking what I'm up to every evening."

The color darkened. Rosi and Nabila were on the other side of the common kitchen, near the ovens. The exhaust was loud enough to keep our conversations separated. I pretended to sigh, just testing how far we could play.

"... Left out again, huh."

He bought it at once. It was hilarious. "O-oh! Oh, I—I wasn't aware you felt so emotional about things like this. Should I add you into the chat so that we could all share secret recipes and things like that? I'm sure it would be very exciting. We weren't deliberately leaving you out or anything. As far as I'm aware, *I'm* the odd one out since, well, you and Chen have known each other far longer than I've known him so I'm sure he'd love to have you in the chat group as well..."

"Okay can't wait," I cut to the chase.

"Oh!" He paused, seemingly surprised. "Brilliant." It looked like he was searching for his phone the next couple of seconds before realizing that he'd left it in his bag at the dining. "I'll do that by the end of the day. Maybe we should be helping Rosi with the dinner preparations." He glanced over at the stove, concerned.

"I mean it's her turn to cook," I pointed out bluntly, but he was already tottering over to the island with cutting boards and raw ingredients all prepped in separate bowls and ramekins, with one casserole dish in the middle.

"Shepherd's pie," he noted over Rosi's shoulder while she was chopping up some carrots and onions. "What's the occasion?"

She turned behind with a blink. "How did you know?"

"It was obvious, actually." Humble. "Just by the casserole dish and the lamb, most would have been able to make a well-informed guess. I also have reason to suspect the presence of dessert, which is very kind of you, I'd say. Besides the green mango salad of course. I've never had anything close to a fruit salad but being fond of Thai cuisine does make one very aware of their cultural palate and I can't wait to taste it. So um... what's the occasion?"

Rosi straight out burst into some cackle before rolling her eyes. "Your wedding I guess." *Okay not wrong but.*

"My wedding?" He blinked, lips maintaining the usual expression of gentle manners. "Oh. Oh, that must have been a joke. I wasn't aware of its humorous quality, but I shall laugh anyway since, um, it would be socially polite to do so." He proceeded to laugh.

Nabila returned from the fridge with some frozen peas before Rosi could redirect the clueless genius back to me and lose a finger from laughing with a kitchen knife in hand.

"Hey, you made dessert?"

The current chef on duty had to calm herself before answering. "Yeah. We decided everyone's getting a minute for an elevator pitch until we make a final judgement, so. I'm pitching glutinous rice balls in sugar cane water tomorrow so I wanna see what you guys think of it first."

I watched the eyes behind his glasses light up at the words 'elevator pitch' and the next couple of seconds featured him scrambling for a mini notepad and pen hidden in the inner pocket of his blazer. It was interesting how he'd leave his phone in his bag and have a notepad in his pocket instead. The tension in his shoulders eased up a little as he was writing; made it seem like something heavy was lifted from his shoulders.

Nabila asked if our classes had decided on a theme. It was an inter-class thing. Some prize money for stores with the most tickets, but it honestly didn't matter.

"Spanish street food." I told her.

She and Rosi looked surprised. "Okay, wow. I'd thought the idiots in your class would go for the dress-up stuff in cafés. Weren't you guys the demon-angel things last year? Are you sure they decided on that?"

To end the conversation, I took both our glasses and headed for the kitchen. "... I only heard the conclusion." They called something after my back, but it didn't seem very important so I said his name and he looked up from his notepad and then followed me back into the living.

Raul had left the couch to poke his nose into Bank's textbooks and Si Yin had just arrived with her gear and all, taking the seat across and demanding to see the report. I told her that we should leave it for after dinner but really, I just knew the papers were somewhere at the bottom of my rucksack, crumpled and possibly torn. I'd been reserving that only for him to see since it would've most likely made for one of his lectures. It was secretly enjoyable.

He ended up coaching Si Yin on her TF courses for test week coming up so I had to be okay with sharing the attention. He would look over occasionally to see what I was doing but I was just staring at him since shepherd's pie was taking long in the kitchen and I had nothing better to do.

By the time dinner was finally served, he hadn't been able to resist sharing the information from Chen and had every graded category listed out on an excel sheet for comparison. Timing wasn't an issue for them but our score for novelty was significantly higher. The others didn't seem very interested, but I could tell from his eyes that he so wanted to get to the bottom of this.

"I could ask Birchwood for her report." It wasn't a dealbreaker but he seemed to think it was. I told him it would be easy.

"Could you really? Emily—another first-year from the school press—she's been trying to do that for the past couple of days."

I was filling his plate with pie and ensuring he's had a good cut of it when he said this and then, at half-past-eight in the evening, someone was at the door. Bank volunteered to get it. Most of the lodge had returned and even if they hadn't, it was unlikely that they'd forgotten their keys. There was some talking at the door but none of us were able to make out exact words until Bank returned with the usual look of confusion on his face. He said something about a first-year looking for Leroy Cox.

Sadly, Leroy Cox was me. But I wasn't very keen on leaving dinner or glasses alone at the table. I asked if he could just get whoever it was to leave a memo. "She look angry when I said that," Bank pulled on the back of my collar. I got up, sighing.

At the door was Violet Birchwood. I wasn't in the mood to talk so I handed her a stack of sticky notes and got one of those blunt pencils by the doorway for her to write with. You can tell I was in a good mood. I closed the door.

"Wait." Her foot was in the way. "Just two minutes—it's about the tag team. Third segment of the school festival? I led my team to victory during the cross-year and you came in second so it makes perfect sense for us to team up. So?"

"Ask Chen. He's second too." I retrieved the writing materials and returned them to the stationary corner by the doorway.

"You're not competing?" She gawked. I didn't like being interrupted over dinner. "But you nearly won the entire thing last year without a partner. Imagine the two of us, cruising through. We'll split the prize money."

"... I nearly won *because* I competed alone." It was the truth. "Bye."

II

VANILLA

Standing idly in front of a train station, cold, alone, and drowning in the muffler picked out by my god-aunt wasn't the most romantic thing to be doing on a Saturday morning and yet, my poor heart had to be racing at awful speeds for such wee hours all because it knew I would be spending the rest of the day with a certain someone.

This person I refer to does not have the luxury of a flexible schedule in which would have made our lives significantly easier by easing the time spent apart. Apparently, being in the same school as your significant other did not necessarily mean frequent meetings or lunches. The last time we'd spent some private time together was on Tuesday at his residence lodge after a brief discussion regarding the cross-year reports. Si Yin and the others weren't exactly the most focused group of people when it came to reading papers and documents, but we'd somehow established a fair tie between Chen's team and ours. The only thing left for us to deliberate on were the remaining two reports, and because everyone else seemed increasingly disinterested in the mystery I'd been so invested in, I had decided to call it a night. Leroy had walked me to the bus stop after that, promising to sate my curiosity by obtaining the reports before arranging a time and place for us to meet on Saturday morning.

That was four days ago. Now, standing idly outside the train station in an old-fashioned, navy blue duffel coat, was me wondering if I was guilty of overdressing—a crime often committed by the overenthusiastic, try-hard social novice on a first date.

The bouquet of pink carnations I'd gathered and styled the night before were starting to look a little out of place next to the four hard-boiled eggs I'd prepared mere minutes before leaving the house, transferring them into a Ziplock bag for easy consumption. Admittedly and most unfortunately, I was never the prime example of a healthy human being—unexpectedly so—and therefore often found myself skipping the meal undeserving of its title of importance, whatever it is nutritionists dub it as. Breakfast was simply impractical, strictly speaking. It required the additional effort of time, effort and energy, which could so obviously be spent on things like solving the 'challenge yourself' problem sums on the last page of each mathematical textbook or reading a book about romantic relationships and how one should be treating their partner. The second option only became applicable to myself as of recent.

Either way, the reason I'd decided to whip up a couple of hard-boiled eggs was primarily due to my reading of the above-mentioned. It took me less than a second to deduce a certain idiot's disinclination to waking up early to do something that required additional effort. Not to mention, his lodge mates had been oddly surprised by his making of breakfast back then, which further proved my point.

And with several premises to support the conclusion I thought absolutely concrete, the eggs were due; two for Leroy and two for myself—to be had on the train to see his mother.

"Hey."

He'd appeared as though on cue, hands in the pockets of his

down parka that featured a hood lined with faux fur. "I like your..." an index finger loosely followed his gaze, lowered to my clothes, "everything."

Strangely flustered, I forcefully handed him the eggs. "I don't know what you're talking about. Here. I timed them perfectly so they should be just about the right consistency in the center."

"What's with the flowers?" He accepted the eggs without quite paying them the appropriate attention I'd hoped he would. After all, they were meant to distract. "Think you got the roles wrong."

"You're mistaken. They aren't for you," I told him, clearing my throat as he led the way, past the entrance and into the station. "Pink carnations represent a mother's love. And although I may not necessarily have the best understanding of whatever that may be, your mother was... well, I suppose she was the closest example I had the privilege of witnessing. Biologically, I mean. She's your real mother."

Leroy's finger was on my forehead before I could physically react to his apparently swift movements. Upset, I'd waved the flowers in his face to block his view but this gave him the opportunity to slip the bouquet out of my grasp. "I'll hold them for you."

"Oh," my initial reaction had been to blink. "Well. Alright."

Clearly, I hadn't been expecting the sudden shift in his tone of voice. Disarmed, both by the oddly thoughtful gesture and how awfully suave he looked dressed in casual clothing, I was rendered speechless for a good minute or two, waiting for him to continue. A tentative glance his way confirmed my suspicions of him having no intention of doing so. The certified idiot wasn't even *looking* in the direction we were headed in.

"Please keep your eyes on the road."

We passed the gantry by tapping our cards on the readers by the electric gates and still, he kept his gaze locked on mine.

"You are. The road."

"You're not making any sense," I told him quite frankly, deciding to check the platform number just in case Leroy wasn't paying any attention to this either. "If this is your idea of some romantic metaphor, I'm afraid a fail grade is due. My seven-year-old god-brother writes better poems."

He had to turn the tables and shift the blame away from himself. "It's your turtleneck," he claimed, reaching over to run a finger along the inside of my collar. "It's fucking distracting."

I shied away from his touch, readjusting the cream-colored vest I'd worn over the old, unfortunately stretched, white turtleneck Aunt Julie had gotten me nearly two years back. "W-well, apologies for... for attempting to dress decently on our first date. If it *is* one, that is. Is it? I can never be sure."

"Think we skipped the date part and went straight to meeting the in-laws, so," Leroy was back at it with his teasing nonsense. "Might as well be married."

Embarrassed, I once again referred him back to the eggs. "Eat them before they freeze. And speaking of freezing, aren't you feeling absolutely *preserved* in just that top?"

"No," he laughed shortly, following my gaze to the wine red, possibly long or three-quarter-sleeved shirt he was wearing, made of thin stretchy material often worn on hot summer days. "I'm not saying you've got bad taste, by the way. The turtleneck's sexy."

"I! W-well..." *Shy* was the kind of embarrassing word I'd never thought of using, let alone uttering it aloud. "So um, I'm assuming you like it?"

"Yeah." Leroy himself appeared fairly entertained by an odd conversational topic quite out of our usual comfort zone. "And the vest."

This one had me displaying an involuntary passion. It had been an expensive gift from my godfather's friend, Aunt Rachel, who'd developed a furious love for made-to-order goods. She got me into the craft of fabric and clothes-making, which soon translated into my appreciation of good craftsmanship. This vest, I had been saving for months to wear on a special occasion.

"Muted chestnut," I told him the exact shade, peering down at my vest and feeling oddly warm. "A nice creamy color. Neutrals are supposedly in trend nowadays, especially among adults."

"So you're an adult?" He teased as we came to a stop at carriage two, door four of platform three and got on the train that was due for departure only fifteen minutes later.

"That's not what I meant," was how I ended up protesting. "I was merely... well, I'd hoped to at least be of decent caliber, dressing wise, walking alongside someone like yourself. So I read up on it over the past couple of days in my free time. Everything seems to suit you perfectly well and it is a disaster for the amateur that I am. All I've ever known were suspenders and dress shirts. It's really no wonder I get laughed at in the hallways back in the private high school I'd attended."

We picked a cozy spot in the middle and had the luxury of arguing over the window seat. And by this, I mean Leroy telling me to take it and vice versa. Decisions were made only after Leroy voiced threats in my ear to kiss me in public, which altogether sounded severely illegal so I sat myself down on the window seat and he took the one next to me.

"Suspenders are cute too," said the criminal whilst shrugging off his coat and stuffing it in the compartment below his seat. I followed his lead. "On you at least."

"I can never tell if you're being serious."

He laughed, resting his usual rucksack on his lap and unzipping the top, pulling out a classic wooden lunch box. "Eggs and this for breakfast."

Expectations exceeded, I told him the eggs were entirely because I'd assumed he wouldn't have had the energy to wake up early and make breakfast for himself. Peering down at the burst of appetizing colors in his lunchbox, I did not feel very accomplished.

"My eggs pale in comparison. You should have told me if you were going to put in that much effort."

He'd had each sandwich-looking thing half-wrapped in baking paper for easy handling, handing me a portion of it. "Not everyone knows how to make a good egg."

"It's only a matter of timing it properly. Other factors have less impact on the outcome," I observed the sandwich-looking food item and identified a couple of primary ingredients. "Seaweed in place of bread. Spam. Lettuce. Oh but yours has cucumber instead. And is that...? Japanese-style omelette."

Leroy took his first, huge bite out of the sandwich. Layers of rice kept the filling separated from the seaweed. "They call it *onigirazu.*"

My first instinct had been to pull out the handmade recipe book of his given to me on my birthday, noting the name and listing every ingredient. It was curious how something so deceptively simple could taste so tremendously good. Other notes included possible ingredients to add or substitute for a different flavor combination.

"Rocket?" He murmured, reading the writing over my shoulder. "And avocado. Yeah I forgot about sugar in the omelette, you're right."

We spent the next ten minutes or so having a quaint and surprisingly ordinary breakfast shared between two human beings, quite resembling the time he came over to make dinner in my kitchen. Private time spent with Leroy was unexpectedly comfortable despite the many qualms I'd had with one-to-one interaction in general, let alone with the very person who tended to send my mind into constant states of dysfunction. Heart palpitations were surprisingly easy to become fond of.

It was when the train began to depart from the station that Leroy told me it was about an hour's ride, and that he'd usually take a nap during this time. On the other hand, I'd been so sure of reading something about 'changed habits' during a so-called 'honeymoon period' in a relationship, dubbed by writers of guidebooks to romance as the most enjoyable two months of the entire bond.

"We're skipping that part since we've technically been married for eleven years," was all he said, folding his arms and slouching in his seat to lean his head against the side of my shoulder. Needless to say, I was left gaping and completely bewildered.

"Leroy, it is, by the definition of marriage across all cultures and dictionaries, impossible to marry someone completely unaware of said marriage's occurrence. No register was signed, no wedding banquet held, no aisle walked down. We are not married." I said this all whilst attempting to stay as perfectly still as I could manage, quietly hoping he found my shoulder comfortable enough to continue sleeping on.

"What if it's an idea?" His eyes were closed, saying this. "If it's just commitment, but people want to see it happening in real life, not in their heads?"

Those words were big and they struck like the crackle and spit of flames, so real that I could almost hear it inside and they sounded so much like the crunch of crisp, red leaves under one's feet that I felt so odd, making such a strange realization at a time like this. I foresaw myself thinking about this for the next hour or so, having never considered such an interpretation.

"What's the point of getting married if you're not committed?" He didn't sound very different from the usual, unamused tone he tended to speak in. "If it's an idea, then I've been married for some time."

Then, after some silence, he added. "You?"

* * *

The hospital was about a five-minute walk from the station we alighted at and Leroy needed no second thoughts about timing or direction; the frightening familiarity he possessed with a place far-away from both his first and second home was something I'd always regarded optional in the life of a human being to which I understood now as a fortunate circumstance I should be grateful for—that none of the people I love, I'd visited in a hospital just yet.

A nurse had greeted him by his name upon our arrival, past automatic glass doors sliding open to a pungent cloud of antiseptic and quiet whispers. The hustle and bustle one tended to associate hospitals with was absent from this one. No emergency cases being wheeled through the door left right center or surgeons rushing from one operating room to another—the atmosphere was oddly quaint. Like a small café on a weekday morning.

"Boy," an elderly man hooked up to an IV line and bringing it around raised his other hand as we passed, flashing a toothless smile at my companion. "What did you bring this time?"

"Quinoa ratatouille. I'll leave it in your room." It was the first time I'd seen Leroy give a proper smile to a stranger, so I assumed he was far familiar with the man than I was able to perceive at present. The patient, dressed in the characteristic blue gown, reached out to give his shoulder a pat.

"I remember that one... it was good alright, five stars," chuckled the man, airy and slightly breathless. "Say hi to your mom for me."

I watched them nod and wave, even as the man turned the corner and looked back, my companion had stopped to watch him go and in his eyes was the warmth of a candle I'd gotten so used to associating with a different kind of heat that the one I was witnessing at present seemed almost foreign.

Wordless, we continued down the hallway and took a left into a second lift lobby, where we waited and then took the elevator up to the third floor, quieter than the last. We passed a couple of open-door rooms and were undisturbed until we arrived at the end of the hallway and turned to the last door. His mother's room was smaller than the others but a tad brighter—lit by the angle of the sun at half-past-nine, filtering into the room and warming the bed.

"I brought someone," he said very casually after knocking on the open door and crossing the room to the full-length windows, drawing the day curtains for the comfort of our eyes. "He brought you flowers."

I tottered in after him before standing idly by the bed, not quite knowing what to do. He was on the other side, where the chair was. "Hello Mrs. Cox. Apologies for the intrusion... I'm Vanilla Julian White. I um, I've grown up now. It's alright if you don't remember me."

Leroy laughed, curling a finger for the flowers in my arms. I handed them over and he stuck them in an empty vase by the bed. There were other things on the nightstand, apart from the vase, that made the room appear rather lived in. What appeared to be a jewelry box rested beside an old-looking flip phone, worn after years of use. His mother had a nasal cannula attached for respiratory support, and I wasn't too sure if being in a coma meant having breathing problems but it could have something to do with how she'd got into this state in the first place.

"She remembers." My companion said in her stead after clumsily putting the flowers together and pulling up an additional stool. "Sit."

"Not yet. I simply cannot see how you did those flowers any justice. Let me do it," I took over at the bedside table, producing a pair of snipping scissors I'd prepared beforehand and beginning to cut the stems of select few carnation stalks. In truth, I did not have the slightest idea how one should be speaking to a comatose patient, let alone Leroy's mother whom I had so awfully disappointed years ago.

There was no saying she'd forgiven me for the ambiguous part I'd played in the closing of her diner and more directly, the letting down of her only child. I wasn't going to assume that just because I was a child back then, she'd never harbored any bitter feelings towards myself.

"He's been doing that ever since we met again," he was laughing, resting his head on the mattress of his mother's bed. "I can't argue 'cuz he's being honest. And it's the truth anyway, so. I told you how he fucks everyone up with facts—"

"Leroy!" I was aghast. "That, don't you... mind your language when you're speaking to your mother?"

"She knows." He had the same laugh in his eyes before turning back to her. "Another reason to love him."

Again, I was sent further into a spiral of insanity. "W-what an awful way of breaking it to Mrs. Cox. I'm so sorry, ma'am. We'd never meant to put it that way, or or or at least I never did. Delicacy is clearly not within Leroy's realm of abilities but, um. Yes, he is... rather fond of me."

It was at this final straw that my companion tugged on my arm for me to sit, and I did. And all he had to say was: "She knows."

"He also made eggs this morning. He thought I'd be coming with an empty stomach. He's not wrong, since that's what I do most of the time, right. I don't do breakfast. It's like he knows me too well... but also not well enough 'cuz I made some in the end. He doesn't know how much I think of him."

Leroy was saying all this, talking to his mother as if she was awake and checking the feeding tube and a folder he'd obtained from the front desk downstairs upon entering, scanning its contents as though this was something he'd done hundreds of times. And here I was, hearing it all—all these awfully intimate things he was telling her about *myself* and it all felt so frighteningly embarrassing. This also being the first time I was hearing him do all the taking and speaking more than five sentences without pausing.

To be the subject of such talk was blush-inducing, heat drowning, fire blazing. I was far out of my comfort zone.

"We celebrated his birthday Monday evening. You should have seen the look on his face. Also, he told me to return the pen I worked my ass off to get. Think it was twenty hours extra in total. Anyway, I was pissed so I wanted to take everything back but he wouldn't let go of the recipe book I made. So I said 'fuck you' and kissed him... they didn't cut your nails."

Leroy was clearly out to embarrass me in front of his mother and he was doing all this whilst tidying her hair and then checking her nails before noticing they weren't trimmed. Apparently, the nurses were supposed to do it.

He turned to me then, as though he hadn't been saying all those infuriatingly terrible things about me and narrating that night with that limited vocabulary of his, asking if I had a nail cutter. I, a stunned species, could barely respond with a 'no'.

"I'll get one down the street," he said, grabbing his phone and wallet. "Stay and talk?"

This all, he'd made seem so effortless and simple. As though he'd been asking for the kind of favor that merely involved me getting him a glass of water; even back then, I'd never had to speak to the parent of any supposed friend of mine, let alone *now*, the mother of my, well, my significant other. Clearly, I had reason to be fazed.

Drowning my protests in a series of excuses provided by the rational mind, stating that, while being anxious was a natural reaction, Mrs. Cox was really just another human being. I could, after all, speak to her and tell her just about anything without the fear of instant regret, often found in the body language of others.

"So um. I brought you flowers, like Leroy said," was what I'd chosen to begin with, after a long moment of silence in her son's wake. "Pink carnations represent a mother's love and I like to think that you are—as in, not think, because, you *are*, as a matter of fact—one of the most honorable mother I've come to know. Personally, I mean.

"You must be wondering how Leroy is at school. He is kind. And clever. And well-liked by practically every other student. He's popular even here in the hospital, did you know that? Well he is. Very charismatic. And charming. But also very bad at AB, accounting basics. I'm teaching him that now.

"Oh and I'd like to... correct Leroy's account of, well, Monday night. If I may. I'm sure you'd understand why I'd tell him to return the pen. It cost at least a hundred and fifty, you see. I don't think anyone would be in the right mind to spend that hefty sum on a mere fountain pen. The recipe book on the other hand, was bound by hand. He'd put them together with string and tape and the cover itself, recycled from an old, hardback diary likely from a thrift store! Clumsily made but the very reason I'd found it so endearing. Any sane human being would have understood its importance, especially since someone like Leroy, well, I'm sure you know, would never try his hand at craft.

"A-and I'd also like to assure you that the kiss did not, um, occur... so abruptly as he'd described it. I'm determined to put it into words but it is till this very date that I cannot."

Words failed me, as though on cue, and I soon turned rather still and awkward, seated by her side and swallowing hard, listening to the beep of the heart monitor filling the silence.

"Illegal would be the word. What do you think?" I waited, finding this all very odd but at the same time, strangely comforting. Speaking to someone who wouldn't respond.

"He's wrong, by the way. I do know how much he thinks about me. O-or at least I think I do, I suppose. Can't allow one to get ahead of himself."

And it was at this point in the one-way conversation that the flip phone on the bedside table vibrated once, catching my attention. I'd turned to it on instinct but there was no further indication of a call of any sort, so I was about to turn back when, again, it vibrated.

The flip phone had a tiny digital screen on the front that would display the caller ID or the date and time of the day but flashed on it in black dots was an all-too-familiar name I would recognize just about anywhere.

ALFRED DEMPSEY

It didn't take me long to figure out who the owner of the phone was since, after all, I knew how Leroy's looked like and it certainly wasn't mine and judging by the model and its frugal nature, the natural conclusion was that it belonged to no one other than Mrs. Cox herself.

Frankly speaking, my curiosity was piqued. After all, Uncle Al had never said a thing about keeping in contact with Leroy's mother and, even if he did, he would therefore have known that she was... well, in the state that she was at present. There was simply no logical reason or line of rational thought that would lead to a sound conclusion.

After watching the display screen light up several times from the multiple texts sent by, apparently, my uncle, I picked up the phone and flipped it open.

It was not password protected. I hadn't encountered such a device even at a younger age and though it confused my digitally-acclimated mind, I found myself staring at a messaging inbox. The style was old and the conversations were difficult to view all at once so I ended up guiltily scanning the previews before accidentally, whilst trying to figure out how to scroll, pressing a button that allowed the user to view the conversation at a glance.

From: A. DEMPSEY

16/10

You were right about his friends wanting to celebrate his birthday. Julie and I were overly anxious… it is, after all, his first time abroad and living alone.

* * *

From: A. DEMPSEY

16/10

What about the fountain pen? I hope you didn't actually get it for him. It would have cost a hefty sum and I would be terribly embarrassed if you were troubled on his behalf.

* * *

From: A. DEMPSEY

16/10

And apologies for the late response. I've been intending to send a message of gratitude for making our Vanille feel at home.

Nonsense, was what this all was. I couldn't understand how or why my uncle would be sending these texts minutes ago when Leroy's mother couldn't possibly have been typing out responses and having a conversation with him. I used the arrow keys to direct the conversation further upwards, viewing its history and altogether committing the greatest sin of my lifetime—invasion of privacy.

Goodness, the urge to find out what was going on was clearly getting hold of my moral values.

From: A. DEMPSEY
28/09
Vanille never said a thing! Well, second place is absolutely wonderful. Thank you for such wonderful news.

* * *

From: A. DEMPSEY
20/09
Overnight camps out in the wild are the absolute worst. I remember my time in culinary school but nothing of that sort. I must call Vanille immediately.

* * *

From: A. DEMPSEY
17/09
Yes, the 56. You've heard of it? Admittedly I was a little rash in signing him up for residence. Do you think the tastings have become a little harder over the years? I barely made it past number 30 when I was his age. Some beetroot of sorts.

* * *

From: A. DEMPSEY
10/09
I've just checked in on him. You see now why I wasn't all that keen on letting him go off on his own? Nearly losing his tongue on the first day... goodness gracious. I hope he didn't cause your son too much trouble.

* * *

From: A. DEMPSEY

30/08

We've just arrived at the airport and are heading to his accommodation. It's an apartment a station away from school. Perhaps you'd like to drop by.

* * *

From: A. DEMPSEY

Attached: picnicwithfamily2.jpg

16/04

They grow up so quickly.

* * *

From: A. DEMPSEY

12/05

It has been some time. Vanille has been making plans on attending culinary school. Would you happen to have any recommendations?

From: You
To: A. DEMPSEY
9/03

How is he?

* * *

From: You
To: A. DEMPSEY
29/08
So how is he?

* * *

From: You
To: A. DEMPSEY
10/10
Did you celebrate?

* * *

From: You
To: A. DEMPSEY
14/02
How is he?

* * *

From: You
To: A. DEMPSEY
Attached: Freshmen Registration.pdf
13/05
This is the school Leroy has been looking at.

* * *

From: You
To: A. DEMPSEY
19/04
He looks the same.

* * *

From: You
To: A. DEMPSEY
30/08
Sorry. Can't go. But I'll send Leroy soon.

* * *

From: You
To: A. DEMPSEY
20/09
He lost to a banana. You should have seen his face.

* * *

From: You
To: A. DEMPSEY
28/09
Second place.

* * *

From: You
To: A. DEMPSEY
5/10
Don't worry. Everyone loves him.

* * *

"What an idiot."

How poorly everything seemed to fall into place, staring at these rectangular digits and alphabets coarsely put together by someone that clearly wasn't Annie herself and had no dignity whatsoever to even *pretend* that he wasn't the person he was—an idiot, after all.

There was no deliberation to laugh or cry and the mechanical beep of the monitor keeping pace through it all but I wanted so much to ask how she'd managed to raise someone so awfully impossible not to think about for the rest of my life like the still and unmoving candle he was, short of the fire I feared but possessing every bit of the warmth I so hoped to be able to touch.

"You would be laughing. Here, look... listen to this. This utter nonsense he's been—well I hope my uncle doesn't actually believe you text like that, Mrs. Cox. Unbelievable. *He lost to a banana?* Was that all he could—*I'll send Leroy soon?* What does that even mean? And just how many times has he been asking how I am when... when I so clearly wanted to... to know how he was, too?"

What an odd feeling it was, to be overwhelmed by a burning flame one thought to be small. I'd always wondered how Leroy had miraculously identified me by my name back in the infirmary since, admittedly, I was no longer the four-year-old child I was back then with glasses slipping off my nose and a bow tie on my neck.

To think he was the very definition of twisting fate and altering paths for them to converge at a single point that was now.

"'Do you think anyone would ever feel like they could spend the rest of their life with me' was a question I asked my godfather's husband once and all I remember is feeling awfully upset when I heard his answer. I still don't think anyone would. As in, no one deserves to be put next to me for more than two hours straight, let alone a lifetime. But... but I suppose I'm regressing; becoming selfish. Is that what love does to someone?" I paused. "Is this love?"

She began to cry.

III

⌒✿⌒

LEROY

They had ice cream and I assumed it had been a while since he had it. The flavor he liked. It was like they knew I was coming and decided to put every tub by the aisle I'd found the nail clipper in; the expensive kind that was at least three times the price of a usual tub but they were having a one-for-one promotion, so. I wasn't the kind to miss out on a good deal.

In the elevator back up to Annie's floor, a nurse recognized me and pointed out the odd sizing of the ice cream tub. "Those look like they're for babies!"

I told her they were cutting cost and she laughed like it was a joke. We got off on the same floor but she went down a different hallway. There was something happening down the one I was headed for. You could tell from the voices.

At the end of it was Annie's room so it was easy to tell when the doctors were over for a visit since no one else would have to be wandering around that area. I ran into a nurse speaking over her shoulder, a clipboard in her arms. She sounded calm enough for everything to be okay, going as far as to reassure the one I'd left Annie with. From the door, I sped through the key markers in the room—heart rate, tubing, bed, drip. Nothing came out of the assessment.

"Something up?" She was coming out of the room so I stopped her for a bit.

"Oh! You're Annie's son," the nurse angled her head to glance past the door and back into the room. "I was wondering if you'd gone and changed your entire image or something. Your fellow visitor called for assistance when he saw that she was tearing but you know that sort of thing, it happens all the time." She smiled and it was apologetic, but I wasn't the kind to be bothered by pity.

"Yeah. Thanks."

She nodded and then excused herself, heading down the hallway. I peered into the room. To register the scene required some time and effort; I wasn't expecting him to be open and familiar in the span of fifteen minutes or so, let alone holding Annie's hand and seated, like he usually would, unbelievably straight in the stool. Just him sitting on it gave the impression of a velvet armchair instead of hardware store plastic.

His eyes were slightly red and he was sniffling, so even at a distance, I could tell he had been crying. The reason behind this wasn't something I could connect the dots to since he didn't come across as an emotional kind of person. More rational than anything else. Things like heightened emotions from being in a hospital didn't seem like something that would affect him.

Annie remained still in her bed. Eyes closed. He was holding on to her hand like it was a bird with a broken wing, nestled in both his hands, cupped and careful. This entire thing seemed to have absorbed him completely and he only appeared aware of my presence when I stepped into the room and removed my coat, draping it on one of the chairs.

He reacted to this by standing up and turning around to hide his face, wiping his eyes with the back of his hand and pretending to be cleaning his glasses. I waited.

"That took you awfully long," he said after taking his time, which I gave as well. "Your mother appeared to be reacting to something I'd said because, as you know, I am a poor conversationalist, and had begun to cry. I'd assumed it was a sign of waking but the nurse who came in had told me otherwise..."

I removed the nail clipper from its packaging and left the rest of what I'd bought on the edge of the bed. "I see you missed me."

At this, he turned around, averting his gaze and sniffing once. Quietly. "I don't see how you could have inferred that from whatever it was I had been saying but admittedly, you aren't entirely wrong. Please take over. You're an idiot but charm is your saving grace and I would prefer not to have your mother in tears, comatose reaction or not."

It wasn't as though he'd said something uncharacteristic or dishonest, but I could not help noticing the way something was amiss from the general atmosphere and tone of his voice. He continued to criticize his own conversational skills until I heard it; the occasional trembling words, like leaves in the wind.

If he was hiding something, there was reason to be.

I wasn't going to pry it out of him. Whatever it was he wanted to say, they were his choice and the least I could do was respect that.

I offered the option of dessert, hoping he'd take it. Fingers crossed.

"O-oh," he made a sound of surprise when I held out the plastic bag of ice cream tubs, sitting by Annie to trim her nails. "Ice cream? Well it's been some time since I've had... oh. Oh it's," he was staring at the label on one of the tubs. *Rum & Raisin*. Eyes lit like a pool on a midsummer day before swiftly trying to hide his excitement by clearing his throat. "It's a... how much was it? I'll pay for my portion."

"Dumbass," I reached for his forehead. He let out a startled squeak. "What did you guys talk about."

"... nothing much," he said after recovering, oddly reserved. Not quite looking me in the eye either. You would have realized by now how easy it was to tell if he was hiding the truth, let alone blatantly lying through his teeth. Yet, it was precisely because I was aware of this—that he wasn't the kind of person to lie—that I understood the gravity of the situation when he actually decides to. Altogether, it was unsettling.

"Really." I couldn't see why he'd choose to lie. It wasn't like him to hold back on the truth, ugly or painful.

"Of course," he was looking down at his tiny tub of ice cream and uncapping it, peeling off the plastic and taking out the complimentary wooden spoon. "Oh. I might have mentioned the ghastly state of your mathematical skills. I understand how that would have warranted a good minute of tears."

I laughed, leaning back and giving him the finger in a lazy attempt to protest. Eyes wide, he pushed it aside with the kind of look he'd give to a porn magazine before hurriedly sitting down with his tub of ice cream and digging into it quietly. I returned to trimming Annie's nails, briefly remembering the previous time she'd reacted like this—tears streaming down her face. It had been months back, when I'd stopped by for an hour and was telling her about the busy week I had. Nothing special. Even complaining about her husband never made her react in such a way; a constant refusal to show any sign of waking or agitation.

"Do you... um," he was looking down at his ice cream while speaking to me. I waited. "Are you perhaps, maybe... I was wondering how you managed to get in contact with my uncle for the birthday surprise. You would have required a phone number, at the very least, to coordinate a Skype call or sorts."

The glance he gave was angled upwards, sideways straight at me and the word he was so found of using became solely applicable in a time like this. He'd called it 'disarming'. Part of the problem was that the weapon rested in his hands.

I wasn't expecting him to point it out. Details were often overlooked in the heat of the moment and for him to have traced it all, back to some point of contact, felt almost characteristic regardless. I had to think fast.

The sentence repeated itself three times in my head before actually triggering some form of an answer.

"There's something called Facebook." Nope. Nope, but could have been worse. "Si Yin's got your info, apparently." Halfway through I'd realized a fatal mistake of calling myself out since technically, I wasn't the kind of person who'd be on social media either. Si Yin was my next best bet.

This got him looking visibly startled. "I-is that so? Well she did mention something about... knowing where I live and who my relatives are..."

I broke eye contact and he looked away just as I did, going back to his ice cream. Leaving the conversation like so and allowing it to sink quietly underneath the surface of his waters was the option I picked out. Either way, I was finishing up Annie's nails when I told him to pass the tub of ice cream I got for myself, nodding at the plastic he'd left on the bedside table.

He removed it from the bag and was handing it over when he paused; staring at the flavor.

"You must be joking," he stared, wide-eyed at the label. "Vanilla? As expected, your taste buds have issues."

I peeled off the plastic and dug in for a first taste. Firing back had somehow become a habit. "It's called having cravings." *Average. Crystal percentage was nothing impressive are far too light for the rich, denser mouthfeel that good vanillas had. Even so, it managed to taste bland. The brown, black specks were probably fake.*

"For one to crave such a... a plain and boring—"

"You've tasted the one at my workplace." Just stating the facts. "You like it."

He became visibly embarrassed by this, blushing to the tips of his ears. It was nice. Dusted red. "H-how did you..."

Realizing that the only reason I'd known this information could only be explained by the fact that Si Yin had sent me a link to his blog, I opted for the truth. This one wasn't so much of a challenge. "I read your writing."

The expectation was for him to feel terribly embarrassed, and since his face had already been the shade of peaches, it didn't take him much to exceed them. The next thing I knew he was indignantly stuffing his face with ice cream and giving himself a brain freeze. Getting out a thermos of hot tea, I poured him half the cap and held it out. He gave me a look before hurriedly accepting it out of oblig-ation.

"The recent one was good," I told him. "Apple crumble."

His reaction had been to glance over, pleasantly surprised but alternating between the floor and up at my face. "Oh! Oh yes, um. The one from the school patisserie... you read that? I'd done it on a whim. The crumble was apparently seasonal and I didn't want to miss out."

"Couldn't read half the words in the first paragraph by the way," I teased, only because we'd made a mutual agreement on his being superior in academics in literally every aspect of it. "Googled nearly everything."

"I suppose you could do with more reading practice then." His mood picked up and he was clearing his throat, hiding the emotion he'd always been too embarrassed to show. "I was planning on doing a feature on the upcoming school festival. A listicle could work—fif-teen must-try take-outs at the upcoming thanksgiving food market. Keith said it wouldn't make the cut unless the visuals were strong and the price points were low enough. I'd have to work on the curation, which means finding out what the other classes are doing and coming up with a list of interesting picks from their menu."

I barely understood half of what he was saying. The solution had been to read his eyes and connect the dots whenever he turned to me. I learnt it was my cue to respond.

"Like I said, Spanish street food. Paella, empanada and... some fried milk thing."

"Leche frita," he finished promptly, nodding and taking it down on the back of the recipe book I'd given him. "That's quite a range. Do most classes opt for more than two items on their menu? Is it encouraged? You'd probably need more manpower, I assume."

"We did five last year—Filipino cuisine—and I was on three items at once because everyone sucked."

He seemed torn between offering a look of pity and one of exasperation. "Well I'm sorry you had to do that. At least you're fond of showing off... there must be a reason Miss Birchwood asked you to be her partner in the tag team competition."

By then, I was done with my tub of ice cream and was waiting for him to do the same. The cup was insanely baby-sized and I'd started later than he did. He was the kind to appreciate every bite.

"Well? She did go out of her way to ask you, Leroy. I've heard how difficult it is to win her acknowledgement and praise."

"Yeah?" I snorted, amused by how nicely he'd put it. "That's why she's so stuck-up all the time?"

"Being hard to impress doesn't make someone a bad person," he went on to defend. "Mind you, she was bawling by the creak at the crack of dawn during the cross-year. Either way, I think you and her are particularly alike in certain aspects of your personalities. You're rather hard to impress, too."

I was about to break it to him, remind him of the millions of times I'd dropped him compliments and very clear signs of being mindlessly in love in his everything, when the weekend doctor doing his rounds came by with his equipment and clipboard in hand.

"You brought a cousin?" He looked surprised. "A friend?"

"Future husband," I corrected with a straight face. The doctor burst out laughing. I blinked.

Aside, my companion appeared visibly exasperated and flustered at the same time, going as far as to bury his face in his hands whilst shaking his head. It was cute.

"Right?" The doctor turned his attention to him. "I can never tell if Leroy's being serious or not. His jokes are great, though." *Okay, but it wasn't really a joke.*

Him coming in meant that it was our cue to go, but the standard procedure involved a nurse, who hadn't arrived just yet so I figured we had a little more time.

"Have you checked the report?"

I nodded. "Yeah."

"All good?"

I nodded again, throwing the rest of my belongings into my bag and clearing the trash; giving Annie another glance. *Ten months now.*

There was knocking on the door and we all turned to it, watching a nurse update the daily check-up schedule outside Annie's room before entering.

"We'll get going," I told the doc, glancing over at future husband slipping on his coat. "Ben?"

"Mr. Cartwright should be back in his room by now, waiting for the community chef. I heard it's ratatouille today," doc laughed, clapping my back as we passed. It's funny how I can't decide if I want Annie here or not. Waking up and recovering meant going home eventually, which was ironically the last thing I wanted to be doing; considering how the hospital felt more like home than home itself.

VANILLA

It was barely two o'clock in the afternoon by the time we arrived at the station we'd met in front of in the morning, having enjoyed a quick bite on our way back. Food trolleys needed some getting used to, for sure. The options given were terribly vast and being the proper decision maker that I was, I'd consulted the trolley lady several times before making a well-informed choice. One could easily tell just how often Leroy had encountered the trolley lady over the past couple of months simply from the time he'd take to pick out a sandwich. It felt almost routine-like, the way he'd point it out seconds after her arrival.

I digress. This all had been to distract myself from the fact that I'd realized how close our first date was in coming to an end.

Admittedly, time had passed a little too swiftly for my liking, and I'd always imagined starry skies, completed by the warmth of street lights above whilst walking them home—not that I would have constant fantasies of what my first date would be like, per se. Just, well. High hopes, I suppose.

We came to a fork not far from the station and I'd turned to Leroy without quite looking at his face. The ground was comforting and fiddling with the straps of my tote bag kept my fingers busy.

"So, um. I guess I'm this way—"

"Can I stay over today?" I heard.

Looking up at once did not quite solve the mystery since it had never really been a habit of his to utilize the art of expression. And meeting his gaze was asking to be singed by flames. I had to physically reach up to ensure my jaw was intact.

"Leroy. I-is the word 'planned' ever going to... going to be in your already *limited* vocabulary?" I managed without breaking down, hoping he hadn't noticed the stammering. The processing and all took longer than usual. "Today is... *today*. That means *now*. A-and I'm not quite sure how I should be reacting. A heart attack is what you're giving me half of the time."

It was by far unfortunate that Leroy did not correct myself, nor did he appear to have any intention of taking back his words at all. He seemed to be waiting, hands in his pockets, staring down at me.

Standing in the middle of the forked road was not a very appropriate thing to be doing so I tugged on his sleeve until we were out of the way.

"Okay so firstly, the refrigerator is unstocked. Second, my bed is small. Third, there is absolutely no entertainment system whatsoever and you might get terribly bored and not to mention, my clothes are most certainly not going to fit you. My apartment is not prepared for an impromptu visit by you." I made sure to lay out before breathing deeply and allowing this to settle in that fiery head of his. The other reason was because it bought time for me to calm my nerves. "That said, I don't... I mean I don't particularly *mind* you staying over—"

"Let's go then," he cracked a smile, already starting in a general direction that took me a second to correct.

"This is not the way to my apartment building," I told him, falling into step. "Where are we going?"

"Shopping for underwear," Leroy said this as though he was stating the obvious, "unless you'd prefer I... put a hole in yours or something." I told him he was being ridiculous, and that underwear was, by its nature, stretchy.

We'd spent nearly an hour in the department store picking out his underwear only because I'd been so amazed by the several different cuts and designs that I never knew could exist in the realm of male underwear. In truth, Leroy had picked something out in less than five minutes upon entering the undergarment section and those five minutes were spent looking for his size. I never knew sizes existed for underwear. I'd always assumed they were stretchy for a reason and Aunt Julie had been the one who did the shopping most of the time.

By the time we'd arrived at my apartment with groceries for dinner and the brand-new apparel that Leroy had got himself, it was half past three. I say 'apparel' because even though my companion had so blatantly claimed that underwear was all he slept in, I'd insisted on the legality of it (illegal, strictly speaking) and thus suggested he bought a cheap, comfortable shirt to wear along with it. I'd stood my ground and told him I wouldn't leave unless he bought a shirt, even going as far as to offer my wallet just so he would have no excuses to buy one. "You simply can't do that. It is illegal."

"*That's* how much you want me to cover up?" He'd laughed before purposefully picking out something absolutely ridiculous: a black shirt with the words 'Impress Me.'

At present, he'd changed into it just as I was keeping myself occupied with the groceries, arranging them neatly in the refrigerator. "We could start prepping as soon as you're ready. I believe the soup takes about two to three hours for it to taste minimally decent."

"Two. ABC's easy."

"And the rice?" I reminded him of the absence of a rice cooker and he paused. "There's only one stove too."

We ended up settling on a general schedule of soup, homework, soup again and then rice. As usual, Leroy never failed to completely side line kitchen owners by delegating the most insignificant of tasks their way. I was given potato peeling while he busied himself with the pork ribs and making of the soup stock. In the midst of mindless peeling, I brought it upon myself to part the clouds and get to the bottom of his intentions. A-after all, staying over while we were, strictly speaking, officially dating, was a far and unprecedented progression in our relationship. I figured something must have had happened with one of his lodge mates.

He'd shrugged for a bit. "Didn't feel like going back," was all he had to say, skinning the carrots with his knife faster than I was going with a peeler and roll-cutting them before I was halfway through a potato. "They get fucking noisy on Saturdays."

I coughed and cleared my throat just so he would know what I mean without me actually saying it aloud. He'd rolled his eyes and given me the indecent finger then, all whilst cutting up his second carrot. I was barely done with my first potato.

"I've always wondered where this all came from," I told him, referring to the general idea of curse words and vulgar hand signs. "Your mother never came across as the kind of person who'd be fond of such language, and I'm pretty sure you started building such a vocabulary at an early age."

Leroy proceeded to snort, not quite getting rid of the smirk on his lips. "Stay in the kitchen long enough and you'll pick it up too."

"The kitchen?" I did a double take, pausing to think. "Easily I can think of examples that would falsify such a claim. My godfather spent nearly three quarters of his life in the kitchen and I assure you, he's never said a single curse word his whole entire life."

"Then he's not human." *Fair point.* Ribs were thrown into the pot, followed by sectioned sweetcorn, carrots and dates. I was working on my third potato and Leroy was already cutting up the second one I'd peeled and added them into the stock.

"Think I was four when he first brought me into the kitchen. On the line," he went on and I found myself slightly taken aback. "That was after he taught me how to hold a real kitchen knife. With two hands." He hadn't quite identified whoever it was he was referring to but it seemed to him almost natural that I would eventually figure it out. I did.

"Real production kitchen, by the way. As in, the one in his restaurant. Not the one we had at home." He finished cutting up the third potato I was done with and proceeded to add that before placing a lid on top of the pot and cranking up the heat. "*Flying fucks* was the first one I learnt. But Annie told me off when she heard me say it, so we compromised on *shit* 'cuz she used it too."

All I could do was sigh since, well, I could technically see where he was coming from. "I'm glad my place remains outside of it all. The kitchen, I mean. The least I can do is speak and write in a refined manner, worthy of a critic."

"I'll teach you one day." Leroy had the gall to wink and I was very naturally beyond frightened by such disarming and illegal gestures and expressions.

We soon left the soup to simmer and fuse whilst the matter of homework and assignments were addressed. I had on my list a couple of essays due the week after the next but nothing particularly urgent except the headline drafts and curation I'd promised Keith, so I got out my laptop and began doing my research.

Leroy on the other hand, was a professional at distracting me. He pulled up a digital version of his recipe book (a neater, much better-designed version of the one he had handwritten and given to me) that was supported by one of the school instructors. It was under her guidance and encouragement that the printed version would be published among the school's exclusive alumni and student collection.

"Not sure when, but it's either going to be on Amazon or just the school bookstore." He seemed rather nonchalant and indifferent about all this when being a published author had been a distant dream of mine since I was three. Ironically, my author is particularly fond of projecting her desires onto me.

"All these," I was referring to the food photography that complimented every recipe in the book. "You did them yourself? That's what the camera in your room was for?" He didn't deny this, so I assumed. "They look highly professional... I'm thoroughly impressed."

Leroy wasn't taking this very seriously because the next thing I knew he was pointing at the words on his shirt and I was rolling my eyes. Naturally, I was feeling terribly excited for him, having gone through the recipes in a single night and then close read the very next day with annotations included. They had been expertly curated.

We spent the next hour doing individual work and were surprisingly focused despite having to split the tiny studio apartment into our own personal spaces. Leroy took the dining table while I remained at my usual spot by the full-length windows, on the floor with a foldable bench thing. I very unfortunately could not resist the temptation to glance over every now and then and because Leroy apparently possessed a similar weakness, we ended up meeting gazes three times. It was awfully embarrassing.

Our tables were about twenty feet apart and we were both plugged in to music but the second time our eyes wandered, he had the gall to wink and the *third*, he'd altogether stood up and advanced till I practically ran into the bathroom and told him to make the rest of dinner while I took a shower.

The last thing I saw was the finger.

Thank goodness I'd prepared my pyjamas and bath towel earlier on and placed them in a basket by the sink, or emerging from the bathroom after searching for cover would provide yet another layer of embarrassment. Fifteen minutes in the shower and I was out toweling myself dry, slipping into a navy blue, satin favorite of mine before unlocking the door and peering out into the room.

Leroy was setting the table, placing a bowl of rice and a serving of ABC soup for us each. Despite being the host, I was being utterly pampered by the guest. Tottering over, I slipped into the seat across him.

"This is... well I promise I'll be doing most of the cooking next time. I appreciate your hospitality."

I'd thought he would be snorting and pointing out my roundabout statements or proving his point by emphasizing on the two words I was having trouble saying but what happened next was completely irrelevant.

"Do you shave?" He was staring at my legs that were out in the open. Since, well, this particular pyjama set featured shorts instead of an ordinary pair of pants. I followed his gaze.

"For hygiene purposes, yes. Is something wrong with my legs?"

He continued to stare but I was hungry and couldn't resist the temptation of food no longer and so asked if we could start eating. He then snapped out of it and we had dinner in silence. This very naturally launched my mind into a flurry of possibilities, of which included the fact that shorts were childish and unappealing despite their breezy comfort, and that Leroy was not very pleased with what I often wore to sleep.

"I could change into something else," I offered for clarification, since I'd technically made him do something about his sleepwear as well. It would have been terribly unfair if I'd disregarded his opinion.

"You mean... take it all off?" He raised a brow as though the words coming out of his mouth were not part of a joke. I reached over the table and successfully dealt a blow to his forehead. My first official flick.

"Get yourself in the shower," I told him, "leave the dishes to me." He was surprisingly quick to cooperate, leaving his bowls and utensils in the sink before I showed him where the toiletries were and handed him a bath towel for his own use.

"Chamomile-scented shower gel?" Leroy wasn't about to let me off the labels on my bottles and I closed the door in his face just as he was beginning to laugh. And as though this was all a game and he was keen on having his revenge, the idiot decided to emerge from the bathroom minutes after in just the bath towel around his waist.

Just the towel.

"E-excuse you." I was physically unable to look at him. Physically. "Where in good heavens is your brand-new shirt?" Clearly crisis-inducing. Though this wasn't exactly the first time I'd seen him without a shirt on—the one other time being back in his lodge, in the morning—this was the only time with glasses and with the only other garment being something highly inappropriate.

"Stained it earlier on," he claimed. I could practically hear the teased flickering of a candle in his voice. I kept my right hand up between us, shielding my eyes. "No apron, remember?"

"No use pinning this on me, Leroy. An apron is a luxury. Plus, you're the school's number three! You... you don't *spill*, t-this is... this is not, clearly, legal l I think you'd have to be arrested for..." I trailed off, stunned and quite incapable of speech. Halfway through, I'd made the mistake of being exasperated enough to chance a look at him but good god, was that not the best of ideas.

It promptly reminded me of the mysteriously rigorous workout regime that culinary students were made to do in separate instances of gym class whilst exempting nutritionists and critics alike. After all, one couldn't possibly be built like an athlete what with food being central to their very living and being unless they were unfairly blessed with the gift of superior metabolism. Leroy was one such fortunate soul.

A pity he'd somehow traded in a good deal of his intelligence for, well, a fine set of physical traits; the idiot did not seem to have the slightest idea of the consequences wet hair could bring. Parts of his bare skin remained concerningly damp, including droplets of water dangling off the tips of his hair and some, clinging to his back.

"Please tell me you're wearing something under that towel," I said to him, slightly relieved to be observing his back instead of the um, the rather distracting front view. Well, technically speaking both were equally high up in their disruptive qualities but I suppose we'd all have to pick our poison at some point in our lives, so. Either way, he appeared to be searching for something. "Is everything alright?"

"Underwear," he laid out, unzipping his rucksack and reaching in before moving on to the grocery bags by the couch. "Can't remember where I put them."

"You mean the box you only just purchased from the department store?" I nearly sighed, pointing him in the direction of the dining table. "They were with the carrots and potatoes in that bag over there. You put them there yourself just this afternoon, Leroy. I can't believe the state of your memory!"

"Just trying to see if I could get away with losing them and not wearing all that to sleep," he had the gall to dodge my words entirely and fire a teasing flame in return. It was practically a crime.

"I'm sorry Leroy but underwear isn't 'all that' when it's the only thing you're attempting to put on at the moment. Let me see the shirt." I knocked on the bathroom door he'd closed for privacy and a hand, along with a bunched-up mess that was his brand-new 'Impress Me' shirt, presented itself through a gap in the door. My companion emerged as soon as I'd accepted it—this time, without a towel but thankfully (or, perhaps on second thoughts, not so thankful after all) clad in a pair of boxers.

"Alright, that's enough," was all I managed after a single glance that confirmed an increased likelihood of fainting spells. "Stay in there and I'll go get you a bathrobe. You're not walking around my apartment in that."

He'd laughed, glancing over his shoulder with a roll of his eyes. "In what?"

"Underwear, obviously."

Less than a minute after I'd pulled out my one and only precious bathrobe from the closet and handed it to Leroy for its appropriate use, the alarm in my phone gave its prompt reminder of bedtime. Naturally, I wasn't going to mess up my sleeping schedule all because a certain someone was over and thus, I'd urged him to don the robe and get into the far end of the bed before hitting the lights.

"At *eleven?*"

The look he gave me was not as appreciative as I would have liked it to be but then again, he appeared to me as a vague condescending blob of human without my glasses and I could very well have mistaken the expression on his face.

"Yes! Eleven. Is there a problem with that?" I made my way towards him, adjusting the covers so that the two of us would have an equal share. "Let me know if it's cold on your end. I'll do something about the heating."

He only seemed to watch, rather still from his end of the bed as I sat on the edge and slowly, carefully slipped under the covers on the other half. Frankly speaking, I wasn't exactly in the most comfortable state sleeping beside the very person I was supposedly dating—an idiot rudely clad only in his underwear had it not been for my generous offer of a bathrobe to sleep in. Well, at least he wasn't completely undressed.

"It's fucking small," was all Leroy had to say as soon as I'd joined him in bed, doing my best to avoid as much physical contact as I could. Admittedly, he was right; it *was* quite the squeeze. Though considering the other options we had, in which included my sleeping on the couch since, well, I wasn't heartless enough to actually suggest he spent the night freezing on that thrifted furniture, this had seemed almost feasible.

"Well then you're welcome to sleep on my doorstep, Leroy Jeremy Cox, self-invited guest," I told him in return, unable to lay bare the squishy creature that was really my heart. For extra measure, I pretended to be making myself comfortable on the extra pillow I'd had to pull out. After all, I couldn't possibly be sharing a pillow with Leroy.

"I'm telling you to come closer, dumbass."

This was followed by a snort and an immediate sensation of a hand on my waist, pulling me in. "You'll fall over like that."

"I-I'm not a child, Leroy. You don't have to go around concerning yourself about thing like me falling off a bed. It sounds completely ridiculous."

Needless to say, the unwarranted physical contact had had me startled. My companion on the other hand, didn't seem to care very much about leaving me in a stuttering mess and merely proceeded to continue on this path of action—soon enough, having my back plastered to his front—though in a manner so initially odd, I couldn't seem to figure out what it was I was pressed up against.

"Those cannot possibly be what I think they are," I whispered-shouted, far too outraged to actually register the fact that I'd accidentally brushed against his, apparently, open bathrobe.

I could nearly hear the smirk in his voice. "What?"

"Bread rolls," I struggled to turn under the covers, far too bewildered to think about anything that wasn't figuring out the mystery that was his abdominal muscles. "Just how often are culinary students made to... to physically, um, exert yourselves?"

"You mean abs," he followed my gaze before returning; staring rather intensely.

"Yes I still can't believe they make it necessary, all those additional field rounds and morning routines and what not." I prodded them out of curiosity and, as biology would have it, they were hard.

"Yeah." He was agreeing with me, albeit to my surprise. Still staring, right down my iris like there was something beyond it that he was looking for. "As though standing from nine to nine and having the stamina to run a line isn't enough as it is. Guess it's why we're always champions in the inter-majors."

"What's that?"

"Sports day, thing. Kinda lame."

"So the majors compete in different segments? Culinary, baking, critics and nutritionists. Like an inter-house sports carnival. The kind they have in every school during the summer season."

"Yeah."

Granted, I hadn't expected *casual conversation*, of all things, to be the source of my returning attention narrowing in on the sudden realization of our close proximity and the sheer clarity of his face despite my vision of poor nature. I tugged on the sides of his bathrobe that had come undone, giving it a quick fix whilst clearing my throat. "There. Much better."

Turning back to the empty space I had been facing—away from the source of my present anxieties—I forced my eyes shut and commenced my first attempt at sheep counting. Alas, it proved futile.

"Night, Vanilla."

He was awfully close. The sheer proximity factored into my general discomfort and heightened self-consciousness, all-too-aware from the clarity of his voice that he had chosen not to turn away from my back and sleep facing the wall. This was further supported by the odd sensation of his abdominal muscles on my back, through the fabric of my pyjamas and the bathrobe he was wearing. Again, as above-mentioned, they were very hard.

Perhaps the entire world was mistaken and that being well-toned wasn't exactly the most positive physical attribute for any human species after all since, well, that couldn't possibly make them very pleasant to hug. All of a sudden, I rather pitied my godfather.

Floating thoughts were unfortunately ineffective in aiding my task to fall asleep and before long, I felt my companion shifting on his side of the bed, tossing and turning for quite the long moment.

"As expected, the bed is small and uncomfortable." I said, strangely nervous. "I apologize. I'll sleep on the armchair. I mean, the couch. You can have the bed." I sat up at once, which was a huge mistake since I definitely would not have appeared the slightest bit sleepy or at least pretended to look the part.

This was very surprisingly followed by him doing the same. Sitting up in the dark.

"I need to jerk off."

"Ah," I'd said on instinct, preparing to shuffle out of bed to let him do as he pleased, whatever the words meant, before pausing and stopping short. It took some thorough scouring of my mental dictionary before I finally realized the absence of the last two words in his sentence, which then warranted some good ol' blinking in the darkness.

Outside, the street was unusually quiet for eleven o'clock on a Saturday evening. There was, however, a warm glow coming from the street lamps downstairs and the odd chill of moonlight combating the orange mist, filtering through the window.

"Is that a bad thing or a good—"

"Masturbate."

Oh, was what really went on in my mind before a pregnant pause ensued and thus ruined the otherwise peaceful, everyday dynamics we had between us since the day we reunited in culinary school.

I mean, there were escalations and the like but *still!* Never to such an extent, dear god these were foreign waters. Very foreign, highly dangerous. Practically lethal.

"U-um. I... well, I."

In the darkness, I knew precisely how I would have looked with the lights turned on. The heat on my face was unbearable and spreading fast, backwards to the very tips of my ears and up to my head for a dizzy moment. Then, it was the neck and everything below that.

What I did not expect was for Leroy to switch on the lamp stuck to the wall on his side, triggering me into a panicked scrambling for the covers in my lap to hide the embarrassment that was my face.

"What are you doing?" He was very clearly laughing, though I wasn't too sure what it was, exactly, he found so awfully amusing.

"Nothing," I kept my face buried in the covers that were bunched up in my hands. Again, he made a sound that was a cross between a snort and a... a don't-know-what and was very soon inching closer, sheets and fabric rustling and—oh god he was trying to take the covers away. "No! No, Leroy, these are my half! You have yours!"

I struggled. I fought. I was unfortunately defeated.

Bare face out like an open book with nothing to hide behind, I refused to have my gaze wander anywhere near his face. This, too, happened to be another mistake of mine. I attribute all blame to the misbehaving bathrobe that was clearly open in all its enthusiastic glory.

All of a sudden, I was acutely aware of the blood rushing downwards and pooling below my midriff. The air was oddly warm and the temperature, rising in a steady motion, played with the thoughts in my head.

"Do you... really need to...?" My eyes drifted somewhere near his neck and, since I wasn't exactly able to make out the exact details of Leroy's body, meant that I could afford looking at body parts I wouldn't usually find myself looking at.

"Yeah."

I tried to make out what was happening under the folds of the covers and his bathrobe by squinting. "Would, um. Would a cold shower suffice? I mean, you've already showered but..."

"You need one too?"

Now he was staring at me. In fact, the direction and general acoustics of his voice made it so that I could tell he was very clearly observing the activity around the lower half of my body, which I, too, had been doing so for him. Except I don't have twenty-twenty vision. Which he had.

Not to mention, satin pyjamas weren't exactly the best at concealing apparent involuntary excitement. Or *instincts*, as I like to call it. Nothing more, nothing less—a perfectly ordinary physical response that needed no attention whatsoever! Instincts weren't going to sweep me off my feet, no. I'd never allow for that; instincts were easily conquered.

At least they'd always been to me, in the past.

"No! No, most certainly not," I told both Leroy and myself. "It'll go away if I leave it and think about the grammatical mistake I'd made in the email I'd written to the Baker's Times for an internship application. It was the very reason I received no response and no one can convince me otherwise."

He had the gall to snort, musing to himself. "Don't you have other ways to get rid of it?"

Admittedly, such a question had indeed made its way across my mind over the years of puberty but entertaining it was a completely different matter. It was in this very moment that I'd decided to give it some genuine thought. In fact, the pause to think had ended up being longer than I'd expected and thus somehow resulted in a fair intensifying of the heat on my face.

Not good.

"I... th-this level of inappropriateness is beyond my capacity." I concluded intelligently.

This proceeded to trigger a smirk on his face that, even without my glasses, I could tell foreshadowed something highly illegal. Leroy was leaning into the conversation, or whatever it was we were having, closing the distance and then in the panicked frenzy that I was experiencing on the inside, brushed something against my upper thigh.

This all had happened in quick succession but because he'd gone and filled my entire field of vision with the upper half of his face, I could only attend to the movement of his gaze—flitting downwards to something below my nose and then back up.

"I'll help you. If you help me."

LEROY

He made me wait for two whole seconds, skin coloring several shades darker than what he first started out with.

"Y-you... you honestly think I'd take you up on that offer?" Disbelief. His eyes struggled, a glimpse into the battle inside. Reason up against instinct. And honestly, he wasn't doing too bad, having re-sisted this far into the flames. He had his waves under control, that's for sure.

"Why not?"

I was at a distance that made it easy for him to observe the details on my face, just so every piece of information was laid out for him, crystal clear. He was having trouble meeting my gaze, though. It was cute.

"Skin," he let slip by mistake and from the way his eyes widened and peered up for my reaction, it only furthered his embarrassment. "I did not mean that. I don't even know why I said it." His gaze lowered to my crotch, mostly because he couldn't look me in the eye. "Were you always this tanned?"

I followed, finding myself highly entertained by his embarrassed, wandering thoughts. "Could be the light."

What I did not expect was for him to continue staring at my crotch, eyes round and, like a pool on a midsummer night, glistening. I couldn't tell if he was curious or amazed or just, turned on by something daunting in his realm of knowledge.

"I mean I'd see why that could be the case but it's ridiculous how I'd never noticed—" I thought he needed some encouragement, what with his drifting attention and with his lips inches away, it wasn't all that hard to lean in for a long one.

It was deeper than usual, unintentionally, so by the end of it, he was holding onto my shoulders for support and then resting his hands on my chest whilst trying to catch his breath. I took one of them in mine and guided it lower, down to where had piqued his interest.

His breath quickened from soft, gentle panting to a series of startled stammers. "Leroy? Where are you—what is the, I-I don't think I..."

"Please?" I'd thought this would make him cave but it was clear he'd known me far too well to fall for one of my tricks. Almost immediately, his eyes had hardened. He knew I wasn't the kind to beg.

"The... the look in your eyes says it all, Leroy. That's no *plea*, that's nearly an order disguised as one and you know perfectly well that it is. I'm not allowing any of th... I... i-is that...?"

His fingers were cold. It had been a matter of taking it out and letting it stand, all whilst helping him out by positioning where and how his hands were supposed to move. Not really what I'd been expecting, but he was keeping both his hands occupied. First, the tips of his fingers and then, the heart of his palm.

Naturally, I was rock-hard.

"Leroy, you're... this... clearly, you're making a, a mistake I-I..." He'd kind of positioned the rest of his body for easier movement of his hands, resting on my length and sort of just holding it there. A single glance at his face confirmed nervous glances and a general expression of extra care and concern for my dick in his hands. "I certainly hadn't *handled* any, sort of, well, body part that did not belong to me, let alone a-a rather specific private area not exactly meant to be handled by just about anyone."

'Handled' was a funny word. I kept that in mind.

Loosening my grip on his wrist, I leaned back to give him some space and rested my weight on the hands I put behind for support. I let him decide.

For the first time, he was chewing on his bottom lip, occasionally peering up with his hands just frozen in place. I didn't say anything to pressure him; just maintained eye contact to let him know that he had all my attention.

"This heat is... it is very unfamiliar," he voiced out of obligation, fingers wrapped around my length and I could see just how he was on the brink of malfunctioning, just realizing what exactly it was he was holding onto.

"I-I should... well, I should remind you that I've never... even to myself, it isn't something I'm entirely familiar with and I'm... I'm admittedly not going to be very good at this. I might even end up hurting you."

This was him. I lifted a finger, beckoning. Still leaning my weight on one hand, I reached for the back of his neck as he neared and, with the momentum, went for another one that was long and deep. From the way his lips had stiffened by surprise and the clear lack of breathing through his nose, I could almost hear the counting in his head.

"There's a first for everything," I told him after he started thumping against my chest as a sign for 'let me breathe.' He sighed, kneeling on the mattress and keeping his hands to himself. Still panting slightly. Satin button-down a mess.

"Short disclaimer, um. I'm no expert. Also, do sound out if, say, I'm hurting you in one way or another. A-are we clear? On this?"

I rolled my eyes, giving him a simple 'yes' but also just leaving it there for a pause, waiting for him to collect himself. He was fixing his shirt—fingers trembling just enough to render his buttoning abilities useless. His shorts were riding up his upper thigh, which was mostly the fault of my wandering hands during the kiss.

Either way, I was about to tell him I'd take care of it myself in the bathroom when he, all of a sudden, went into breathing exercises mode, closing his eyes and all. In the seconds I was distracted by his breathing, he'd sort of leaned into me, head angling in a way that I thought he was going for a hug but instead, reached for my shaft.

"Hey—" I thought of telling him to slow down, or at least warn him against forcing himself but there was something in his eyes and it was fucking full-on-*concentration*.

It was so like him to be setting his mind on pulling something off, no matter how far it was beyond his capacity of knowledge or experience. For him, even in moments like these, to be doing his best was personally the ultimate turn-on.

I found it hard not to stare at his face. He was blushing, that's for sure. And then swallowing because he was nervous; then, occasionally, peering my way to check for reactions. For some reason, I could tell the things going around in his head were just about crazy.

He had both his hands running up and down my length in gentle strokes, resembling mere brushing of his fingertips at times that anyone else would have mistaken for deliberate teasing. His inexperience was clear as day—almost as though the concept of jerking off had never been an issue legitimate enough for him to include in his mental capacity. His touch was soft, slow and unsure, mostly careful with no sense of rhythm and visible worry written on his face.

"Does it, um. Are you...? Is there a proper way of doing this?" He finally asked, having observed zero reaction on my face. His gaze continued to alternate between the heat in his hands and up at my own.

I reached for his waist, pulling him closer to laugh in his ear. "Wow, you really suck at this."

He blushed indignantly at my amusement and stammered a protest. I slipped a finger down the back of his satin shorts and tugged, along with the band of his underwear. "I'll teach you."

"What! Th-that is not how—"

"Watch closely."

"Good god Leroy Cox this is no ordinary practical lesson with step-by-step demonstrations!" He was pressed up against me, fingers still somehow wrapped around my shaft but frozen in place. "You're not going to... you cannot possibly be thinking of..."

I coaxed the back of his neck into leaning forward, just so that he would rest his head on my shoulder for comfort, then stripped his bottom half. I checked his state for permission before reaching between his legs.

He had been trying to look at what I was doing or where my hands were about to go, but we both knew he wasn't the best multi-tasker around, so while he attempted to jump-start his malfunctioning hands, I stroked him once.

His reaction was immediate. Trembling—almost violently, in the middle of saying my name before shutting down in a whimper. It was soft. Barely audible. But he was close enough and I was looking out for signs in the first place.

He was untouched, for sure. The skin I was caressing between my fingers, feeling in the heart of my palm. Pale, pink at the tip or at least from what I could tell under the dim light. His skin was smooth. Almost soft.

I stroked twice, then with my other hand, reached up to run along the sides of his waist, covering as much as I could while he seemed to be almost leaning into my touch. This was before I found a pace he responded to the most, kept at it for a couple of strokes and then, picking up.

"That's... y-you're not..." He wasn't in the state to speak, let alone piece words together for a sentence. Somewhere along the way, he'd left my length and reached for my hand that was stroking his own, brushing my wrist or whatever it was he was trying to grasp. "That's just—that's going to... to dirty your... you don't have to..."

If this was him trying to stop me from pleasuring him, it wasn't really working because his attempt was feeble and also, he was also clearly crumbling under instincts; unconsciously leaning into my touch, along with his entire body just giving in and inching, closing the distance between us till he had his face buried in my shoulder. It muffled the sweet things threatening to escape his lips. His breathing picked up, hard and uneven against my neck and the scent of his shampoo, mixed with the chamomile tea he had before going to bed and his pyjamas was sending me over the edge.

"Leroy?"

I turned, just to observe the look on his face but instead, stared at his ear that was a mere inch away. I licked it.

He gasped, clearly surprised and turned several shades redder the moment he heard himself. I laughed, nuzzling down his jaw and picking up the pace of my hand that had been doing the stroking, thumbing the tip several times till he was unable to internalize the physical pleasure he was going through—hips bucking and back arching into his high.

He came in my hand. For a good moment, he seemed to have lost all control of his system. Fingers clinging on to the bathrobe on my back and pitched, adorable sighs escaping his lips. I let him rest his forehead on my shoulder whilst catching his breath, coming down from his high.

I'd always imagined his resistance to be a lot lower. Like, coming from a kiss, low. If this was his first time receiving a hand job or jerking off, even, then I'd say he was doing pretty well. It surprised me. Would have to correct my stance on this.

"Oh god I'm so... I'll get you some tissues."

"No need," I told him, holding him in place with my other hand that was clean, knowing that what he needed most at the moment was some time to patiently wait it out, let the high of his climax slowly make its exit. We stayed like this for a good minute or two—him resting his forehead on my shoulder and me wondering if my erection was ever going to go away—till he promised he was alright and that I could let go.

He brought a box of Kleenex over to the bed and I asked, teasing, if he was ready to put 'observation into practice.'

"That was barely observing," he started out, back to being overly self-conscious already. "I-I... I was in your neck nearly half the time." I wiped my hands and pulled him closer to wipe him down too. Meanwhile, he was looking around for his shorts, slightly dazed.

I wanted his full attention.

"You were really weak right here." I thumbed his tip without warning and went for his ear once more and it was enough to send shivers down his spine.

"Leroy, please." He looked serious, albeit teary-eyed from the prior and immediate pleasure. "No more."

Seeing that he wasn't in the state to respond or continue, I let him off the hook and cleaned him properly, handing over his shorts before helping him with the covers. "You sleep. I'll be in there."

He followed my gaze to the bathroom, slightly stunned. "W-what? But I thought we were... I mean, you haven't exactly...goodness. Why am I so tired from... how is this possible?"

"Ejaculation releases a hormone called prolactin, ever heard of that?"

"No... no, I haven't," his eyes were half-closed, "I must have missed it out on the biology thesaurus I'd read five years ago. I must have sped through it..."

"It makes you tired," I went on, as a distraction. I was really just waiting for sleep to hit him. "Also associated with 'recovery time.' It's the break people take between rounds of sex."

"O-oh... oh, I see..." He mumbled something about research and having to go back to that biology thesaurus before completely falling asleep. I made sure he was comfortable under the covers before heading to the bathroom with the past ten minutes still fresh in my memory.

* * *

I was up before he was and it had pretty much everything to do with that huge window behind the bed without its curtains drawn, leaving the sun all up in our faces and the urge to reverse it back down the horizon just at the forefront of my head. I'd gone to bed at least fifteen minutes later than he did, minutes after taking care and washing up, then making sure he was fast asleep before lying next to him.

Sitting up, I checked the time. He didn't look like he would be waking up anytime soon and I was reluctant to move. The bed wasn't too bad. Small, but comfy. He'd chosen a good duvet. Everything smelled like him, too; refined, a little reserved but still soft and soothing. Chamomile. I felt for my phone and snapped a picture. Then put it aside.

There was something about his face right now that said a lot about the things he liked to hide behind those glasses of his, often like a mask. People used to hearing big words line his every sentence, said in a tone so serious that he'd be mistaken for an icicle, wouldn't see past the dangers of honesty and the complexity that was the web of his mind.

Without the active shield of words and knowledge, he looked defenseless. Almost soft, breathing into the side of his pillow like ripples in a pond.

Staring at him first thing in the morning didn't cross my mind as a bad idea but it soon did when I felt instincts rushing down south so I got back up and checked the general state of my situation under the covers.

Hm.

I had to get up either way, which meant either doing so now at a low risk of him seeing all that versus giving it a gamble while we were both awake and heading to the bathroom to brush our teeth.

The safer call would be the first, even after factoring in the possibility that he'd wake from my climbing across him to get out—my side being a wall, so.

I made it out safely after carefully adjusting the covers so that they replaced my warmth and then, supporting myself on both hands beside his head, rolling out. He didn't stir. Also, I almost stepped on his glasses. For some reason, they were on the floor. So then it was brushing my teeth and washing up, dealing with morning wood, wearing some pants just in case he'd get a heart attack minutes into the waking world, then searching the fridge for anything breakfast worthy.

Sure, it wasn't part of the usual routine. I skip it most of the time since it meant a couple more minutes in bed, especially on weekends when I set the alarm for noon. Still, he was the kind who needed some distraction after first times, regardless of the context. Giving him something on a plate to critique was a good idea.

"Two eggs," in the egg rack. I nearly laughed. His uncle wouldn't be pleased to know how often he'd been resorting to microwaved box lunches. This fridge was basically unstocked without me.

I checked the freezer for some leftover bacon, and then after fishing out a red and green pepper from the bottom of the vegetable drawer of expired stuff, mapped out a vague menu of frittatas and rosti. Fortunately, we had a couple of potatoes leftover from last night.

Getting the burner going made an unnecessarily loud sound so I turned over to check if he stirred. Surprisingly, he didn't. The assumption was that giving (not entirely) and receiving a hand job for the first time had been extremely exhausting. Studying, reports, essays, exams were easy for someone like him but it all came down to one activity that drained all the energy otherwise spent in the world he was comfortable in.

I caught myself on a dangerous thought. It had to do with hoping he'd say something about liking it, or any form of green light that meant he would be okay with progressing further. Or at least be okay with what we did last night. I had to settle for a low bar; partly because I'd always been the one who knew exactly what I wanted for a longer time. We never really talked about sexuality, or the fact that asking him out actually came before said talk.

I was crisping up the bacon strips, getting a good char on both sides whilst dicing up the peppers and keeping an eye on the bed when I caught him stir at the corner of my eye. This sadly distracted me from the bacon and it was the smell of an overdone char (okay it's burning but I don't want to admit it) that brought me back to the pan.

"Leroy?"

I don't usually panic but it was the combination of having to hear his reaction to last night and burning fucking *bacon* that altogether made me switch off the flame and stop functioning for a moment. He called me a second time and was already sitting up, rubbing his eyes and squinting in my direction.

I gave my hands a quick rinse before going over.

"Hey."

He struggled to sit up straighter, momentarily dazed as soon as I neared. Assuming he could make out my general features at this distance. "Leroy? You're... I," and then he was turning pink by the second before finally retreating back underneath his covers. "I slept surprisingly well."

Okay. Wasn't expecting that.

"Yeah, happens after... yeah," I finished intelligently only because he was giving me this wide-eyed, innocent look that made it hard to go on with the sex talk. Not as if I had any practice either. Being awkward and stiff applied to me as much as it did to him. "Everything okay?"

He blinked, staring into space before slowly lowering his gaze to my bare chest. "I, um. Yes. Are you...? I'm... so so sorry I fell asleep during... i-it's just—"

I wasn't going to put him on the spot so I pretended to cut him some slack and relieve him from my gaze, glancing over my shoulder at the kitchen countertop. It's obvious how looking at him in a way put pressure on his response. Like he said, 'candles.'

"It's nothing. How's your body?"

"A-absolutely nothing we did warrants that question and you know it, Leroy," he couldn't bring himself to look me in the eye and was searching for his glasses, groping around the bed after checking the bedside table. I told him it was over on the dining table. "This is odd. I can't seem to remember how I used to look you in the eye."

I gave him the usual and his response time, slowed by embarrassment and another streak of emotion I couldn't make out, made sure I landed the flick. He didn't react very much to it, only reached up to rub it lightly and blush even harder. At this rate, I was going to catch his awkward embarrassment.

I pointed this out.

"Well I'd like for you to know just how shameful I feel about falling asleep without... taking care of your needs. It was extremely rude of, of me."

His words never failed to amuse and entertain but this was a step farther than his usual. I helped him out of bed and brought him his glasses before going back to the burner. He headed for the bathroom before emerging, moments later, with a toothbrush in his mouth.

"Did you like it though?" I cracked the eggs into a bowl and added to that whatever milk he had left in the fridge.

He blinked, mouth full of toothpaste. "Hm?"

"Did you like it," I repeated, lowering my gaze so that he had more to work with. The added suggestion provided some grounding but it still took him ten blank seconds to figure out what I was referring to.

"Physical pleasure is, a-after all, pleasure," he managed after rinsing out the toothpaste and then coming out of the bathroom all shy and cute. "It was an escalation of our, um, of us. An escalation, *but*, not unpleasant."

Things were looking up. "Okay," I told him, trying not to let the amusement show on my face but then again, I wasn't the best actor. "So there's a next time?"

"That... would not be inaccurate. I must admit, this all isn't... I mean, I'm not entirely sure about something as complicated and beyond my realm of knowledge as sexual attraction or, well, orientation or anything of similar categories or labels but I can be sure that on my part as, um, a-as your... your partner—are we? Is that how you'd... because the term 'boyfriend' sounds so oddly childish that I can't seem to wrap my head around it—but as I was saying, yes. I take full responsibility for... for not, you know. Fulfilling my duties of, of our seesaw-ing. You had to do everything on your side and I was practically a pebble. You might as well have been seesaw-ing with a puppet."

I'd finished frittatas and was in the middle of buttering the pan for the next dish when he started spiraling into an abyss of self-blame and just basically coming down way too hard on himself. So I got a fork, stabbed it into a triangle of frittata and presented it in front of his face.

"You're not going to be 'seesaw-ing' your part of the play as long as you aren't ready for it," I told him, guiding the end of the fork to his lips so that he'd distract himself with the food. "Just... take your time. You need a day? A week? I'll wait."

"But Leroy—there's no acidity in this by the way, you're missing tomatoes and I have lemon-infused olive oil up there in that cabinet but I suppose you're not going to be ransacking my pantry at eight in the morning, so—you see, I... I want *not* to take my time. Does that make any sense, grammatically? It's just I've always wanted to understand myself, o-or my attraction towards you, specifically, on a greater scale."

I cut myself a triangle and sent it in for evaluation. No surprises, he was right about the acidity. "Your fridge is unstocked. No tomatoes whatsoever. You've got a bottle of sour cream so I'm using that to go with the rosti. There's your acidity on the plate."

"Oh. Oh, alright, um. That works... but Leroy, were you listening to me?" He sounded anxious and this was kind of what I'd feared the most. "I mean to say that I, believe it or not, do not dislike the progression in our relationship last night and I'd like to, well, I'd like for it to... to continue. And not be sent back to sleep before you're satisfied yourself."

I plated breakfast for two and nodded at the dining so that he'd set the table. He did after hesitating. We sat across each other and I picked up my utensils but he refused to start, waiting expectantly for my answer.

"Hey," I sighed. "I know what you're trying to say. But we both saw how much you froze over last night just from trying to give me a hand job. Or just, having your fingers on my dick." He flinched at the word and it only seemed to prove my point. His version would have been 'reproductive organ' or something along those lines.

"S-so... you don't think I'm ready?" He sounded hurt. I felt worse than before but knowing how this could possibly lead to something worse than him just being mentally hurt kept me under control. "Even though I'm telling you that I am?"

"It's not just a gut feeling, Vanilla. You're the rational one. You sure jumping into this with zero knowledge about sex is the better decision?" I laid out, pouring him a glass of apple juice. "I don't want to hurt you."

VANILLA

Admittedly, that conversation with Leroy had taken its toll on my confidence level and general faith in the capacity of my mind for precise decision-making and superior judgement. While mundane texts continued to be exchanged and everyday conversations about flavor combinations and accounting basics made up the most of our digital back-and-forth, the topic of mature activity never once resurfaced after that day.

It had come down to a point in which I was desperate enough to be filling up whatever space there was left in my mind with the necessary knowledge. Leroy had claimed my insistence on progressing further in our relationship to be a matter of poor judgement primarily due to my inexperience (true) and my lack of theoretical study (also true). Thus, I figured I had to be doing something about it.

The basis of research should never start with the internet, just in case you're wondering. My first and accurate instinct was to consult science, as it should be, always, and after reading 'The Hormonal Theory of Sexuality' and several other biological texts, I finally moved on to prose and manuals, of which included 'Instructional Modules on Sex Education for College Students' and 'Values in Intercourse: From Principles to Practice.'

Admittedly, these were all very informative and provided a fair enough foundation for my branching out to keyword searches on the internet. Googling unknown terms did aid in my process of understanding this field of knowledge but had, unfortunately, raised more questions than I started out with.

Needless to say, I was far too embarrassed to be consulting Uncle Al with my woes or Aunt Julie with, um, sexual activities between two males and my only other friend who wasn't Leroy was Si Yin, who, herself, seemed rather clueless about such things. So then the only person left on my list was most unfortunately, another awkward pebble soul unable to have a conversation about things that happen behind closed doors.

"So um, Leroy and I... well, we had a row—"

"Oh dear, that's terrible!" Moments after catching up with my godfather, I'd decided to jump straight into the topic at hand and as usual, Chip was extremely enthusiastic in his reactions to whatever it was I had to say. Up until this point, all he knew was that Leroy was my childhood friend and that we were dating.

"But then soon after, he kissed me and not a single rational bone in my body could remain mad at him." I backed out a little but it had also been the partial truth. He'd done so just to break my shell and get breakfast going.

"Evil!" Chip had exclaimed. *"Pure evil!"* For some reason, I felt like he'd been through something of similar nature. *"What was it about? Did he steal the pudding you had at the bottom of the freezer, reserved for a special occasion?"*

"Well um. Not exactly, but I understand where you're coming from. I've been... I mean, we've done some..." Good god, this was harder than I thought and not a single word related to the events of that night could be pieced together without me dying of embarrassment. "I've just been doing some research on... on, y-you know. The kind of night-time activities human beings do behind closed doors. More specifically between men."

"B-but Vanilla! That's... that's very brave of you but aren't you fifteen? Um, i-isn't this, I mean, no judgement, really, but of course you have the right to be curious so I suppose being curious about it isn't a bad idea and um... Xan! What did I tell you about drying yourself before coming out of the bathroom?"

"I... I understand but," at once, I began to see how Leroy had had a point about my diving into this. "It's knowledge, regardless, and yes I may be rushing into things but I... dear god, you're right. I am taking things a little too fast. I suppose it's the nerves of coming into a relationship without knowing anything. I can't seem to find a reason for my attraction to Leroy. *Specifically.* I struggle under the category of sexual orientation. It's all so confusing."

"Oh Vanilla, sweetheart, these things can take a lifetime to figure out! Some people realize their orientation past their fifties. It's not an answer you're going to get in less than five minutes like a mathematical problem... and if that's what you're worried about, we can talk about it over Thanksgiving! J-just... night time thingies should be taken slow and do your research if you must but back in my day, I was as clueless as you are but um, Xander was very u-um good at, the um, the leading part, so..." From the other end, I could hear laughing in the background.

"That's another thing that had me confused. Must there necessarily be a leading figure? A-and I've read things about the um, the entering from the back and well I was wondering about the pain and all because I'm pretty sure the muscles down there aren't—"

My godfather's husband had left me a text the very next day warning against conversations of similar nature or he'd soon have to hunt me down for causing husband malfunctions. Chip later on apologized for that and told me it was good practice for his kids in the future, which ultimately meant that I'd come upon crossroads.

Even with the next couple of days packed with first-quarter assessments and minor projects, I continued to read up on scientific texts that would further my understanding of, um, the future activities that Leroy and I would preferably be... *maybe* engaging in. Either way, texting was the closest interaction we could squeeze into our busy schedules and our lack of tutoring sessions, mostly due to every class' school festival prep work out of curriculum hours, soon garnered the attention of our friends.

"So did uh you and Naruto-boy get into a fight? Is there no more Naruto-Einstein? Should I be worried?" Si Yin had been resisting the urge to ask this particular question since a week ago when I first turned down her invitation to lunch with Raul and the rest while Leroy was on Line Production duty.

"I'm not avoiding him," was what my intelligent self decided to go with even without her mentioning anything close to that. "I-I mean we had our opinions. On which we disagreed. But neither of us are giving the other a cold shoulder and this is not a cold war so no, you should not be worried."

Si Yin had shot me a fair look of pity regardless of my explanation and given my shoulder three pats. It was later on in the day while Chef Palmer had once again entrusted me with the handling of school festival duties that I ran into Raul. A small of team of volunteer classmates, including myself, had stayed behind after school hours to set up our food stall for tomorrow.

While electricity and gas were mostly provided and set up by the school technicians, decorating the booth with signages, a fancy menu and relevant props were perhaps even more important than producing good quality food. Nowadays, a picturesque storefront for the purposes of social media ranked first among consumers' decision-making factors. At least according to CR04 Industry Knowledge, it was.

Raul and several of his classmates were hammering away at a several recycled wooden planks, combining them into a single, decent-sized signage for their booth, which was... right across ours. At once, I was looking out for a certain idiot. Fortunately, he was nowhere in sight.

We were putting up a row of scarlet lanterns across the awning, just below the signage that was in traditional Chinese characters we'd agreed on—with a rough English translation in a smaller font—when Leroy's lodge mate decided to call out to the few of us and asked if anyone had decent handwriting.

Si Yin had been the first to point her fingers at me.

"I just need you to write the menu here," he gestured to a blackboard laid out on the ground space between their stall and the one owned by the class beside them. "It's going up near the back so can you make it big? And cursive? Cool stuff."

I picked up a stick of blue chalk and, according to the menu Raul had keyed into his phone, mapped out the menu items and their respective prices in my usual penmanship. He was easily impressed.

"Thanks man. You and Leroy, uh... no more playdates?" His Italian accent seemed a fair bit thicker and from our past experience of working together during the cross-year event, it meant that he was nervous.

"Oh we've just been, um, a little busier these days. I'm sure he'll be needing some help with AB soon after the school festival, so. Plus, the holidays are near."

"Yeah but no I wasn't talking about the AB, I was talking about the playdates," Raul insisted, oddly serious. "And yeah, the holidays are coming but you know they're all preparing for the interschool, right...? Dude's just going to get busier so... yeah."

"But that's not due till January, is it?" I straightened up, dusting the chalk of my hands. "The school calendar has it on the week after new year's."

"Change of plans. L'Assiette doesn't wanna host the W-interschool any more. CSS said they can't either so it's on us this year and the dorms can't fit in that many people during the semester so they're doing it right before Christmas when everyone's home."

I blinked in surprise. Leroy hadn't said a word about spending Christmas in school. I'd even considered inviting him to Uncle Al's annual party since, well, since it might have been several years since he'd attended one.

"He didn't tell you," Raul gave the look on my face a glance and sighed. "Maybe it's not important."

I shook my head, denying his attempt to ease the discomfort

in my chest. "Um... we'll figure it out. Thanks for letting me know though." He appeared rather distraught by my response, not quite reacting to the small wave I threw in his direction before retreating back to where I'd come from.

"Hey!" Si Yin was on me as soon as I returned, dropping the calligraphy brush in her hand and coming up to where I was. "Everything okay?"

The front of our Chinese street food stall looked decently pleasant, filled with dangling lanterns and scrolls of Chinese characters read from up to down, right to left—which was really just a fancy version of the menu. The traditional woks, fryers and pans we'd requested were provided in abundance and with the other volunteers working on the fake firecrackers we'd thought of hanging up on both sides of the stall, it wasn't looking shabby at all.

I'd even proposed a photo booth section at the end of the collection queue, specifically for customers to snap a quick photograph right after they'd received their food item fresh off the pan. Overall, it looked just as I'd imagined it to be.

"White? Where should we put this?" Freda and Lavinia, patisserie and nutritionist respectively, were part of the few who'd stayed behind to help. They were holding up a string of convincing fire crackers each.

"They look wonderful. Thank you—don't worry about putting them up. I'll do that."

"Nah I'll do it," Ariq intervened all of a sudden, taking them from me and dragging a chair behind him towards the far right of the booth. "I'm the tallest around."

Both Freda and Lavinia rolled their eyes but I was quietly grateful for his offer since, having made the mental projections and estimates, I would have eventually had to ask for his help. Admittedly, this was all a matter of not allocating any volunteer more work than they'd already signed up for. After all, we were five out of the twenty-odd students of 1B.

"So! The fire crackers are done, the menu's all good... you gonna head to the ice cream parlor now?" Si Yin was back at it again, shuffling into my line of sight and searching my eyes for any sign of truth. I told her and the rest that they were free to leave.

"I'll be, um, doing final checks on the crockery first. We've got to ensure everything's in place when the ingredients arrive tomorrow at five in the morning, so... have a good rest, everyone."

Ariq was dragging the chair back to its original spot while Freda and Lavinia picked up their bags and waved, leaving Si Yin to whisper-shout in my ear.

"Vanilla! What's going on? Why are you avoiding your man?"

"I-I'm not *avoiding* him," was all I could intelligently come up with, adjusting the frames atop my nose. "We're both incredibly busy. That's no equivalent to avoiding somebody."

"Uhh yeah it is," she was on the roll, jabbing me in the chest. "You've checked the crockery list, like, five times. Everything's in order! Leroy's class has their booth right across ours and you're not concentrating because of that, am I right or am I... right?"

I tried for a different approach. "Well Si Yin, what if I tell you that the reason I'm, well, finding accuses to stay a little longer is because I'm just... you know, waiting for him to appear over there? Help Raul and his classmates set up their booth? They're far from done, as far as I know."

This got her pausing.

"Oh. Oh!" Her frown dissipated into nothing and she skipped over to counter where she'd left her bag sitting. "Alright. Don't want to be a third wheel then... oh yeah and remind me what it was that you needed me to—oh right. Five o'clock with the Polaroid camera," she said after checking the wallpaper of her phone, presumably where she'd put all her important reminders.

I thanked her for remembering, then waved over my shoulder. The list attached to the clipboard in my arms wasn't the longest of its kind. An anonymous vote had made Chinese street food out to be the theme of choice and getting a hold of the crockery and ingredients proved to be rather effortless with the school's vast connections and well-stocked pantry. While most of the class hadn't seemed all-too-enthusiastic about the festival, no one appeared vehemently displeased by the result of the vote.

It took me an additional twenty to thirty minutes to ensure that everything was present and in place—and some perfecting of the fire cracker angles and taping the ends of the scrolls down so that they wouldn't collide at every gust of wind—before leaving the plaza at eight in the evening.

The desire to have the next twenty-four hours sped up and done in the snap of a finger were crashing waves in a storm that rocked my boat. I needed it all to go away and for this to be out of my realm of responsibilities before directing all my attention to personal issues, which was precisely the reason I'd set my eyes on pulling this off flawlessly.

Alas, this was not to be.

Five in the morning, hours before the sun would peek above the horizon, the booth we had so painstakingly decorated was in a state far worse than we'd started out with. To say that it was in shambles was an understatement for at least then, there was proof of us having put up *something* but no—the stall was bare; robbed of the lanterns, fire crackers, signs and every scroll, every streak of red. A mere skeleton.

IV

⚛️

VANILLA

My first instinct had been to check the booth number indicated at the corner of the striped awning in a hopeless attempt to prove my wandering eyes wrong, frantically searching under the tables of crockery and then the gas and the grill for a sign of some prank of poor taste, but even the aluminium bars holding up the stall appeared bare and untouched so much so that I'd begun to question my sanity and entertain the possibility of this being part of an unwarranted dream.

It was dark out and there was barely a streak of sunlight over the horizon at five, leaving the rest of the plaza ghostly quiet except for the occasional gust of wind. Being the first to arrive meant the absence of an immediate consultant and, surveying every nearby stall and booth, I came to the conclusion that everyone else had decided to ignore the school's scheduling of ingredient delivery for an hour's worth of additional sleep. Not to mention, I'd also been one of the last to leave the night before, having double, triple checked every single aspect of the booth to ensure everything was in perfect order. The state of the school had resembled a graveyard by the time I'd left, so who could have gone to the extent of... of arriving after ten in the evening and before five in the morning for some silly, *childish* sabotage?

I was no more furious or frustrated than I was tired. Exhaustion was heavy on the shoulders and for a moment, dropping my bag on the ground had not seemed to lighten my load.

With most of the plaza unfortunately empty, the only solution had been to come up with hypotheses of my own and, accordingly, map out possible routes of action and the remaining options I had. I was about to start searching for students down the lane our booth was on when, to my pleasant surprise, several male students whom I'd recognized as Leroy's classmates from yesterday began to filter into the plaza with cartons marked 'fragile' and ice boxes over their shoulders, headed for their booth.

"Hi, hello," this was the fastest I'd ever gone up to strangers for a chat. "Sorry to bother. You're the only ones here and I was wondering if—"

"Oh hey." One of them seemed particularly enthusiastic. "You're that first-year guy Cox chose to be on his team for the cross-year."

"Yes. That I am," I caught on quickly, hoping this would provide him enough incentive to converse with someone like myself. "I was wondering if you'd perhaps been here earlier than five o'clock in the morning? Or, if, by chance, you'd seen anyone wandering around our lane late last night or early this morning... something's wrong. My class had our booth decorated and all but..." I'd trailed off, turning to the stall across theirs.

Almost at once, there was a chorus of boy-gasps. The general 'ohh' sound they tended to produce at something shocking or in a general bad situation when they knew not what to say.

"*That's* you guys?"

"There were lanterns all over the awning just yesterday, right?" One of them set his ice box down and I nodded vigorously, glad that there were at least witnesses who could remember what the stall looked like before. "They're gone?"

"Feels bad man." "We honestly just arrived and got a call from our representative about the ingredient pick-up, so..." "But Cox was here late last night, wasn't he? Setting up the deep fryers."

I was all ears at the name, turning to meet the gaze of the student who'd mentioned his presence. "Leroy? He was here? But um, exactly how late did he...?"

"Like, about eleven-thirty-ish, maybe? I don't know. You want me to call him or something?" He was nice enough to offer but the logic in my head had gone several miles ahead as soon as I'd heard his name.

Pure rational reason would have concluded that Leroy was not a witness to any suspicious activity occurring the night before since if he *did*, he would have texted me right away or warned me about it because one, he knew our class was the only Chinese street food stall in the entire plaza and would have identified that as ours and two, he had no reason to be hiding something like that from myself. Even if he did, he wouldn't have put up with such behavior occurring right before his eyes and because the school closed at midnight sharp, that would have to mean that the incident occurred between four, the school's opening hour, to five in the morning, when I'd arrived.

The only premise that would destroy my entire claim was my unwavering faith and trust in the subject.

"Um, no it's fine. You don't have to call him," I said to his classmate, thanking the rest of them with a brief nod. "Thanks for your help... I guess I'll just contact the authorities."

"Oh. You sure?" He seemed surprised by my confidence—which was perfectly justified since, well, even I was taken aback by the sheer lack of doubt in my decision not to contact him.

"Yes. I'm sure. Thank you, again."

I gave the time a quick check whilst returning to my booth across the lane. Two hours till the instructors make their rounds for the quality and hygiene check. The festival briefing the other day also mentioned something about giving each booth an electronic machine for coupon scanning, which would be keeping track of the numbers for every class and the total number of customers they'd served. The top few were entitled to keep a portion of their earnings and were also said to be given priority in upcoming learning journeys.

There was much at risk, considering the competitive nature of our school's culture.

"Vanilla?" I heard Si Yin's voice from afar and turned, relieved to see her approaching from the far end of the plaza stairs. "Sorry I'm late. The traffic was bad and Sebastian had to make a detour down small roads. What's..." Her voice trailed off as she got closer. Then she stared at me in disbelief.

I shook my head, resisting the urge to avert my gaze. "I... I know what it looks like but—"

"This wasn't how it looked like yesterday, right?" My best friend took one look at the bare, empty mess before returning to me, shaking my shoulders. "My memory can't be *that* bad, can it? Oh my god Vanilla, do something with your magic hands."

"I-it most certainly did not look like this," was all I managed, silently relieved that the first of her thoughts hadn't jumped to identifying me as the perpetrator, 'caught in the act.' Just as I'd trusted Leroy, she, too, had complete faith in me. "I'll check in on the group. Could I entrust you with getting an instructor here? Or any form of authority. Just, someone from the organizing committee."

She gave a swift, but slightly panicked nod before taking off in the direction of she came from, then u-turning because the organizing committees tent was in the wrong direction and she could tell from the way I was snapping my fingers at her back.

Okay Vanilla, nothing wrong yet. You have two hours to set things straight so just... just calm down, I could hear my head telling the frantic creature in my chest, thundering in a crazed beat. I composed a text on the volunteer group just to check in on their whereabouts, hoping they'd somehow know something about this or that they'd miraculous moved the props somewhere else due to unlikely weather conditions o-or—*good god* was it hard to convince myself.

Then it was taking a picture of the state of our booth with the intention to send it in the class group chat after composing a suitable accompanying caption but then I was hovering over the send button like a malfunctioning bot.

While Si Yin had been loyal, trusting and kind enough to understand my plight, the ultimate truth remained: we were best friends. The rest of my classmates on the other hand, weren't exactly on the greatest terms with myself and by god, were they not going to be happy about this. The worst-case scenario was something I often preferred mapping out before everything else, especially during dire situations that required much preparation of the fragile heart for damage.

I was going to have to take the blame if we never find out who the perpetrator was. Or at least for now, it was bound to happen first. *This was all very insane. And how could this... why would anyone... how* could *anyone—*

"Is it me or is our booth kind of, not, ready?" This statement indicated the arrival of several other classmates on the early morning shift, of which included Jingrui Li and Jesse Meyers, culinary majors whom I've worked with prior to the food festival. And by that I merely meant being on production kitchen duty together. We weren't all that chummy with one another; nor were we on generally pleasant terms.

Knowing at once that I wasn't going to be spared the opportunity or time to dish out a full-length explanation of what happened, I devised a two-pronged approach: sending the early ones to search for the missing props and décor, and having the others quickly remake the elements of the booth in less than two hours.

Either way, I'd arranged for there to be additional class members on ingredient prep duty, which was a relief because imagine if I hadn't tried to foresee issues—not to an extent like this, no, but still—occurring at such an untimely hour.

"It's not like we expected to win anyway," Li had said soon after receiving my instructions to look for the missing props in designated areas I'd pointed out, ones with a higher probability rate. "1A's killing it with their café so... why try?" Meyers had responded to this by sighing so loud that people across the lane turned.

They left, ignoring Si Yin who'd returned with an official from the organizer's tent. After exchanging a word or two and explaining the situation as quickly as concisely as I could, we were told that a report would be filed and our instructors informed.

"Guess the Polaroid camera's kinda useless now, huh," said Si Yin as soon as the official had left us to speak to the school's security team. "I was honestly so pumped up that I remembered. Oh and isn't that your man's class across our booth? Why didn't I see that yesterday?"

"I think you did," I cleared my throat, gesturing towards some leftover paint cans stowed under the tables we'd marked out as the ordering counter. "I've asked if they'd seen anything but... good god. Whoever did this had the brains to take whatever was left of our sign, too. We haven't got anything to paint on."

"Are you saying their clever or that they're like, crafty. Is that the same thing? You're *actually* complimenting whoever did this?" She clutched her chest in disbelief. "I'm gonna just circle the plaza and ask around for extra wood. The least we could do is piece together some scraps and paint over them..."

I congratulated her for thinking on her feet before re-directing my attention to Ariq and Freda, members of the volunteer group who'd done up the décor and basic dressing of the booth across several days.

"We're going to have to remake key elements within the next two hours."

"Yeah we saw your text," Ariq appeared to be in the worst mood I've ever had to see him in, which wasn't a very good thing since he nearly seemed to be permanently upset and disappointed in the world. "Motherfuckers' better be expelled for sabotage or something or I'm quitting school myself."

LEROY

I was on ingredient prep for the morning shift even after being the last to leave the night before, setting up the huge cast iron pans for the paella and then the deep fryers for the leche fritas. It wasn't part of my plan to be up before the sun was but the probability of him assigning himself the morning shift was high. And since watching him mend his class' booth, which I saw last night was right across ours, seemed like a good idea, I went along without complaining.

Another plus would be the similar break times, which meant that all I had to do was look out for him from where I was and then go over to hang out once he had the will to actually remove his apron and give himself a break. They'd done a pretty good job with the décor. It looked more festive than our own and even Raul admitted it over text.

I figured it had to be his idea, since no one would actually be dedicated enough to have everything written in both Mandarin and then English in small text, just for continuity. Even the scrolls were made of the exact material, which Si Yin probably helped him source for—and it's gone.

"Hey I was about to send you a text man." I dropped my bag over at our booth, still looking over at his. "What took you so long? We went to collect the shit without you."

This wasn't really within my realm of concern at the moment, considering the fact that he'd literally just had weeks' worth of his hard work turned into nothing. The well-decorated booth was now a skeleton of aluminium frames holding up a white tent, which was what everyone had started out with.

The lanterns, scrolls, firecrackers—even the sign that caught my eye last night—all gone. He had his head lowered, fingers on his forehead, speaking to someone rummaging underneath the counter. My first instinct had been to go over; ask if everything was alright and then offer some help but I could tell from his face just how exhausted he was from explaining and re-explaining the situation. Every additional person he had to entertain was unnecessary stress.

That, and he wasn't going to feel all that good about himself if our first interaction in a while was something like this. Knowing him, appearing incompetent and weak or asking for help was the last thing he wanted to be doing in our kind-of mini-cold-war-thing. He was the type to pile everything on himself and have it all bottled up, either way, so I simply kept an eye on the situation.

If there was one thing I knew about him for sure, it was that he'd never back down.

"You know anything about that?" I got this over to Raul, who looked like he'd arrived only minutes before me and was putting on his apron. He handed me one before following my gaze.

"Oh, what? Wait... seriously? Wow how could I miss that oh what the fuck," his eyes were popping out of their sockets just from registering the missing décor of the stall across. "Ho man, but then don't you need to go over and talk to playmate? He must be crazy sad and angry." I mean, yeah. Couldn't argue with that but still, I wasn't sure if it was my cue to actually go over.

"Hi I've been standing here for like ten seconds and neither of you have eyes, apparently."

Raul turned first. I'd kept the corner of my eye on his stall while giving the ingredients in the ice box a quick quality check. He then nudged me in the side, which was usually what would happen when things required my attention.

"Hello? Leroy?" Birchwood. "I'm assuming you're trying to show off by bringing my attention to your work ethic or whatever mise en place you have going on so far but, hm, guess it isn't really working." She was doing something to her hair a lot. Something's different.

"So obviously, my class is waay ahead of everyone else. We've had everything down to the second and I mean, it's barely half-past-five but we're soo done with the ingredient prep. We're even training our waiters and waitresses down the hallway." So that's why she's dressed like that. "I'll let you know where we're headed for the next learning journey I guess. And I mean, we did talk about hosting a party with the prize money but, mm, a chalet's kind of small. I was thinking more of a villa."

The mussels weren't looking too good. Knowing the school, they practically did quality checks on their suppliers twice a week. The shrimp was okay but honestly not the best I've seen. I buttered a pan and cranked up the heat just to give one of 'em a go. Rough gauge of how fast they would cook.

"Birchwood got a perm," Raul was whispering. I didn't get why. "Dude, she's trying to impress someone. It looks hella expensive. Even my mom goes for the cheap kind."

"—honestly wouldn't be enough, even if our count was a thousand and above. I mean, really, what can you do with five-hundred dollars? That's not going to get you *one* night at an average villa."

On medium heat, about twenty, no, twenty-one on each side. This cast iron needs a little warming up. I grabbed a torcher from one of the boxes behind me and, facing it away, turned the knob.

"So, about the tag team competition this afternoon, I have the aprons and the tags. Make sure you conserve your energy, don't work yourself too hard 'kay? I need you in your best at two o'clock sharp."

I was torching the pan when I heard this, and it had me pausing, blue flame blasting the cast iron till it was orange. The mussel I threw in had popped and was black beyond recognition.

"Oooh, it's you," Raul was back at it with the whispering. "It's you she's trying to impress. Okay you're frowning."

Killing the flame and turning to Birchwood, I stared. "What."

She sounded surprised. Looked that way too. "What do you mean 'what'? I told you I was having your name down on the signup sheet, didn't I? You said nothing so I thought you agreed! Silence means consent."

"No it doesn't," I laid out. "I ignored you."

By now she was very clearly offended by my words. Honestly, there weren't many people in the world who could put up with my shit. "What!" Already, she was raising her voice, pitched unusually high all of a sudden so much so that heads were turning from all the way down our lane. Including the stall across ours. "How is that even politically correct? You can't *ignore* offers made by someone giving you an opportunity, Leroy. What are you trying to say?"

So I was annoyed, no surprises there. Also not including the fact that she had basically the entire plaza of students prepping at their booths turning to stare. Raul was doing his best at bomb defusal.

"Hey hey hey, Birchwood, no one's saying anything, okay? See? Cox isn't saying anything. He's quiet. We're all quiet. And don't you have to prepare for the instructor's taste test? It's soon. Maybe just go back?" The others who'd returned from collecting packaging for the food had not been expecting our guest. All they could do was walk around her and quietly mind their own business.

Birchwood wasn't having any of that.

"Oh my god, now you're all ignoring me. Well I hope your little booth gets *ignored* by everyone coming to the festival." She was practically shouting. Listening to all this wasn't worth the burnt mussel, no matter how poor its quality. "Seafood paella? Done to death. Leche fritas are so last year and they look ugly too."

I was surprisingly good at keeping my mouth shut. Or generally just blocking out stupidity. It was the one thing the other parent was sane enough to do—wire his son for selective processing of information. There were things the world did not need to entertain and brainless shits were one of them.

I let her storm off.

"Woah, hey... she got your name down on the tag team contest," Raul had to remind me. I shrugged it off and helped him with the seafood sorting. "You just gonna pull out from the list then?"

"Guess so," my eyes were wandering unconsciously and I knew just where they were going. They ended up on exactly where I saw them heading for and by some miracle, our gazes met. Being the awkward little thing he was, averting his gaze and pretending to be adjusting his glasses was his go-to reaction. That, and not realizing that his ears were red.

He probably heard all of that; Birchwood wasn't going easy on her tone of voice.

"You think she has anything to do with the uh, the decorations and everything?" Raul must have thought we were out of earshot, like he'd always seem to think whenever we're back in the lodge, so he hadn't really thought of lowering his voice.

Fortunately for him, the others were there to entertain. "Dude, if the press gets wind of this, Birchwood's gonna hunt down whoever started the rumor." "Yes, talk about it but *softly* but also not *too* softly 'cuz we want in on the stuff too." Otherwise, mostly warnings.

This wasn't the kind of conversation I wanted to be a part of, so moving on, I sped up on two boxes of seafood to sort through. Once that was done, I looked over at Raul and told him I'd do his. "Go check on the stall across."

He gave this a double take, eyes wide. "Uh, you mean you want me to talk to playdate for you or..."

"I'm doing you a favor," I gestured to the box of shrimp he was taking forever to sort out. Part of ingredient prep was to ensure every morsel served was of a certain level at base quality. Raul said something under his breath before removing his gloves and then heading over to the booth across, quietly observing the situation from afar before sliding into a conversation between two first-years re-decorating the booth.

He returned after a good ten minutes looking fairly triumphant. I didn't know if I could trust the look on his face; by then, I was already done with the seafood sorting.

"So I was talking to some classmates of his—they're pretty cute by the way, is it a thing? Is his entire class cute?—and they said something about not making uh, new props or anything and no one's found their old ones yet so they just gonna remake the sign and sub out the scrolls for something simple on paper, I guess. Yeah but they're gonna have a plain booth, you know. 'S probably not gonna work out."

I was in the middle of getting out the short grain rice, double-checking the sack to confirm that it was the variety I'd told them to request for. Bomba. Or Arborio, if they couldn't get their hands on that. "Did you see him?"

"Playdate?" Raul was smirking and I didn't need to look at him to know that he was. "Yeah you know, obviously stressing out. Plus, you guys haven't been talking to each other so you can imagine how sad he is right now—"

"Bring one of those over," I nodded at the pair of standing industrial fans the others had brought around while Raul was over on the other side flirting with girls. They were part of my list of requests. "Just put it in front of his booth. He'll know what to do with it."

"Okay but what's he gonna do with a big big fan?" He sounded like he was rolling his eyes. "It's kinda cold at their booth. And by the way this is the last order I'm taking from you. It's not like you did *all* my prep..." He trailed off after I pushed the pan of sliced chorizos his way. And the marinated ground beef. "I was gone for ten minutes!"

"You can cook a meal in ten minutes," I told him with a finger. He clicked his tongue and gave me the same.

I watched Raul rope in someone else dealing with the food packaging, keeping an eye on the cast iron pan and peeling the shrimp all at the same time. They were lugging it over to the booth across and then having someone call for the person in charge, which was no one other than *him* so I chanced a glimpse at his reaction.

The fan was throwing him off. I could tell from the look on his face that it was. He was staring up at Raul and the other guy, confused for a good second before looking the thing up and down and taking over with a huge smile of relief. Si Yin came over to help move the thing, and I could almost hear her thanking him for the additional welfare but it really wasn't about keeping those on duty sweat-free.

I saw him directing her towards the grill while they struggled to move the industrial fan over. It was the exact position he should be having it—facing the stir-fry woks and grills, above where the steam would be and out towards the rest of the lane; then he was looking up and glancing over. I looked away before he could catch me red-handed.

* * *

The organizers had come by with the ticket machines and stickers for passing the quality examination two hours ago and most of us hadn't bothered to attend the opening ceremony down at the field so by the time the school gates were open to the public, we barely felt like this was a festival.

Most visitors were parents and alumni going around with complimentary coupons and the occasional stack of 'em, if they could actually figure out where to buy more. There was music blaring across the plaza to keep the spirits up but it was nine in the morning and no one was in the right fucking mind to be listening to house at this time of the day. Plus, those on the morning shift have been up since four-thirty, at least.

The paella had turned a couple of heads, for sure. The smell wasn't something to resist and the fan helped by bringing it farther down the lane. Still, people were holding on to their coupons like they were some scarce resource and fifteen minutes into opening, we'd barely served three people.

"I don geddih." Raul was on his second serving of seafood paella, slotting his coupon into the machine to increase our counter. "Thih ih gooh shih. Why ahnt peepo comih to eah thih?"

A question I didn't know the answer to. It was tough trying to look welcoming up front so I told the others to swap out, keeping an eye on the empanadas while all they had to do was serve paella on order.

The other booths around us were picking up, appearing a lot more occupied with their line of three to four customers. Across, their class wasn't exactly doing so well either. They've had one or two since opening—though I gotta admit, whatever it was they were serving smelled like something out of heaven.

"Tasting samples," I told Raul, knowing it was our only way out of the slump. Doing below average wasn't something I was used to (cocky, but just stating the facts) so none of the requests I'd made could account for something like this. There was no back up, which meant I hadn't thought of giving out free food and there were no plastic sample cups we could use.

"Yeah like we didn't think of that while you were thinking of it but we got nothing to hand them out on." It was some other guy.

Nutritionist. All of us turned to the stack of paper towels. No, it would only make us seem desperate—

"Hi." We looked up, thinking it was a customer. He had on a red Chinese apron, which was what they wore in the booth across. He didn't look very happy. "White said you can have this." He directed this at me, handing a plastic bag over the counter.

Raul took it and peered inside without asking. "Woah, dessert cups! And *biodegradable*."

This was sexy and staring across the lane at him, I could tell he knew I liked it.

Sample-giving had probably made its way into his multiple probability cases and being him, he wasn't the kind who'd miss out the opportunity to fill every gap. Still, the décor thing. No one would've seen that coming and for someone as orderly and disciplined as himself, it must've been a heavy weight to bear.

"Thanks. Tell him that."

"No I don't want to," the first-year was feisty and just overall in a bad mood, turning and heading back to his booth. "You tell him yourself."

We got round to handing out paella and empanada samples at all corners of the plaza and when it was my turn to go around with a tray, I mostly just stood around till people decided to come over. I was really just banking on my reputation.

I hate talking.

"Cox?" "What's that? Can I try some?" "You're handing out free samples? Hold on, I'll text my friends to come over." "You look really good in that." *You mean that tastes very good*, I wanted to correct but it involved talking so I ended up deciding against it. Either way, they seemed surprised after trying the paella.

"Dude, man, this is sick." "This is actually... super good." "I mean it's you, so, I guess it makes sense..." "Okay that dude was soo wrong about the Spanish booth. I didn't even know it was your class mend-ing it!" "Yeah we would have surrendered our coupons right away." "Totally."

I got that group to pause, narrowing down to the last couple of comments. "What'd he say?"

"Mm, nothing much," the girl was a freshman judging by the single badge pinned to her collar. "That the food's sub-par and that the ingredients weren't fresh, and I mean I honestly shouldn't have believed him. He's literally, like, a first-year too, so. But seriously though I thought he was legit 'cuz he said his class had their booth right across the Spanish one."

Her group of friends chipped in, adding something along the lines of that being the reason they believed him too. Whether or not I bought their stories was a different thing altogether and frankly, both the rumor and their reasoning behind it was pretty dumb but I wasn't all that surprised.

What really did it was the fact that this dude, whoever he was, had something to do with Vanilla's class. Heck, he could've been one of his classmates.

I got this over to Raul and the others when I ran out of samples and had to return, but the motives and intentions had me stuck at trying to explain why anyone would spread dumb rumors for no reason.

"They could've been jealous," some girl shrugged, not really caring as long as business was picking up from our handing out of free food. "I mean, their booth isn't exactly the most... uh... I mean, it looks stupid now, doesn't it."

"Yeah but we're not the ones who messed with their décor," Raul wasn't getting any of this and ten minutes into the conversation, he was still trying to come up with conspiracy theories. "Just so you know, I had my money on Birchwood. You saw the look on her face when she walked off. Angry. Liva. Livid. Whatever. Maybe she dressed up as some dude and went off just to frame some other sad soul in case you found out. That girl's great at stirring shit."

"It's too much effort," I snorted, not really wanting to entertain the idea but the moment he said it all, the entire thing was stuck in my head. "She's not even smart enough to come up with something like that."

"Really, Cox?" Raul. "She literally just equated your ignoring her to, uh, *consent*? Birchwood is great at overthinking. She blows up every little thing and makes it into some pizza, you know what I mean?" I let him be, throwing a couple of dredged leche squares into the deep fryer.

I expected someone else to entertain him since, well, they'd been so eager to talk about Birchwood all morning but everyone on duty had lapsed into this weird-ass silence. I glanced up from the fryer just to see what was going on and there that mother fucking kick-ass legend was. Yamazaki Shin.

"Hi, hi, good morning everyone. I tried your sample paella and it was so good, so. I came for more. Plus, they gave me some extra coupons to spend so can I make that, um, two? For me and my wife." He had his hands behind his back, composed and quiet, but not the least bit intimidating. Beside him was the person he pointed out. A woman with an infant in her arms. A girl.

"You're Chef Yamazaki!" Raul stuck out a hand and reeled him in. He could hug the president and forget about flinching. "Dude, dude you're awesome. I love your YouTube channel. The ah, the aesthetic. And all. Oh I read your cookbooks too. Sign my shirt?"

Everyone was too distracted to actually prepare his order so I took over while they got their arms signed. People down the lane were stopping to stare. Also the people in the booth across.

"Oh! Oh, uh, yeah okay haha... I'll—I'll sign your shirt, sure." The legend searched his pockets, presumably for a pen. "Uh, honey? Anh, honey. Do you have a pen?"

"Yes but Shin, it's the strawberry one," his wife whispered not-so-softly and everyone was practically lining themselves up in front of our booth to get his autograph. "Lemon's going to wake up once I pull it out. She can smell that thing a mile away." *That's a nickname. Right?*

People began to offer them permanent markers and sharpies from several booths down and before we knew it, there was some unofficial signing event going on and Yamazaki's paella was getting cold. I gave it away to the customer after him and made him another two.

"You're the one who made this?" He directed this my way after clearing the line of fanatics but it took me some pausing to register that I was having a conversation with some culinary legend.

"Yes."

"Wow, it's really good for someone your age," he glanced at the badges on my collar. "My wife asked for a second sample on the spot and she's never liked paella. I couldn't even get her to try it."

"Thanks."

"What's in your herb blend? Chopped parsley, olive oil, lemon juice and... something else."

"Garlic."

"Garlic?" He looked surprised. "Not the soft heads, then."

"Yeah. Hard heads. The purple kind."

"Wow, I... I couldn't tell. I never knew there was so much of a difference, used in a herb blend." I could tell he was trying to be friendly and nice and, don't get me wrong, he really was, but I wasn't very good at dealing with... famous people. He even got his wife to come over to introduce herself.

"Hii, uh, sorry, I can't really—oh, okay yeah you hold Lele—hi," she extended a hand. "I'm Nguyen Thi Anh. Your paella is super. Shin couldn't even cook like that when he was your age though he was *very* good at proof-reading my fanfics."

Yamazaki was holding his daughter and laughing nervously at the same time, which I assumed was his original state of mind. "Uh, I uh, still am, though. Right? I'm still good at proof-reading your writing."

They exchanged a look. I handed them the boxes of paella.

"Actually, you look very familiar," Legend went on to say while his wife opened the box and started digging in without him. "I've seen you somewhere."

"Cross-year recordings?" I said to throw him off, knowing where this was going. It wasn't the first time with other celebrity chefs too, since I was basically a copy of the other parent when he was younger.

"Hmm, maybe. Way before that, too? Do you maybe have a picture of you when—"

"Oh my god, honey. Shin. Honey, look." His wife had turned around and was pointing at the booth across us. "Isn't that... you know, at Mr. Honeycutt's wedding? The, the boy with that super pale hair and cute blue eyes and those glasses? He sent us a picture of them not long ago. At the airport, remember?"

One line and I knew exactly who it was they were talking about. They'd moved up front so that Raul could serve the others behind them but I was, for once, intrigued by people who weren't him.

"Where? You mean the... oh. Oh, yes. Yes that *does*... yes it *is* him. Alfred Dempsey's nephew, the uh... gosh, I forgot his name but Chip's told me dozens of times—"

"You know Vanilla?" I cut in. The couple did a double take.

"Oh yes, that's him!" Yamazaki's wife was taking her excitement up a notch. "Doesn't he look adorable? *And* he stuck with the glasses! Gosh, the last time we saw him in person, he came up to my knee or something. Are you two friends?" There was a glint in her eye that reminded me of Si Yin but at the same time revealed the exact number of levels she was above her.

I looked away for a second and at Yamazaki behind her, noting some dangerous spark in her eye to which her husband dished out clear warning signs of imminent chaos in a single glance. I turned back to his wife.

"He's my—"

"*Boyfriend sounds childish.*" "*F-future husband? Leroy, what were you thinking?*" "*Yes, we're dating, yes but um, 'lovers' is such a... such a terrible term it triggers the immediate malfunctioning of the heart.*"

"—ne." Yeah that works too.

The spark in her eyes turned into flames and I could literally see her, in her eyes, sipping tea in a house on fire. "Confidence king!" Then as though unable to resist a conversation with her husband, said to him over her shoulder. "I can't tell who'd win. Him or Mr. Jaxon. Oh wait, we haven't got your name my dear." She returned to me and continued wolfing down the rest of her paella.

"Leroy."

With Yamazaki around, I was pretty sure my last name was going to be a dead giveaway. They were among the top few alumni who'd made it big on a global scale and he'd at some point given classes while Yamazaki was still around as a student, so.

Neither of them pressed any further during the handshakes, which I appreciated.

"You're very talented, Leroy. My guess is that we'll be seeing you at the W-interschool," Yamazaki flashed a smile and most students around me would have equated this to being blessed by a god. "Sorry for holding up the line and um, causing a commotion in front of your stall. Now if you'd excuse us... Anh just looks like she's dying to pop by that Chinese booth right across."

"Thanks for coming by." I nodded, watching them wave and cross the lane. Their daughter's sleeping face poked out over Yamazaki's shoulder. She was drooling.

Business picked up after his visit and by that, I meant a line that snaked round the booth and cut into the space of the stall beside ours. Naturally, people weren't very happy about that, so we had to improvise and start handing out ticket numbers and call them out whenever their order was ready.

A couple of hours passed like that and with people constantly in front of the stall, I wasn't exactly given the chance to be stealing glances at someone in an apron across the lane. Needless to say, I'd wanted to see the look on his face if Thi Anh had somehow casually pointed me out to him.

At least they seemed to be acquainted beforehand, and it wasn't like they were riding on his sudden spike in fame or that his uncle was a renowned culinary critic.

"Cox," Rosi arrived at the stall, tapping her wrist. "Break time. I'll take over whatever you're doing."

I nodded, handing over my apron and briefly telling her what to do for the rest of her shift. Mostly just order taking and frying up the leche fritas, which for her standard was pretty easy. She'd put aside an airtight bag whilst gathering her hair into a bun and I saw that they were a bunch of coupons.

"Can I have some of these?"

She followed my gaze. "Oh. I mean, Chef Palmer said it's for class use and everyone's entitled to one each, so." I slipped one into my pocket before glancing over at the stall across. As expected, everything about him looked like he needed a break. Yet, there he was taking orders from a surprisingly long line, calling out, serving food, and probably forgetting the definition of 'shifts'.

"Uh, you can go now," Rosi was waiting for me to give up my spot. I got out one of the disposable boxes and piled on a serving of paella. "Oh I get it, you're waiting for someone and you want to spend your break with them but they're busy and you're stalling 'cuz you, don't want to waste your time off." She stabbed my back

with a finger at every 'you' and I flipped her off only because she'd
nailed it.

Fuck.

"Just go." She nudged me out of the booth. "No one's timing you.
I'll, like, close an eye or something. I'm counting this as a favor so
we're even now, since you saved my ass from Marseille on Monday."

I went with this, heading for the stall across and joining the end
of the line just so he would have to regard me as a customer and forget about making excuses not to entertain my requests. A glimpse
of the menu was enough to confirm the lengths he'd went to. Every
item on it was a solid product of research, and to ensure complementary flavor profiles whilst guaranteeing the ease of eating on the
go, he'd narrowed it down to three items among the hundreds that
were part of Chinese culture.

I missed the chance to snap a shot of his face the moment I got
up front to the ordering counter, only because I was too busy musing over the look in his eyes. He had been calling out the order of
the person before me over his shoulder and quite obviously didn't
see this coming. The moment he returned to serving me, his next
customer, was the moment we locked eyes.

"Oh!" His blues went wide and I could see in them, a ripple on
the surface. "U-um. This is... an interesting change of, well, events."
He was referring to the swapped roles, since I'd always been the one
taking his order at the parlor and he had a point—this was more
amusing than I thought it would be. "How can I, um," wow, he's adjusting his glasses again. Nervous. "What do you—"

"Hi! I'll take your order." Some girl in the same Chinese-style
apron he had on cut in with an empty notepad and directed this at
me. I didn't respond and she took this as her cue to address the person she'd just casually brushed aside. "White, right? Uh you can go
take a break now since it's technically my shift."

He paused for a good second—stunned, alternating his gaze between me and the girl. I was distracted by whatever he was wearing.

"Oh... but, um, Davis, I thought you'd just extended your break till..."

"Nah it's fine! I can take it from here," she flashed him a smile, nudging him in the direction of the flat grill. I saw him glance over his shoulder at Si Yin and some other girl over at the woks and grills.

"So what can I get you?" She was back to asking for my order, which I didn't really appreciate. After all, I'd joined the line just to tease him.

I held out the paella in one hand and beckoned with my other. "Him. To go."

Characteristically oblivious despite my blatant flirting, his first thought was to assume that I'd been referring to something written on the menu behind him (yeah, like I'd beckon to a *food item*) and had continued to remove his apron but then his classmate blinked, and, following my finger, caught his attention.

He must have seen the smirk on my face because the next thing I knew, his ears were bright red. He'd flinched, too, before averting his gaze. As though he'd wandered a little too close to a burning flame.

"Um. I hope you're waiting for me to point out that grammatical mistake because I think you used the wrong object pronoun it's 'that' as in, a food item, instead of 'him' and I don't quite know what else to say."

This was full-on entertainment but there was a line at my back and I didn't want to be holding up the stall he'd worked so hard to run smoothly. I caught his eye.

"I meant *you*, dumbass." He looked startled by my words, folding his apron into a neat square before placing it aside. There was reluctance in his movement and I saw that he seemed concerned about the running of the stall, glancing over at Si Yin and the other girl at the grill. "I'll meet you at the fountain."

* * *

"It's *Cong You Bing*," he said, holding out a palm-sized craft paper bag and adjusting his glasses at the same time. "Deep fried scallion pancakes. They're more like flatbreads layered with spiced scallion and then deep fried. Si Yin says it's her favorite breakfast item."

I mused quietly, appreciating the fact that we'd shared the thought of offering the other a taste of our food. I exchanged his for the paella I'd packed and he seemed fairly surprised.

"Oh. And... this is for me?"

I nodded, taking a bite out of the scallion pancake. The kick was crazy. "This is good."

"Thank you." Even on casual occasions like these, he had his tie in perfect condition. "Can you taste what's—"

"Pepper. Ground. *Sichuan*."

"Hm! Okay, you win." He cleared his throat adorably and continued to avoid peering directly into my eyes, popping open the box of paella and going in for a forkful. I waited for his verdict.

"Smoked paprika. That's very clever, using it to substitute the smoky flavor one would get from cooking on a wood fire since, well, those aren't allowed. The shrimp is also perfectly cooked. And hard head garlic instead of the usual white ones in your herb blend. Oh we never stood a chance..." It was cute how he'd thought of our stalls—right across one another—as rivals and I had to resist the urge to dish out some mini-challenge for 'loser does as winner says.'

We took a right down the first lane of the plaza and I let him lead, just to get an idea of what piqued his interest. Turns out, he was merely following a list on his phone whilst finishing his paella.

"It's the background curation I'd come up for the listicle I mentioned. Granted, there's no fixed framework for this but I had to ensure I could start somewhere. The article has to feature at least ten classes, with pictures and a verdict. Plus, I don't actually have a photographer with me this time round so I've got to do this entirely by myself."

I scanned the checklist he had and noted a few I'd heard about. Birchwood's café was one of them. Still, having to busy himself with article-writing during his break time wasn't exactly ideal for his mental state. He'd dealt with a thousand over problems in a single morning.

"What happened to the decorations?"

He looked up, biting his lip and then looking away. "I don't know... we never figured out. But I've reported this to the authorities and they said they'd check the security cameras. I mean, at least we're not stuck on an average of a single sale made every fifteen minutes. Chef Yamazaki came by, and he really helped out. A-and the fan Raul provided us with. It was ingenious. Most customers stopped by and it had nothing to do with the décor."

Mm. "Depends how you use it."

Glasses rolled his eyes and came to a stop at the end of the first lane. "I knew it was you, Leroy," he huffed, then peered up, sideways. "You're unbelievable. I was all over the place. It also doesn't help that most of my head's been, well, filled with... um, information and knowledge about biological health and we haven't exactly talked since... then."

I was caught off guard. "You searched it up?" I said, careful. Watching him closely. "I thought you were scared."

"But I've been telling you I wasn't!"

"Yeah but," I gave our surroundings a second's survey before playing with his ear. "I thought you were lying to make me feel better."

"That will never happen," he laid out without an inch of hesitation and I didn't exactly bother hiding my amusement. "I always tell the truth and you know that! A-a-and why would I spare your feelings? It's not like I love you or anything." He stared down the second lane and I followed, giving him the finger that was accompanied by a short laugh.

"Fuck you."

"Language," he seemed almost used to it by now, keeping his eyes on the booth signs and looking out for one that was on his list. "I'm going to have to be interviewing store managers while I'm on break because Keith needs this article out by the end of the day."

"You're spending break time doing up your article instead of me," I laid out, just to be sure.

"I think you missed a preposition right there, it's 'with' you or else the prior verb 'do' would have to be associated with the latter subject and that wouldn't have made any sense, grammatically. And yes, the article takes precedence."

"Fine," I gave up, going for his forehead. "There's that drink stall three down on your right. Blue pea lemonade."

"Oh! The galaxy sunset," he noted, giving his list a check before getting in line. "Hm. It's nice having another pair of eyes on a hunt like this. There's simply too many people around."

We talked about stuff like this morning's incident and how he'd managed to work things through but when it came down to details about his classmates and that supposed rat spreading rumors about the Spanish stall, he closed up a little and wouldn't let me in. I thought of pressing him for more but he looked tired and stressed enough as it was. So I didn't.

When we got to the front of the queue, I stepped aside for him to do whatever he needed to for his article and watched him order the only two drinks on the menu soon after. *Galaxy Sunset* and *Milky Way Aurora*.

He was collecting his order—one drink in a hand—and heading towards me when I had the idea of preserving this scene. So I got out my phone and snapped one just as he was holding out one of the drinks to me for, uh, safekeeping.

Unfortunately, the sound of my phone camera went off and he nearly bubbled with bewilderment. "W-wha—was what a... Leroy, I held this out to you so that you'd free my hand! I need two shots of these beverages for the article!"

I continued snapping away because he was frantically searching around the lane for a spot to place the drinks until he realized there was none and finally calmed down enough to reward me a glare.

"When you're done with that, perhaps you could take this drink and free one of my hands so that I, too, can take a photo for my article."

I clicked my tongue, turning the screen of my phone towards him so that he could see the perfect candid snap of himself panicking with drinks in his hands. "Just use this one."

"That is absolutely not happening I look horrendous in that photograph can you please delete that," he'd delivered this monotonously enough for me to get the message.

"Okay I'll take another one," I rolled my eyes and took the drink as he requested me to do. "Hold yours out. Like this." I had mine in the left of the frame and nodded at him to fill the right with the other drink in his hand before snapping a photo with shallow depth.

I showed this to him for quality checking. He frowned.

"I admit, it is a decent shot... but borderline cheesy. I'd pass it off as something out of a couple's Instagram post about some carnival date and the street food they'd enjoyed. Look, even our hands are in the picture. It's far too casual."

I shrugged. "Exactly. That could be your angle. Street food for a date."

He was a mess.

"I-I can't—I can't have all the pictures in my article feature your hand and mine in the same frame holding out the same food in the same pose for an... an article with an angle like that, it would be extremely scandalous!"

"We're on a date," I told him with a smirk. "Being scandalous is allowed."

Still a mess.

He tried out the drinks and wrote down his verdict and comments before we moved on down the lane and came upon the main area of the festival that was in the middle of the plaza, between the four lanes of street food booths. I hadn't seen the entire set up since we'd been busy with our own stalls but there was apparently a stage for key events. Like the tag team thing.

Which was about to commence in... three minutes.

To the side was Birchwood and some other dude she got to replace me. There were other contestants too but I could barely recognize them. Tenner and Chen, number one and two, had not bothered entering the competition.

Either way, I was surprised by the attention the event was receiving. The main area beside the fountain was packed. And by that I mean people all the way from the front of the stage to the steps of the fountain, seated on the ledge with umbrellas to shield themselves from the water splash.

Birchwood had a fanbase; and though, not to brag, it was common to have one as the school's top-celebrated culinary students often do, I was pretty sure Tenner had started off with something of a smaller scale, even back when she was a third year. Birchwood was only a freshman.

Already, she had signs and colored boards and light bands and even a fucking *cheer* team. There had been stuff going around about her giving benefits to her fans but even so, wow. This was taking things far.

"Hm. I think I see some of my classmates up in the front. With the banners and all." I turned to my companion, sipping on the last of his blue pea lemonade and staring past the crowd.

It was a far-fetched idea.

That Vanilla's classmates may have overheard Birchwood's outburst in front of our stall and, to get back at me for all that, decided to spread shit about us. Even for soap operas, it would have sounded stupid at the very least. Fans were... fans. They weren't psychos.

Still, the thought of there being people in his class possibly familiar with the act of sabotage was concerning. I turned to say something about this but all of a sudden, the entire crowd had their eyes on us, over their shoulders.

VANILLA

I find myself fond of being described as 'observant' or 'attentive', words I've never once heard in my lifetime of 'odd' and 'know-it-all'. I'd say paying attention to my surroundings and, well, generally being aware of whatever was going on around me had become a critical characteristic, what with the need to assess problematic situations and, in seconds, deduce the several probable solutions.

At present, I'd realized just how walking around with someone who tended to have all my attention could make this critical characteristic of myself entirely obsolete. It was hard being hopelessly smitten by an unwavering candle. One never really knew when to look away. Or how, for the matter.

"Is something going on behind us?" I said to this very being, glancing over my shoulder and following the general direction of whatever it was everyone seemed to be interested in all of a sudden. I spotted a lone mother pushing her baby cart around the fountain but nothing else seemed to warrant the attention of that many people. I turned back. "Oh."

Leroy had snorted, then shifted his weight so that he was now between me and the crowd of spectators.

"Nothing. Let's go."

I felt his hand on my back but a glimpse over his shoulder confirmed that the entire crowd gathered in the middle of the plaza—before the stage and all the way up to where we were—had continued to stare openly. Violet Birchwood and her partner had taken center-stage beside the announcer and they, too, appeared to be looking our way.

"Um. Miss Birchwood," the announcer's voice sounded nervous, even over the PA system. "I don't think that's... I mean, I'm afraid inviting guest students into the contest isn't really, uh, allowed...? It's purely registration-only." Almost at once, I pitied the awkward student, probably a member of the logistics club who hadn't the slightest clue how to deal with difficult situations.

Thankfully, Leroy and I had caught on pretty quickly; Birchwood had invited the two of us to compete against her in the tag team competition, just by calling out our names as we passed. Needless to say, this was rather absurd. We'd exchanged a look, which practically conveyed the extent of our shared amusement. Or so I hoped it did.

"Yes, but they're *late*." Everyone could hear Birchwood pointing out on stage. I tugged on Leroy's sleeve and made a small gesture to leave, exercising maximum discreet. Adding to my pool of numerous enemies was not going to do well for the rest of my high school days and mind you, I've got three and a half years to spend. "Leroy and whoever that is can sub in."

We'd started in the direction of the third street food lane, away from the plaza fountain and everyone else when Birchwood had so unfortunately made the poor decision of not remembering my name, which, of course, had to be the one sole thing in the universe Leroy was not going to stand for.

"You're kidding," he stopped, hand on my wrist. "She doesn't know your name?"

"She's clearly in the mood for laughs, Leroy. You cannot possibly be provoked by such a... no, you're not—no no no don't go! She knows my name! We've had a meaningful conversation back then at the SOY and she was in tears! We're friends!" Taking me on a U-turn, he ignored the hundred blinking eyes and silly whispers, heading straight down the side of the crowd and up to where the stage was.

I was a fool for thinking he'd be somehow persuaded by my words and that love had the power of changing destinies and, what, re-writing the stars. Good god, he was a flame.

Somewhere at the bottom of the stairs that led to the stage, a member of the organizing team had thanked us under her breath, afraid that she'd lose her credibility as soon as Birchwood decided to throw a tantrum and run to her father for help.

I turned to Leroy, who, very naturally, looked like he was up to no good. "I can't believe it. We're simply giving her exactly what she wants." I could confirm this by glancing around, pitying the organizers who appeared helpless in the face of the headmaster's daughter, anxiously gazing up at Leroy and myself. "She's not royalty, no one's obligated to meet her demands. Please let's walk away now before it's too late."

At the top of the stairs, we were quietly handed a clipboard each with registration forms attached to them. My companion had, without question, started filling it up. Head lowered, he'd chanced a sideway glance my way and the most disarming expression one could ever possibly imagine. "Teach her a lesson then."

Startled and anxious, I asked what he meant by this. "She's only going to feel worse than she already is. And how do you know we're going to win? I don't wish to make any assumptions but I certainly have reason to believe that she isn't the nicest loser around either." Not to mention, I wasn't very keen on being a prime witness of her sour mood escalating into some murder of her partner. After all, I'd heard her every curse at the waterfall, directed at her cross-year team.

Leroy had other plans.

"Come on." *It was that look again! O-outrageous!* Needless to say, I was weak and severely disarmed.

"You cannot be serious!" I whisper-shouted, turning in my completed registration form with a hesitant sigh. "Yes, I am very fond of you, but there are... are limits to the compromises I can make and and and it's not very nice of you to, well, use my fondness for you against me. I'm supposed to be writing an article. A-and didn't you say this was a date?" We were led to the second decked out station on the makeshift stage and given an apron each. "If so, then this is the worst date I've ever had."

"At least it's a memorable one," he had the gall to tease. "And what are you talking about? You've only ever been on dates with me. I'm your first. All our dates are bad." And *wink!* "So bad."

I was beyond bewildered—gobsmacked into outer space and mumbling to myself along the journey past the milky way, clearly defeated. "You are absolutely illegal."

"I'll make it up to you the next time," he laughed. "Promise."

By this point, I was adding up and multiplying my calculations of just how hopelessly smitten I was to overcome every rational bone in my body and give in to the fire that he was. Halfway through the announcement of a change in the line-up, I began to notice the presence of baking utensils: an electric mixer, whisks, rolling pins, spatulas... and then, glancing over at Birchwood's team on our right, noted that her partner was a culinary major.

"—the same. One main dish, and one dessert. Five minutes to ideate and make a list of ingredients you're requesting, and then it's an hour and a half to the judging. Oh and of course, tagging your partner in and out every ten minutes, we uh, can't forget that..."

"Leroy," I turned to him. "Leroy, this is a huge mistake. I have never made a pastry or dessert or, or anything like that in my whole entire life."

"Yeah but you've tasted many," he laid out, as though this piece of information should be the decisive factor. This warranted much correction.

"That's ridiculous. Culinary and baking skills are two entirely different things and you know that," I bit my lip, somehow wishing I'd spent more time in my godfather's bakery instead of reading planetary encyclopedias in my room. "You need to be precise. There is no room for mistakes and we both know how we feel about things like this."

"That we're always gunning for the win?" He laughed and I couldn't resist the honeyed softness that he the flame turned everything into. "Yeah."

"I'm not going to deny. This is a lot of pressure," I said under my breath, all whilst giving the crowd before us a quick survey. It seemed a lot more substantial now that we were up here on the stage, faced with more than a hundred pairs of eyes. Birchwood and her partner had a considerable amount of the crowd to themselves, filled with banners and fancy decorated boards with her name assembled in colored cut-outs of what looked like cakes and pastries. "And the strangest thing... I don't dislike it."

"All part of the fun," he'd turned to me with a wink and almost at once, I could hear gushing near the front of the stage. Apparently, being the school's number three also came with complimentary magnetic forces. The crowd had thickened.

"We're monsters. This isn't how human beings react to external stress and pressure."

At the far back of the fountain, more students and visitors were stopping to stare and as though misfortune was the one and only creator of the universe, I soon realized I had been returning the gaze of my classmate Ariq, who, on his break, had been strolling alone with a cob of grilled corn in his hands. We exchanged the oddest look. He then did a U-turn and headed off in the very direction he came from.

"—so if everyone could just scan this QR code, yep, uh right on up on the screen, it leads you straight to SurveyMonkey. Vote for the theme and the results of the poll... they're coming in and... oh. Oh, there's an overwhelming response for 'Nature' and I'm haha, honestly not surprised." The announcer sounded oddly nervous, as though he'd forced out a lie through his teeth.

Alarms ringing, I consulted my companion. "You think...? Could it be that—"

"She told her supporters to vote for a theme she already prepared for?" There was a smirk on his face and it wasn't going away. "Even better."

I was rolling my eyes before I knew it. "You really like a challenge."

"One can tell." He winked. In my head, I was drafting an arrest warrant for Leroy Jeremy Cox.

Given an option, the theme 'Nature' wouldn't exactly be at the top of my list. Besides being vague and wholly idealistic or clichéd, every ingredient in the culinary world was somewhat parked under that umbrella. The logical conclusion would be to emphasize the dish through its plating and preparation technique.

Leroy had ideas. And by that, I meant simply laying out whatever it was he felt like having for lunch.

"Phad Thai." He said the moment we were given five minutes to discuss and a piece of paper to list the ingredients we needed. "I'm starving."

"And losing your mind," I pointed out. "How would looking at a plate of phad thai give the impression of nature?"

"Hunger is nature," he shrugged and I was not going to let him continue with the jokes so I gave him the look and he finally came up with a proper explanation. "It has the most vibrant colors for a main dish."

"Alright I see where you're coming from. Shrimp, lime, cilantro, chilies, peanuts, bean sprouts... it's just—the rice noodles. It's part of the appeal but the color wouldn't stand a chance against the extravagance Birchwood is going for."

"Vermicelli instead of the flat ones." He seemed to agree, marking that down as our very first ingredient and then the rest of the dish. "They're easy to dye." He snapped his fingers, meeting my gaze.

"Color change. The drink we had earlier. Blue, yellow. Then purple after mixing."

"*Galaxy Sunset?*" I blinked. "Yes, well. They used blue pea flowers as a dye for the flower tea and a lemonade slushie at the bottom. You're thinking of dyeing the vermicelli blue and then changing it to purple with lime juice over the top? That's pandering. It doesn't sound like you."

"Isn't," he admitted, smirking a little. "But beating people at their game sounds fun."

Fairly stunned by his competitive spirit, I stopped him in the middle of his listing of ingredients, telling him to cross out the blue pea flowers. He gave me a look. "Yes but I don't pander, competition or not. Use black goji berries—they do the same thing. The least we can do is introduce a new ingredient that isn't an overrated darling of the internet."

This somehow warranted the display of his indecent finger amidst disarming smirks, which seemed to startle the announcer who soon came over to remind us of public press making their rounds.

"You know replacing that gesture with a kiss would cause way more trouble, right?" Leroy had the gall to suggest in front of the poor student, finishing up our list in casual scribbles. "It's self-censorship. The middle finger's 'I wanna make out with him but we're in public and he'd complain' so now you know."

"Leroy, you are frightening in long sentences," I was pink with insanity, unable to look at him *or* the announcer in the eye. "Please exercise some restraint."

"I'll just leave you two alone," the sophomore concluded with an awkward laugh before slipping away, reminding us of the remaining two minutes we had to discuss the menu and key ingredients.

I shot my companion a look before closing the case. It mostly meant 'I'll deal with you later.'

"Is there a way we could run with this color-changing theme in the dessert too? Well it's nature and what's that without a display of flowers, I suppose... so the raindrop cake. Have you heard of it? Crystal clear jelly—"

"The Japanese dessert?"

"Yes, that. I've seen them do cherry blossoms in it. Almost like a snow globe. We could replace that with the black goji berries and injecting some acidity into the topmost layer would have it turn from blue to purple. I-it's really intricate and a technical nightmare though, so I wouldn't be surprised if you're against the idea."

He had a laugh tugging on the corners of his lips and I paused, wondering just what it was he'd found so amusing.

"Remember what I said about taking risks?"

I sighed, averting my gaze. "That I'm 'learning'?"

"Yeah," he returned to the list, adding agar powder and brown sugar to it. Something experimental I wanted to have in case we had the time was soy milk. He added that too. "Scratch all that. I was wrong. My guess... you actually *like* taking risks."

Clearing my throat in an attempt to appear half as embarrassed as I truly was, I began to see just how badly I had wished to disassociate myself from disorder and uncertainty—the primary pet peeves of a certain fictional vulture I'd so adored and admired for the longest time. Leroy on the other hand, had seen through my guise.

"Well. If, among the premises of your argument lies the personality of the human being I am hopelessly charmed by, then... I don't see why your conclusion isn't reasonably valid."

Admittedly, he had to pause, frowning for a good second or two before figuring out the exact meaning of a sentence packed with double negatives. After which, the middle finger seemed to be due.

* * *

To be frank, I wasn't a fan of having conversations in the middle of mise en place, or any form of the whole culinary process. Admittedly, I'd never really been a fan of any form of multi-tasking at all—which Leroy would gladly agree with—and yet, this was the very component characteristic of a tag team contest.

Needless to say, I wasn't the best communicator around. Not in the kitchen. Not outside of it. Not anywhere. Not in this universe, I wasn't. Unsurprisingly, I'd stood rather idle by the side of the station while the clock was ticking down the first ten minutes into the cook-off, keeping an eye on the mental checklist my partner had in mind. After all, Leroy seemed perfectly fine on his own. No need for yelling out instructions or hand-clapping to the beat of 'hu-rry-up'—unless you were Miss Birchwood's partner and perhaps worked better under such conditions.

It was odd, knowing we were being watched by a crowd of curious people. Still, our silence seemed to have caused quite some concern amongst the organizers and alas, the poor announcer they sent to check on our progress, had also been tasked to raise this.

"You guys seem really quiet. Some sort of telepathic thing going on?" He laughed in bouts, stiffer than before. Leroy didn't look up from mincing garlic and Thai red chilis, which meant that he'd left it up to me to come up with something intelligent.

"We don't like to talk." Intelligent. "Plus, he's doing exceptional without my help."

"Really?" The announcer seemed fairly amazed. "Um. Okay. Sure, but... maybe some kind of communication? Like, 'what are you going to do next' or 'don't forget the fish sauce' you know? Stuff like that."

"He's an expert," I blinked, rather frank. "He has the next ten steps in his head, maybe even up to fifteen. He's not going to forget something as important as fish sauce either."

At this, the poor student seemed to back down and honestly,

I hadn't meant to frighten him. *Goodness, Vanilla. You need to watch your words.* He left our station after a timid 'sounds great' and a feeble wave. I could only watch him go—wrought with guilt.

"You know," said Leroy, amidst preparing the blue noodle dye, made from infusing black goji berries in water. I'd told him earlier on to ensure the soaking up of its unique taste by the vermicelli. "I wouldn't mind listening to you go off."

"But... but you don't like being told what to do," I'd observed, unfolding my arms.

"Not by other people, yeah," he had amusement in his eyes. A constant presence in our conversations. "Just you."

"Well it so happens I don't quite prefer ordering people around either. I like correcting people in my head, yes. Just, not—Kosher salt, not Himalayan—not aloud. Oh. Look, I'm doing it already."

"Do it all you want," Leroy had the gall to send a wink in my direction. In *public*. Not as though doing it in private would have made it any less illegal but still. "I'll have my fun when it's your turn."

Clearing my throat to conceal the slightest streak of intimidation I'd felt at his words, I reminded him to get started on the dessert since, well, we'd have to be accounting for its chilling time in the refrigerator.

"Be precise. It's a four-to-five ratio on that agar powder to sugar. Leroy—use the weighing scale."

"Because every chef loves to eyeball," he fired back with a playful spark in his eye and I was silently thanking the rolling pin, cupcakegods above that we weren't walking around with lavalier mics at our collars. "And the milk jelly?"

"A two-to-five."

"So you just happen to have everything stored up there?" He tapped the side of his head and I rolled my eyes.

"Well. Agar is merely a polymer made up of subunits of the sugar galactose, so all one really has to do is work out the chemical equations in their head, bearing the chemical formulas of the pre and end product in mind. Balancing the equation gives you the ratio."

"Mm." Ah, the indecent finger. Served with a side of disarming smirks. Indeed, a fatal combination.

And now even more so, thanks to my partner's prior elaborate explanation of what the display of his middle finger actually meant. *But hold on... was this not a gesture he's particularly fond of using in front of Raul and Rosi and, well, most of his lodge mates?* This was fairly concerning, considering the fact that it would have implied some form of frivolous character or i-infidelity.

"What does it mean, exactly? This... this gesture of yours," I referred to his indecent finger by raising my hand and simply pointing to the one in the middle. "Since its definition appears to differ from time to time and person to person."

My partner looked up from his mise en place, gaze flitting to the digital clock above our heads before resting on me. "It just means 'fuck you'."

"A-ah." Oh. "But earlier on, you—"

"For other people." He laughed under his breath. "For you, it's..." he left the sentence unfinished, returning to the chopping of cilantro and licking his lips. Leroy was very hard to read at times like these, partly because he'd supposedly given a detailed explanation of what it meant earlier on but at present couldn't even conclude.

Admittedly however, there were concerns far more immediate and alarming than the one I had in mind—primarily the fact that Leroy would be tagging me in in less than thirty seconds. We'd made the clever decision of having him go first, to get the mise en place (my major weakness, considering the unfortunate state of my technical knife skills) out of the way and then have me start on the actual seasoning and flavoring of the specific ingredients.

The ten-second countdown accompanied by the chorus of our audience made the signal to swap roles all the more nerve-wrecking, specifically leading up to that single instant. They'd announced the remaining time we had on the clock before hurling words of urgency at Birchwood and I, somewhat encouraging the competitive spirit.

Not to say I wasn't any less competitive than Birchwood was, but already I could hear her start yelling at her partner to, well, yell at her. Tell her what to do. I wasn't about to have Leroy do any of that; in fact, I hadn't quite bothered sparing him a glance. Logically, it'd only add another layer of nervous embarrassment to the whole thing, so. I assumed the most professional state of mental concentration.

First up on my list was to check the dyeing of the vermicelli. Tasting the natural blue dye, I told my partner it was a little blunt, and wasn't going to bring out the fruity flavors of black goji berries once tossed with the other ingredients.

"Drain it out? Make another bowl of dye."

"Mhm," I got out a mixing bowl from one of the cabinets. "I'll just make this one a little more concentrated than before. And then soak it again. We have time."

"While you're waiting for it to infuse, get the agar mixture going."

"Yes I was thinking of doing that."

"And while that's on the heat, taste the herb mix. Then butterfly the shrimp. Don't forget to remove the veins."

"You're *enjoying* this—ordering me around," I pointed out, controlling the extent of my bewilderment whilst separating goji berries in a mixing bowl of water. "I am well-aware of my incompetency. Multi-tasking was never my thing."

"Want to be flash-frying the shrimp instead?" He teased, further capitalizing on my poor technical capabilities to which I admitted he was clearly superior in. "I could start yelling if you want."

"No, no. There's quite enough yelling going on over at the other station."

"You know that's how people establish dominance in the kitchen, right?" My partner laughed, folding his arms and leaning against the counter as though we were back in my apartment and this was a private occasion. "Birchwood's looked over more than twice in the last two minutes."

Placing the vermicelli back into the dye that was now more concentrated, I produced a pot pan and began filling it with distilled water. "To think I'd expected your answer to be a little more refined. How exactly does yelling in the kitchen equate to an establishment of dominance? There must be some other way of doing so. Um, well. Not that I would ever wish to execute such a display of dominance. Also not that I wish to be dominated, for the matter."

I caught a glimpse of the expression on Leroy's face. He seemed genuinely confused. "How are we not married yet?"

* * *

The issue with color-changing dishes soon came to light ten minutes before the judging: that the sauces and ingredients of the phad thai, when stir fried with the vermicelli in a traditional wok, had the color of the noodles turning invariably grey due to the shade of the sauce and herb mix and the acidity of it. While we'd expected to pull off the showy display before the judges by topping the noodles with lime juice (and therefore changing the color of it in front of them), this all seemed to be happening as soon as Leroy had the noodles stir fried in the wok.

"Three tries," he reassured right after things went wrong, having separated the vermicelli bundles into four and used one of it. I pieced together the possible reasons for our failed plans and devised several solutions.

"One, it turns into a noodle salad. Which means no stir-frying and therefore no tampering with the acidity of the ingredients and the sauce. Two, we have them get us a pH meter and, you're not going to like this, but we balance the pH of the sauce and herb mix *before* it goes into the wok of noodles instead of adding it one by one. We'd most probably be compromising on the taste but I trust you're sharp enough to make the best out of what we have."

Leroy got one of the errand students to come over, telling him to fetch a pH meter as quickly as he could. "A noodle salad's not going to win. It's the easy way out." He said just as I predicted he would. "I'll get the raindrops while waiting for the monitor."

"No, hold on." I stopped him, feeling the adrenaline in my fingers. "It's two of us in the last five minutes. Let me handle the dessert, I just need you to check on the jelly. Then double the phad thai toppings because we might need all three tries."

He'd laughed, turning and checking on the agar in the refrigerator before chopping up more cilantro, and pounding peanuts and chilies with a pestle and mortar. "Exciting enough?"

"I can't imagine being a culinary major and having to go through all this nearly every day of the week."

"Mostly three times a day. Sometimes four on weekends before practical exams. Which adds up to..." He frowned.

"Four times seven, Leroy," I nearly laughed out loud. "It's twenty-eight. A hundred and twelve in a month."

"..." "I'll spare you. They're back with the pH meter." I directed his attention to the errand student hurrying back with the instrument and a bottle in his hands before placing them on the counter and zipping away. "Are you doing alright with the toppings?"

He shelled a couple more shrimp before readying a new mixing bowl and then grabbing the pH meter. He stared at it with three minutes left on the clock before partners could join. "How does this work?"

"Um, oh yes you just—first, turn it on," *I forgot he's home schooled and has probably never been in a chemistry lab.* "Yes. Then place the pen-like node into the buffer in the bottle and press 'calibrate'. Once it starts beeping, you can dip it in the sauce mix."

He left the electrode in the bottle to calibrate and immediately started mixing the sauces in the bowl. "What should I try first?"

"Half fish sauce half soy? Then a couple of drops of sesame oil before you throw the cilantro in."

He did as I said and once the meter started beeping, removed it from the buffer, wiped it down, and held it in the sauce and herb mix. "Six point two."

"More cilantro. And a little sugar and then add the spring onions and bean sprouts. Everything but the shrimp and the peanuts.

We were so occupied with balancing the mixture that we hadn't noticed just how much the crowd had grown in the final stretch, up until the signal for partners to join in for plating minutes. It must look rather strange from their perspective; us using the pH meter.

"Seven point two."

"Perfect, but you have five minutes to stir fry *and* plate this. In three tries." I placed the tray of jellied desserts out and removed a clean needle syringe from its packaging.

"What happens if I pull this off?" He said, turning up the heat and oiling the wok. "You've met Annie. Do I get to see your family?"

Besides having no time for flustered embarrassment, I was almost certain about another thing. "There's no 'if you pull this off', Leroy. Frankly speaking, three is an overkill. You'd be perfectly comfortable with *one* try."

He rolled his eyes, laughing all the same. "Again, overestimating my abilities."

We didn't speak for the next three minutes—the final stretch before judging—only because everything unfolded in their natural state, smooth and without interruption. I'd injected the lemon juice into the pale blue raindrop agar and a purple-blue gradient began to form, resting atop a soy milk cream jellied base and coated with a sheer syrup for an added shine.

The fragrance of our main dish had turned heads, apart from the flash sizzling of the phad thai in a wok, mostly thanks to the high heat and the direction of the wind. We'd plated two servings for each dish, even though only one was required and, strictly speaking, I hadn't had the chance to taste the dessert myself.

By the time we were both done with the plating to the fearful chorus of a ten-second countdown, Leroy and I had chanced a glimpse at each other's work. His reaction had been the slightest movement of the corners of his lips, gaze leaving the dessert plates to meet mine.

I'd offered an under-the-table high five. Something I'd always dreamed of doing, having read numerous forms of exceptional teamwork and observed in every one of Xander's volleyball competitions Chip would bring me to see. He was the coach.

Admittedly, I'd never entertained the thought of being part of something like that. A team, or anything of that sort. Group work in elementary school was barely a challenge and having skipped my way through middle and high school at an early age, never really had the most familiar or friendly project team.

This was, simply put, my high five debut. An alternative to see-saw-ing at the playground; the rustling of red leaves above and its crunch under the—

"Marry me," my partner whispered, refusing my open palm by showing an indecent finger in return.

"All I wanted was a high five, Leroy. And you wouldn't even give me that."

V

VIOLET

I stared down at whatever we had on the table and almost at once, couldn't believe I had the gall to pick someone who had zero grasp of complementary flavors or even the concept of food. Granted, Park wasn't my first, second, or even my third choice when it came to partnering up for any sort of duo contest. Landing someone with the same level of expertise with savory dishes as I did with sweets wasn't easy, and with Tenner's absence for the past three weeks and number two being another yellow, Cox had been my next best bet.

Watching him take his dish to the judges up front wasn't the most pleasant experience. Right next to him was Park with his lackluster gnocchi that screamed 'subpar' in presentation, fragrance and overall first impressions. Frankly speaking, none of the judges looked a tad bit impressed by either of them which was, like, a relief since it sort of meant we had this in the bag. Glasses boy wasn't going to produce some miracle dessert that could beat anything I made, anyway.

"We'll start with Team A's gnocchi."

The female judge in the middle was the only one I couldn't put a name to. The one on the right was Chef Marseille's wife, some food journalist from the Times and the one on the left was the dean of a rival school. I'd seen him once at a cocktail dad hosted over the summer break. His son was pretty decent but he'd butchered the word rendezvous and I can't possibly date someone without basic conversational French in their head.

Park was a third-year. Yet, he'd almost made his gnocchi with just flour and eggs so naturally I was like, *what?* No one makes gnocchi without potato, everyone with common sense knows that. How else is he going to get that light and fluffy texture? And does he really think he can beat anyone with flour and eggs? Wow.

If I hadn't told him to add fresh beetroot juice for that natural color and flavor, he'd be serving the judges his last meal or something. A single glance at whatever Cox had made sort of confirmed this either way—their dish was a contender. There was nothing the judges could find fault with.

"The texture of the gnocchi is something I'd have in a restaurant. Good job on that." Marseille's wife has common sense. "The color on it too, is fantastic. I like the sweetness of the beetroot. It complements the butter sauce and gives the whole dish a very natural look, with the edible flowers too."

The rest of them sort of agreed. I say sort of because they didn't seem to have anything else nice to say and were wiping their mouths, loading their pistols. Already, the guy from the rival school was shaking his head with the worst kind of smile on his face.

"Julia. This is not gnocchi." Wow. He was picking at his plate. "This is food for a rabbit. It's tasteless. Bland. Did you even season this?"

I was the one who'd reminded Park to lay off additional rounds of salt and pepper. One, two cracks was fine but more than that would've messed with the edible flowers and, wow, if some dean of a culinary school didn't know that, he's... he's kinda stupid. Yes, I was offended.

"Yes, um. A little bit of salt and pepper." Park was silly enough to look over his shoulder, right at me with those weak eyes of his and I was ready to smack my forehead and just leave.

The other judge in the middle simply nodded and sighed, writing something on her papers before moving on to Cox's dish. "Alright. Team B."

I wasn't getting the clearest view from where I was standing, right behind the station. They'd set up a projector screen behind us, right before the backing of the makeshift stage, but turning around felt oddly sentimental. Like I was worried they were going to win or something.

Either way, I could tell they had cameras zooming in on the dish being presenting and projecting whatever was in the frame onto the huge screen behind us because the audience wouldn't shut up. The only people who weren't transfixed by Cox's dish were my loyal supporters, who of course, brought banners and handmade signboards that were super cute. They were the nicest people around.

"Describe your dish please," Marseille's wife was frowning at the plate in front of her, as though having a hard time deducing what it was. "I've never seen anything like it."

"Vermicelli phad thai, topped with shrimp, cilantro, beansprouts and crushed peanuts. The vermicelli, we soaked in black goji berry tea and... with a little bit of lime," he added, presenting a show of squeezing fresh lime juice with a spoon underneath, over the noodles, before giving it a light toss.

I saw, first-hand, the vermicelli turn from a shade of pale blue to stunning lavender. It was insane—and apparently, I wasn't the only one with that thought. A chorus of oohs and aahs made the entire thing a lot less bearable. This was, like, a disaster. A nightmare.

Cox was good.

"Not blue pea flowers?" The middle judge was visibly more impressed by their phad thai than she'd been with our gnocchi.

"Black goji berries do the same thing," said Cox. Marseille's wife offered an alternative name. Something along the lines of... something wolfberry. Cox then turned to glasses at their station and the latter nodded, so he relayed the message. *It was his idea?* I had to process this. It took a while.

"That's interesting, using an ingredient out of the norm. We don't really use wolfberries in Western cuisine." And that was the end of dishing out compliments because, again, dean of rival school had differing, entitled opinions. He needs to, like... get a life or something.

"Color-changing noodles." He snorted, a snarky laugh that made him look like a turtle with bad hair. Do turtles have hair? "This isn't pre-school, young man."

Okay, w-o-w. I had to keep track of my mouth opening on its own thanks to the number of phones people were holding up in the audience whilst maintaining my composure. The chorus of boos coming from their side of the crowd sort of made my point—Cox's dish was hands down something I'd order from a café if its picture was on the menu. The pale blue of the vermicelli adorned by the plump redness of fresh chili shrimp, crisp green onions and beansprouts; natural colors put together in a fragrant street food dish that had been elevated by its creator. It was barely street food.

Sure, I hadn't actually tasted it but, like, common sense? That's what everyone does when they dine at some restaurant for the first time, pick something on the menu that has nice pictures of it or a decent description. If anything, the color-changing aesthetic was my thing. This dude needs to chill and—*who even is he?*

"Tastes better than it looks," he had the decency to admit, writing something down on his notepad. "I didn't come here for unnecessary gimmicks." He said this looking up, directing it at the audience whilst shaking his head. "If this is what you kids over here consider winning then I'm sure our students will find this year's W-interschool a breeze." The entire plaza went quiet.

I scoffed. *So he's picking a fight, this... dean... from L'Assiette Vide?* He must be, judging by the way he's spitting all over our food over some minor issue of preference. Explains his standards I guess. They *do* have one of the best plating courses in the culinary world.

But, still. People who can't keep up with trends are just the worst, stuck in their old ways. Like, wow—don't they have Instagram? A phone? A *life*? He's obviously exaggerating about the presentation. Cox's dish was in no way tacky or overdone like amateurs in wannabe hipster cafes owned by actual boomers. Honestly, the dish looked professional. Just saying.

The fact that everyone else cleaned his plate of phad thai while Park's had his barely touched also showed a clear winner and that I was right. Well at the very least it proved my point about it both looking and tasting good, which I guess sucks to be that over-critical dean. Probably a critic. Critics all need to get a life, I swear.

"You're lucky it's him you're going up against," he was going on and on with that snarky laugh and, wow, I can't believe the thickness of his skin. "Tacky things like that should stay on the internet. Never in a contest."

Cox's response to that was surprisingly mature. He'd laughed shortly, hands behind his back and eyes sort of hard to read. If you don't already know, he's very hot. "Think I agree."

"Really." The critic couldn't be satisfied with people *agreeing* with him and by this point I think everyone in the audience dubbed him slightly mental. "No boy, I don't think you do. You don't understand how important this is, how your food looks. It's a fact that the eyes are the first to eat. No professional chef would serve *color-changing noodles* in his five-star restaurant."

From where I was standing, I thought I saw Cox's face darken a little. Like he'd been triggered or something. It disappeared the moment I caught it so I guess props to him for hiding it well. Curious, I glanced sideways at his partner at their station. The critic boy with pale hair who wouldn't stop talking most of the time. He was slightly more readable. Obviously anxious.

They flashed the tallied scores on the screen, giving Park a surprising 68 out of 99 (surprising because I thought it was a bare pass like a 51 or something) and Cox a 71. The breakdown of his score was displayed a little below that in small text and lol wow, that dean gave his presentation score a measly 2 out of 11.

Before I knew it, they were calling for service so I got out my beautiful creation from the freezer and, of course, everyone gasped in awe.

I could tell the dean was in love with my dish even before arriving at the judge's stand and by the time they'd cleared Park and Cox's plates for mine and the dessert from the other team, I was greeted with ear-to-ear smiles.

"Classy," Marseille's wife said to me and then... then turned to the other guy too. "These look gorgeous."

"I see you two are way above your partners' leagues." The dean from L'Assiette Vide had a different sort of smile on his lips and I was at once, like, super confused by his mood swings. Dad needs to have better friends. Like, normal ones who aren't condescending male chefs with PMS.

"Well, sir, um. It's a tag team contest, which means that both, us and our partners, had some sort of role to play in, well, the making of both the main dish and the dessert." All of us at the judging stand turned to stare at glasses boy who'd clearly spoken out of turn and as usual, he's got the guts. It happens every single time. "My apologies. Excuse me..."

The PMS guy was back to his snarky laugh and *wow*. Way to go, four-eyes! His mood is ruined and he's about to judge both our dishes. This is sabotage. It's obvious I'd be up first so he probably said that to, like, get something out of it. Even if he didn't, what's the use of pointing out something we all knew but didn't want to admit? If it's under the carpet, keep it there. God, he was going to struggle growing up.

"Okay then," the lady in the middle broke up the awkward silence by getting us back on track. "We'll start with Team A's stunning dessert that, I can see, suits the theme perfectly. What is it?"

"It's a black forest tiramisu tree with chocolate branches, and..." I picked up a stray branch I'd placed perfectly by the side of the plate and ran it through the bubbles filled with dry ice fog placed strategically around the plate, creating the perfect 'black forest' display with edible flowers and a beautiful caramel biscuit crumble doubling up as soil. "The base of the trunk is the tiramisu and the chocolate branches are dark chocolate pieces I'd tempered and shaped by hand."

I could hear the applause and the cheers and the whistling, everyone completely blown away by my display which was, of course, natural. Who else would've thought of preserving dry ice fog in edible bubbles? I had to request for a specific machine and thank goodness my dad had bought that for one of the food experimental classes recently.

"This is quite, *very* extravagant, young lady," Marseille's wife was obviously impressed, removing a chocolate branch from the tiramisu base and holding it up. "It's exquisite! You made this in one and a half hours?"

"Less than that, actually," I pointed out with my little girl smile. Judges loved that smile. "Since it's a tag team."

They tasted it; every aspect of it and all the elements both separately and together. Needless to say, they loved it. End of story. I won.

"Team B's dessert. Now this is something I'm fairly curious about," the lady in the middle had turned her attention elsewhere, narrowing in on critic boy's... jelly, looks like. "Nature at its finest. A literal raindrop. It reminds me of something I've had at Yamazaki's some ten years ago."

"It's actually a traditional Japanese dessert called the raindrop cake. Or, um, *mizu shingen mochi*, excuse my butchering of the pronunciation."

"Yes, I know it's Japanese but that's not what I was referring to," she actually corrected him. It was kind of entertaining. "It's the presentation—the style you've chosen to present it in. Frankly, it's frightening how simple it looks and yet because of how simply it is presented, you can see every technical difficulty involved in the making of it."

They each cut into the raindrop and tasted a spoonful.

"You injected lemon juice," the dean of L'Assiette Vide was looking at him with an unreadable expression. "It balances out the sweetness of the berries and sugar. And it's also what gives it the purple gradient?"

"Yes. That is correct."

He nearly smiled. And that was when I started to feel a little uneasy. "You are taking a big risk, young man. In terms of technical difficulty, tiramisu is nowhere near the raindrop cake. Put some ingredients together and you have it. No heat, no precision. You here, have to be calculating temperatures, acidity, pH levels, and better yet... you have nothing showy to cover up your mistakes like this young lady over here with her... fog bubbles and edible flowers."

Alright this guy is officially mental. He has worse mood swings than mom used to have and she was, like, bad.

"It's very similar to Yamazaki's style," Marseille's wife agreed. "Because of the simplicity in presentation, there is less area of messing up. Mistakes, if made, would be clear as day... you're lucky there are none." I mean, she isn't wrong. It *is* lucky of him.

"Leroy—my partner—he did the agar and soy milk mixture. I have nothing to do with the technical parts of it and, well, him being him, I'm pretty sure he knows what he's doing. I... well I'd just like to say that I don't think this is a product of luck."

Oh my god is it still talking? I stared at him, jaw dropped and, like, just, unable to conceive his existence. He's way too honest! And blunt. And just, tactless, overall.

"Okay," the dean scoffed. "So what did you do?"

"I merely designed and plated the dish. I suggested it have a soy milk base and the clear agar on top of it, with black goji berries preserved in the clear parts while infusing its essence in the soy milk—instead of milk, due to soy's alkaline properties and would hence remain blue even after injecting the lemon juice. That's... that's all I did."

Marseille's wife gave him a curt nod before making some notes, presumably marking him down. Don't get me wrong, I'm glad she did. But sometimes I just can't get what's going on in his head and his, like, obsession with truth and honesty. I mean, he could've just kept quiet about that and got the credit all the same. Eventually, their scores were going to get tallied and he'd just be pulling their overall downwards.

Our attention was directed to the projector screen at the far back for the scores and of course, I was... I was—*what?*

Everyone must have been just as shocked as I was because the entire plaza had gone so deadly quiet that you could have heard a pin drop. They'd given glasses an 85 and me an 89.

An 89, for god's sake! Only four *whole points higher than a stupid tiny raindrop cake with no showmanship. It's official. They're mental.*

They'd even given him a full 11 out of 11 for technique and me, a point less! Creativity was the exact same which was honestly just blasphemy because that included theme representation and I was obviously so much better at interpreting 'Nature' than he was and *plus*, the showmanship? *How??*

"157 to 156. Team A will advance to the semi-finals!" That stupid announcer had this ridiculous smile on his face, all cheery and joyful when I, the winner, was clearly not feeling any of this.

I mean, there was clapping and whistling and all, the usual stuff I was used to but not a single vein in my body could accept this... this victory. It was downright humiliating! And not to mention *unfair*. Just how high was his initial score for them to mark him down and still be just four points below me? They'd... they'd almost made it a draw!

I can't believe it. Dad needs to hear about this.

"Hi. Hello."

"What?" I snapped, turning around at someone tapping my shoulder. It was critic boy. *Great.* "What do you want?"

"Well I was wondering if you'd like to have a taste of the dessert we made. Leroy, I mean, Cox insisted on two servings instead of one so we ended up with some extra. Would you like some?" He was holding out another serving of his raindrop cake and by this point, I was in no mood for entertaining anyone else, let alone him, but something in me wanted to know exactly how this stupid little thing won the hearts of some three judges with mental issues.

"Give it here."

He appeared slightly taken aback by my accepting of his offer, handing me a dessert spoon and the plate before adjusting his glasses and, like, waiting by the side for comments. I pushed some leftover of the tiramisu I'd cut out to make the tree trunk towards him. Again, he looked surprised.

"It is a good black forest tiramisu."

"Yeah of course it is," I snorted, going for a second spoonful of the raindrop. Why does he talk so weird? "What else would it be?"

He seemed all of a sudden apologetic. "I—that wasn't what I meant... your presentation skills were excellent and innovative. It was a winning show."

"Then?" I frowned, glancing over at Park getting ready for the semis. "Why are you looking at me like that?"

Critic boy literally looked like he'd swallowed a snake and was trying to cough it out but actually contemplating if he should just let it remain in his stomach. "Could I, perhaps, avoid having this awkward conversation by, instead, dropping you an email?"

I looked at him weird. *Email? Who the hell uses that sort of thing unless they're a boomer?*

We didn't continue from there because his partner soon came over after returning his apron. He, too, had some leftovers of his phad thai and slid it across the table towards me. "Julian White."

"What?"

"That's his name," Cox said, straight-faced. Barely readable. "Remember it." Critic boy was weirdly pink and embarrassed over this little thing and was all up in Cox's personal space, nudging his side. Wow. He has got to know his boundaries.

I rolled my eyes at them to end the conversation and headed off to where Park was. Plus, my supporters were waiting with the new merch I'd released. I mean I did promise them I'd sign it all.

VANILLA

By the time Leroy and I had checked off every booth and café on the listicle I had due tonight, it was ten minutes to five and the sun was about to set. Admittedly, he'd been the worst sort of distraction anyone could think of, purposefully snapping candid photos of myself and suggesting I use them for my article and then further teasing me by actually setting a collage of the worst ones as his wallpaper. I'd told him I looked ridiculous and all he did was laugh and flick my forehead. Completely underhanded.

Either way, we had to be returning to our stalls for the final two-hour shift till seven—the closing time of the open house festival. Guests would then be asked to leave and organizers would go around collating the tallied results of our coupon machines.

I'd arrived back at my booth just in time to see Si Yin speaking to Chen by the flatbread grill, waving her steel griddle around in a dangerous fashion. The patisserie major had spotted me as soon as I'd stopped in my tracks, standing by the takeout counter with his hands in his pockets and winking in my direction. Si Yin followed his gaze and turned to meet mine, doing something with her hands and, sort of, sliding them across her neck. I couldn't quite understand that gesture.

"Hey," Chen greeted as soon as I neared the takeout counter. "Saw you on stage this afternoon. Never knew you were that good at desserts too," he laughed, reaching over to ruffle my hair. Taken aback, I nearly spewed some quality nonsense in his face. It happens whenever I feel severely offended; my mental dictionary automatically pieces words together to form new ones and dishing them out was my only form of expression.

"Oh, um. Thank you." Come to think of it, Leroy and I had

never really made our relationship known to, well, the public or our general surroundings. In the first place, what *would* be considered appropriate between participating members of a platonic relationship? Was hair ruffling acceptable? Still, Chen wouldn't have known about Leroy and myself. Perhaps it was his way of saying hi and I was overthinking. "Well, I did have a good partner."

"Cox?" He laughed. "The guy barely knows a thing about sweets. You probably did all the work."

"Oh um... no, not really. I mean, no. We were fairly even, or so I do believe." The urge to change the subject heightened. It was not something I wished to delve further into or harp on for more than two sentences. "Is there anything I can get you? Have you made your order?"

Chen flashed a smile. "I was just asking your friend if she's seen you around and she said something about you leaving early. But you came back, so. Guess it's my lucky day."

Words escaped my lips in the form of nervous laughter. It was all that I could muster in situations like these and, glancing over his shoulder, I could vaguely see a struggling Si Yin attempting to end our conversation by loudly scraping her steel griddle on the teppanyaki grill. I gave her the eye. She sighed and put the equipment away before removing her apron and passing it to me.

"Well, I apologize for making you wait and um, unfortunately I have to be getting back to work since it's my shift right now, so..." I left it there, which was likely enough to get the message across but, but but but Chen had very *casually* waved it aside. In fact, he'd leaned in.

"I have news about Tenner," he said in a lowered voice, leading me to a quiet corner. "She's quitting school."

"W-what?" Stunned, I had no control whatsoever over the expression on my face. *Good heavens.* "Impossible. Does... does Keith know about this? Does anyone? The rest of the student body or, or the top thirty-five? Or her team for the cross-year segment, at the very least?"

Chen shook his head. "No one knows if it's because of the cross-year. I was called in to a faculty meeting last evening. They're making me number one next week. Cox will be two. Birchwood's moving up to nine after the midterm assessment."

The midterms were a set of theory and practical exams with a twenty to thirty percent weightage on our final grades at the end of the year, usually held a week before the thanksgiving holidays. For first-years, it would be the first official assessment of the year and therefore our very first chance on the ranking board.

"But. But midterms haven't even started yet," I pointed out. "How would they know if she'd do well enough to... unless you're saying that..."

He'd averted his gaze, not too keen on finishing my sentence. "Thought you'd like to know."

"Does Leroy—um, Cox, know about this?"

Again, Chen shook his head. "Not yet."

Our attention turned to the booth across the lane, glancing over at our current subject of interest who seemed fairly occupied with clearing the line. Over to the side were a group of female students lingering at the store, laughing at something Raul had said but with their eyes fixed on Leroy.

"You look at him a lot."

I did a double take, turning back to Chen. "I'm sorry, who?"

"Cox," he nodded in the general direction of the Spanish street food stall. "You guys know each other? Apart from being on the same cross-year team, I mean."

"Well yes," I found myself scrambling for words, mind going blank almost at once. "We know each other. I mean we're close. Childhood playmates, to be exact—I'm not sure if he's ever told you this and now that I've said it, I remember how his friends had laughed at the term and now I quite regret saying it. Forget play-mates. I, um. We're... we're um..."

This was no longer a matter of searching for the right words. In fact, I'd known exactly what it was I'd wanted to say and yet, this was the first time I struggled to say it aloud. The truth.

"Any chance you'll consider me your playmate too?" Chen suggested out of the blue in what I assumed was a mood for jokes. Even so, my already-awkward smile seemed to stiffen and freeze in place. I had to pause.

"I'm sorry?"

He laughed. "I'm doing a video on Dalgona coffee. Some trend that's been making its way around the Internet and I need your help, coming up with something unique. I wanna see what else I can use besides coffee. Was thinking of making a cake out of it."

"Ah," my godfather had sent me a picture of his very own perfectly executed first attempt. "Well if it's stabilizers and colloids you're talking about, it's entirely food science. A text on food particle density or fat content might help you with that."

"Which is why I need you."

Well, I'm not a textbook and Googling helps, I caught myself daring a thought like that and killed it at once, having had quite enough of conversations for the day. I busied myself with putting on the apron and inching towards the class booth. "I'll think about it," I told him as politely as I could, elaborating on my lack of availability the next week since, technically, I, too, had midterms to prepare for.

Chen said something about 'hitting me up', which was terribly confusing since the phrase was by no means in my mental dictionary.

VI

VANILLA

I must confess, there was never once in my life in which I would entertain the mere thought of flying alone at the age of fifteen. Four months ago, Uncle Al and Aunt Julie were by my side every step of the way, unsurprisingly anxious about my 'living alone' and 'early pre-adulting', ensuring I was comfortably settled in my apartment before boarding a plane back home. It had taken me less than a day to realize that I would eventually have to experience flying by my own since, well, what with Thanksgiving and the winter or summer break and my lack of acquaintances living in the same part of the world, the chances of having a flight companion was a near zero.

Zero was *also*, very apparently, a certain idiot by the name of Leroy Jeremy Cox because here he was, seated beside me, on a four-hour flight back to our hometown. This idiot was a natural, a born champion of exceeding my expectations of the external world. He'd successfully checked off my list of 'last things to expect in the next ten years' in the span of three months, crowning himself the king of 'impress Vanilla Julian White' just because.

"Anything I should note?" He turned to ask in the middle of this movie we'd agreed upon and hit play at the same time. *The Favorite.*

"About my family?" I blinked. "No, not really." He laughed low, seemingly unconvinced. I stuffed his earphones back into his ear because I wasn't going to miss a single second of this masterpiece film.

Mind you, this entire arrangement had all escalated rather quickly. Just last week in the middle of exams, Uncle Al had dropped me a text reminder of the thanksgiving dinner we were going to have over at our place, mourning over the untimely extension of our house renovation. Apparently, something had gone wrong with the Victorian mahogany banisters and we currently had no staircase.

One thing led to another and my godfather Chip Honeycutt soon suggested we hold the dinner party over at his place instead, while Aunt Julie and Uncle Al continue to stay at a nearby hotel whilst our house continued to be in a... stair-less state.

The idea had been for me to sleep in one of the rooms on the same floor, which Uncle Al soon got to arranging and by the time he'd told me about it, had already booked a 'nice little suite' down the hallway. This was around the same time I'd overheard Leroy speaking to his mother's weekday nurse over the phone. He wasn't allowed to stay after visiting hours.

"Could I, maybe... invite someone else to thanksgiving? A friend from school. Um, you probably know him," I'd went on to say, recalling the... well, the text messages he'd exchanged with 'Annie'. "Leroy. From kindergarten."

My uncle, a world-renowned food critic, had then very monotonously redirected me to the proper person for such a request. Our host. Needless to say, my godfather was not going to say 'no.' In fact, I highly doubt he'd ever turned anyone down in his whole entire life of fluffy goodness. "I-is he that boy?" He'd said over the phone, four days ago, in an excited whisper. "The one you've been talking about? Oh I can't wait to meet him!"

I hadn't the heart to lie but neither was I feeling too bold that very day and so I'd simply kept quiet on my end and blushed my way out of the conversation. It was a tragedy.

"So... I can finally see your room?" The distraction was back at it with his primary purpose, glancing sideways with a smirk on the corners of his lips.

"Unfortunately for you, my house is currently under renovation and, well, that would mean... no."

Fortunately for me however, Leroy and I had agreed that he return home for two days tops—for thanksgiving dinner and to collect some old things from the landlord of his mother's old diner—since being too physically distant from his warded mother for long wasn't the best idea.

"Where are you sleeping then?"

I could feel myself turning into an inanimate object of embarrassment. "My Uncle's booked a hotel room for me."

"And...?" There it was; that disarming, illegal spark in his eye.

"And I asked if he could make arrangements for an additional bed," was all I quipped in response, turning away.

I caught him rolling his eyes and flashing a sideway smirk. "As if I'd actually use it."

Save me. "You aren't, by any chance... nervous, are you?" I'd posed to my companion only after ringing the bell of my godfather's new place. They'd moved in just two months ago after adopting their third child, Atlas, and having found a nice little place with just enough bedrooms for everyone and a front *and* backyard for their daughter Rory's outdoor hobbies. The address had, indeed, required some thorough research online but upon pulling up in the cab and taking in the wafting fragrance of cinnamon rolls, all doubts had vanished.

Leroy had given me yet another sideway smirk, snorting at my thoughtful concern for his wellbeing. I rolled my eyes and felt instantly regretful for paying him any sentimental attention, adjusting the collar of my neatly pressed dress shirt. In the distance, half a tiny little head could be seen peering out of the kitchen window. I waved.

"Yeah. I am."

I turned, surprised by the words of my companion. And his candor. He had on his school dress shirt and tie (which he declared were the only pieces of formal clothing he had in his wardrobe), done up by yours truly yet again due to said owner's lack of expertise. Only an idiot would pair a well-done tie with the monstrosity of a bomber jacket, which happened to be the only outerwear he'd brought along. And true enough, there was something surprising in his eye without the certain stillness of a candle flame. It flickered once.

"Well," I returned my gaze to the front door, realizing that I might have been staring. "I feel the same."

I heard him shift. Or more specifically, his half-empty rucksack containing travel essentials. Of which included one pair of jeans.

"Ice cream boy!" No doubt, Rory was the one answering the door, sailing down a makeshift ramp that took up half the front steps and past the front yard on her hoverboard. I'd always imagined her words appearing above her in permanent capital letters. It suited her well. "You're early. Check out my new hoverboard!"

Some thirty feet away, I spotted Miki, youngest of the Honeycutt-Jaxons, with half his head peering out from behind the front door—presumably still frightened by the prospect of answering it.

"Hello Rory," I greeted politely as she neared the gate and proceeded to unlock it. "Yes, I have observed the presence of your new gadget. You seem to like it very much." Her eyes had zeroed in on Leroy halfway across the front yard, curiously distracted from the conversation.

"Yeah. Uh... yeah, I like it. What's a geh-jut? And, who's he?"

Rory was never one to beat around the bush and her cutting to the chase had been very well within my expectations. She'd looked my companion up and down with wide, open eyes. The recipient of her gaze simply stared back, blank in the presence of an entirely new species: children.

"Rory, this is Leroy," I began by explaining. "He's from the school I am currently attending and he's joining us for thanksgiving." Chip's daughter had her gaze locked on us the whole journey up the front yard, all the way to the door. She and her hoverboard were one. "Leroy, this is my godfather's second child, Rory Jaxon-Honeycutt."

"How old are you?" She chose to open with, glancing at Leroy's bomber jacket for the third time. "I want that. It's cool."

"Taste," was all Leroy had to say, nodding. I sometimes think he should consciously dial down on the attractiveness. Nods should not be that attractive. "I'm sixteen."

Rory was all aboard. "Sick! Think you can talk Xander into getting me something like yours?" Already, she was lighting up. "He flips me off when I tell him people say I've got taste for nice clothes!"

I couldn't believe it. Refused to, even. I myself had taken more than a year to learn the ways of Chip's daughter and somehow get her to warm up to the boring little god sibling I was, all for the sake of speaking on a decently conversational level. And that was all *with* purposeful adapting and having met her at least ten times.

This however, had not been the case of Miki Honeycutt-Jaxon.

By the door, dressed in suspenders and a little bow tie that both appeared awfully familiar, was the nine-year-old angel I'd absolutely fallen in love with the moment my godfather had introduced us back when he was a mere infant. He was hiding behind the front door whilst politely holding it open. Impeccable manners.

I pretended not to notice the miniature force that had welcomed us with the magic of doors opening on their own, casually removing my coat at the entrance and stowing my bags in an empty cabinet Rory had directed us to. Leroy had followed suit.

"Vanille, Vanille," he did this little thing with his toes, tipping them up and down. It was his show of hidden excitement. "I'm here, behind the door."

Naturally, I was at once filled with the blessings of a thousand heavens. Miki's tiny voice embodied every streak of graciousness in his good behavior. Being well-spoken and fond of books was an added plus. Leroy on the other hand, seemed almost apathetic do the wonders of angelic figures.

I'd turned to the boy behind the door, leaning down with my arms open. He'd run up to my waist and threw his arms around it. *Oh. He's a little taller than I remembered him to be.* "Miki, you look absolutely stunning in those suspenders. I missed you so much."

"I missed you too, Vanille!" He whispered excitably, holding onto my arm while his sister closed the door behind us. He then peered up at me and, farther behind, noted the additional presence. Leroy was in the middle of listening to Rory's latest hoverboard adventure in the park when he'd caught my eye and glanced, over his shoulder, at Miki. The boy, slightly started, subconsciously weaved behind my legs for cover. "Oh. There's someone else."

"Miki, this is Leroy." I told him, gesturing at the idiot in front of me. "We go to school together and he's very nice."

"But he looks a little scary," whispered Miki into my elbow, unaware of my companion's unbelievably superior sense of hearing. I could tell Leroy was trying hard not to laugh. "Like daddy when daddy's not around..."

The tiny nine-year-old even let go of my arm to catch up with Rory instead, just so that he could be five more feet away from the burning candle.

"Smile," I muttered under my breath as soon as they were leading us down the hallway towards the kitchen and slightly out of earshot.

Leroy nodded once, seemingly understanding what I was getting at before flashing a winning smile at Miki, who'd chanced a teeny glimpse of us over his shoulder.

Needless to say, this was a huge mistake and had resulted in the boy's further retreat into his sister's side while the two of them led us past a large empty living room and into the kitchen. I couldn't help but notice how the house was a little quiet and empty. The lights were mostly turned off, save the warm glow coming from the kitchen and in the middle of it all, a lithe figure in a strawberry-printed apron, humming a forgotten tune.

My godfather turned as soon as we entered the kitchen, lighting up upon his daughter's announcement of our arrival. "It's ice cream boy and his very cool friend. I'm calling Xander to ask how long he's gonna take. He needs to see this bomber jacket a-sap."

Chip was one to skip all the formalities and go straight into gushing. It had been nearly five months since we last saw each other. Aunt Julie had said something about him doing away with all-day contacts recently and opting for the comfort of glasses instead. He'd chosen a pair that were, in my opinion, the height of fashion.

"Uwaa Nillie!" Open arms were the first thing I saw and then it was the smell of cinnamon and pumpkin. Chip was an inch or two shorter than I was, so I'd somehow started observing the fragrant notes of whatever he'd been baking in his hair just a year ago. "You're early! And why do you seem so much taller than I last saw you? O-or have I shrunk? I sure hope that's not the case... how was your flight? And and is this your friend?" He came out of the hug and peered over my shoulder with curious eyes. "Should we be introduced?"

I turned to the figure standing in the doorway, unable to catch the expression on his face. He had his arms crossed, leaning against the doorframe with a distant gaze turned away from the kitchen and in the general direction of Miki and Rory, who'd returned to assembling puzzle pieces in the living room.

It was times like these that I sometimes realized exactly why I'd found myself so drawn to him despite being his polar opposite. He had been giving Chip and I our private space.

"Leroy."

It caught his attention, glancing over his shoulder with the flicker of a candle in his eyes. He straightened up from leaning against the doorframe, uncrossing his arms as he walked over with an extended hand.

"Thanks for the invite," said Leroy, other hand uncharacteristically going for the back of his neck as though uncertain of his standing. Chip was practically beaming throughout their handshake, eyes sparkling. "Wasn't really expecting to be welcomed."

"Aw but why not?" My godfather gave his apron a quick tidy before presenting us freshly baked hot cross buns on a warm tray. I reached for one and gave half of it to Leroy. "We're more than happy to have you over. Hehe. Vanilla's never extended an invitation to anyone at school before. He must like you a lot."

The idiot had the gall to flash a sideway smirk in my direction. In broad daylight. In front of Chip. "Yeah. He does."

One could tell the extent of second-hand embarrassment my godfather was currently experiencing just from the look on his face. "O-oh! How... how very honest. So very sweet."

I cleared my throat and jumped at the timely pause during their conversation. "So, um. Where is everyone?"

"Xan's gone out to pick Giselle up from her studio," Chip was back to busying himself with dinner. "Your aunt and uncle are on their way with your grandmother and Gretel and Shea are just about closing the bakery. Do you mind waiting for a bit? It's only a little past five so I have more than an hour to, um... whip up a thanksgiving table enough for twelve people." He displayed slight panic on his face. It also involved waving a wooden spoon about like it was a wand. "Oh this isn't good for the heart. Your uncle's always been the one hosting thanksgiving and we have a little more people this year with Atlas and Leroy, s-so... um..."

"I'll help."

My companion had apparently stuffed his half of the hot cross bun into his mouth and was, already, rolling up his sleeves before I was even registering his response—as though he'd been anticipating this particular scenario and was simply waiting for it to occur. He even topped it off by loosening, and then removing the tie I'd taken ages to perfect, successfully rendering both Chip and I completely speechless and bewildered by the idiot's bold gesture.

Well, he best not be having any thoughts of taking over the kitchen or Xander wasn't going to have the best first impression of him, I found myself projecting quietly, far too distracted by the possibilities. Dazed, I'd somehow gained the additional item of 'Leroy's tie' in my hands and looked up just in time to catch him passing me with a private wink.

Gobsmacked into outer space, I was.

"W-would you? Really?" Chip had recovered a little faster than myself, I suppose having had nearly twenty years of experience with the devil himself. "It's quite a mess now. I'm honestly embarrassed that I don't even have the menu straightened out just yet a-and I really feel bad because you're our very important guest of the night."

Granted, I hadn't really given Chip or the rest of my family a thorough run-through of Leroy's exceptional culinary skills and general mental and physical capabilities. In fact, the only thing they bothered to ask about was nothing at all—blinded by the mere mentioning of his name, considering my complete lack of human relations since birth.

"I'll help with the menu," I offered, sighing shortly before privately glancing over at my companion with an eye of warning. *Don't you dare try anything funny.*

The candle in his eyes flickered in play.

LEROY

I say that, but I really wasn't going to. He probably thinks I'm playing, but truth was: I needed something to distract me from the nerves. Helping out in the kitchen was at the very least keeping me in my element—a safe space away from everything else throwing me off. Thanksgiving. Thanksgiving throws me off.

"I'm so glad you offered to help out," Chip was the kind of person to try and fill the silence. It was just the two of us going full speed ahead for dinner. A certain someone had been tasked to entertain the kids after menu planning and if anything, bless this occasion for sparing me a glimpse of how cute he can be. Not that he wasn't on an everyday basis. "You're really good at dicing onions!"

One every seven seconds. "Do I get brownie points for that?"

His godfather was someone you'd call enthusiastic. And helpful. Or... more like, just someone who prioritized the comfort and happiness of others before his own. He seemed a little confused by my statement, turning to me briefly before going back to his turkey gravy.

"O-oh. There's a point system?"

Probably where he got that streak of cluelessness. Crazy how he can solve the entire 'challenge me' pages in my AB text in less than five minutes, *upside down*, and casually turn my wordplays into an English test by correcting my grammar.

"To get in someone's good books, yeah," I explained a bit. Keeping the conversation light. Chip had been stealing glances at my chopping board, visibly impressed by my knife skills.

"Oh! Oh, you mean to say... you mean, mine?" His lips were an 'o'. "Well as a parent of four, I *do* find it comforting when boyfriends or girlfriends seek approval and permission from, y-you know. But at the same time, who am I to do the approving or, or... permission giving?" He went on, checking the pumpkin pie in the oven and wearing his mittens. "Take good care of each other. And, and no strawbe—I-I mean, no embarrassing... night-time activities just yet, okay? Oh dear." I nearly laughed. He'd turned around to the kitchen top with the asparagus and carrots and faced them instead. "Get yourself together Chip! You have three kids and you'll have to be giving the talk sooner or later!"

Some fifteen minutes into prep, we were down to the last two dishes for the evening and among them was the genius idea of getting Chip's husband to eat asparagus without forcing it down his throat. It involved twist-wrapping an asparagus stick with pastry and bacon strips, alternating between the two, and then baking the stems in the oven. That, paired with a nice parmesan sour cream dip.

"They'd sold out on brussels sprouts in every grocery store nearby. Can you believe it?" Godfather went on to account for the asparagus, somehow worried that his husband might not like it.

This all felt pretty distant at first. It's clear how their relationship could be toothache-inducing, especially for people like me who hadn't exactly seen the best parent examples. Both Chip and his husband seemed like the kind to give in after a mere sentence from the other, so I couldn't see how the asparagus was going to be a problem. He *was* going to like it.

I don't know what to feel about someone liking my cooking even before the first taste. In easy terms, they'd be biased. Some might say they are in love. But if it is, then I guess I'd be better off without people loving me. But then if it is... *does he feel that way?*

"Chip? We're here and Alfred's brought that stunning Scotch that Xander loved last year." Some people were at the door and godfather was torn between checking on his rested turkey and going out to receive them so I told him I'd take over. He thanked me and went out to greet his guests in the hallway. *Uncle Al and Aunt Julie.* I spent the ride here memorizing names.

They had a short chat outside the kitchen before Chip returned with a woman who looked vaguely familiar. I'd seen her before. The logical assumption was that she'd often be the one picking my only childhood friend up from my place.

"Where should I—oh!" She noticed my presence almost immediately. I turned around to nod. I didn't exactly know what to say. "Leroy? Yes, Vanille did mention that you were joining us tonight and... wow you've... you've grown so much and and you're so *handsome!*"

"Uh, thanks," I froze up, more speechless than before. I heard her call for someone by the name of Betsy. I thought I screwed up for a moment because that was *not* a name I remembered saying but said person soon came into view and it turned out to be grandma on a wheelchair. *Nana*, he calls her.

"Julie? But the appetizers are on the... oh. Sweet holy banana bread, you must be Levi." Wheeling her to the bar top by the kitchen was him in pinkish cheeks, hiding behind his glasses with his head lowered. I actually liked the name she gave me, so I went with it.

"That's me."

"You're... hella fine, you are," she ignored the hand I extended and went straight for a hug. I had an apron on. "So you taking care of our boy? He doing good in school?"

"He's great," I glanced his way. "Acing everything." It was the truth.

"Got a lot of friends like you now? Bring a couple more next time?"

"He's pretty well-known," I offered instead, giving an answer he'd be comfortable with elaborating on if needed to. "I gotta go. Helping Chip with dinner."

His nana said something about postponing it to breakfast but then Julie took over and wheeled her away from the kitchen and back into the living room. From where I stood, I'd caught a glimpse of his uncle handing out what looked like souvenir snacks to the kids. Somewhere along the way, one more of them had been added to the party of two. He didn't look like a kid.

"Vanilla, I'm so sorry to ask but do you mind setting the table? That's the centerpiece over there and the tablecloth's in the cabinet to your left. O-oh! And I made sure to get it in the checked colors you were raving about in your blog, hehe." He and his godfather's interactions were something I could watch all day. It felt almost as though he was back to being that tiny suspender-wearing, encyclopedia-reading fawn.

"I see your comments all the time. They're really insightful! But you must be so busy, with the kids and the bakery and all..."

"Oh no no, Miki loves your blog! We read it before bedtime and he sometimes writes the comments instead of me."

I was stealing a glance every second before I knew it until we actually got to work, setting the table and laying out all nine dishes, counting chairs and dishing out empty plates. The turkey smelled amazing, and wasn't the least bit dry after taking it apart. The aromatics he'd used in the stuffing paid off, and he'd even added a couple of bacon strips on top for flavor. His husband was apparently carnivorous.

All these expectations and prior knowledge of Xander Jaxon-Honeycutt eventually came down to the actual meeting of him in the flesh. The guy had arrived with someone by the name of Giselle, who I've been told was his artist sister and they all flocked to the table at once, greeting the rest of the family.

"Zelly!" Rory basically jumped at her. "Holy shit you have to see this bomber jacket. It's so cool. You know what I'm thinking of thrifting one and then..." Her aunt held up a hand and then magically produced a black bomber jacket with a red Chinese dragon embroidered to the back, wriggling her brows. "What the! How did you know??"

"Xandie told me," said her aunt, helping Rory into the jacket. "So I made it last week. You love it you love it?"

She got Chip's daughter screaming for the next minute or so while they hugged and I was just standing idly by the side waiting to introduce myself or for someone to introduce me because hell, this just got a lot more pressurizing than it was a couple of minutes ago, but then Rory turned to me and said in a lowered voice: "I'm calling off the plan. I got the best dad and aunt in the world."

Can't relate, but must feel nice huh.

Xander hadn't exactly left his husband's side since the second he returned, and while he got to looking at the bottle of scotch Alfred had brought along, he didn't seem as intimidating as Miki had made him out to be. All I could tell was how open he was about him and Chip. He'd swoop in with a glass of iced water and hand that to his husband after kissing him on the cheek. The latter's reaction was to be mildly flustered.

Another thing: the guy had aged well. Kinda unfair, if you ask me. It's bullshit how he'd managed to maintain that build all the way through and, according to Shea, Chip's youngest sister, seemed to have even more appeal than before.

"How old is he again?" I asked under my breath, retrieving my tie from the expert and purposefully reaching all the way down his back pocket. He'd jumped and given me a look.

"Thirty-five."

We both turned to Xander.

"Think I could look like that at thirty-five?" I played and he nearly laughed, rolling his eyes.

"Wouldn't be surprised if the world had made your existence illegal and thrown you into outer space by eighteen but, one can dream."

I had to pause and register the meaning behind his sentence. By the time I'd come up with a good comeback though, Chip had waved me over to point at the oven. The baked asparagus sticks were done.

We got to arranging them in a glass jar and separating the dip into three portions when Xander decided to enter the kitchen in search of old-fashioned glasses for their whisky. He looked over once and then, whilst getting out the glasses, asked the question.

"So you're the guy?"

Chip was the one who reacted before me. "Xan!" He was whisper-shouting. "I told you his name yesterday."

"Leroy." I held out a hand after wiping it on a Kleenex. The hand-shake was the firmest one I'd had to date.

"You're that kid. From the kindergarten," he seemed to remember, eyes amused. "You were a rude mother fucker."

Mm, sounds like me. "Still am, I guess..."

He actually laughed, helping out with the ramekins we'd put the dip into. He took two out of three, and left Chip with just one to carry. "Not bad. So you remember what Julian used to call me."

I paused, searching. "Not really."

"Mr. Handsome." He finished, almost straight-faced, save the smirk that was basically incorporated into every inch of his existence. I was taking notes. He was that good at it.

I settled for something else: "He calls me other things."

Okay so I shouldn't have said that in front of possibly future godfathers. It wasn't so much their reaction that spelled out 'you screwed up' but the fact that I'd just embarrassed Vanilla in front of his relatives behind his back. Chip was blinking and then blushing so hard he turned into a physical strawberry. His husband on the other hand, just looked a tad bit surprised by my comeback.

"He's lying." Came a voice from the bar top and I recognized it at once. Probably too anxious to actually leave me alone, knowing how difficult Xander could get. Okay, so he heard everything.

"Clearly—I-I mean, the only other term I use is 'idiot', which is by far the most suitable word, believe me."

It was hard not to laugh and give him the finger.

"W-wha!" His godfather looked so immensely traumatized by this interaction that he needed to put his ramekin down on the countertop and steady himself. "No middle fingers! It's banned in this household and and and you two are... are still too young to be... t-to be..." He had a wavering gaze fixed on his godson, lips quivering as though he might start tearing up any moment. "Nuu I can't let him take you away!"

VANILLA

To say my family was fond of Leroy had to be the world's greatest understatement. Charmed by his disarming smile and the witty little things he'd inject into conversations every now and then, I quite paled in comparison—reduced to a mere pebble watching from the side lines as my companion advanced to greater heights of 'blending in' more than I could ever imagine myself doing.

Atlas, my godfather's eldest adopted son, had been my unexpected partner for most of the evening. Our conversations, however, had mostly involved the idiot seated in the center of the room, particularly invested in a conversation about the younger me skipping through private high school and actively avoiding every single human being around me.

"—nearly losing himself on the first day of school! You have no idea how worried we were, sending him off and leaving him to fend for himself on foreign lands," said Uncle Al, having had one too many despite Aunt Julie's multiple attempts at stealing his old-fashioned glass. I was brave enough to continue listening. "If we hadn't known you'd be there, we'd—"

"I had him on my back," Leroy was back to letting them in on my embarrassing moments at school. "For about ten minutes. The whole way, racing track to infirmary. Barely three hours into orientation. The classmate he had with him couldn't even remember his name."

I wanted to protest. Still, those were the facts and... and, well... everyone else seemed sufficiently entertained by his stories from the way they were laughing and egging him on. Good-naturedly, of course. Apparently, the lack of unfortunate events and mistakes in my life had made it difficult for my family to consider myself a part of the human race.

"First day of the cross-year segment—lost his glasses. Right off the bat. Dropped it in a running stream. Couldn't see a thing for the rest of it but saved our asses and pulled a second."

I gave him a look, unsure if he was actively trying to drown me in mixed feelings of being both insulted and complimented at the same time. Rory and Shea kept asking for more, and Uncle Al seemed happy to hear more about my school adventures, which, admittedly, I have been keeping to myself most of the time. Chip kept leaning over for a side-hug.

"Frequents the ice-cream parlor I work at but refuses to order ice-cream," he went on, diving further into the details. It did a great job in keeping everyone entertained. "Has an insane palate but a fridge stocked with microwavables."

He looked over with a smirk. "Sleeps over but insists on wearing pyjamas to bed."

Oh.

*Oh um, that was...*intimate. I found myself struggling to stomach the words he'd so casually said aloud and internalizing the sudden silence in the room. Offering some short, nervous laughter, I made the timely announcement of fetching the souvenirs we got and giving them out before we forgot to do so and *then* pulling Leroy aside.

I'd initially made for the entrance where we'd stowed our bags away but then decided against it halfway through and made a detour, instead, down right towards the stairs. My companion had followed.

"Too much?" He stuffed his hands in his pockets, raising his gaze to meet mine. I was standing on the bottom-most step, leaning against the banister and staring at the doorway we came from just to see if anyone had decided to follow.

"A little." I nodded, sighing after a good moment.

He did the same, shoulders falling. "And I was doing so well all evening."

"Unlawfully well, I might add," I'd added under my breath, laughing shortly. He winked in return. "They like you. A lot."

"You think so?"

"I certainly know that as a fact," I offered, folding my arms and looking away as soon as I was beginning to feel the burn of his gaze. The next sentence was hard. "Among many other things which happen to include... well, that I haven't really... consulted my aunt and uncle about the, um... us." Finger pointing.

I saw him pause. "Okay."

"And basically everyone else... except my godfather. Nana. Chip's side. His kids. But his husband probably figured out from the conversation you were having with him, so. Um." I breathed in once, heavy and deep before returning his gaze.

"They let me come to thanksgiving without knowing about us?" Leroy was straight-faced; unreadable at present. Flame unflinching, almost glowing in the shadow of the stairs. "They'd let a friend do that?"

I swallowed, starting to see the cracks in the alliance of fire and ice. "I should have told you. I'm sorry."

"Your family's too nice."

"Well... it isn't exactly about being nice or not since I'm sure they wouldn't have turned me down, knowing that... well, that I've never once mentioned the name of anyone else besides fictional characters and scientists, let alone invited a friend over to dinner, so—"

"Friend." He said quietly. "You just said friend."

I was wide open, eyes, face and all and I'd begun shaking my head a second too late because he'd looked away and backed out of the shadows, heading back where we came from and *everything* had just, just escalated far too quickly for proper damage control that, by the time I'd gone after him as calm and collectedly as I could, he was back in his chair and, and smiling and listening to what everyone else was saying.

I felt it then—a slow burning of the chest and the wretched flame that, though much smaller and weaker than the flame of a candle, left marks far darker than the fires I was used to putting out.

* * *

The strangest thing about having a brain is having it cease to exist in the most important of times, quite literally forgetting its own presence in the head and allowing, instead, a dark silence to fill the void. I was fortunate enough to have never been on the receiving end of this shadowy abyss, scrambling for ground and having every next possible solution fall through. To confess: I did not know what to do next.

And as though standing in the doorway, just barely out of sight, was going to somehow provide me with a concrete answer to an endless question, I'd dug my feet into the floor and stayed in that exact position for a near minute or two—waiting for the recovery of my mind and listening to the faint laughter coming from the living room.

We had to talk. That much, I knew; yet the steps in which I would have to take seemed almost frenzied and warped in panicked thoughts, somehow involving the immediate kidnapping of Leroy regardless of the consequences or the stopping of the entire thanksgiving dinner.

Those thoughts, they were child-like and selfish—as though for a moment, my mind had been reduced to the workings of a four-year-old on the brink of losing his only friend. *This was no mind.*

"Nillie?" Chip had neared the blind spot I'd chosen to think in, returning to the kitchen with two empty glasses. "Did you find the souvenirs? Is everything okay?"

I threw parts of myself together, straightening up and adjusting my glasses. "Oh yes. Yes, everything's fine. I had to, um, recall where I put them and I was just admiring the design of this archway. Distracted. I-it's a beautiful archway."

My godfather was the most unsuspecting person to ever exist. Yet, he'd paused in his tracks and placed the glasses on the bar top before slowly turning to me with gentle eyes. "Giselle designed it. There's an eagle and a sparrow carved into the wood on both sides. Miki loves it. But... the Nillie I know doesn't have to recall where he's put his things, does he?"

Those words were heavy and at present, I was at a loss for truth and lies. "The bag's in a cabinet by the entrance."

"But, so," he searched my eyes. "You're going to get the goodies or... is there something you'd like to tell me?"

"I-it's nothing," I settled quickly, relieved he'd given the option of an urgent escape. "Thank you. I'll be right there in the living room."

Then I was fetching everything from the cabinet and handing them out one by one—trinkets, the soapstone figurines I'd got from Brazil, the exclusive culinary handbooks—consciously avoiding the gaze of anyone specific, fearing that the look in my eyes were dead giveaway of the rocky waves within.

I'd managed a private conversation with Uncle Al upon handing him a handwoven trinket basket for his cufflinks, conveying my general discomfort. "It's a migraine. I'm really sorry."

"Goodness gracious. Sit down, I'll ask Chip for some medication."

"O-oh I wouldn't want to cause any trouble..." I held on to his arm, panicking slightly. "I probably just need to lie down. Would it... could we perhaps head to the hotel anytime soon?"

It was half-past ten. Any later than eleven, I wasn't quite comfortable with. The sooner I could speak to Leroy alone in our room, the sooner we could have this resolved. And I say that, 'resolve', but I really mean explaining myself and hoping he'd see where I was coming from after, of course, listening to his side of things.

"But we haven't had Chip's pumpkin pie just yet, Vanille," the critic in my uncle never seemed to have a day off. "You know we can't leave without having a slice of it. Those mochi waffles of his... one would never think they were bake by the same person. We'll leave right after."

Chewing on my lip in unease, I gave in without another word. Uncle Al was well aware of my unconditional support for any sort of pastry made by my godfather and insisting on my request would have seemed all the more unnatural. Either way, an additional ten to twenty minutes of pumpkin pie couldn't possibly hurt and might even put Leroy in a better mood, as Chip's food often does to the human heart.

I had to, in the meantime, distract myself from the various probable instances that had, already, unfolded in my head like a deadly storm. Revealing our relationship or going as far as to be as open about it as my godfathers were at present entailed many other questions to be asked and answers, demanded. There was, among many other things, the expectation of 'coming out'—of revealing one's orientation having introduced a partner whose gender wasn't quite as society would expect. And if that should be the case, I, too, would have to be sure of my own sexuality, apart from never having raised the matter in a conversation with Leroy. Therein lies the truth: that I had no answers to these questions, regardless of their seeming importance.

"How is it?" I noticed how Chip had decided to seek the opinion of Leroy before everyone else, after handing out slices of pumpkin pie on dessert plates. He'd even added a dollop of whipped cream on top of every slice. "The crust and the filling?"

Most of the room had started digging into their pie and Leroy had been one of the first to do so, slicing through the perfectly-set filling and tender, flaky crust. It came to me, and perhaps, to everyone else, a surprise when my companion's final verdict had been put across in a manner so blunt and monotonous.

"It's a little bland. But I like it."

Stunned by his comment, the rest of the room had momentarily paused and glanced down at their slices of pie, perhaps even wondering if he had been given a different, store-bought serving. I scrambled for a forkful of it, knowing exactly how precise the culinary students at school had trained their taste buds to be, but he was wrong. As expected, the pumpkin pie was, objectively speaking, gently spiced but bursting with the flavor and sweetness of fresh pumpkin, rich and smooth.

I'd even went as far as to consider the inconsistency of the filling but logically speaking, that was impossible given the fact that every slice had come from the exact same pie. Further, Chip was that experienced of a baker not to make such a mistake.

"I disagree. I think it's quite perfectly flavorful," said my uncle, unable to resist an honest opinion. Aunt Julie had given his shoulder a nudge.

"O-oh, but... hm, tasting it now, I see what Leroy means." My godfather, as usual, was the kind to mediate. His husband sat beside him, surprisingly quiet. "I was um, a little light-handed on spicing it."

"Yes but the trick is *not* to over-spice it or that would only ruin the true flavor of the pumpkin. Spices are meant to bring out the flavor of the dish's highlight, not overpower it."

"Alright Alfred, now that you got us educated can you just enjoy your pumpkin pie?" Nana got to prodding Uncle Al with the back of her fork. "Boy's said it himself. He likes how it tastes so I don't know what you're defending." The room fell silent soon after, save the faint clinking of forks against plates. Miki and Rory had resorted to hiding behind Atlas and nibbling on their shared slice of pie. The former feeding the latter.

Needless to say, I'd found myself both a little confused, crossed, and ultimately, disappointed. Leroy had never once come across as someone particularly petty or childish enough to be taking out his emotions on any external entity, let alone, my family. No matter how upset or piqued he was with me or my words, I would have pegged him as having decent control over himself.

Or... or perhaps he would only show this side of him to certain people, if, at all, I say to convince myself. *Maybe our relationship was something so important, something he cared so much about to warrant such emotions and behavior.* After all, we were, admittedly, amateurs at the whole thing. These were emotions, new, and how to handle them was not necessarily something that could have been picked up in books and TV.

"Aunt Julie?" I approached my request from a different angle this time. She smiled, leaning in. "Do you think we could..."

"Get going soon?" She finished knowingly, sighing. "Yes dear. The check-in period ends at eleven too. And your nana's doctor said she shouldn't be staying up past midnight either."

Aunt Julie then spoke to Xander and Chip aside, exchanging hugs and kisses with the latter. I felt my heart sink a little, knowing that this was all far too brief, far too sudden a parting for my liking. Uncle Al on the other hand, was a fair bit tipsy and had in the midst of goodbyes given each and every one of Chip's dishes a verdict on the way out.

"Will we see you for Christmas?" Miki tugged at my sleeve, peering up with his large, cinnamon eyes. He was unconsciously doing the tippy-toe thing yet again. "I like decorating the tree."

"Of course, Miki." I told him, opening my arms for a hug. He settled in gently. At the corner of my eye, in the far back, I spotted

Leroy speaking to my godfather's husband. Neither were smiling, nor did they seem to express any form of aggression or displeasure. It seemed like a neutral exchange and yet, not knowing the exact contents did strike me as fairly worrying.

"Promise you'll call me," Chip had said into my shoulder during our hug, and I'd given him my pinky for reassurance—something he'd taught me when I was a lot younger. How promises were to be made.

And after several rounds of goodbyes that never seemed to be enough, the five of us, including Nana, headed out the front door and down the path towards the gate. Aunt Julie was slightly ahead with the car keys, while Uncle Al busied himself with guiding Nana's wheelchair. Past the gate, Leroy had stopped in his tracks and looked up, knowing we were out of earshot.

"I'm that way," he said, jerking his head in the opposite direction and causing quite the earthquake in my chest.

"Oh. U-um, what do you mean? The car's—"

"I'll sleep at my old place. You should take care of Betsy."

The horror that seized my mind at the sound of those words felt very much like a terrible, burning flame. "No but we were supposed to be sharing a room. It's really just going to be the two of us."

"And I guess the reason why your uncle agreed to that is because he thinks we're friends," he stared, straight into my eyes.

If this was a war of words, no doubt, Leroy had emerged victorious. Yet, the candles inside burned much lower than before. As though in defeat. I scrambled for protests.

"Vanille? Nana's ready," Aunt Julie called over her shoulder, waving at the two of us several feet away from the car. "Let's go!"

"Thanks for the dinner, Julie," Leroy went up to her before I could stop him. "But I think three in the backseat's going to make the ride a little tough. I'll sleep at my mom's diner." Behind his back, I was shaking my head and waving my hands, quietly hoping Aunt

Julie would refuse his sudden change in plans but she'd glanced, un-
easily between us, before offering my companion a ride at the very
least.

That, too, he'd declined. "Betsy's tired. She'll need the space."

"Leroy—"

"Thanks again." He backed away, starting in the opposite direction. Then, lowered his gaze at me. "See you."

I was looking at his back in less than a second, watching it shrink
as the distance between us grew farther and father and then, it was
that odd feeling; so painfully familiar—the feeling of only knowing
the way he looked from behind. Far, far away.

* * *

No luxurious cranberry bubble bath or silken cozy pyjamas could rid of the storm inside my head, resulting in both an inner and outer tossing and turning, the ultimate enemy of sleep.

I was in bed, closing my eyes to the faint playing of Clair de Lune
on my phone; which defeated its purpose since I'd placed it on the
nightstand, within my reach, and was checking the lock screen every
minute or so. Nothing, for the past two hours.

It was midnight by the time we'd arrived at our rooms, having
taken some time checking in and ensuring Nana was comfy and settled in her suite. Washing up and getting into bed had taken about
half an hour. Sending him a couple of texts and waiting had taken
another half and, after giving up at exactly one in the morning, I'd
ended up being unable to sleep for the next hour or so.

I'd even drafted and sent my godfather a 'thank you' text to distract my mind from wandering, frenzied thoughts. It unfortunately had not helped very much.

Leroy, sleeping in his mother's closed diner—alone, most likely without any form of electric heating since, clearly, no one had been living there for at least the past one and a half years. *Was there even a bed?* Knowing him, he'd settle for three old, dusty diner chairs put together but what of the cold? And hot water to shower in? I'd offered my very own bottles of shower gel and shampoo for his use and it was the very reason he hadn't packed his own.

A brief calculation of exactly how long he'd been away provided several answers to my questions, sparking a couple more along the way. Not only was there going to be an absence of electric heating, the building's insulation would have needed to be checked for repairs. And since he'd lived with his father before high school, was there even...?

I sat up and reached for my phone, googling for current wind speeds. They were strong. Possibly a little too cold for his liking.

Leroy. He'd made a trade; sought to reduce the intensity and destruction of his fire into a single, burning flame of a candle, all for the sake of protecting others from himself but could a candle survive against the might of the wind?

Alas, this very thought had me out of bed and pacing in the room. I had to see him. Still, I couldn't possibly go running to Uncle Al or Aunt Julie at nearly two in the morning. They'd only be anxious and worried about my state and it wasn't as though I was going to be any good at explaining myself and the entire situation at present.

Not Nana. And certainly not Chip either since he, too, was as prone to overthinking as I was and would eventually not be able to hide it from both my uncle and my aunt, knowing his inability to tell any sort of white lie. He probably wouldn't even be able to get a good night's rest just from thinking about my worries. Plus, he must've been exhausted from a day's worth of thanksgiving preparations... *and so I had my answer.*

There was only one person I could settle for.

He'd picked up on the fourth ring and was the kind to wait for the other person to start speaking first. "Mr., um, Xander?" I'd started off in a whisper, standing idly by the only chair in the room, huddled in a corner for some odd reason.

"*You don't have to whisper, Julian,*" I heard him say in a non-committal voice. He sounded surprisingly awake. "*This is a phone call.*"

"Oh. R-right." I cleared my throat, struggling to gather my thoughts despite knowing how it was with my godfather's husband when it came to telling him things. He needed them fast and straight-to-the-point. "Well it's nearly two in the morning so, I'd thought..."

"*There's no point in whispering if you've already decided to call someone past midnight and they answer the phone, awake. Anyway, you sleep at three when you're a parent. Atlas' light only just went off.*"

"O-oh no. I meant... I meant you and Chip." This had been the foremost concern on my mind before making the call. "I wasn't, um, interrupting... anything, was I?" It would've put Xander in probably the worst mood and at the same time alerted my godfather to the help I was seeking.

After all, most of our phone calls had for some reason summoned the devil's work in the middle of it and would often end with him being unable to keep his hands to himself. That, or Chip would choose to pick up the phone in the middle of their night-time activities in a heartbeat. Everyone knows how time difference can be the greatest enemy of phone calls.

I heard a snort on the other end. "*I don't force my husband to have sex with me when he's that tired, Julian.*"

"Ah. I see." It should now be obvious to anyone reading this; how I have remained a speechless little pebble in terms of my ability to have a conversation with my godfather's husband. I was never truly able to get over just how intimidating he can be in the absence of Chip but in all truth, he was the one remaining adult I could go to for help.

I explained my situation, reading out the concise, revised summary I'd written on the hotel notepad and doing my best to appeal to whatever that was left of his human heart. "He's probably sleeping in a chair. Without proper heating. And I'm... well I'm just, really... really worried."

I heard him sigh on the other end and, as I have come to learn, understood it as him giving in. "You shits. I'll be there in fifteen."

Relieved and absolutely drained by the pressure I was under throughout making my request and just praying he gets where I was coming from, I breathed a trembly 'thank you' into the receiver—only to realize that he'd already hung up.

And as promised, a family seven-seater pulled up at driveway of the hotel a little more than fifteen minutes later. I'd changed out of my pyjamas and headed down to the lobby right after the phone call so by the time I was downstairs, Xander had just turned in.

He nodded at the passenger seat after meeting my gaze so I took that as permission to get in. "Thank you. Um. Here's the address." I showed him the map on the screen of my phone and he waved it aside after taking a glimpse. I fastened my seatbelt.

"No one said having kids meant driving them to their boyfriend's place at two in the morning," he said, straight-faced, moments after hitting the main road.

Granted, I hadn't exactly been the best godson to him and Chip; and hearing him say that, including me in the same category as Rory, Miki and Atlas, made me feel absolutely terrible. "I'm sorry. I... I was really going to wait till seven to call but I couldn't, well... I couldn't—"

"Not talking about the time. I mean I didn't sign up for this in general."

I felt the weight on my shoulders grow. "O-oh."

And all of a sudden I was back to being that four-year-old child outside kindergarten, waiting for his uncle to pick him up. *Just how was I stammering so much?* Perhaps I was beginning to see why Chip hadn't quite kicked his habit even after twenty years of knowing his husband.

"I'm really sorry for dragging you into this," I thought of apologizing yet again, not wanting to be dubbed as the unappreciative child taking the adults around him for granted. And, well, honestly because I was truly grateful and sorry for adding to his troubles. "He's not... we're not usually like this. It happened because I was... I wasn't ready to tell everyone about us. No one else knows except for you and Chip, by the way. A-and Leroy didn't... he didn't take it very well when I told him that. Which is perfectly understandable. I mean I invited him to thanksgiving so it's only natural for him to think that the rest of my family knows about us."

My godfather's husband did not say a word in response. Keeping his eyes on the road.

"I was hoping we could talk about it but he was really upset and... and I don't want, I mean I can't stand the thought of him resenting me because he's really the only person my age who would... who would put up with my nonsense and poor social skills and still so openly express his affection for me.

"I-it's just a plus that he's so disarmingly attractive and criminally good at what he does, aside from being highly knowledgeable and skilled at anything related to the culinary world. Anything that isn't math, I would say.

"I simply have no idea how to go about telling anyone about this, about us, without them questioning my orientation or, or expecting me to... 'come out.' A-and honestly, I don't quite know if he's the only person who'd ever want to spend the rest of his life with me, but... but I'm pretty sure I'd very much like that."

Somewhere along the way, my vision had started to blur and after releasing my knotted emotions in the form of words, received a plain silence in return. Xander had kept his eyes on the road all the time, and when I chanced a glimpse at his face in an attempt to gauge his reaction—whether I should be apologizing for going off—I observed a cross between a weary look of frustration and monotony.

"Okay look," he sighed. "Like I said to you when you were four, you're still *young*." He'd started off very slowly, as though speaking to that very four-year-old he was talking about. "You're fifteen for fuck's sake, you don't need to be figuring out whatever it is you're worried about."

"But—!"

"Yeah, there's gonna be a lot of people expecting the shit they want to expect and answers to the questions they have, sure. And you're the worst kind of person to live in a world like this because you like having answers to every question around but some questions *don't* have answers and people need to learn to deal with that shit. You don't owe them anything and those people can just fuck off. Nicely. "

I had to pause for a moment, filtering out the curses and deciphering his philosophy before finally taking it in. Naturally, I wasn't at my maximum capacity for thought and to be lectured honestly felt so much better than being the one doing the lecturing, which was the effect Xander tended to have on myself, specifically. He and Chip had very different ways of parenting.

"Thanks Mr. Handsome." I sniffled.

"I'm your godfather, you little shit." I saw him swipe at the tissue box through blurred vision before shoving a bunch of whites in my face. "Stop crying or I'll send you back to kindergarten."

* * *

"Do you have a brain?" The girl answering the door had on a nightgown and curlers in her hair. "Who'd be selling anything at two in the morning?"

Moments ago, Xander had pulled up across the street right outside the diner and I'd taken a moment to recognize the storefront I had frequented nearly thrice a week back in the day. It looked shabby now. Almost dilapidated without the warm lights coming from within and the homely hand-painted sign that used to welcome every customer.

I'd peered through the display window while Xander insisted he wait in the car, not wanting to be part of our 'romantic reunion'. Well, he was wrong. There's nothing *romantic* about staring into pitch black darkness and searching for a doorbell only to realize that all they had was an old-fashioned knocker. And since Leroy had neither responded nor read any of my text messages, I'd knocked several times in urgent concern, wondering if something ill had happened to him. O-or that he was just sleeping.

Unfortunately, I had narrowly missed a probable scenario—one that happened to include a stranger answering the door.

"I... hello, I'm sorry," I said to the girl, stunned and deeply apologetic but unable to stop myself from glancing over her shoulder. "This is an ungodly hour. I um. I was wondering if anyone by the name of Leroy Cox has um... do you know him?"

She frowned, inching the door shut. "Yeah and I don't think he's in the mood to see anyone right now."

I placed a hand on the wood. "He's here? W-well, I'm his closest friend. That is to say, he's very important to me. Could you, um, perhaps tell him that I'm here, waiting for him? I'd very much like to speak with him. Just for a moment—ah, unless he's asleep. In a bed.

Comfortably." Again, I chanced a glimpse over her shoulder, but all I could see were empty tables and chairs in disarray.

"He's not here," she said, clicking her tongue. I did a double take.

"But... you mean to say, he... um. Hold on, do you own this diner?"

"No, it's been closed since like, the ice age," she scoffed, rubbing one of her eyes. "My mom's the landlady. We live upstairs. Can I go now?"

But then, Leroy and Annie... they no longer own this place? Wouldn't he have the rights to the diner by now? Then... then where exactly did he go after dinner, and, did he even come by at all? But since she did say he wasn't in the mood to see anyone, she must have seen him, at the very least.

"I'm really sorry about this," I tried one last time, doing my best to keep the door open. She was leaning on it. "But could you please tell me where he went? He dropped by, is that correct?"

The poor girl seemed increasingly exasperated by my constant efforts, which was understandable considering the fact that she was nice enough to actually answer the door and try to converse half asleep. "I don't know. He didn't look very happy, that's for sure. Picked up some of the old things they left here and left like, two hours ago. Why would he tell anyone where he went?" She closed the door in my face, officially ending the conversation. I hadn't even gotten the chance to say thanks.

I'd returned to the car and sent Leroy another text along the way, telling him about the diner and asking where he was. Deep down, I was struggling to come up with any other option he had in these parts of town, at this hour. At some point, I'd even considered having to make a police report.

"He's not—Xander? Are you, um," I tapped my godfather's husband on his shoulder. He looked more than half asleep. "Are you alright? Again, I'm so sorry for roping you into this... but Leroy isn't at the diner. I don't know where he could've gone." I watched him open a bottle of water and after a couple of gulps, poured some right over his face.

"Fucking idiot," he breathed, slapping himself awake before taking the wheel. "You sure he hasn't got other family in these parts?"

I was about to shake my head. "I... well... he's never mentioned anyone."

"You guys are a mess," he concluded, starting the car and heading down the street in a crawl. "He can't have gone very far. There's no bus operating at this hour and the cabs around here don't drive around past midnight that often."

I was, once again, on the verge of dreadful tears. To be witnessed in such a poor and distasteful state was downright embarrassing. Xander did not seem to care very much about my reputation, however, which was the only blessing amidst this chaos.

"Evergreen Kindergarten for Future Leaders." I heard all of a sudden and looked up, passing the back of my hand across my eyes to clear my vision. "That's your school, right? We used to live further down, right up the hill. The only bus stop nearby was the one opposite this kindergarten."

It was. Xander must have remembered since he'd used to walk and take the bus around instead of driving a car. They didn't have one back then. And then there was that one time he'd offered to send me home. O-or rather, wasn't really given a choice.

"That's... where you first met him too," I told Xander. "Leroy. He was there beside me."

My godfather's husband rolled his eyes, as though I'd stated the obvious. "Yeah, but more importantly isn't that where *you* first met him too?"

Slightly dazed, I'd given him a blank look in return before glancing over his shoulder and across the road. The gates were closed. Everything else about it, however, had remained quite the same.

Even the benches that my fellow classmates would hang around after school, waiting for their parents to pick them up. It was either
there, jumping up and down and balancing on the back rests or
busying themselves at the playground by the...

I lowered my gaze to the screen of my phone. Nothing.

"Do you think he's—"

"The dumbass basically has nowhere else." Xander put forth
bluntly, pulling over and reclining his seat. "Just go. I'll wait."

Alas, I was, yet again, on the verge of tears. "Thank you so much.
I-I'll be right back." I hopped out of the car, closing the door behind me and making my way across the street towards the kindergarten—down the fenced-up area and all the way to the back where
I remembered the playground was.

The November breeze had the foliage of red and burning leaves
above swaying in its wake, heavy and crisp. The ground, cloaked in
a flurry of dead and dried leaves, browned and papery, trembled at
every passing gust of wind, picking up bits and pieces of whatever
that was stray in a momentary, floating whirl until it led my eyes to
him—crouched up in one of those hollow crawl tunnels meant for
children, head between his knees in the most uncomfortable position.

I crossed the distance but he soon noticed, raising his head a little and uncrossing his arms, presumably in surprise.

"Vanilla?"

He made an attempt to straighten up, ready to turn and slide
himself out of the tunnel but I stopped him just in time, crawling in
and stubbornly blocking his way out. He stared.

"How did you know?"

I fidgeted uncomfortably. Seconds in and this was not doing well
for my neck. "You're an idiot for not answering my texts. I was about
to involve the police!" I'd started rather frankly, only to observe a

twinkle of amusement in his eyes. I reached out to give his forehead a taste of its own medicine.

"The diner," I went on. "It doesn't belong to your mother anymore?"

Leroy nodded. "She sold it for the extra cash so that we could move to someplace near school... then came the coma so I had to spent quite a bit on the bills."

"Does your father know about this?" I asked, chewing on my lip.

"I don't like asking him for help." *As expected.*

I sighed. Uneasy. Glancing over at my companion, I unfolded my arms and shifted slowly to face him with open arms. He stared, then met my gaze with a hint of his signature smirk.

"What's this?"

"W-well I was offering you a hug."

"Dumbass." He leaned over, closing the distance and gently taking control. He tasted surprisingly of... of *alcohol*—only that I wasn't exactly sure what kind.

I confronted him at once. "Was... was that...?"

He seemed to pause, guilty. "Early evening. Your godfather's husband gave me some over dinner to cook with," he explained, holding up a silver flask. Gobsmacked into outer space I was.

"B-but you drank it?"

"I was cold," he reasoned, candle in his eyes flickering again and again and naturally had me soft and anxious beyond belief. "The wind's fucking me up."

Almost immediately, I'd removed my coat and draped it over his shoulders, confiscating the flask and replacing it with a hand warmer in my back pocket. "I can't believe you were willing to spend the night out here over... over some silly misunderstanding."

He slapped my hand aside. I looked up, frightened. His eyes were dark.

"Because I'm scared of loving someone more than they will ever love me?"

Those words stole every string of thought I supposedly had, locked and loaded for firing upon seeing him. In a broken voice, I told him that I was sorry. That I knew he'd always been the one so willing to express his affection in such brave and honest ways and that these had been the very walls I could hide behind.

"But please don't think that I... that the extent of my emotions is any less than yours because I do, very much... more than you'll ever imagine, I do love you.

"A-and you, walking away like that, turning your back, I used to think I could put up with the distance—that I could be happy, satisfied, contented just by watching you from afar while you walk ahead but I've come to realize that I would very much prefer to be... to be beside, or... or seated across like when we were—"

"Playing on that seesaw." He finished, staring straight into my eyes with a flame that was now bright and intense. This continued for some time and I, somewhat affixed, enchanted by the flame, began to feel the words fade into silence.

His eyes then rested on something over my shoulder. I followed his gaze.

"Leroy, um. We're too heavy for that."

He laughed low, taking my hand. "You never know."

VII

⚘

VANILLA

"Gay, I guess," said Leroy without so much as a blink or a pause at the question I'd posed. It hadn't been an easy one. "I'm attracted to you. And you're a guy... unless you're not."

Xander had dropped us off at the hotel after begrudgingly swinging by an all-day convenience store and buying each of us a hot beverage and cup ramen, insisting we had all that before going to bed (and that I draft a text to Chip whilst filling my tummy just so that the details of our adventure remained fresh in my mind). I'd put some water in the electric kettle as soon as Leroy made for the shower, preparing our cups of ramen before gently laying the question upon him when he emerged i-in a bathrobe.

"I'm pretty sure you've seen me without my pants on and I do identify as part of the male species, so." I handed him a pair of chopsticks, mildly distracted by the forward confession he'd made about his attraction towards me. He was running a towel through his hair. It looked much darker when it was wet—as though singed from the heat. "And no, that's not quite the answer I was looking for. You can be something other than gay and be attracted to me in a... attracted to me, sexually. That's my current stand on things, by the way. I find

I like you in that way. I mean I find you very asdkljf and I am, at the same time, aware that I am not attracted to other men."

You must understand that this was all going on at half past three in the morning and considering the fact that we'd boarded the plane at six a.m., our nonsense was... well I'd say it was justified.

Leroy's response was to blink, reaching over to receive the pair of chopsticks before staring at my hands and then back up at me. "That's why you didn't tell them." He seemed to understand now; why I had been struggling with the expression of truth, that dealing with something as foreign as my orientation wasn't exactly the easiest thing.

"Yes. I'm still confused and not entirely sure what's happening just yet," I confessed rather quickly, meeting his gaze briefly before nervously looking away. "I don't mean to keep you a secret, or anything like that."

My companion was quiet for a moment, gazing at the steam circling and rising from our sinful cups of midnight ramen. I pushed one towards him and started first, blowing on a couple of strands I'd caught with my chopsticks. He on the other hand, had a tongue incapable of understanding the concept of temperature and had straight up sent a generous portion into his mouth and down his throat.

I let the silence settle in, staring out of the window as it did and all of a sudden, registering the fatigue rested upon my shoulders. He seemed to follow my gaze, watching the streets down below and the occasional wind passing by, whistling against the glass.

"Think there's something for people attracted to intelligence?" He posed rather casually, halfway through his cup and I was, very naturally, immensely bewildered and illegally disarmed.

I couldn't words, so I simply returned his question with a look of absolute confusion and absurdity.

Leroy had the gall to square his shoulders like he'd just made a wild guess at the last question of his AB test. "Would explain why I'm so turned on every time you say something."

"So you'd go to bed with Albert Einstein or Edith Stern."

He gave that a thought. Well, he better. "... don't know the second one, but okay I get your point."

Admittedly, I couldn't quite tell if he was being serious about this whole thing but regardless of his intended purpose, he'd won a smile and then because I could so clearly see him hiding a smirk behind his cup of noodles, it worsened into a laugh. *What an idiot. Has me wrapped around his finger and is perfectly aware of it! Someone, report him to the authorities.*

He gave my forehead the usual after confirming the lightened mood.

"But does it matter?" He came up with soon after, staring intently at the side of my face that I could practically feel the burn without so much as have him in the periphery of my vision. I reached over without quite looking at him, gently directing his head elsewhere so that I could actually concentrate on having a conversation without heated eyes on me.

"Well my godfather's husband said the same thing. He says it isn't important. That we don't need to feel obligated to have an answer to that question. Initially, I'd somehow arrived at the conclusion that I, myself, wouldn't require a label, but that others would. And after listening to what he had to say, I suppose we don't have to arrive at any conclusion either way." I addressed the window. The view. More specifically, the reflection in it. "I mean. If you're okay with that."

He did not turn—somewhat obliging with the direction I'd put his head in—but met me in the glass with a testing smirk. "So... I'd be right to say that you like *my* dick. Specifically."

"This conversation is over." I finished up the last of my ramen, snatched up his empty cup on the table and put them back into the plastic bag they'd come with before securing that and properly disposing of it by the front door. "And I'm setting the alarm for seven in the morning as punishment."

I could hear him laughing in the bathroom, brushing his teeth.

* * *

To say I was an absolute disgrace to my reputation of having the most impeccable manners in all of teenaged human species was, by the very next morning, an understatement.

Leroy and I had ended crawling back into the waking world at eleven o'clock with the worst of eye bags and an inability to carry out basic functions like putting on a pair of pants or remembering where I'd left my glasses the night before. Most importantly, Uncle Al and Aunt Julie had reminded me just the night before about coming down for breakfast at nine; which meant that they'd gone nearly three hours either waiting for me downstairs or without a single text message.

Twenty-four missed calls.

Naturally, being late was a phenomenon I'd never before experienced, and to think it wasn't Leroy but myself who'd mistaken the vibrating phone for the alarm I'd set and continually hit the 'snooze' button! Down the drain my spotless reputation went and even for my uncle and aunt who'd basically known me for my entirely life, this was exactly how their perception of me was—which, strictly speaking, was highly accurate, as far as I knew.

But perhaps that was all before sitting up in bed and registering the presence of a lion's mane poking out of the covers, completely oblivious to the multiple alarms and phone calls I was receiving. Leroy Cox had not stirred one bit despite my frantic attempts at returning the calls I was receiving from both my uncle and grand-mother.

Thank goodness neither of them were worried enough to actu-ally use the spare keycard they had to enter the room, most likely under the persuasion of my aunt. Who'd... probably made a couple of wild guesses regarding the situation at hand.

They would've needed an ambulance had they done so; Leroy's bathrobe had, as usual, come magically undone in the middle of his reckless sleep. He was the kind to move. A lot. And then stay in a specific, unbelievable position once he'd found that miraculously comfortable enough. This time, it involved sinking his entire face into the pillow, arms wide open, chest down with his back some-what covered by the robes that for some reason, refused to stay on his shoulders.

After having a brief conversation on the phone with my uncle, apologizing for the mess that I was and reassuring that I was, indeed, alright and that I'd... overslept because Leroy had arrived rather late, I was informed of the hotel's check out time. Twelve noon.

The next hour was spent in quite the frenzy. Waking my compan-ion and ensuring that he sat up *with* his robe done before struggling to find my glasses and then struggling to change out of my pyja-mas and then, just, well, struggling in general. Aunt Julie met us downstairs at the lounge of the hotel lobby, wagging a finger in our direction while Nana was all over Leroy once more, tousling his hair and patting his shoulders.

"Where's Uncle Al?"

"He's gone to settle the bill. And you have a lot of explaining to do, little fawn," Aunt Julie crossed her arms and I recoiled on in-stinct, knowing how she'd used those terms on me when I was much younger. It first happened when they found out I'd dropped by the bookstore on my way back home and secretly bought a collection with the lunch money I'd saved up.

"W-well um. Leroy said he needed to drop by his mother's diner to collect some of their belongings, so. So he turned up pretty late last night at about um, midnight. And... we played some games and had some snacks before we slept." The events were to a certain extent, accurate and believable. Which was what made a lie convincing sometimes. Have details, but not too many. "The alarm was... that was my fault. We overslept and I'm really sorry for making you worry like that."

I don't play this card very often. Lying. And both Aunt Julie and Uncle Al know me well enough to trust my judgement of when I'd resort to dealing such a hand and the extent to which I'd do it.

She breathed a sigh, giving my nose a pinch. I sneezed. "You deserve that. I don't recall you spending late nights playing games or, or snacking back when you were in that high school! Should I be worried about this culinary school of yours?"

"Julie," Nana smacked my aunt's thigh and I could tell from the corner of my eye how hard Leroy was trying not to laugh. "The boy's acting like a normal teenager for once and you're concerned about that? Has Alfred finally rubbed off on you? I'm not allowing no more of that. Maybe you should spend more time over at my place."

Aunt Julie pursed her lips. "But Vanille's *never* overslept. Not even when he's spent hours burning the midnight oil for some pop quiz in senior year he's most likely going to ace anyway."

Again, I apologized. "I promise. It won't happen ever again."

"Good. Because Alfred says the next hotel giving us a free night has the best breakfast buffet in town, so you and Leroy *have* to be there, on time."

"Thanks A... Julie." My companion was this close to making a fatal mistake that would have sent my flying into outer space but to my surprise, Aunt Julie had laughed and, after glancing at Nana, said that he could call them whatever he wanted to.

The conversation went on to details of our school life that gave insight into the curriculum, stuff like the classes we were attending and the kind of core modules we were supposed to be taking according to our majors. Uncle Al returned sometime later, and upon hearing about my side of the story from Aunt Julie, told us that we should be setting off to our next accommodation very soon.

"Unless you two have something else to do? Someplace you want to eat at before flying back?" He'd directed this at Leroy more so than myself, since I'd told them about the short period of his stay.

"I was thinking of a place, yeah." My companion surprised me by nodding. I quickly pulled him aside.

"What did I say about impromptu plans?"

"I was thinking of going alone though..."

I blinked in return, glancing over his shoulder to check on everyone else before coming back to the whispered conversation we were having. "Well... I mean, it's not that I object to you going alone but today's s-sort of... it's the last day we're seeing each other. Until the end of the week-long holiday, that is. Not to say I wish to spend every single second of it with you, that would kill me, no doubt. I... just thought you'd like for me to go with you. At the very least."

My companion laughed low, leaning in to give my forehead the usual. "I'm going to see someone. This time's... not a good idea."

"Why not?" I probed, uncharacteristically nosy thanks to the terrifying seed of insecurity that had, for some reason, taken root somewhere within. This conversation was a great job nursing it; I simply couldn't bear the thought of there being another person he wanted to spend time with and at the same time, refused to let me meet them. Still, as I've learnt from multiple awfully-written protagonists of romantic fiction, taming the green monster inside was a necessary part of making any relationship work. "Not that I mind. Just... sorry I'll stop asking."

He sighed. "It's my dad. And we argue. All the time," he laid out bluntly. "So yeah. Don't want you to see me like that."

I paused, registering how stupid I must have sounded and promptly dilating the blood capillaries under the skin of my cheeks. Ultimately, I was childishly relieved of the weight on my shoulders. "Yes um. I respect your decision. A-although I wouldn't mind tagging along some three quarters of the way and then waiting nearby so that you'd at least have some company while you're traveling."

He took a moment to think about this, glancing over at the rest of my family seated at the lounge. "You... not gonna spend some time with them?"

"We've made exciting plans over the rest of the week. Redecorating the house. My room. Shopping for new furniture."

Leroy laughed shortly, then groaned under his breath as though giving up. "Fine. But when he comes, you're stepping out. The guy's a professional at involving bystanders."

"Okay," I nodded, unusually excited and guiltily so. The last he'd ever spoken about his father seemed about ages ago, back when we were playmates. "I'll go ask my—"

"I'll ask." He reached out to block my way with an arm, glancing over his shoulder with another one of his disarming smiles.

Moments after we'd sought permission to leave for the rest of the afternoon and rejoin over dinner at the next hotel, we were on our way to a restaurant, or so Leroy had divulged. It was really all that he told me on the bus and, as a human being with a great distaste for limited information, I felt around for snippets of more.

"It's your father's restaurant?" I offered him a chocolate mint. He gave the box a glance, laughed shortly, and shook his head.

"He wouldn't waste his time on someplace quiet and out of the way. They're in New York, Shanghai, Manila, Singapore. The new one's somewhere in Europe."

Needless to say, I was mildly surprised. "You've been keeping up with him."

Leroy uncapped the bottle of water we'd purchased at the transfer station to share. "He's still my father. We just don't get along."

The words had so coincidentally struck a bell in my mind and I was at once reminded of the problematic issue raised by Chen on the evening of our school's open house. "Oh um, speaking of not getting along... Chen was telling me—Layla Tenner is quitting school. Consequently, he's going to take her place as the school's number one and you'd be moving up to second. And and and Birchwood will be joining the top thirteen as number nine. Did you know about this?" I searched his gaze, waiting. He was unexpectedly calm.

"What about you?"

That was not the answer I'd been expecting. It was practically another question. "What do you mean?"

Leroy clicked his tongue, rolling his eyes but with the corners of his lips turned up. "The ladder. You're not in?" Initially, I couldn't quite understand why he was asking this.

"Well clearly I didn't make the cut or Chen would be telling me about it," I pointed out with a smile, flattered by the indirect compliment he was making.

"Yeah, bet he'd love to come running to you with good news," said the idiot under his breath who, apparently, wasn't as good at taming green monsters within compared to myself.

In fact, I was admittedly so surprised by his reaction (had I not made it obvious enough that Chen was barely an option for my attention or attraction?) that it'd taken me a minute to gather my thoughts. "All he's been asking for are favors and quite frankly, I'm not so kind as to agree in a heartbeat. First, it was to join his cross-year team against my will and then now, he wants my advice on Dalgona-style desserts like cakes and pastries and and and going shopping for the ingredients together. And, again, if you knew a thing about being polite, I was turning him down in the most socially accepted manner by coming up with some form of an excuse."

He was listening to all this—or at least I hope he was—while staring at me before finally cracking a smirk and leaving me speechless with a private display of his indecent finger. "Knew he wasn't competition."

I rolled my eyes, pointing at the vulgar gesture in his lap. "Keep that up and he will be."

He had the gall to challenge me by doing so for the rest of the ride (cramping up twice) and for some completely irrational reason, managed to leave the both of us unable to sit back in silence without a smile threatening to surface. He'd changed from his right to his left hand as soon as the former had cramped up. It was absolutely *idiotic*.

This lasted for as long as thirty minutes until we'd arrived at our stop, alighted, and headed down an empty street. Leroy led the way and as we seemed to near our destination, the flame in his eyes darkened and dimmed, leaving our moment of smiles some way behind.

The restaurant we arrived at was not something one would expect to find in a quiet, narrow street, void of life and pretty much home to one or two pigeons roosting above. It had a pair of Italian flags on both ends of the storefront and a colorful row of fake flowers in a makeshift balcony dangling above the sign. A casual would have passed it off as borderline fancy but to the keen eye of an expert, trained, it was trying a little too hard.

Glancing past the immediate foreground of the display window, one could make out an elderly man behind the counter adjusting the reading glasses slipping down his nose. Before him were folders, papers and documents scattered around in a haphazard manner.

"That's your father?"

"Grandfather." Leroy corrected shortly, hand on the front door. He didn't say anything about staying outside so I followed him in and waited for the signal instead. Needless to say, curiosity got the better of me; that, and the sheer surprise of registering the presence of an extended family. After all, he'd never really mentioned a word about anyone apart from his mother.

The elderly man looked up from the documents he was deciphering as soon as he heard us enter. It was only after removing his glasses that he seemed to recognize his grandson. Unfortunately, his response had been to turn away and sigh, rising from his seat and retreating to the coffee machine on the other end of the counter.

Leroy did not waste a second. "Siegfried?"

"Your father just left this morning. Didn't he tell you?" Both those words and the tone he'd said them in felt almost stifling. His grandfather clearly wasn't in a mood to entertain customers, let alone family—pouring himself a cup of coffee and holding it up to his lips.

Leroy did not back down. "Do you know anything about the diner?"

"What diner?"

"Annie's diner."

"Oh, that," there was a snort. "Yeah, what about it."

The look of frustration on Leroy's face was an unbearable sight. The flame in his eyes burned, fierce and stronger than ever, flickering and reaching to spread its heat but he'd shut it down in a blink—killing the flames and reducing it to the still silence of a candle. He'd turned to me then with a look and I, hesitantly, excused myself.

And I was inching towards the door, the last I heard was a snippet of Leroy's elaboration. "I was there last night. He lied about the landlady. The place is under his name but he hired someone else to..."

This was no proper way of piecing things together considering my limited knowledge of the supposed selling of the diner but if the place continued to be under Leroy's father's name, then wouldn't that have meant he was the one who'd bought it over? But then there was the landlady. And then I could only watch him speak to his grandfather from a distance. From the outside, they looked almost like strangers.

LEROY

Just an hour ago, I was kissing him on the forehead in front of the departure hall and appreciating that stunned, pink shade dusting his cheeks while he struggled to come up with something coherent. He ended up settling on 'I'll let you off just this once only because we won't be seeing each other for the next week.'

I'd reminded him about downloading Skype on his laptop at the hotel last night. His reaction back then had been to pause and think for a really long time, before coming to the conclusion that facetiming or any form of video calling was 'not good for the heart.' I'd given his forehead the usual and told him not to come begging for a picture once he starts missing me too much.

"I assure you, that will not happen."

He's right, by the way. Don't know how he does it but he always ends up being right about things and here I was, on my flight back, itching to send him a text every now and then. You can't do that on a plane so I ended up drafting and queuing eight messages in total. Then scrolling through his appreciation album. And then going back to whatever boring movie I was watching on the entertainment system. And then scrolling through his photos again.

It wasn't until the movie I happened to be watching started featuring some crazy obsessive ex that I glanced back down at the phone in my lap and deleted all the queued messages.

The rest of the week sounded impossible for now. To think I settled with getting ice cream for him at some nearby parlor after I was done talking at the restaurant. But then again, I was spending more than half my energy trying to keep my fire in check, so doing anything more exhilarating than ice cream would have put our mood at risk.

Hugh had been an asshole, to say the least. Fact that Siegfried turned out so obsessed with money and fame and running away probably had something to do with it. He'd spent about an hour running in circles and leading me along as though he knew the reason behind the diner being under his son's name and then laughing when I finally snapped and told him to spit it out.

At least I tried.

To: Braised Chicken
Miss me already?

* * *

From: Braised Chicken
I see that you're safe and alive

* * *

To: Braised Chicken
Split second reply?
Wow you miss me

* * *

From: Braised Chicken
All I miss is your ability to make proper inferences Leroy Jeremy Cox
My mistake, it never existed

"Fuck you." I laughed under my breath before realizing a second too late that I'd cursed aloud and caught the attention of everyone else standing in line waiting for a cab. Thank fucks for thick skin. *And how did I end up here without knowing?*

By the time I was back in school and craving for a nap, he and I had exchanged an hour or so's worth of high-quality banter and it was just the shit I needed to survive the rest of my day without him. After taking a quick shower and crashing for two hours, I woke up at seven in the evening and gave him a text to tell him that I was awake and about to order some food.

He slapped me with a 'you're a chef in a culinary school and you're about to pay for delivery and unreasonable prices for mediocre food?' So I got my ass out of Cayenne and headed for the marketplace to get some ingredients. Not before sending him a *shef* meme.

Sadly, I ran into someone along the way. I wasn't expecting humans because, yeah, people go home for thanksgiving because most people have families. But then I remembered not everyone celebrates thanksgiving and felt like a little shit for assuming. Chen, apparently, was one of such people.

"Cox? Woah, you're back."

I nodded in greeting only because I wasn't going to give him the chance to slide into my—*his* DMs and complain about me ignoring him in the hallway. On instinct, I'd decided not to entertain or pay him much attention for more than a second's worth of my time but he stopped right in front of me and said something about meeting Layla Tenner for the last time before she leaves.

This got me frowning. "She's here?"

"Yeah. We're in kitchen nine. Booked it out for her farewell party—it's all in the chat group, Cox," he laughed. "Which you're in."

My first thought went something along the lines of: *thanks Tenner you were great but I don't love you or parties, so.* But two seconds passed and Chen was still standing there, in my way, which soon got me thinking about the insider info I could be getting for a certain writer and then, taking a leaf out of Xander's book, maybe earn myself some brownie points.

I gave in and Chen seemed just as surprised as I was with myself, which probably meant that he wasn't expecting me to actually go along with him. We made a short run to the marketplace for some nachos to go with a dip someone had made before arriving at kitchen nine to some half of top thirteen lounging on kitchen countertops half-drunk.

Over at the instructor's station was a bunch of party food and a Bluetooth speaker playing sad music beside a cocktail mix that obviously did not involve *just* fruit. That aside, everything else seemed... surprisingly chill. They'd even ordered pizza, which was great evidence so I snapped a photo of that and sent it to Braised Chicken after captioning it 'shef'.

"Royroy?" Tenner was her usual self, sliding off the counter as soon as Chen and I came through the doors. I noticed a slight change in the way she was smiling. Missing some spark. I didn't really know what to say so I just stood there and waited for her to come over. Wasn't expecting the hug though. It happened very quickly. "Aw you naughty little shit. I missed you and your stupid face... where's your cute friend? The boy with soft hair and great tongue?"

"Back home," I cut things short and went straight for it. "Are you really leaving?"

I felt her pause and put me at arm's length out of the crushing hug. Jean Mercier came over to hand me a plastic cup of the cocktail mix I spotted earlier. Definitely did not smell like fruit.

"Well I haven't really... got a choice," Tenner sighed. "You didn't get to hear the story 'cuz you were late but in short, I'll... find an internship or something. Like a gap year. Like I'm graduating early or something."

"Without a certificate? Without the credentials?"

I knew it was a little too much. You'd be having the IQ of a goldfish if you'd actually thought she was making the active choice of leaving halfway, just when she was about to graduate at the top of school. But this was something he would ask as a journalist. Something he'd want to get to the bottom of.

"There are reasons," she was sighing a lot and it wasn't usually something people would associate her with. "And I can't tell you now."

"Well... Violet's going to be ninth and she for some reason, won that cross-year." Chen was going around handing out what looked like cookies which he claimed were the original Dalgona sugar cookies. "Don't you think the headmaster's got something to do with it?" He sounded salty despite the sweets he'd made, even shoved one in my face and I accepted it just so that he would leave.

Biting into it, I noted that the texture wasn't something I was used to but could see it being an acquired taste. Though the flavor itself was... a little dull. Wasn't as sweet as I thought it would be. Which may have been a good thing. Wow, I forgot how to be objective.

"Lindy's her stepmother and she was one of the judges too." *But Lindy isn't that kind of person.*

"Quiet down kids," Tenner was rolling her eyes. "I don't know what you've heard but I'm pretty sure it's not just the work of one or two people."

There was a pause.

"What do you mean?"

"Never mind," Tenner backed out as quickly as she'd cut in.

"What?" "You can't do that we're suing you."

"It involved people outside the school, okay? I don't know how but they made some sort of agreement to get me to leave. And they've done it. Birchwood doesn't know a thing. I've talked to her."

Chen snorted. "She could be lying...?"

"She's too stupid to lie. I've seen her done it before and she's actually really easy to read. Also cries very easily." Okay point taken.

"Think we're going to lose the W-interschool?" Mercier dropped in the middle of a long-ass silence which I was happy to participate in. Or stay out of. Whichever I was doing. Number six after Mercier was the first to pull Tenner into a hug, and then before I knew it, they were turning it into a group thing probably because, yeah, Tenner was competition, but she was also the reason why interschool stuff were pretty easy to win.

I went into some corner to lean awkwardly by the window but number one spotted me and demanded I join the hug. "We'll just win without her," I said so that she'd give me the finger instead.

* * *

Third night of thanksgiving holidays; I was working on the third and final draft of my book, making minor changes to phrasing or repositioning text and photos when someone decided to knock on my door.

My first and expected reaction was to ignore it. But then it went on and realistically speaking, having spent the entire afternoon testing and refining recipes in the lodge kitchen without running into someone else, I'd automatically assumed I was alone in Cayenne.

A ghost then, I got up and crossed the room, unlocking the door and swinging it open. Disappointed by an obviously human girl, I was about to close it.

"Hey hey, wait up," she laughed, hand on my door. I stared at it. The other one was in her hair, twirling it. "I'm Chloe. Third-year nutritionist. You're not... busy on a holiday night, are you? I mean... someone like you shouldn't be alone." I think she smiled. I honestly can't tell.

I must have missed her point because—where was it again? She wouldn't move, shifting her weight and then doing something that resembled blinking but with only one eye which wasn't a wink because I'm pretty sure winking doesn't look like that. My eyes narrowed.

Chloe clicked her tongue, rolling her eyes with a laugh before dragging a familiar someone into the picture. Raul. He'd been standing in my blind spot, beside the doorbell, not looking very proud to be involved in whatever was about to happen. Either way, I couldn't really catch the look on his face since he had his head lowered and a hand in the way of his forehead, presumably to avoid my gaze.

"So Raul over here says he's your best friend..." She let that settle in.

Yeah. Zero clue what she was on to and I barely recognized her, which meant she was definitely breaking some rule about letting non-residents into lodges over the holidays. Sure, I wasn't the friendliest person with the best memory around but at the very least, I could roughly make out who was and wasn't a part of Cayenne. Sort of.

"So?" The girl a year older than Raul and I finished in a weird, high-pitched voice. I was getting nothing out of her so I turned to Raul with a look. All he did was clear his throat and avert his gaze; code for 'don't ask me.'

I refused. "Thought you were in Milan."

"Yeah, uh... now I'm back," he laughed, sheepish, hand going to the back of his head. Chloe finally had the common sense to actually get to her point.

"So we were thinking. Maybe the three of us could have some fun tonight. Since we're, you know, the only ones here." She was clinging onto Raul's arm like he was some kind of trophy, and in the middle of her sing-song offer, started to reach for my hand. I pulled away before she could.

"I'm not casual."

Chloe blinked. She didn't seem to understand. Glancing between her and Raul, I could tell the latter was trying hard not to sigh. And I was trying hard not to fuck him over too hard.

I had to lay it out word for word; "I don't do hook ups."

"Oh," was all she said, visibly surprised. "Oh I thought... just by how you look..."

I snorted, shaking my head at her sheer stupidity and general lack of common sense. In my head, I was already planning what I'd be saying to Raul the next morning. Either way, the conversation was over so I shut the door and let them walk away.

They were talking outside as soon as I'd left them alone, going on for a minute or so before I could hear the click of heels heading back down the hallway. Couldn't hear another set so I re-opened the door and there he was, standing with his head in his hands.

"She going?" I leaned against the doorframe, giving him the stare.

He was awkward, needless to say, chewing on his lower lip and refusing to meet my gaze. "Yeah."

"Tonight or tomorrow."

"Tomorrow..." He confessed, finally looking up. "Sorry man. I just—it was just a 'yeah Cox said he'd be back' blah blah and she came up here so fast and and and plus, I don't even know how she knows your room number 'cuz we literally just met. On the train here." That got me kind of surprised since I'd assumed she was his new girlfriend. Would've made her number ten. Or eleven.

"No excuses," I flipped him off with the kind of glare we'd exchange on a daily basis. He laughed, doing the same. "Stop having them over then."

He apologized again before I told him to get out of my sight, then thanked me with a laugh before heading back to his room down the hallway. Not exactly giving it a second thought, I went straight back to work. Bad idea.

Ten minutes later, I was hearing amplified sex noises through the wall and trying hard not to flip my shit. I debated between kicking the wall and throwing something into his half-open window before finally taking a deep breath and plugging in, turning up the volume to near max. The old me would've gone with the kick. I mean, it's the reason for that greyed spot under my desk—Raul was *very* casual.

Not that I'm pissing on hook-up culture or anything; I'm just not part of it. He respects my view and I, his. But still.

I mean, he's got to have his limits. And feeling a rhythmic impact on the wall my desk was facing while I was trying to position a picture of my best beef bourguignon... that's got to annoy anyone at some point. Full volume music wasn't doing very much to keep the slight tremors out of my worries so I gave up, packed my essentials for work and headed out the door. I made sure to slam it real hard, just for extra measure.

I'd grabbed a chicken thigh and a bunch of leftover asparagus from this afternoon's experimentation on my way out, just in case. Leaving the lodge, I made for the school kitchens whilst getting my phone out to check the forecast list. Number 8 was free for the next two hours, so I had that booked before heading down.

Wasn't long before I was back on track and speeding through corrections from page to page, plugged in, pretty much appreciating the space and the fact that I was the only one here at this hour. Kitchen 8 was one of the bigger ones with about ten stations down each side of the hall and to top it all off, a high ceiling and tall windows spanning the entire length and height of the wall on the left.

The appreciation lasted for about half an hour.

I was surprisingly beginning to feel the hole, seated at the instructor's table and staring down the rest of the empty stations, the walkway; the absence of him in a space so big, left to stomach alone. It wasn't something I'd say I was familiar with. Rather, it wasn't something I remembered feeling a couple of months back at all.

I used to like the space. Can't even remember how many times

I'd do something like this: book out the kitchen on a whim, seven to midnight, randomly coming up with recipes and testing them back in freshman year. Come to think of it, I'd only started caring enough after Annie's situation. After giving in and using her phone to send a couple of texts for my benefit.

Back then, I was under the impression that his uncle had forgotten about us but the texts soon became an actual conversation and I'd somehow managed to slip some info about the school into our casual back and forth. I wasn't naïve enough to be thinking I'd actually *see* him here or imagine us coming this far but just hearing about his interest in becoming a food critic... it'd all of a sudden become so much easier to willingly improve at the very thing I hated doing. That was how I got to acing every culinary exam and topping my level. Just so that someday, a certain critic would show up.

In glasses. With a bow tie. Or suspenders.

Beep. I reached for my phone to check if it was a text from him but it wasn't so I ignored it. Turning back to the screen of my laptop made me realize I'd been stuck at rephrasing some three words for nearly fifteen minutes—daydreaming about a frozen lake.

I got out the chicken and asparagus I'd brought along and stuffed into the freezer under the counter earlier on before heading to the pantry in the back for some essentials. Nothing expensive or noticeable. Wouldn't want to be using something meant for a class next week. Plus, there wasn't really a point to effort; cooking itself wasn't something I actually enjoyed with him out of the picture, so naturally, cooking for *myself* was only ever going to be at a level of 'edible'.

Though unlike him, I was one to factor in my protein intake. He on the other hand, with those microwavable boxes of frozen shit stacked up in his fridge...

I snorted out loud and noticed how the sound felt almost piercing in the empty space, with extra reverb that went on even after that. Then it was the sound of sizzling butter on a pan, complete with the fragrance of fresh rosemary and thyme for flavor and then, the chicken.

Think I was four when Siegfried first showed me how to do something like that—pan-grilled chicken—and in two hours, he'd made me stand on a chair and replicate the exact dish. Twice. With the basting on the second try, which I'd messed up because the cast iron pan was a little too heavy for just one hand and you needed the other to be doing the basting. And I didn't have three hands, so.

Fact is, he was the one who signed me up for culinary school in the first place, coming home after a week of flying around to grab my shoulders and take me out to dinner, for 'celebration purposes' which turned out to be getting me into his beloved high school. Get this right: he didn't even pay for the fees. Just got me through by talking to some people and left it all up to Annie, which was the only reason why I actually agreed to it. Because then he couldn't come along with us and Annie and I could leave him for good.

"Braised chicken..."

I didn't have that in the cookbook. Or vanilla ice cream. I still remember privately scooping myself a cup back in the parlor on a bad day. Medicine for loneliness. I was seas apart from the place I'd grew up in, without Annie to talk to or anyone else, for the matter. Speaking of the parlor... I had the morning shift the next day.

I'd been absentmindedly basting the chicken, just going through the motions, before adding a bunch of asparagus to the pan and then turning off the heat. Not quite bothering with a plate, I decided to eat off the pan itself.

Already, I could hear him in my head. *You look absolutely ridiculous! A chef like yourself, standing over a pan, stabbing into a whole chicken thigh without a knife in sight. I need to lie down.*

I was laughing to myself. Out loud. Then instinctively reaching for my phone to snap a picture and send it to him just so that he'd wake to some good shit. Pity he can't taste it. But kind of the point, you know what I mean? So that he'd crave it.

It was in that instant that I finally understood the gravity of him being the entirety of my driving force in the kitchen; the whole purpose of me continuing down this path. Questions like whether or not I actually liked cooking, or if I liked cooking for *him*—those kind of questions, I already knew the answer to. After all, they crossed me several times in the last couple of months.

I just never really thought beyond that. Beyond why I was still *here*. Why I was in culinary school, training to be a chef, to cook food to be eaten by other people I didn't really care about—judges, guests, customers, instructors. Whether it was okay to be basing my career, my future on just one person and to be someone because of *them*. Whether it was okay to be going this far for someone else that wasn't myself.

* * *

From: *Braised Chicken*

That does look mildly appetizing. You seem to be doing very well. We've managed to paint the entire living room today. It's in a stunning lapis blue and I've never seen any color go better with the gold rimming on our new ceiling. Oh, and the bookshelf I ordered just came in today. No spoilers, but here's a picture of it with the rest of my room blurred out. Also, Chip and the kids came by to help with the furniture moving and he's never been this traumatized by any comment more than what you'd said about his pumpkin pie. He even made a new one thinking you were still here.
I told him that I wished you were too.

It's Sunday. The last night of five long days, deprived of wit and intelligence. Sadly, the people already back in school didn't happen to include the one I was hoping to see. Dinnertime passed and I'd spent it finishing up the final draft of my book before heading down to the kitchen I'd booked out again with some ingredients for an extra braised chicken recipe I thought about including last minute.

I arrived at kitchen 9, eight p.m. sharp, only to see a couple of kids still hanging around inside with a countertop and sink full of pans and tools they'd yet to clean. The bunch of them had turned around at my entrance but lost all interest as soon as they saw me starting towards the station farthest away from the one they had been using.

Yeah, it wasn't the reaction I was used to getting since being number three *usually* came with people recognizing you left right center and bowing in the hallway when they did, but. Didn't matter.

"... for real. I mean she won but literally with that guy being a deadweight."

"Only makes... so much better... why doesn't..."

Apparently, they also didn't bother entertaining the bare minimum level of respect one should have in the kitchen, especially in the midst of strangers. No shit talk. And the fact that they continued to speak at the volume they were conversing at before I came into the picture gave the impression that they owned the school or something. Wasn't as though I could afford plugging in to music whilst dealing with knives and fires.

Turning around, I casually called out and told them that I'd booked the place from eight to ten. They sort of stared for a while, and in the brief pause in between, I somehow recognized them as his classmates. Others from 1B. Two of them, male, were the skivers on duty at Line production with me the other time. The girl, I didn't quite make out but looked vaguely familiar.

My guard raised without question. They exchanged a shifty look before slowly turning to their pots and pans, cleaning up their station at the slowest fucking pace I'd ever seen. Like it wasn't their mess to begin with. Turning away from their haphazard cleaning attempts was the only way I could deal with this shit so I started pulling out the knife block and cutting board to get my ingredients prepped for recipe testing. I had a notebook out on the dry counter with a baseline to start with, then along the way would scribble down the changes I made as per routine.

"She's so nice, picking someone like Park and giving him the win." As though they weren't already loud to begin with, the girl decided to raise her volume to the extent that I could hear every single word of what she was saying to her friends. Logic. "It's like she's letting him experience the glory. For free. Without even doing a damn thing."

"His dishes were kind of stupid... who makes gnocchi in a tag team contest? With a *nature* theme?"

"Can't you tell she was disappointed in him though?" Says the guy who didn't know which *knife* to use for dicing onions. "Her face while she's watching him from the side. I'm surprised she kept her cool to be honest."

I didn't know if they couldn't actually tell if their voices were loud enough to bring the conversation to unwilling parties or if they actually thought unwilling parties had no idea what they were talking about even if they could hear them. I caught on at gnocchi, since it was the dish my phad thai was up against and then pieced together everything else. Side inferences include that they were somehow hardcore supporters of Birchwood, dishing out compliments like that. Knowing this felt disturbing. *Add that to them being in his class...*

"She's probably experienced worse. Those people talking shit about her desserts behind her back? She's so nice to her supporters and her cakes are the best. This is why critics never have a good reputation. Because they love ruining other people's."

They laughed. My chopper paused, hovering over the right leg joint I was about to severe. Something was burning.

"Seriously though, he's, like, so boring? Have you ever heard him try to have a proper conversation?"

"He can't can he—"

"All he ever does is talk about assignments and deadlines and like... why some flavor combination doesn't work. Remember that time we were supposed to be having a *discussion* about the menu for the stall and he basically shot down our ideas like he hates us?"

"He did that to Violet too didn't he?"

"I don't know, I've only heard him do it behind her back. Serves him right about the décor. Nobody's gonna search the barn and suspect wood scraps."

I was done prepping the chicken and moving on to the onions when everything slowed to a stop. It didn't take long for it to sink in—that they were somehow involved in it; shameless enough to sabotage their very own class to prove a point and let someone else bear the entire weight of being discredited.

The kitchen knife in my hand was shaking. I stared at it. The blade, I'd sharpened minutes ago I now sunk into the cutting board and it stood upright, trembling a little at the impact. Something else was crackling. They were too busy talking to notice. It was loud, in my ears. The sound of a fire.

"Right? It's practically fraud, what he's doing. No one can identify ingredients just by *tasting* them. How does he get so stuck up about—"

I hadn't expected it to land. The pan. It was the closest thing within my reach that would've made a sound loud enough but the speed and strength at which I'd grabbed it and threw it across the room, I'd overestimated. I knew as soon as it left my hand that it was feeling lighter than usual. I was used to cast iron. It was on the side of his face with a dull smack, strong enough to make him stagger before turning, with red seeping down his jaw and an expression of shock and fury.

The girl screamed. The other guy was shouting something before crossing the room and grabbing my shirt, spitting in my face—I held onto his wrist, hard, searching for something to put out the fire but *fuck* it was too late and I knew I'd fucked up, hard, when the girl took her phone out, other hand over her mouth and pointed it at the bleeding guy but no, I liked it. I liked the fire and it thrived, burning big and spreading fast I could feel it torch the walls and fury was its fuel because it grew with words and the look on their faces. As though they'd done nothing wrong.

"—the fuck is wrong with you?!" "Li? Li are you okay? Oh my god you're bleeding." "Jesse, punch the fuck out of that guy."

Footsteps. Someone from the pantry. "What the hell?"

Oh fuck, just when I thought it couldn't get any worse.

Kitchens 8 and 9 are connected by a shared pantry. The guy must have heard the pan when it fell to the floor. I didn't bother looking at his face but everyone else seemed to pause for a moment. He saw the blood first and then turned to us on the other side of the hall, stunned. "Who was it?"

The other guy loosened his grip, massaging the wrist I was holding. "Him. He's fucking mental. Threw that shit out of nowhere."

I could feel Chen staring, surveying the rest of the kitchen and trying to figure out what the hell was going on. The three of them were back at their station, fussing over that dribble of blood and occasionally shouting over their shoulder. I stayed, numb from the flames that seemed to have no end. Chen was speaking to me.

"You threw the pan?" He breathed; words shallow in disbelief. I didn't respond. "Did you throw it?"

I wasn't even looking at him, struggling to focus all my attention on putting out the flames that scorched every inch of reason and just staring at the three clueless fuckers who hadn't an idea of their wrongdoing. The urge to snap something boiled and rose to the surface and I couldn't stop it. I couldn't put it out.

"Cox."

Chen was in front of me, blocking my field of vision and forcing me to look at him. "Your eyes look like they belong to a fucking animal. Breathe."

I was losing it and I knew I was. I knew I'd fucked up the moment I let go of the pan. Or the moment I heard Li say a word about him and as though all I could hear was the crackling of flames combusting every rational thought, I couldn't think beyond the now—let alone form words to tell anyone what had happened.

Chen didn't have that number two handed to him on a silver platter. He worked for it and sometimes, it showed. He unlocked it and typed something on the screen before sliding it across the counter and turning his attention to the other three.

What did he say about White?

I felt my eyes close and the fire retreat very briefly. He was telling the girl, stunned and standing frozen to the side, to get medical help from a nurse over at the administrative building. I slid his phone into my hand, staring at the blinking text cursor before typing out the first couple of words that came to mind.

He read them with a blank expression before turning back to Li and reminding his friend to keep the pressure on his wound. "You'll be fine. Stop whining. It's barely a scrape."

"I have a concussion." "Yeah! He got hit by a frying pan, dude. He could've died."

I saw Chen roll his eyes with his back faced towards them before fishing out something like a handkerchief and telling the other guy to bring Li to the bathroom down the hall. "Take a good look at yourself in the mirror and you'll know what I mean. Wet this and hold it over the wound. I'll be there in a minute."

"And him?" They shot daggers my way. I stared back. "You gonna report him?"

"I'll deal with him. You deal with his wound before he fucking 'dies' or something," Chen scoffed, nodding towards the door while Li and the other guy pretend-limped out of the kitchen. Neither had leg injuries. Li would not stop groaning, even out in the hallway.

Chen sighed. He leaned against the counter I'd been using, arms crossed. I was prepared for it; braced myself for the shit he was going to give me, be it a lecture or a wake-up punch. I waited. Then looked up. He was glaring at me.

"That's just going to get you expelled."

Yeah, like I don't already know, I wanted to say, but knew this wasn't the time to be dishing out the usual off-handed words I liked using against him.

"They probably got cameras on it. There's one in every corner," he glanced up. "And I'm pretty sure you know how bad it's going to make you look." Again, stating the obvious.

"Don't need to salt the wound," I clicked my tongue, already mad at myself for failing to contain the fire. "I'm admitting to it when the girl comes back with a nurse. Go on. Be happy. Do your dance. I'm finally out of the way."

Ah, fuck. What was he going to think? Going to say? It was beginning to sink in, the reality of it all, and I wasn't exactly excited to be imagining the look on his face tomorrow anymore.

"Look." Chen breathed in, then sighed the loudest I'd ever heard him express an emotion besides anticipation and condescending joy. He straightened up, pushing away from the counter he was leaning on. "We don't get along and we both know that. And no one gets away with talking shit about White and doing what they did, sure—but you doing what you did isn't going to help our case because now they have a free 'get out of jail' card with that injury and can easily have you expelled.

"Which, honestly speaking, isn't the best thing for me because I want to win the W-interschool. And with Layla gone, we both know what you are. I can't afford having the best culinary major sitting out this season, so when whoever it is comes through that door later, you're going to say that it was all an accident. You understand?"

His voice was surprisingly louder than the crackle and spit of flames inside and for a second, I felt them pause. I hadn't been looking at him the whole time but now I was. Staring back at him in disbelief.

"The cameras?"

"You think I haven't done anything stupid back in my first two years?" Chen scoffed. "I'll handle that, and you handle the account. All they know is that you hit someone with a literal flying pan and said *nothing* afterwards."

"It *flew.*"

"Soap on the handle."

"That's stupid."

"Trade." He said this as though I'd missed an obvious point. "I'll drop them a note about their sabotage while you find the evidence. If they insist you did it on purpose, we get them suspended for bullying. Plus, they can't enter in competitions for the rest of the year."

He had me. It was a dangerous idea and I was roped in before

I knew it, so stupidly seduced by not wanting to leave his side and foolishly believing that I could, actually, get away with something like this.

Frankly speaking, I'd never seen Chen so willful, ambitious, cunning, careful with his every step that it seemed as though he was, all of a sudden, on my side. He saw that I was wavering and took the opportunity to land his final blow.

"And would I have been stupid enough to dirty my hands? No. But did I like what you did?" He flashed a smile I never got to see. "Yeah, kinda. They deserved it."

VIII

VANILLA

"Your man's looking sharp," was all Si Yin had to say through a pair of binoculars she had produced from her bag before the start of assembly period; which, today, consisted partly of the headmaster's speech, followed by an official re-ordering of the school's top thirteen students on the ranking board. With the rest of the school seated comfortably in red cushioned seats, nearly half of them were falling asleep. "They're kinda just standing there, huh. Pretty boring. Oh, the Birchwood girl's got this really nice crown braid thing."

The thirteen of them were up on stage, standing in a line a couple of feet behind the announcer's podium, waiting for their segment and mostly just staring into blank space. I felt oddly empathetic. Leroy had texted me near midnight, an hour after I'd arrived at my apartment and fallen asleep on the bean bag and it was the first thing I'd woken up to this very morning, leaving me rather anxious and confused.

I'm screwed, it said.

My immediate instinct had been to give him a call and then, because he wasn't picking up, send a series of texts asking if he was alright. It was only after I'd given my academic inbox a brief scan that I understood what this morning's assembly period encompassed, which gave some insight into why he wasn't exactly responding to my text messages.

Admittedly, Leroy wasn't the kind of person I'd consider easily flustered. For him to be thrown off by something completely beyond his expectations and actually use those words felt nearly surreal, and if anything, I couldn't stand seeing him on stage, quiet and alone, unable to wholly appreciate the new title he was about to receive.

On the outside, he looked just about how Si Yin had described him as. 'Sharp.' Which, frankly speaking, felt like a term for icicles and the cold, more so than candles and flames.

We were dismissed at the stroke of one, held up by sleepy students funneling out of the auditorium at a crawl. Si Yin had shooed me towards the general direction away from the door, assuring that she had next period's Chef Lindy 'all covered.' I thanked her for reading my mind.

"Hi. Are they backstage? The thirteen," I asked, going up to a photographer at the front of the stage with my media pass. He nodded.

"You're the writer on duty? Need a camera for the interview?" He was about to walk me down the side of the stage to the back of it but I told him, upfront, that I wasn't the writer he was looking for and then hurried off backstage.

I spotted about half of them through the curtains as soon as I was making my way down an unlit corridor, speaking in hushed tones and appearing mostly irate. I was thoroughly surprised by the odd desire to see someone seated deeply in my chest since, if this were any other person I was looking for, I'd probably given up at this point and left a clearly unhappy group of people to themselves. But I came forth.

"Hi. Sorry. I don't mean to interrupt, but I'm looking for—"

"Vanilla?"

I heard his voice and turned at once, relieved. The look in his eyes was unusually guarded, making it particularly difficult to observe the size and brightness of his flame, perhaps due to the lack of lighting. I let him take the lead down the rest of hallway after thanking the group, following him out of a side exit before finally asking if he was quite alright.

He stopped in his tracks, leaning against a wall by the stairwell. Meeting my gaze. "Can I lie?"

"W-well," I blinked in return, mildly surprised. "Lying is... it's not against any rule. It's unfortunately a part of being human, or so many will say. But you know I prefer the truth, which is... what I'm trying to say—that you're allowed to hurt me and that I will not hold it against you if you do because I do not wish for there to be an obligation to lie in order to protect my feelings. Though exceptions are allowed, in which case if you're willingly making the decision to lie, then yes. You can."

I could see the candle in his eyes again as he laughed, low, and it eased the ache in my chest. "I missed you."

"... that's your lie?"

"No, dumbass." His gaze flickered before I felt him pull me into his arms. "It's the truth. Fuck, I hate being number one."

"Number two," I corrected, oddly intoxicated by the physical contact we were sharing in broad daylight.

"One for culinary majors."

"Ah, yes." I said dryly. "Everyone must hate you more than they already do."

He held me at shoulder length, only to present his indecent finger soon after. "I'm serious. Not everyone falls at my feet."

"Well, most people do," I pointed out. "It's a lot of pressure, to be keeping up with expectations whilst defending your title. And yes, you like winning. I do too. Everyone does, at some point. It's nice to be the strong one without any apparent weaknesses but that is unfortunately not how it works in reality. People *can* be number one even with their vulnerabilities and weaknesses. Besides, if you come to dislike your standing any more than you already do, we could stop the AB tutoring and get you a fail grade aaand you'll drop ten ranks tops!"

He pinched my nose while I was laughing and made me sneeze. Then it was the usual to the forehead before a conclusive kiss. Mildly flustered by the last part, I gave our surroundings a quick survey.

"Where do you learn all this?" Leroy's expression was a cross between a smirk and a frown. We started down the stairs together.

"Books." I provided some vague answer that would make for a roll of his eyes. "They can surprise you. Change your life, even."

Every kitchen, classroom and experiment lab in the school came armed with their very own emergency phone box attached to the wall behind the instructor's desk, which, on certain days of fortune and luck, would interrupt an otherwise 'boring' theory session with a shrill ring.

It came in the middle of homeroom period, which Chef Palmer was obliged to answer after settling administrative matters (travel declaration forms for the upcoming winter break). She'd put the receiver away within seconds and called for Si Yin and myself to report at the auditorium right away. Most of the class had been reduced to private conversations and chatter, which felt mildly reassuring considering the fact that we would have otherwise drawn much unnecessary attention.

"We're not in trouble, right?" Si Yin asked in sheepish laughter, rolling down her sleeves and straightening her ribbon. "Why are we going away? I like free per—I mean. Homeroom."

"It's a briefing for W-interschool participants," Chef Palmer pulled up an email on her laptop and gave it a scan while we stood idly by her desk. "Apart from the thirteen, class representatives are nominated by default... ah shit I missed this out last night 'cuz I thought it was just a delay announcement. Sorry about that. They called because it's past reporting time and you guys haven't turned up. I told them you're on your way."

"Oh. Hold on, but we weren't exactly inform—" Si Yin and I were promptly shooed out of the classroom before I could finish, even pointed towards the auditorium just in case we weren't set on departing just yet.

"You know, this is kind of, a hundred percent *her* fault...?" My best friend sped down the stairwell at a pace I could not afford to keep up with. "It'll look sooo bad on us when we arrive! Like, everyone else is there and we barge in, that kind of thing. Oh, and did I ever agree on being the sub representative?"

"Well, your name *is* technically under the class's vice president position," I told her, slightly out of breath even though we had a couple more blocks to go. We passed the corridors of the administrative block, making our way down Roth hall before crossing the connecting bridge towards the Marriott Pavilion auditorium.

And by the time the two of us had arrived in one piece, Chef Lindy was waiting outside the main entrance with a clipboard and a pen, repeatedly tapping the latter on her chin. "1B? You're twenty minutes late. Might as well be removed from the list," she teased with a roll of her eyes, giving the list in her arms a glance before nodding at the door. "There's a stack of papers on a table in front of you once you're in. Take one each."

"Yes, Chef Lindy. We're terribly sorry."

"Yeah but it wasn't even our fault." I tugged on Si Yin's sleeve to cut the conversation short and she gave in with a sigh, groaning once before following me past the double doors.

"—*siette Vide* and the Culinary School of Shanghai. The 150 participants for this year will each receive a welfare bag during their complimentary stay on campus consisting of school souvenirs, food vouchers and marketplace coupons. As you all know, this is a great..."

We'd entered the hall as quietly as we could but as soon as the announcer looked up from his papers to present us with a marvelous glare, nearly half the heads turned. I quickly swiped two copies of the summarized briefing from the stack of papers Chef Lindy mentioned before eyeing the nearest pair of empty seats.

It did not cross my mind to give the surroundings of those holy available seats a proper survey. Regrettably, the situation turned out fairly eventful.

"You could have picked anywhere else," Birchwood hissed under her breath, folding her arms and turning away from Si Yin and myself.

I offered a sigh. "Good afternoon to you too, Miss Birchwood."

"Oh my god you're so pretentious. Why are you even late? I thought you weren't the kind of person to be late. Why do people always disappoint the expectations I set for them?"

"I... never knew you thought so highly of me," was all I could whisper in response, mildly surprised by the compliment she was so obviously paying me. Birchwood scoffed.

"Yeah well obviously. I'm talking to you, which already says something. I don't talk to idiots, if you haven't noticed."

"I have."

"Okay good."

Our conversation ended then and there. Which, albeit rather short, had been one of the most pleasant experiences we've shared since the first day of school. Quite the improvement, I must say.

"...since we're hosting the tournament this year. Your assigned buddies from the other schools will be allocated to you by the end of the month by email... so check that constantly. I see some of our *late-comers* look visibly confused so I have no choice but to repeat the key dates I've pointed out earlier on. This Friday, the 14th of November, is the start of the month-long W-interschool training for the fifty of you. Details on the reporting time and place are all in the handout given to you. On Wednesday, 12th you will be moving into your allocated lodging. 13th December is the start of your winter break and 30th is when the students of other participating schools start moving in. 1st January will be the first day of the W-interschool and yes, your winter break will be cut short by a week, replaced by the tournament. Any questions?"

I frowned. This much, an idiot could gather just by reading the handout, which I just did in less than ten seconds. The dates were all marked out on the third section on the second page, which hopefully meant that Si Yin and I hadn't missed out on much.

"Did he say... free lodging?" Her eyes lit up as they turned to me, alternating between the words projected on the screen up front and the ones on the handout in my lap. She hadn't exactly looked at her own.

"Apparently, yes. They're providing us with a room each... it must cost a considerable amount."

"But we're just first years! You think they take requests? I like the Hudson apartments. I've always wanted a loft. And a cool roommate. I want a roommate."

I gave the handout a further scan, noting the additional information in small font about balloting and first years also being given a room since... ah, the training schedule. There were five AM and ten PM slots too. It made sense to have everyone move into the campus for the sake of having a stricter regimen.

My distracted, lovestruck heart had a way of directing thoughts into the unfortunate darkness lit by a single candle; in fact, I was thinking, searching, *looking* at the back of his head before the conscious mind could register that I was. Seated beside him was... Chen. At first, I'd assumed they were somehow obliged to sit in order (meaning number one followed by two and then three or four) but then number nine was seated right next to me, arms folded and legs crossed, glancing at her nails every now and then before opting for the act of endless scrolling on her phone.

"You're not seated with the top thirteen," I observed aloud, hoping I hadn't phrased it in a way that offended her.

Birchwood rolled her eyes, which was mild considering the many other things she tended to do. "You're not making any sense. We weren't told to sit together or anything."

I blinked, suddenly confused.

"Again, the school would like to emphasize on the importance of teamwork and forging closer bonds with budding culinary experts from all across the world, which is a great opportunity since you will be working with some of them in particular segments of the tourna—"

"I think I spot your man," Si Yin whispered a minute too late, pointing him out, seated a couple of rows down. "He's sitting with someone... who isn't... you?" She looked at me then, as though confuzzled by the alternate universe she was in. "That's not you."

"Well, I'm seated here," I said, oddly calm. Pleased, even. That they were getting along. "That's Chen in the yellow scarf."

Both Si Yin and I were clearly taken aback by this piece of information, so much so that it became our key point of interest throughout the rest of the briefing. After all, this was *very* new, and certainly not an unpleasant development—which I made sure to point out as soon as we emerged from the auditorium, together with Leroy, Raul and Rosi. They, too, were class representatives.

"They even had lunch together," said Raul in a heartbeat, to which Leroy responded with his usual finger. "Probably W-interschool talk. It's all about the strats you know."

I turned to a certain idiot with a teasing smile. "Who knew you could get along with someone other than myself!"

"Woah, woah I think that's a different 'get along' right there,"

Raul did not hesitate to cut in but a single glance from his best friend made it so that continuing necessarily came with punishment, leaving me mildly confused.

Either way, Leroy appeared to be avoiding the topic of Chen entirely and though I wasn't sure if it was due to embarrassment or general unwillingness to admit that he was wrong about his new friend, I decided not to probe. I noticed, however, his gaze resting on the general area below my chin and following it immediately, could not quite make out what he was looking at.

"Is my badge crooked?"

"No. Your tie's loose," he leaned in, reaching for it and in that instance, as though the tie was a part of the human body, I felt the warmth of his fingers and shied away at once. What an embarrassing reversal of roles!

"O-oh. Yes, we were, um. Late. And quite hurriedly making our way down," I excused whilst fixing my own tie, feeling the heat on my ears and the back of my neck. *Ah Vanilla, you put beetroot to shame. There's your only talent.*

I caught him smirk at my reaction before pulling back, returning his hands into his pockets. Si Yin took the opportunity to flash a devious grin my way, which soon developed into a rigorous back and forth of ridiculous faces before all of a sudden, an unknown force shoved past my right shoulder from behind.

I was falling face first before the registration of other relevant information but someone to the left had caught my upper arm just in time, allowing me to regain my balance and raise my gaze to whoever it was that did. How incredibly awful it must be to possess inhuman reflexes, a criminally attractive face and unmatched skills all at once. It therefore explained his complete lack of aptitude in math, which must be made extremely heavy in order to properly balance out a character like himself.

"Watch where you're going." A familiar voice, a foot or so in front of me by then, made in cold warning. I recognized it only after spotting the person beside him. Meyers? So then the one beside him must be Li from our class. Si Yin was shaking her fist at their backs but all I could register was how unrecognizable Li's face was.

He had an unholy bruise the shade of wine down the side of his face and up on his head, a gauze patch taped and wrapped around the circumference. It looked as though he'd gotten himself into a huge fistfight.

I'd turned to Leroy just then, hoping to reassure him of my well-being and that I was quite alright so that he wouldn't be burning in flames while people were shoving me around but peering up at him, I realized that I didn't have be saying a word.

He appeared oddly calm; the flame of a candle in his eyes still and unmoving... in perfect control. I retreated, mildly relieved but at the same time, strangely concerned that he wasn't his usual fiery self.

LEROY

I was with Annie in her room when he told me he got put in Cinnamon for Wednesday's moving in. Naturally, I was disappointed. He was, too. We were never the kind to drop emoticons here and there but when his text came in at ten in the evening, all I saw was 'It's Cinnamon, unfortunately :c' which made the whole exchange a hundred times cuter than it would've already been.

The whole of Monday passed in nothing less than pain. By lunch, Chen had the camera footage settled and the deal made with the three of them at the infirmary. I had my doubts about the whole thing—not to mention a stubborn unwillingness to lie—but he went on to explain that the trade-off was saving all three of them who were involved in the sabotage of their stall, which was the better offer just by considering the numbers. And just when I was beginning to think I could no longer stare at frozen lakes and summer pools, the interschool training forced all thirteen of us into full speed ahead.

I started to miss him more than I missed him over thanksgiving. Texts never seemed to be enough and calls were shorter than usual since both he and I had separate training regimens and schedules. Some days, he had to be up by five in the morning. Some days I was going to bed at one.

It was the reason I'd hoped he was put in Cayenne. That and the fact that my last visit to his place had been nearly more than a month ago. Which meant that we hadn't done anything more than fleeting kisses for four whole weeks.

I get that the school needed us scattered and separate, mostly to entertain or interact with partner school students moving in before the tournament. Raul said something about it all being 'friendly', which I'm pretty sure meant something else. Chen was on the other end of the spectrum. He told me he wasn't here to make any friends. That there wasn't anything 'friendly' about competition.

Either way, November sort of passed in a snap. Because Cayenne and Cinnamon were all part of the spice lodges, we shared a study and a gym. The former was more like a reading room thing, and once, I'd passed it after spending an hour on the treadmill before advanced plating when I caught him reading curled up in a corner. My phone wasn't with me at that point, so I just stood out there behind the glass carving the image into my mind when he noticed he wasn't alone and quickly assumed a proper sitting position with his legs down... until he realized that it was just me and huffed with a smile, leaving his book on the sofa seat before coming out to say hi.

"You understand that what you just did could very well be reported to the authorities?" Like I said.

I'd teased by telling him I'd then never look at him again if he so wished. The slight panic on his face was nothing less than endearing. "That... that was *not* what I meant."

I then asked if he was free on Christmas for a party Raul suggested hosting. Vague plans were made the night before and he did say I could invite anyone outside of Cayenne, so.

"The second and third-years in Cinnamon haven't any plans for Christmas a-and it's really only been the four of us so I have been rather lonely as of late. Not, not saying that you haven't been providing any company. You have. In the form of text and calls but. Well, I've... I mean I have naturally come to miss your presence. Physical presence. Does that make any sense?"

I told him that I'd make out with him if I hadn't been running for an hour. But I had, so. At least he got the hint and blushed nonstop. "So you in?"

"Yes, of course." He seemed quite excited about it, which felt nearly contagious since the next couple of weeks started passing a lot faster than I thought; actually having something to look forward to made getting through hours of stupid shit a lot more bearable.

Plus, Raul had made it a point to cancel the random gift exchange thing we did last year and replace it with a compulsory 'get everyone something of whatever price but it'll be anonymous' kind of thing. It felt a whole lot more reassuring, since some people actually ended up with nothing during the random gift exchange and I for some reason, had four boxes with my name on it.

It's not a nice feeling, having to face the empty hands of others and look at your own. I prefer being on the envious, lonely side; not the one being envied.

The Christmas thing had him really excited. He and Si Yin had made their rounds in the new mall thirty minutes away, shopping for gifts like they were part of Santa's factory. Hands down, Si Yin would pass the test for an elf with that pixie cut and him, a reindeer. The small one. Tiny antlers.

"I grabbed a leather-bound Filofax diary organizer for Si Yin while she was away in the next section looking for Rosi's gift. She mentioned just last month about starting on a daily planner as part of a new year's resolution, so. And I got Raul a nice bottle of thyme-infused olive oil. I-I haven't quite decided on yours yet."

He told me one night while I was walking him back to his lodge, wondering if he was simply putting up a strong front despite the bags under his eyes just so that we'd have a conversation. He was clearly exhausted.

"Don't stress over it. Sleep early," I'd told him at his doorstep and was about to lean in for good, long one when his lodge mate stepped out for a smoke and greeted me by chance. I didn't even know them. I'd turned back to him but he was already embarrassed and shy so I let be, sending him in before heading back.

Fast forward to a week later, four in the afternoon, people were already starting to filer past the main door of Cayenne—which Raul had decided to leave permanently open. 'Just in case anyone's curious.'

"Welcome to the Christmas party for, uh, lonely people in lonely lodges. Because obviously, Cayenne is not lonely." No one was telling Raul to shut up, partly because they were all over the food on the dining.

We'd decided to have it potluck style, meaning everyone had to be bringing a dish regardless of the time they'd intended to spend at the party, just so that no one would end up pointing fingers at non-contributors or potential dish washers. Which was me. Last year. Because I hate cooking, remember?

This time, I'd slipped under the radar with something simple and easy: Vietnamese netted spring rolls. The lattice wraps I'd found in the marketplace were just the trick to making them look deceptively classy. Someone else made beef lasagna, which was also kinda clever. Most of everyone brought their own version of party food—no-brainer, affordable shit that thankfully did not include alcohol because the last time someone added a bottle to the fruit cocktail, some girl from another lodge threw up all over our carpet.

When he'd arrived alongside Si Yin with his mini eggnog pavlovas topped with rum syrup though, I think most of us thought he'd brought it to the wrong party. They were obviously made with much more effort compared to everything else on the table so much so that once his tray of pavlovas made it to the dining, every ramekin was taken. Naturally, I wasn't very happy about it. I'd never had the chance to give his desserts a go, so this would have been my first.

Though after giving it some thought, I would've preferred my first to be something he made specifically for me anyway. So. I let it go.

The next couple of hours was mostly food and games, though we were sort of playing our own, in private—stealing glances every now and then, across the room, catching the other looking over behind a glass of fruit punch. I would wink. He would roll his eyes and turn away, which only served to provide me with a clearer view of his pink ears.

"Can everyone just join the line? Like, I'll hand you the boxes with your name and you can go off. That way, we're not crowded round the Christmas tree like a bunch of hungry zombies," Rosi shooed the rest of us away from the middle of the lounge so that we ended up making a line that snaked across the room.

The average gift counter was something like four or five per person, which wasn't too bad although there were about twenty people in the room. He was a couple of turns before mine, so I was watching him and crossing my fingers for a six. Or five. He walked away with three, looking mildly surprised and awfully pleased, unlike the others who'd received the same number he did.

"We got a winner," Rosi said to me when it was my turn, not forgetting to roll her eyes. "Eleven for you."

How the fuck does this happen? I'm not even nice to anyone, was all I could think after balancing the stack of boxes in my arms and heading over to the couch where he was. His eyes were brightly lit, gleaming in anticipation—fingers already hovering over the ribbon of his first gift. It wasn't mine.

"As expected, Mr. Cox, you are highly sought after. Those gifts look... well, they have very fancy wrapping don't they."

I turned back to the boxes all over my lap, not quite knowing what was fancy and what wasn't. The last time I received an actual Christmas present apart from last year's party was way back in nursery. From Annie. Then it was living with Siegfried, which meant no Christmas, so.

"Should we... start with the one who's got the most to look at?" Raul was rubbing his hands and smirking in my direction but I wasn't having any of that.

"No—"

"Yes!" *"Eleven."* "Pick one." "Just open them, hurry up." "Oh and guess who it's from or something." "Oh my god yes."

Ah fuck. I didn't want to unintentionally offend people by getting it wrong either, since I clearly didn't even know eleven names around here to begin with. Most importantly, could I have a good night's sleep if I got his gift wrong? The answer: no.

The first thing was a Himalayan salt block and no doubt, I actually fucking laughed after opening the fancy-ass box since whoever gifted it made extra effort to disguise its true form. I'd seen it in restaurants and TV shows. Heck, Siegfried uses it over at his Michelin stars.

"Thanks," I said in general, then caught a gleam in Si Yin's eyes while sweeping the room. She then laughed out loud so everyone else turned to her and knew she'd given it away. "It's cool."

It was. Really. But whether I was going to use it felt like an entirely different story. I might have...? But with the cookbook done and nothing more to experiment and exams not exactly allowing for special tools like a *Himalayan salt block* unless stated, I hadn't any reason to be fully utilising something like this.

Not to mention, experimenting with food was never within my realm of interest to begin with.

Still, I thanked her.

"An... egg timer," I held up the next gift and the entire room broke down crying in laughter. "I really need this."

"As the school's top culinary major, you sure do," Raul clapped me on the back and almost immediately, I knew it was him. I gave him the finger and he did the same. All good.

Then it was a whisk from Rosi. And fish sauce from Bank. And truffle oil from Nabila. Then a couple of people chipping in for a mini *kebab grill*—the vertical standing kind—which got the rest of the room going crazy with envy and then there was me, thinking:

where the hell I was going to put this without space in my room *or* the kitchen cabinet.

I caught his expression when everyone else was fawning over the kebab grill. He looked almost nervous, now that I'd opened most of everything and hadn't gotten to his just yet. I asked if he was okay and he nodded vaguely, smiling a little before stating that everyone seemed to know exactly what I liked.

I found this surprising. *Was that how it looked like to him?* Because I sure wasn't feeling very understood. Frankly, I was starting to feel the disappointment—which, apart from the appreciation that everyone actually made an effort to get me something, at all, was honestly great by itself—surrounded by culinary tools and whatnot.

It's not their fault, in any way. It wasn't. I'd come to accept it: that I was, in their eyes, Leroy Jeremy Cox, top culinary major, and with only two years of official experience. Part of the kitchen. A chef. The label I was never really going to live wi...

That one.

It hadn't looked very exciting. The plain brown wrapping. No tape. Just paper. And to be very honest, my lowered expectations hadn't really helped with the suspense. Outside, it didn't look as enticing as the reflective, sparkly wrapping that the rest of the gifts happened to have but looking inside, it was instant—I knew who, exactly, it was from.

I glanced over.

"Woah dude. JBL?" Raul was the first to react, taking a closer look over my shoulder. "A flip five!" A wireless Bluetooth speaker.

I was starting to feel weird. Dizzy; confused, like I wasn't expecting the sudden transition away from disappointment and experiencing the high of something akin to relief but also, not quite.

"Who's it from?" Rosi asked.

I caught his eye and he promptly cleared his throat, looking up from his glass of water. "Well. You've always been been fond of listening to music plugged in but... so I thought, perhaps, sometime in the near future, you'd be more open. With sharing. What you're listening to."

The room went quiet. I thanked him then. "I like it." A little differently from how I thanked everyone else. Not because we were in a romantic relationship; or because he'd given me something different from everyone else. "Thank you."

But because it was then that I realized what exactly it was—some sort of undertone, some underlying message that he himself might not have even realized had been unconsciously conveyed.

The gift was an answer to the question I never had to verbalize.

Vanilla did not see me as the school's number one culinary major. He did not see me as the chef I did not want to be, or the heir to Michelin star restaurants, or the favorite of instructors and the future of culinary progress.

He saw me as ordinary. As human; one who had interests beyond the immediate show of participation—one who could fail, one who was no product of perfection. Who played games and liked cup ramen and vanilla ice cream and listened to music on long train rides or study periods.

And for that to be the person he'd fallen for.
Think I could spend the rest of my life with someone like that.

To say that Vanilla was pleased with what Leroy had gotten him was an understatement. He was madly in love with the pair of adjustable, dark leather suspenders—the slimmer kind, to match his physique—that were incredibly suited to his wardrobe. The fact that they were adjustable were an added plus, since it meant that they could last for the next couple of years even if he were to grow.

Quietly, awfully pleased, he'd thanked Leroy with a reserved nod, stating that he was, still, very concerned about the price.

"That JBL probably cost you more than a hundred bucks. Just shut up and keep it," was all the latter said, stealing a kiss. "Wear it to our next date maybe."

IX

⁘

LEROY

He was walking alongside someone I didn't know.

Three days before the start of the tournament, lodges had shopping carts parked outside and student ambassadors positioned around to facilitate the whole moving-in process. Being a part of the ranking board meant that I was an ambassador. I pretended not to know. Currently, people were arriving in buses and cars and directed towards their respective lodges, along with their assigned student buddies from the host school. Which was us. And he'd just been introduced to one of his student buddies.

"Cox," Lee Jungwoo. Seventh. He'd done something to his hair. "You look like a serial killer." We were standing in a row, several feet away from the registration counter, with name tags on, in our school tracksuits.

The other ambassadors up front in registration would come to us with people and say something along the lines of 'show him to Xu from Hudson.' Then we'd search for the Hudson buddies standing around in the grass patch some hundred feet away, closer to their lodge, and drop them off there. Rinse and repeat.

By the end of the day, most of us would have met our assigned two; one from LV and one from CSS. I say meet because I didn't intend to show them around or take them out to dinner like the instructions suggested for us to do. Hosting was clearly not my forte. Conducting a short tour for them to get acquainted with the school was the more than enough, and more than a quarter of them had to be seniors. Meaning there was a chance this was their second time here for the tournament.

I was crossing my fingers for one of those. Preferably two.

"Heard they're giving us a budget to take them out for new year's or something. Since they're spending it here." Some guy down the row. The girl beside him mentioned fifty bucks each.

"Assiette didn't even do a thing about new year's last W-interschool." I was there. They gave us a sparkler each. Lasted for ten seconds.

Frankly, I'd be happy without the fifty bucks if the students I was assigned to had new year plans of their own. Wasn't uncommon. Logically, people would rather spend time with their schoolmates, exploring the mall nearby or going further out before a week of non-stop competition and stress. Ideally, they weren't even interested in talking to me. That way, I wasn't obligated to entertain anyone since... I was bad at entertaining in general.

That, and I had plans. With a certain someone.

My eyes went to him on instinct, taking in a second student handing him half her bags. Without complaint, he'd sorted them gently into a shopping cart before starting in the direction of Cinnamon, glancing over his shoulder at every three to five steps just to ensure they were keeping up. I hadn't noticed Jean Mercier calling me from the registration counter until Lee beside me snapped a finger between my eyes. I'd given him a look. It was blank.

"Cox. What the hell? I called your name four times," Mercier flung a couple of bags my way. I caught them. He shook his head, smiling regardless. "Get to work. These are your buddies. Remember, it's a *full tour*. No slacking."

He was flanked by a guy and a girl in casual clothes—clearly first-timers, judging from the look on their faces. Lost. They came up to me as soon as they were handed a welfare bag each and needless to say, awkward silence ensued. The first minute of our journey to Cayenne, none of us spoke.

Still, they knew my name. Mercier had apparently said it four times which was honestly good news since I never really liked introductions. Plus, I was in the mood to ride. Getting this over and done with would've meant extra time, wisely spent down at the racing track with Caspian.

"So, um... Cox, right?" The guy hastened his steps to keep up with me and the other girl. He was a lot shorter than us both. "I'm Maple! L'Assiette Vide. Second year. O-oh and, um. You guys have really long legs but do you mind slowing down a little? Sorry..." Already, he was panting.

Naturally, I couldn't have people dying within a five feet radius so I had to choose between giving in to his request and speeding up so that he wasn't within five feet. But I guess they'd prefer him alive, so... the girl apologized and matched his space. I tried my best to do the same.

"That's a cute name," the girl adjusted the drawstrings of her hoodie. "Hold up. Is that your first...? Or last name."

"It's my first name!" The guy had bleached hair in the shade of mild pink. His roots showed.

"What's your last?" I got it out of the way; not exactly fond of wasting time and memory space since last names were what we'd eventually be acquainted with in the kitchen. He seemed slightly fazed. Smile faltering a little.

"O-oh. Um, it's Pierson."

"Cox." I nodded.

"Hold up, I'm Cox too," the girl burst out laughing, turning to me with a raised brow. "Cox is kinda common over here, huh. You're the second one this morning although back in my school, I'm like... the only Cox. Liqin's my first name. I'm half Chinese, just in case you're wondering. Quarter Filipino. One-eighth Irish and I can't remember the rest. My dad's somewhat American... I think."

"Wow! That's really cool."

I couldn't understand the fractions she was pulling out so I left the conversation at 'quarter Filipino' while the other guy chipped in. They seemed to get along without my input, which was honestly the best thing to happen so far. I wasn't about to cancel plans with Caspian, so.

We arrived at Cayenne minutes later, dropping off their bags and settling the security codes to their rooms. Key fobs were handed out at the entrance and I briefly taught them how to unlock the front door using the weird-ass button.

"You make it look really easy." Pierson had to say. He smiled a lot. He was also a laugher. Fortunately, I had the other Cox to entertain his expressions or I'd be down with a migraine before the end of the day. Both had a lot to say about their courses and I figured, even without them explicitly revealing their majors, that Pierson was in nutrition and Cox, culinary. Lodging stuff aside, they were decently intelligent enough not to ask stupid questions.

I moved on to a brief, *obligatory* tour of key landmarks: Roth, administration, Marriott, commons, plaza. Plus one or two leisure spots like the barn and where best to see the river and that was it. I skipped the racetrack, the vineyard, the rooftop strawberry field right above the commons, tennis courts, the indoor pool, etc. They didn't seem to matter as much anyway, and would've seemed like I was trying to sell the school or something. And wasting my time.

"How's welfare? I heard you guys have access to every facility. We gotta earn service points for that kind of thing," Cox from CSS sounded like she was considering a transfer. Though I was pretty sure her school was at least twice the size of ours. They ran a hotel on campus; part of some new course they came up with two years ago. Been there once with Siegfried.

"Somewhat. We have credits depending on our grades. Or club activities. Gold credits give you access to all kitchens, restaurants and cafes. Things like that. Service is compulsory. We have a roster."

"Oh, oh! We have one too," Pierson. "Sometimes, we're on lunch duty. And there's cleaning and gardening and running the café downstairs too. Our school's a lot smaller, I think. We're in the middle of Cité Rouge so we build upwards... fifteen floors in total, haha. And everyone hates the stairs so we have eight elevators!"

Okay. *Eight.*

Cox was clearly impressed. She might as well be considering a transfer to LV instead, since I wasn't about to start singing the praises of a school I never wanted to attend. Pierson was on the other end of the spectrum. By the time we arrived at the student commons to grab complimentary lunchboxes provided by the school, they were actually talking about applying for a transfer.

"Mind if I use the bathroom?" Cox stopped short before we joined the line, nodding at the red-blue sign. Pierson said something about not needing to go and waiting outside. I vaguely agreed, attention split.

There was no fixed schedule for ambassadors and all, but knowing him... *there.* By the marketplace's juice aisle with a basket, doing his shopping. Or for others. Likely the two assigned to him. He was giving the label on the bottle in his hand a read while joining the line to pay for his basket. I watched him from a distance.

"So, um... do you have any plans for the new year?" I thought I heard something. Pierson was looking up at me like he was expecting some kind of reply so I made the connection that he had been trying to have a conversation. I wasn't the best at small talk.

"Yeah."

"O-oh!" He on the other hand, was very uncomfortable with silence and didn't see it as an option in existence. "What are they? I still don't really know what I should be doing... none of my friends made it past the preliminary selection, so... is there, maybe, some festival going on nearby? Um, on the other side of the river or something? With fireworks?"

I honestly didn't know the answer to his question so I just told him that and expected him to crumble and die from the awkwardness but he just giggled or something and slapped my arm. No reason to do that, but okay.

By the time I returned my attention to the checkout counter over at the marketplace, he was done with the electronic payment and was looking around, probably searching for the students he'd been assigned to. He neared us, tunnel-visioning on the people he was looking for and ended up missing me entirely. I held on to his wrist when he passed, giving him a scare and amusing myself with the startled jump he did.

"Oh good—Leroy!" He sighed after taking me in and already, I could see the words 'idiot' circling around in his head. "Someday, I'm reporting you to the authorities. How did your tour go?"

"Okay," I used the only word that came to mind about non-relevant things. "You done with yours or... anytime soon?" Just a gauge. He wasn't fond of last-minute surprises, so I was planning a couple of hours ahead just in case.

It felt strangely electric; the way I'd skim his waters with my fingertips and watch the ripples fade.

"We've covered the entire right and middle wing so we'd most likely be done in less than two hours. One of them happened to be a senior who's participated in the W-interschool during her first year! It certainly takes the pressure off... and I believe you haven't learnt a thing about manners." He stopped all of a sudden, turning to someone by my shoulder. *Oh. Forgot.* "He hasn't introduced us. I'm sorry for interrupting your conversation like that. I'm Julian White."

"Hi Julian!" Pierson accepted the handshake with a bow. Just a little weird. "I'm Maple... sorry about the name, haha."

His eyes softened. "No it isn't," he reassured and for a moment, it felt as though he was speaking to his godfather. "I-if it makes you feel any better, Julian isn't my first name. It's actually Vanilla. Julian's my middle. Name. And neither of us should feel defined by a term in which the external world requires to... to differentiate existences."

"And we should always carry ourselves with confidence no matter what! And and and hold our heads up high and sign petitions for cute names to be accepted by society!" Pierson added in a voice five times the original excitement, pumping his fist into the air and then holding his other up for a five.

Even for him with a godfather *that* spirited, he'd done a double take and started blushing in embarrassment. He was also far too polite to refuse the high-five.

* * *

It takes about two to three hours of non-stop company in groups before introvert instincts start to kick in. And if you haven't noticed, I'm a high-functioning introvert. Small talk drained the fucking life out of me and oddly enough listening to people rave about mindless things wasn't exactly my forte either.

So by the time we were done with the tour and had met up with the administrative team back at the registration counter we started at, I was sucked dry; the need to be alone kicking in fast and every other meaningless conversation just exhausting the backup power I was currently running on.

You can imagine the sheer relief in the form of 'thank fucks' running in my mind when Cox, on our way back to Cayenne, apologized for not being able to join us for dinner. Apparently, she'd made plans with her friends from school, which was exactly what I'd been hoping to hear. The next natural thing to do was to call it off since 'it wouldn't be the same without all three' so that was what I did and already, I was on the path of recovery.

"Sorry. Lunch tomorrow? Oh but there's the briefing isn't there... we'll figure it out," she dismissed with a wave before heading past the front door first, in a hurry to get her things. Pierson was right behind us so I didn't really think about the closing the door, but then I felt something tug on the back of my jacket.

He was holding on to it with a weird, sheepish smile on his face so I dropped my gaze to the back of my jacket and asked if he could let go. He sort of apologized before quietly requesting for a minute outside. I had to reassess the situation to actually understand why he wasn't particularly keen on talking in the lodge. There were others in the lounge taking turns to give Raul's PlayStation a go.

"Uh, okay...?" I closed the front door so that he'd start talking quick.

Pierson was doing something with his index fingers—each somewhat pointed at the other and then touching like they were part of an E.T poster??? What the fuck am I looking at. Don't even know how to describe it, for sure.

"So, um. I was wondering if we could still have dinner...? Maybe? I really don't know anyone else here and, um. They did say that it's the only meal not provided by the school so I don't really know where I should be going or how I should go about settling it. I-if we could have dinner together, it would be great. It's just... I don't have any friends here." Okay yeah you've said that three times and I'm mean, so. Really just dying to point that out.

Ah, fuck. "I made plans too. It's private."

"I don't mind just tagging along! I won't be a bother. Promise!" Pierson looked oddly persistent, looking up at me with a ridiculous number of blinks in the span of two seconds. I told him no.

Then, out of nowhere, like some meteorite crash-landing in the middle of a motherfucking tea party with scones and shit, he started *tearing up*. Me being the high-functioning introvert without the pros every introvert was said to have ('great listener' 'empathetic human' 'very understanding'), blanking out was the first instinct to kick in and naturally, not a single word came to mind.

"I'm sorry... i-it's just. It's my first time so far away from home and I—I'm just. It feels so lonely and... I just thought it'd be nice to, you know, rely on someone strong and cool like, like you. You know?"

He wasn't making any sense and honestly all I could hear was his sniffling, but what really kept my mind in a state of confusion was his reason for... crying? It wasn't within my realm of expertise. Stuff like being far away from home and dealing with loneliness and having no one to rely on felt like the natural state of things. That, yeah, life *was* supposed to be that way and having anything more than that was a plus. An added plus.

"This isn't..." *something to cry about,* I almost said. Then I heard his bespectacled voice at the back of my head and knew it wasn't exactly the best word-choice at present so I kinda just sighed and kept my mouth shut so that he'd continue talking it out.

"You're really nice. A-and I really want to make some friends here. It's just so lonely and I feel so... so *sad.*"

I was trying my best to listen to Pierson's repeated rambles while awkwardly tapping his shoulder when all of a sudden—again, like a meteorite in the middle of a tea party—he ignored the shoulder taps and went straight for my torso like it was the teddy bear he'd go to sleep with every night. And then topped it all off by sobbing into my chest.

"I don't do hugs," I told him straight, immediately holding his shoulders at arm's length.

Needless to say, this wasn't exactly a situation I knew how to handle. Frankly, I never had to deal with people who were a tad too physical in expressing themselves and hugging it out with a stranger I'd just met barely four hours ago was a far stretch. "Please stop crying."

"W-well then I'll need your shoulder to rest on. Then I'll stop."

VANILLA

I was fortunate enough to be assigned a pair of friendly, relaxed female participants who seemed perfectly fine with the pace of the tour and my subsequent suggestions of places to go for dinner. Going with the flow was apparently their way of life and as such, neither had any complaints about dining at the student-run restaurant with an outdoor seating section that extended out into the river.

The initial plan was to have them dine there for free by spending the gold credits I'd received from Keith before the winter break as a reward for my 'stellar performance' throughout the semester. The girls however, Juanita Castillo and Nia Williams, insisted that I spend my credits on something else and that they'd pay for their own meals in cash. Either way, I was out on the front porch waiting for them to change into their outdoor shoes whilst devising a foolproof plan of paying upfront and pretending I'd never intended to do so. *They did have a buffet option for dinner, so maybe—*

My gaze rested on figures in the distance. Cayenne was the lodge next door, situated slightly north of Cinnamon and higher up on the hill. Still, there was no mistaking that heated shade of bronze, fiery under the light of the setting sun filtering in at an angle. It didn't help that I was originally a familiar friend of his back.

"Which way again?"

"Up the hill and past the vineyard I think. All the way."

There was someone resting their head on his shoulder, arms going around to cling on the fabric on his back. Soft locks of pastel pink were brushing the side of his neck, which soon led to the reasonable conclusion of the mystery person's identity.

"Nice boots by the way."

"Yes girl! They new. Black Friday be blessing my life always."

Maple must have been painfully upset by something to be sobbing in that manner, which found its way into my heart and made the scene oddly unbearable. Our short interaction at the student commons reminded me of a younger Chip I'd never before seen, and had thus made the moment strikingly nostalgic. The mere thought of my godfather sobbing his heart out was enough to break my own and I was oddly glad to see Leroy comforting him. There was something else needling in however, but I wasn't too keen on identifying what it was.

Though knowing that idiot, he'd be appallingly embarrassed if some three people walked in on a moment so vulnerable and private, so I turned around, peering past the doorway to ask Williams and Castillo if they were in a mood for shopping at a new mall instead. Heading to the student-run restaurant would have meant continuing up the hill, which would've made things awkward for Leroy and Maple. The mall was in the other direction.

"Oh honey you don't have to overthink! We fine with that restaurant but if y'all in the mood for some shopping, I'll be in the mood for some shopping."

"I'm fine with anything," Castillo agreed, joining me on the front porch and checking herself in the reflection of a window. "I remember eating at that restaurant in my first year? The food was really really good."

"Ah... yes. I see. W-well then I suppose we could..." I'd made the mistake of glancing at the lodge next door and giving a reluctant response. The combination of both had caught the attention of Williams, who'd only just closed the door behind her and was adjusting her coat.

"You okay sweetie?" She followed my gaze. Needless to say, Leroy and Maple weren't exactly hidden by a magical bush of cherries or the wonders of filmmaking censorship. And perhaps it was my imagination, but they seemed oddly closer than before. "Oh I see you..."

"Where?" Castillo joined us in a heartbeat and I was starting to feel a little more embarrassed than I had been originally.

Williams had snorted after pointing them out to Castillo, then started shaking her head. "Mm... I mean. Maple Pierson... boy, he's got to stop reeling 'em in..."

I turned to her. Surprised. "Yes. That's him. How did you know?"

"If you from LV, you gotta know him... not 'cuz he gay or anything, just... I mean you can tell he gay, he all over the cutie but like, that's not why he famous," Williams laid out before lowering her voice. "Don't at me but he sucked a lot of dick and I *seen* him suck dick, so I'm just sayin'. Okay not like *see* see. But close. Anyway, poor cutie gonna fall pretty damn soon."

Castillo was somewhat laughing about the way Williams had described Maple and, indeed, I'd found it nearly unbelievable myself. Maple had been the sweetest innocent being at lunch today and the mere image of him doing something other than... w-well, than sweet, innocent things felt in every way unthinkable. Perhaps there had been some sort of misunderstanding or miscommunication, which the spreading of information was inevitably subject to.

The fact that someone so important to me had somehow been roped into the description, too, felt uncomfortably problematic. Leroy wasn't going to... well, he wasn't going to cheat on me. That much, I knew and believed. From that perspective, I therefore had nothing to be worried about.

"What do you mean? He set a trap or something?" Castillo squinted in the direction of our neighbors.

"He be acting all princess, y'know? Like he waiting to be rescued all sad and lonely but when they all alone... that's when he start gettin' *very* naughty." Williams laughed when Castillo rolled her eyes, playfully slapping her upper arm. Brows raised and thoroughly amused. "So where we going? I'm hungry."

We eventually settled on the mall because Castillo had forgotten to pack a hairbrush and had been thinking of getting one over the next couple of days. Even then, as we were making our way downhill away from the lodge, a glimpse over my shoulder was enough to tell me that Maple still had his head rested against the other's chest.

From: Just Let Me Impress You
How was your day?

* * *

To: Just Let Me Impress You
Uneventful but rather fulfilling. The student buddies I've been assigned to are really nice. We had dinner at the mall nearby. And you?

* * *

From: Just Let Me Impress You
I had dinner alone
Then spent some time with Caspian

* * *

To: Just Let Me Impress You
Oh! But what about your student buddies? Weren't we supposed to have dinner with them?

* * *

From: Just Let Me Impress You
One of them already had plans so

* * *

To: Just Let Me Impress You
Ah, I see. That is unfortunate. Would that be Maple?

* * *

From: Just Let Me Impress You
Pierson
He's hard to deal with
I'll tell you about it when we meet
New Year's Eve?
You said this afternoon you had plans
Keep the evening free?

* * *

To: Just Let Me Impress You
Again, if you knew a thing about politeness, you would understand
that I was deliberately reserving New Year's Eve for a certain idiot.
Maple was right in front of us! I can't possibly tell him 'no, I'm com-
pletely free as of now and am waiting for
a specific person to ask me out,' can I?
I have the entire day, Leroy.

* * *

From: Just Let Me Impress You
Attached: standing eggplant.png

A picnic by the river on New Year's Eve was perhaps the most romantic state of affairs I'd ever find myself suggesting as a wholly unromantic and serious character without a dash of experience in a heart-fluttering, giggle-inducing romance. My unfortunate love interest, a silly lion with a one-track mind and appalling manners, had prepared a stunning basket of goodies for an afternoon under the shade of a tree and what would have been a pink, dramatic breeze as does every novel of the same genre would have described such an embarrassing scene.

Alas, none of this had happened.

Every participant of the W-interschool received a text message at three in the afternoon, notifying them of a last-minute obligatory meeting at five p.m. on accord of several changes that have been made to the schedule. Needless to say, no one took this very well and, in fact, expressed their dissent by coming to the briefing dressed in party dresses or... um, party pants? The bottom line was that the meeting had caused utmost disappointment in the organizing team and everyone, including students from our school, were boiling in our thoughts.

Most of everyone had made plans to enjoy the last night of their winter break that had, already, been cut short by the tournament. Since it had so coincidentally fallen on New Year's Eve, several lodges had pooled together the fifty dollars provided by the school to rent a bar or a function room in the shopping district downtown.

The briefing lasted for nearly three hours, dashing hopes of admiring the sunset by the river and appreciating a nice pink breeze a-among many other things that, um, clearly did not matter. Most of the participants were suffering from a severe case of hunger and were not in the mood for drinks in an empty stomach.

Leroy and I on the other hand, had agreed to move the picnic to his room after Chen called for another thirty minutes with the top thirteen. I wasn't involved (naturally) but my companion was surprisingly unfazed by the request and went along with it, merely apologizing and telling me to wait in his room.

I'd obliged—clearing some space in his room for the picnic mat and arranging the food and drinks so that they were perfectly placed. Then, for a beginner's shy attempt at romance, I'd connected my phone to the Bluetooth speaker I got him for Christmas before googling for 'romantic music.'

The first option had been something by the name of 'Careless Whisper' but three seconds in and even an amateur like myself could tell the extent of its inappropriateness. I'd had to go through every single track until a playlist of decent suitability was found before sitting back and hoping it was to his liking.

Minutes later, I heard footsteps and thought it was him but then there was a knock and, well, clearly, Leroy wouldn't be knocking on his own door so I opened it and found Maple, his student buddy with two bottles of what appeared to be alcohol in his hands. He'd seemed mildly surprised by my answering of the door and, after learning that Leroy had not returned, asked if I wanted the drink instead.

I'd politely declined and thanked him for his generosity before asking if he was... quite alright. He, startled that I knew about him crying out on the front porch, flashed a smile and said that he was fine. Then, left with a wave.

As expected, he didn't seem a tad bit inappropriate or, well, as others may have described him. Still, I watched him go, slightly confused and not quite knowing what or who I should be believing. Then, just as I was about to close the door and head back to waiting for a certain idiot in his room, he came up to the landing of the second floor by the stairs and caught me standing in his doorway.

Nearly at once, a smirk had crossed his features and I knew exactly what he was about to say before he was even *thinking* of what to say and so I made a gesture to close the door in his face but he was faster and held the door open with one hand, snaking his other a-around my waist and and and... well, I don't quite know what happened next. Neither words nor images reached my mind that was a blank.

It was only after a relaxed meal in comfortable music and occasional words that I somehow found myself falling asleep leaning against the side of his bed. The picnic then turned into a sleepover after I wholly missed the countdown to midnight and woke up to the same soft music playing on the speakers and him at my shoulder—too—asleep. After dropping my family a text to wish them a happy new year (and Si Yin as well), I'd tapped the lion awake and told him that I should be heading back to my lodge.

Somehow (do *not* ask), I was persuaded to sleep over. Even though the entire thing meant returning to my lodge to collect my toiletries, pyjamas and toothbrush! *Goodness, Vanilla*, I'd thought to myself then, *you're absolutely, problematically lovestruck.*

This morning, we'd made plans to be up by six in the morning but Leroy, who was one to pay no respect whatsoever to his poor morning alarm and had set his snooze to buzz only every twenty minutes, succeeded in making the both of us (more of myself, really) speed through washing up and getting dressed just so that we'd make it to the opening ceremony on time.

By the time we'd emerged from Cayenne and headed down the hill towards the plaza, most of everyone had gathered before the makeshift stage and were forming rows of ten according to their schools and alphabetical order.

Si Yin had spotted us from afar and, having paid no attention whatsoever to the facilitator trying to get her to stand in line, waved us over. Leroy seemed to know where he had to be going so we parted ways and I made for my best friend jumping around and raising her eyebrows in a rapid manner.

"Ooo walking together? You're just on time by the way they said something about starting in three minutes but everyone's like, not getting into their rows and they're still handing out nametags and stuff before they announce how the first segment's gonna go. You think it's a team thing right off the bat? Or individual and then the scores are all tallied or something? They said yesterday that they doubled the elimination process so, like, that means it's gonna be faster, right?" She spoke very quickly and I was about to provide the best answers to her first couple of questions when her gaze lowered to the general area of my neck.

Distracted by how intensely she was staring at my collar, I followed her gaze. "Is something..."

Oh good heavens. I looked up and away, hurriedly unknotting the half-Windsor I'd done up perfectly in front of his mirror minutes ago and feeling the heat on my neck spread upwards to my ears. "Please don't laugh."

Si Yin was already choking on her mirth, face red and eyes completely wide with amusement. "Is this for real? You guys—"

"I-it's just a mistake. We got dressed in three minutes and... oh I must have grabbed the one on the back of his door oh god. I'd done it on instinct and then handed him the other and..." I stared helplessly down at the red-striped tie in my hands before the facilitator going down my row asked me where it was and told me to be appropriately dressed immediately before the commemoration photo was to be taken... in five minutes.

Needless to say, I was then frantically searching for a certain idiot before finally spotting him with a couple of his male friends who... who seemed to be waving me over? Raul was one of them. They were laughing when I made my arrival and, embarrassed, I'd hurriedly held Leroy's tie out to him with a glare while he, smirking and clearly enjoying this supposed moment of embarrassment, took his time *removing* his (my) tie and then handing it to me with a look th-that was just, simply, *bad*.

LEROY

I joined the row of 'C's without thinking twice, spotting the top of Chen's head sticking out from the crowd and just casually sliding myself between two random people and pretending I was there all along. Plan sort of failed because for some reason, people couldn't stop looking at my shirt and I was about to ask why the hell they weren't minding their own business when I felt a tap on my shoulder and turned to face the school's number one, who was great at telling me how bad I was with time.

Then he, too, paused mid-sentence, frowning at something on my collar. "You—oh my fucking god, Cox. You could've just told me you guys were dating instead of baring your fangs all the time." He clicked his tongue, rolling his eyes with an exasperated snort.

I was getting nothing from whatever he had to say and was about to follow his gaze down to my shirt when the gears in my heard started turning right on cue. Three whole seconds later, I could feel my lips stretch into a smirk. "Is it blue?"

He flipped me off. The amusement, I felt in my chest; bubbling. It was hard not to start smiling like an idiot.

"Explains why he always seemed to have some sort of excuse. If you'd told me sooner, I would've backed off, you know," he sighed. "I was under the impression we were on equal standing and that I still had a chance. You were pretty obvious about how you felt but White was, like. Business mode twenty-four-seven."

"Not with me," I laid out and fingers flew my way.

"You fucker," Chen laughed. I did too, before my hardwired brain started entertaining itself with thoughts of him and how he'd, by now, be panicking with mine in his hands and searching for me in the next five minutes before the opening ceremony with red ears and a cute, fucking glare.

Somewhere down 'D' row, Raul was making his way over with Bank right behind him from 'F', I think, or something along those lines. People were casually swapping places all around without the facilitators noticing, so. They came for no concrete reason, probably because Raul was dying to share his party stories which was usually the case. He'd spent last night in some club for the countdown and him walking was already a sign that he didn't enjoy it. Since, well, he wasn't wasted. Or hungover.

I did nothing to the tie I had on—made no gesture to remove it—and Chen, catching on the second I had that thought running through my mind, rolled his eyes and left the chat to start another with Lee Jungwoo some three people down. Don't ask how he got there.

"It started off sick and the music was great but the girls were either very pushy or, you know, like too much... your tie is the wrong color, man." He paused for five seconds. "Oh. Ohh... playdate."

I feigned nonchalance. He shoved a finger in my face before doing the thing with his brows and glancing over my shoulder as though something else had caught his attention. "Ah he's here." Raul raised a hand. Calling out to someone.

I didn't need to follow his gaze to know exactly who he was talking about because if you don't already know, I get turned on whenever he's within my fifty-feet radius. The rest of the group must've spotted him making his way over to us and made the connection, laughing and joining Raul in waving him over. Lee, who'd been so curious about the person I was so 'busy flirting with' was staring at me with wide, enlightened eyes. The amusement was killing me.

He arrived—flustered and trying to catch his breath. I was just taking my time, dragging this out as long as I could, taking in the pink dusting his ears and appreciating the glare of a baby fawn. I was right about my tie. He'd been too embarrassed to wear it around and had removed it, rolling it up into a neat little bundle which he was now holding out to me.

"You should really learn how to respect your morning alarm, Leroy Jeremy Cox, or I'm never going to spend another night in your room. You have absolutely no idea how absurdly embarrassing this is. Thank goodness Si Yin took notice at once."

"Or you'd be wearing it all day?" I removed it. Slowly. Enjoying this. "My color. You look good in it."

The shade of pink on his ears darkened and he was furiously trying to recover whilst waiting for me to hand over his tie. "W-well unfortunately for you, Leroy, I have news and and that is, that, blue is not a color that suits you and it clashes with your eyes if you haven't noticed so although you may very well think this shade of red looks smart on me, we are never not ever, I mean, never making the mistake of wearing the, the wrong tie ever again."

I gave his forehead the usual and he hastily retrieved his tie from my hand whilst gently balancing mine, neat and rolled to perfection, on my shoulder before running off. Deer-like.

"Tone it down, I'm warning you," was all Chen had to say, standing by his word. Backing off nicely.

"Students. Participants of the twenty-second W-interschool." The audio feedback from the sound system on stage was poor and most of everyone was not in the mood to pay the emcee any attention. "I know you're all dying to get back inside but Mr. Jael over here will now be giving out instructions for the commemorative photograph. Please ensure that your uniform is in perfect condition before looking up at the camera drone above."

I could feel my thoughts tuning out, just waiting for them to get this over and done with so that we could move on to the opening ceremony and *then* the prep for round one. We were standing out in the cold for a total of fifteen minutes with cheap hand warmers given out by the facilitators before finally being introduced to the judges—one from each school as primaries and then a guest judge for every segment.

They were big names. Yamazaki was one of them but we'd have to wait till tomorrow to see him since that was the segment he was doing. Round one was a critic from France. Leclair.

"Facilitators are going round with lottery bags. The number on your draw determines the serve ware you will be presenting your dishes on." As expected, the initial instructions weren't the best at giving us an early idea of what we had coming up next. I drew a five right out of the bag and glanced at Chen. Four fingers out of his pocket.

They got to projecting a list of numbers on the screen up front after a couple of minutes and the entire plaza started shifting rest-lessly around. Right beside number one was the word 'Ramekin' and beside two, 'Martini Glass'. Several down, I weeded out my number and felt my imaginary middle finger twitch.

Dessert Glass

I gave four a glimpse and, relieved, exchanged a look with Chen beside me before slipping my number into his pocket. He had his somewhat wedged in the muscles of his palm before shaking my hand. Soup spoons over dessert glasses any day.

"As you can tell by now, the types of serve ware up on the screen are only meant to accommodate the tiniest form of food, be it fine dining or home cooking. The details of the first elimination round is as follows."

Bite-sized Challenge
Type: Elimination (60)
Style: Buffet

Participants: 150
Scoring: Point per portion

"Sixty on the first round," Chen snorted under his breath. "What's the rush? I don't get why they're increasing the number every year."

First rounds were usually designed to weed out amateurs right off the bat while allowing those of the other end of the ladder focus on giving their school a head-start in points without the point cap. Simply put: elimination was a personal problem while the overall score was the one and only determinant of the school in which the ultimate winner was going to come from. Naturally, Chen had his eyes on the second part.

"We have about a thousand guests arriving for a free-for-all buffet of a hundred-and-fifty dishes. As usual, there will be no point cap for the first round so this is your chance to gain as many points for your school by adding to your empty dish counter. Every finished portion counts as a single point, whether it's a shot glass of raspberry coulis or a shrimp cocktail in a martini glass.

"The two-hour buffet has no designated route or restriction, so your guests are going to be picking and choosing what they wish to eat entirely by their own volition. If you're good enough they may return for a second serving or even remain at your station throughout the entire round. Each school will have thirty minutes to come up with a relevant strategy and then spend an hour, *individually* refining their recipes before another hour's station and ingredient prep. The official commencement of first round begins at three o'clock sharp.

"Those who have drawn your numbers, please proceed to the front of the plaza to register your assigned serve ware according to your school—stop walking I'm not done yet. Have your participant

IDs ready and remember to collect the name tag and apron with your name on it. And *check* the name, for god's sake."

I stood in line with Chen for the next five to ten minutes before collecting a silver chef's name tag that had our initials and last name engraved. Not gonna lie, it looked a whole lot sleeker than the one we were given last year and the idea of exchanging mine for a sweet 'V. J. White' after the interschool sounded pretty tempting.

People were being directed to different lecture theatres according to their schools as soon as they were registered but I was taking my time, keeping my eyes peeled for him. Most of everyone else had rushed indoors to escape the cold and after briefly acknowledging a couple of familiar looking faces from the others schools (they came right up to me, so I didn't have much of a choice right there), I spotted him already seated in the front row with Si Yin. Should have known he wasn't the kind to be wasting anyone's time.

A facilitator handed Chen a mic as soon as he entered while Marseille on the other end of the platform up front gave everyone the usual glare with folded arms and her index tapping the side of her elbow. "Hurry up children. Your thirty minutes has started and at the rate you're walking, I can already see us losing to CSS."

I was eyeing the open seat next to a certain someone when they called for the rest of thirteen to get up front and lead the discussion alongside number one. Chen was giving me a look that a hundred percent meant I wasn't allowed to give any excuses so I dragged my sorry ass up the platform and slotted myself randomly between Lee Jungwoo and Jean Mercier with a sad *ah, fuck.*

Chen had a lot more on his plate. He was being briefed by the facilitator while the tech team pulled up some slides on the projector screen and handed him the clicker. He had to be ready in less than a minute.

"Morning everyone." Gotta hand it to him though, that's some quality smiles for an early-ass morning. The theatre was in no mood to respond but Mercier busted out some odd cat-calling and whoop-ing that the rest of the thirteen started to follow except for, I think, Birchwood and myself who just stiffly clapped and before we knew it the rest of the hall was cheering along for the hype.

"Unlike our previous number one, I like getting straight down to business without the fun, so. I apologize beforehand. Um... so can I have those who drew a one, the ramekins, to sit on the right, fol-lowed by the twos, martini glasses, and so on? It's the best way to start getting things organized since we have to decide who's on ap-petizer, main and dessert."

The thirteen sort of remained up front but shifted ourselves to match the general position of our draws. Not to brag, but those with the soup spoons were looking pretty relieved that I was standing in front of them. We were a sad four in total.

My eyes went straight to him a few rows down, seated in front of Birchwood at 'Shot Glasses' with a composed smile on his face look-ing mildly or very sexy. Wow I'm fucking deprived.

"Um, Cox? We're sort of the hardest group, right? As in, everyone else has it easy for ideas but are we seriously going to serve them a spoon of soup as an appetizer?" The person who spoke had two badges pinned to his collar, which meant he was a sophomore like me but I had no clue who he was.

"No. Ever heard of appetizer spoons? Canapé? Not soup."

"Right," some girl in the year above me. "So we'd be on appetiz-ers."

"Most likely." Chen was making his rounds and stopped by to ask if I had any specific dish in mind since, he said, he'd be giving thir-teen their first choice. I told him we'd be on cold hors d'oeuvres, el-evating ordinary soup spoons into something fancy when he asked a good fucking question.

"Asian soup spoons?" He frowned. "Or western. Did you ask?"

I made the stupid mistake of assuming that it was Asian soup spoons they were talking about since the western ones would have made us look like fucking fools in front of the guests because who'd be in the right mind to serve a portion of food on a western soup spoon? After checking with the facilitator and confirming that it was the Asian ones they were referring to, I went back to the team with good news and they all collapsed in relief. It was apparently their first time competing.

"Smoked salmon canapé with dill cream cheese, crème fraiche and top it with caviar or something," I laid out for Chen, who noted it down and looked sufficiently satisfied with my menu so I got back to helping the rest of the team sort their stuff out before then reporting our general category to the person behind the laptop up front. They keyed in our names under appetizers and said I was good to go.

Glancing up at the screen with a list of names and categories projected on it, it was obvious that most of the school and perhaps even the other participants preferred going with the natural categories of 'appetizer' and 'dessert' since they matched the serve ware we were using. Bite-sized. Doing up a 'main' seemed to be what people were avoiding. By the definition the facilitators had given, Chen said that mains were supposed to include carbs in the recipe. So potatoes, then. Nothing else came to mind.

We had about forty names down on the list by the time a member of the organizing team came round with the digital floor map of the buffet hall which was the J. Rosenthal function hall with a hundred and fifty stations arranged in the shape of a square in a square. The moment they pulled this up on the screen, with the names, fire exit and main entrances all marked out, I was searching for his before looking at my own. Hm. Logic.

"Let's take a minute to confirm the categories. We need a minimum of ten people under 'Main', so. We'll go by name, category and recipe. Anton? You're on blackberry trifle dessert. Arnolds. Cookie dough... think we need to change that—"

They'd changed the screen to the floor plan so I didn't get to see which category he'd put himself under. The thirteen of us up front were giving suggestions accordingly, with Lee the top nutritionist giving most feedback on what should be eaten buffet style whilst considering the fact that people were walking around a lot. Menus kept changing and all but mostly for those on appetizers and desserts who... uh, weren't standing up front.

No one's really dared to disagree with thirteen. It's never happened.

"Cox, smoked salmon canapé. Yeah I approved that, so moving on. Cullen, uh, I'm not too sure about having rice on... White." My eyes went to him on instinct. His hand was raised. Not too high, not too low. A well-practiced raise; like he was so used to asking and answering questions. "You have something to say?"

All eyes turned on him. He stood, hands behind his back in a polite manner.

"Sorry to interrupt. I was... I'd just like to point out where Mr. Cox's station is placed. Top left—the furthest away from the front door in which our guests will be entering from. Which, in other words, would mean that they would have gone through at least sixty other stations to arrive at his... *smoked salmon canapé*. If I may be brutally honest, no one's going to pick a cold, bitty appetizer absent of a fragrance pull thirty minutes into the buffet that far into the room because the dish incites neither visual nor the olfactory sense, let alone anything auditory so that one would be left standing in the corner with six empty appetizer spoons max. A-and as I'd observed earlier on, the entire team of soup spoon draws have relegated themselves to the category of appetizers which, I, um, again, my apologies, believe quite unnecessary! Especially you, the idiot standing up on stage. Clearly, you're better than salmon canapé and with your technical skills I don't see why you aren't on the list of mains with something fragrant and strong and perhaps even showy, what with you being placed in the least favorable spot in the room. It doesn't have to be an appetizer just because it's an *appetizer spoon*. Limiting yourself to your draw is doing exactly what this segment wants you to be doing! You can't afford to be tricked." He sat as soon as he finished before dusting slightly pink and then standing again. "I-I meant *we* can't. As in, everyone." Then, sitting.

The entire room looked like they'd been fucked over twice. I think the silence lasted for more than six seconds. Chen was beside me. Mic lowered.

He leaned in. "That was hot."

"Yeah, I know."

At the back of the room, Marseille was trying very hard to hide one of her rare smiles. Most people think she doesn't play favorites but I knew her type. She loved herself a student like him.

"Right, uh... Cox?" Chen recovered with the mic raised and I nodded, eyes still holding the gaze of a frozen lake and feeling a smirk I couldn't quite control just taking over the corners of my lips. I settled with a nice finger because kissing him in front of forty-eight already shell-shocked humans wasn't exactly legal.

"Ch-Chef Marseille?? Cox just did a middle finger—" "Cox do *not* be indecent or I'll make sure you're on production duty for three consecutive weeks." *Okay, she got me.* "The first-year just called him an idiot." "Such a hater." "But Cox flipped him off omg you think he's offended?" "But White has a point..." "He's out of his mind. Speaking like that to the school's number two. Who does he think he is?" "Yeah but Cox agreed to change his category. He nodded."

I hadn't really gone that far into thinking what I was actually going to do with a main dish on some appetizer spoon, distracted by the mixed opinions coming from the floor. Anyone trying to call bullshit on his point doesn't deserve a spot in the W-interschool because they obviously don't have a brain. He'd explained his rationale. Over-explained it, even. All he had to do was point out the fact that I was placed furthest away from the door and everyone else in the room should have been able to see his genius.

"That's actually a really good idea," Lee Jungwoo said down the row, directing this at Chen who passed him the mic. "Pointing that out. It actually gives us a couple more options. We've been trying to come up with a strategy based on our draws, which, easy, yeah, sorts us into sub teams and gets the ball rolling. But eventually, with the floor plan as it is now... you see we can't change where we're placed in the room but what we *can* change is the menu. Our categories. White's right, we're limiting ourselves now.

"There's no reception before the buffet, which means the guests are coming indoors after being out in the cold. They'd want to start with something hot so if we're having all our cold appetizers up at the front of the room, they might skip all that. We want something to warm their tummies."

Everyone turned to stare as soon as he finished and then Lee, ears red, quickly handed the mic back to Chen who was already working with the tech team on having the categories written beside the names on the floor plan.

"Uh... 'warm their tummies'?" Birchwood was judging number seven and doing something with her hair. "Is that scientifically proven? You're a nutritionist...?"

"Okay, okay, it's just... a belief that warm liquids cause stomach muscles to relax."

Both the floor and the platform were having private conversations all over but I had no one to talk to so my eyes were back at him, speaking to Si Yin and then glancing in my general direction. We met. He then averted his gaze by shyly glancing around before beckoning once the coast was clear. Quietly. With his hand on his lap like no one was supposed to see him hooking his finger and reeling me in.

I grabbed a mic from a random facilitator before heading down and handing it to him. Naturally, he was looking mildly flustered.

"W-wha! This was supposed to be a private conversation."

"Oh. Like what you want for dinner tonight, or..."

"Oh good heavens, no. Not *that* sort of private conversation, although, yes, we could have a discussion on that a little later. I was thinking more along the lines of—" So apparently the facilitator had turned the mic on before I grabbed it and the entire hall had stopped talking to eavesdrop. Which was fucking hilarious because he was way too focused on speaking to me to actually realize this was happening.

"—improvising on that strategy Lee mentioned. In fact, we should not only be considering the temperature of the food, whether it's served hot or cold, but perhaps should also devise some sort of plan that would allow the guests to go for something sweet after a savory main dish. In fact, it would be silly if we'd placed all desserts in a corner and relegate main dishes to another. As soon as a guest finished their portion of raspberry trifle, they might seek something savory like grilled jerk shrimp that's a little citrusy with a zest of lime, conveniently located several feet away. O-or that nice French-boned chicken you made the first time you came over for dinner. Think of it as leaving a trail. The guests can't tell which school the participants are from so it wouldn't look like a hard sell when, actually, they are indeed following a route we'd planned out for them and thus get as many hits as we possibly can."

I glanced over my shoulder at Chen. He seemed to have taken this into account and was discussing this with Mercier and the number eight that moved up from nine since the previous semester whose name I, uh, missed out. He was a hybrid. Critic and nutritionist.

"You're a first-year, right?" He had three badges on his collar. Summer pool rippled in surprise when he registered people were responding to him over something he thought he'd said in private. "You haven't taken the buffet design course... I assume? How did you know all this?"

I was about to snort and make some remark about him maybe deserving the spot he had in the thirteen when someone else beat me to it. Was not expecting this to happen.

"He's a nerd. What do you expect?" Birchwood. "Average stupidity?"

VANILLA

As a wholehearted, introspective observer who prefers watching from the sidelines to direct intervention in the unfolding of events beyond the invisible glass separating myself from the world, I had, in the span of four months, surprised myself and everyone else familiar with my personality.

I now apparently have friends. I also have an intimate companion. I am also apparently very capable of removing the invisible glass and stepping into the other side of the world. And at the very same time developing a temporary, spontaneous ability to voice my opinions publicly in front of a very big crowd as long as I wasn't looking at them. For some reason, I am also able to incite a brief 'suspension of disbelief' in which I would so logically conclude that as long as the crowd remained beyond my field of vision, I would, as well, remain beyond theirs. No one witnessed the tremble in my fingers or the redness of my ears; any external manifestation of my nervous disposition was not observed.

"Your feet were shifting." Leroy Cox was a liar and he couldn't possibly have observed such a detail as minor as shifting feet but here he was, walking alongside myself as we made our way to the practice kitchens.

"Ah, now you're making things up." I said, opting for a tactical subject change. "I'm just surprised I got away with speaking like that to you and by extension the rest of the... well, those of higher ranks since technically you'd all agreed to be sorted according to your draws. I... you're not offended, are you...?"

He snorted, going for my forehead. "You realize that saved our asses."

"It's a feasible plan of eighty-five percent working probability.

Everything else would depend on the strategies of the other schools and how the guests respond to having a hundred and fifty food options," I told him, speeding up a little to catch up with Chen who was leading the way. The other schools were filing out of their assigned lecture theatres and heading to the practice kitchens as well. "We could discuss this further when we're at your station."

Participants were given five minutes to move from left wing to Roth Hall where the allocated kitchens and stations were before spending a maximum of sixty minutes refining their recipes. Fortunately for Leroy, the top thirteen students of each school were given individual practice kitchens for focus and privacy.

"Leroy?"

Sweet bubbles of joy were the hallmark of Maple's voice and I'd heard him calling for my companion several feet to our left—him, emerging from the lecture theatre and us, following the crowd up to the second floor. Leroy's selective hearing was a problem.

"Your student buddy." I pointed out. Maple had made his way over amidst the chaos of moving humans before greeting Leroy with the most excitable hug I've ever seen.

Si Yin, who had been speaking to Rosi right behind us, walked into an extinguished flame that seemed just about frozen from the top of his head to the very ends of his toes. After recovering from the impact, she and Rosi shared an all-too-dramatic gasp. Needless to say, I'd paused and registered this rare and miraculous occurrence before being seized by an uncontrollable fit of laughter. This, I'd done my best to suppress.

Leroy was the palest I'd ever seen him without a sign of life in his eyes and seemingly *terrified* while my display of amusement had him snapping out of his frozen state and sending an indecent finger my way.

"Can you not, like, block the entire hallway or something?" Birchwood had been some several feet behind Si Yin having received a bouquet of flowers from her supporters who'd returned to school despite it being their winter break to see her live performance. She overtook the bunch of us stopping in the middle of the hallway before seemingly doing a double take at Maple's very enthusiastic form of greeting.

Her eyes were nearly exactly as I remembered them to be on our first day of school. 'What are you doing here?' 'Who *are* you?' 'What are you *doing*?' Maple on the other hand, seemed to recognize her at once. Apparently, he was one of her fourteen-thousand followers on Instagram.

I was therefore put in a very awkward position of unfortunately being in the middle of Leroy and Birchwood, both of whom were somewhat involved in a budding conversation led by Maple. Thankfully, having read *Social Conventions for Dummies* by L.O. Red back when I was attending a private high school, I was sensitive enough to fall back alongside Si Yin and Rosi, allowing Maple to take my place.

Leroy had glanced over his shoulder nearly at once to shoot me a rather amusing glare, all whilst Maple continued to hold onto the idiot's upper arm within his reach. The two girls beside me were making wild gestures at Maple's back which I'd found mildly confusing. This lasted for some three minutes until the latter arrived at the line production kitchen on the first floor of Roth Hall where he'd been placed and waved goodbye. Si Yin and Rosi were assigned to stations in kitchen nine on the second floor while Birchwood had disappeared down a hallway of private kitchens and Leroy, in the opposite direction.

"I know he reminds you of Chip but—"

"Well, he's clearly taken a liking to you." I followed him into kitchen suite B, producing a tiny notepad I'd filled with ideas during the discussion prior. "I've never seen anyone greet hostile fires with a hug. It's a good thing."

Leroy had his head tilted slightly away from our conversation, biting his lip with a slight frown that seemed unsure if it was amused or skeptical. "Not sure if I can be as calm as you are now if you were on the receiving end of that hug."

I blinked. "You mean if Maple greeted me with one?" He had his hands braced against the countertop, staring down at a basket of basic ingredients and picking up the pencil on top of a notepad placed beside it.

"Anyone, really," he said shortly with a sigh. "I feel like you're giving him a whole lot of leeway because of the resemblance."

Crossing the room to where he was, I held my hand out for the pencil and wasted no time getting him started on drafting out a list of ingredients according to the menu we'd discussed back in the lecture theatre. "If what you're trying to do here is assess my capacity for jealousy, I'd very much prefer if you'd said that from the very start. I am capable of it. Admittedly, I've never had to experience the green smog since, well, this is my first romantic relationship and, academically, I'd long figured out that envy was no rational emotion to be feeling since, with hard work, I'd eventually be able to attain whatever it is someone else has. Now that we are dating, I flinch at the thought of anyone else having your full attention. O-or perhaps even just a slither of it."

I'd nearly finished the list whilst rambling away and, glancing up to observe his reaction, felt him lean uncomfortably low—resting his head on my left shoulder. I reached up to give it a pat.

"Maple is adorable, and I see why and how he can be attractive to certain people. Naturally, I'd be afraid if you eventually took a liking to him. And would I somehow be able to prevent that possible future? If you end up falling out of love for me and liking someone else instead, is there anything I can do but accept that you have? Well the answer is no. Hanging on to someone who clearly doesn't love you isn't the solution to anything and hurts both parties in a romantic relationship. That doesn't mean I stop loving you, by the way. One can never tell that sort of thing. The only remaining option would, speaking from probability, be to trust you and by extension, your love for me wholeheartedly, without question. I may very well end up getting hurt. But that will be my private concern if it so happens. I hope it doesn't. Happen. I'd spent the second half of my childhood concluding that I'd spend the rest of my life very much alone. Which I *could* do. Very much. But do I *want* to?

"Well... no. No, I don't. Given a choice, I would very much to spend the rest of my life *not* alone. Spend it with you, ideally."

I'd completed the list and highlighted several points about the tableware and how the station should be displayed from prep to collection area and had been thoroughly distracted by my doing so till I finally registered the exact meaning of the words I'd said, aloud, and and and promptly spiraled i-into another fit of embarrassment. Clearly, there was something severely wrong with my brain today.

"I did not just say all that." I turned to him in a whisper of dismay, to which he, jaw angled towards my neck, laughed into it.

"So... when's the wedding?"

"... judging from the sheer lack of attention you are paying to the task at hand, I'd say several days after your funeral, since Chef Marseille would murder you for messing up a perfect opportunity to bulldoze the school ahead in points. Ah, and the several-day interval just to ensure you don't somehow return from the dead."

After some awfully embarrassing shared laughter followed by the usual indecent finger and signature smirk tugging at the corners of his lips, we finally returned to running through the list that Leroy had to be submitting to the organizers so that they'd be able to prepare the ingredients beforehand.

"Charcoal stove?" He stopped at the last of the cookware I'd listed on the notepad and I nodded, particularly electrified by the idea of having it in a buffet.

"Yes. The white, Japanese kind. Made out of clay. Squarish. Grilling the *chashu* over charcoal on the spot will not only add an inviting fragrance to your dish, it will also do brilliantly at attracting guests to your station."

Leroy nodded, penning something down in his chicken scrawl before straightening up and frowning at the words. "Yeah, nothing's going to beat that intensity. The natural oils of it done *aburi* style. But the smell. I'd be drowning out the rest of the room."

I blinked. "Ah, you're afraid of overpowering their senses with just your dish... true." Giving it a second thought, that would indeed be a great concern considering the fact that this was ultimately not an individual tournament. "Well. Rationally speaking, it's a dilemma of choosing one's means to the very same end. Should we be thinking on behalf of the school as a team or simply place our hopes on one person who may very well be able to provide such a big point gap that would be able to decide the winner in the very first round? Both are means to the end that is victory. I would even go as far to say that other schools might not hesitate to execute an overpowering dish."

He nodded once, yet again scribbling something on his notepad while I left the final decision up to him.

"Alright I've spent enough time with you. I'm going to check on Si Yin."

The idiot had the gall to hold me back by the waist. A-absolutely unforgivable. Caught off-guard, I'd fallen backwards and into his arms, perfectly immobile.

"You?" He asked, gaze lowered. "What are you making?"

"Oh. Are you, um, perhaps offering some advice? Well... it's panko-crusted shrimp with chive aioli. Simple, really."

He gave that a thought, getting straight to envisioning the dish. "The plating?"

"Just a dollop of aioli at the bottom of the shot glass and a knotted bamboo toothpick through the shrimp, balanced on top of the opening."

He nodded. "Make sure your pan's nice and hot before the shrimp goes in or it's going to have an uneven cook." I struggled to straighten up with his arms around my waist, taking notes in the most uncomfortable position but doing so in a professionally efficient manner. Having Leroy around made one an expert at filtering out unnecessary distractions. "Don't crowd the pan. Rest the shrimp on some kitchen towels once they're done so that the oil doesn't end up dripping onto the aioli in the shot glass below it."

Nodding away and keeping my attention fixed on registering and understanding the logic behind the information, I hadn't noticed my companion closing in from behind so when I finally looked and and and *did*, I was naturally reduced to a flustered mess.

"It is broad daylight." "So?" "We are in school." "Your point?"

"Illegal activities are forbidden, you moron," I had to lay out with a heat on my ears and he laughed, leaning in. I factored in his relatively pleasant behavior for the past week and the fact that he hadn't been very demanding about physical intimacy and decided upon a fleeting butterfly kiss on his cheek. "That is the most you're getting." I told him, lowering myself back to the ground after the tiptoe.

The flame in his eyes softened to a bud before growing into something that w-was just, simply *bad*. "You call that a reward?"

He had a hand wandering its way down my spine all the way to my lower back and clearly, I wasn't in the proper state of mind to be thinking rational thoughts save throwing out random words from my mental dictionary when all of a sudden, the door swung open to reveal an initially animated Chen.

Red as cooked shrimp, I slumped to the floor and curled up into a ball.

I heard the school's number one sigh in the most disappointing manner. "Cox, I told you. Not in front of my fucking salad."

X

VIOLET

It was twenty minutes to open doors and naturally, I'd had my strawberry mousse in white chocolate shot glasses all laid out, perfectly arranged to the exact millimeter before deciding to run to the bathroom to give my hair and make-up one last fix, since, well, I had some time. On my way out of the function hall, I saw glasses boy several stations down with his panko-crusted shrimp. The shot glasses he'd chosen weren't too shabby but that's literally it—I could see him fumble with the induction cooker and gingerly flip the shrimp he'd butterflied terribly onto its other side and immediately, anyone could tell that he had the technical skills of a potato.

I came back from the bathroom, expecting his station to be all good to go but he was still frying up his shrimp so I went over, grabbed a sample, examined the color on the shrimp and tasted it with the aioli. He panicked slightly but the shrimp was already in my mouth.

Right off the bat I could taste the parsley and red pepper flakes he'd combined with the panko crumbs that were crunchier after frying in the pan, coating a good, seasoned shrimp that had a mild sweetness which might have been a thin brushing of honey or something, I couldn't tell. The chive aioli was the creamy citrus he needed to be cutting through anything sinfully fried and the textures, altogether, were actually...

"Not bad," I snorted. He seemed relieved. Shoulders relaxing. "You plate like a garbage boy though."

Startled, he picked up one of the shot glasses in front of him and held it to the light, as though that would give him the answer to what plating like a garbage boy meant. I told him to set it down because he was making himself look stupid. "You're taking too long to clean your plate. And it's because the opening of the shot glass is small so the aioli you spooned inside is all over the place and needs some cleaning up so *think*. Use a piping bag. And the tail ends of your shrimp aren't facing the same way. If you're making it face the end of the toothpick, then the rest of it should be the same. Standardize it." I referred to the rest of his samples laid out on the table.

"A piping bag... that's a brilliant idea," he was smiling and there was something about the way his lips were perfectly curled that honestly didn't sit well with me 'cuz, like, who smiles like they're at some PR event twenty-four-seven? It's like he's practiced it in front of the mirror a thousand times and honestly, I wouldn't even be surprised if he did that at some point. "Thank you. I've been struggling with the dollop of aioli, so. I really appreciate that piece of advi—"

"Okay bye I'm busy."

I returned to my station because I wasn't going to spend the last fifteen minutes having a conversation with a nerd when I could so obviously be Instagramming the white chocolate shot glasses I'd made in, like, less than thirty minutes with a blast freezer. Just in case you're uninformed, Instagram *is* advertising. That is a hundred-percent free. Whether it's a story or a post, as long as the picture is stunning and people were looking at it, they were going to come.

Though I can't be sure the invited guests were familiar with the dessert or pastry scene that I was established in but even if they weren't, as long as I could get them to take pictures and maybe use a custom tag...

"Hey. Birchwood."

I looked up from the screen of my phone. Jael. "What."

"Did you see L'Assiette's pink Himalayan salt block? And that grana Padano cheese wheel." He held up his camera, scrolling through the photos at lightning speed. I couldn't even tell what he was talking about. "Where'd they even get that at such a short notice?"

I scoffed. "A cheese wheel? Wow, they must be stupid. Cheese and carbs at a buffet. What, is it a cream sauce pasta in a ramekin or something? Are they actually trying? People aren't going to come back once they'd made their rounds of a hundred-and-fifty other dishes. It's too filling."

"Haha, yeah, uh," he stopped scrolling through the photos on his camera to give me a look. "The thing is, they're up front. First one through the door."

I paused. "Wow. *Wow*, fuck them."

"They have a pretty good strat, if you ask me. Most of their dishes are showy. Some huge setup that'll attract the guests—all that flambe, the chocolate fountain, grilled filet mignon on the salt block... and it's all pretty filling. Like they aren't giving the guests a chance to try anything else after they had theirs."

"People make better decisions at buffets," I chose to believe. Giving my immediate surroundings a scan, I realized it wasn't hard to differentiate between the stations manned by CSS and LV students. The European cuisines with a lot of classy showmanship screamed LV while CSS had some sort of global... international theme going on.

"Geographically diverse, I guess? I don't know," Jael said after I pointed this out to him. "It's not a bad strat. I saw, like, three different types of grills on the right. Kebab. Plancha. Satay. And like a huge Chinese wok or something. I mean it's how their courses are organized too. Culinary majors choose a cuisine to specialize in and I heard it's pretty widespread. Okay, gotta run. Ten minutes to door."

I dismissed him with a wave, going back to crafting my Instagram post, editing the photos, choosing the selfie to go with it, and then the filters. Honestly though, I was having a hard time concentrating because, like, ten seconds after Jael left to prep for the open doors, the station beside me had its owner ringing his call bell *non-stop* before some member of the organizing team finally arrived.

At the same time, a serve counter dressed formally in black came over to my station. I told him to stand a little further behind so that he wouldn't end up getting in my way. Since I was one of the few contestants utilizing edible serve ware, I was given a manual counter instead of an electronic device that weighed the empty dishes to keep track of our score. He caught the attention of the guy from the station beside mine.

"Hey, the air conditioning is really weak. Half of us are dying," I heard him say and honestly, I wasn't getting where he was coming from. The air conditioning in the function hall was fine. "Could you turn it up a little? Like, the air flow or something?"

"Sorry but we can't do that. We're dealing with food here and turning up the blast is just going to rapidly chill everything out of a pan."

"Yeah so what about the desserts? You're just going to let people have lukewarm cream or stale pudding?"

My serve counter looked at him like he was a three-year-old. "Dessert stations are equipped with cooling—"

"So if you're at some five-star hotel, dining at a buffet, you're expecting the guests to walk around sweating their pants off?"

I was looking at him like he was crazy; I mean, he was, to be equating this to 'sweating someone's pants off' because I sure as hell felt fine but apparently, the entitled L'Assiette boy had some of his pals in their stations down the row backing him up and I had to stand there, listen to all that bullshit before watching that member of the organizing team give in and leave to consult the rest of the team about lowering the temperature of the room and turning up the air flow.

This was all before I saw the guy beside me bring both his trays of samples to some other dude way across the hall and... and *swap dishes* and then place martini glasses of shrimp cocktail, which belonged to the other guy) on his station while several other people started... doing the same thing! The people around who were not in on this or, like myself, did not get the memo that swapping out stations was allowed, were looking a hundred-percent confused.

I glanced at the clock. Five minutes to opening. Then returned my gaze to the station beside me and lo and behold, he was nearly done swapping stations—transferring more than half of his equipment and samples to the other table while the other guy took his place behind the counter. Exactly how far back they'd had this planned, I did not know.

Then, I was freaking out because this was practically sabotage and being downright unfair to those with stupid-ass stations at the far back like Cox and then with the stupid air-conditioning thing... oh my god that guy got a spot right under the vent. It's *perfect* for his lobster salad on cucumber appetizer things and I'd be lying if I said I was anything short of enraged by the fact that someone stupid had just one-upped me even though he technically wasn't on dessert.

The rest of the hall was up in a buzz and several people were rushing around, speaking to the organizers once they got wind of the swapping stations (Chen being one of them) and I was just standing there in the middle of the chaos minutes before bubbling with rage.

Looking around, there were several unfortunate souls on hot

food prep whose stations were directly under the now freezing air conditioning vents and White was one of them. I wasted no time in heading over and telling glasses boy to pack his things.

"I want this station."

He was freezing, hands rubbing the sides of his upper arms whilst looking mildly disturbed by the fact that his pan was so *obviously* rapidly losing heat and nearly had his entire hand right on the surface of the metal.

"Sorry, what?"

I clicked my tongue, leaning in and hissing under my breath so that we were out of earshot. "Don't you get why your pan's taking so long to heat up? At this rate, all you're going to get is an uneven cook on that stupid shrimp of yours and it's all because of that silly—"

"Yes, I've realized the sudden drop in temperature and the fact that the air conditioning vent right above me somehow feels like it's a part of some snow storm but there's barely three minutes till the guests come running in and none of us had any idea about swapping stations being accepted which also brings me to the fact that I *don't* have a choice but to—"

"So hurry up, you moron," I nearly strangled him right there and then. "I don't have much, so the swapping is going to easy. Turn off the induction cooker and take your trays. Two at a time."

He stared at me like I'd gone insane and for a while seemed unable to process the entire situation when he finally snapped to his senses and mumbled something like 'you're on dessert' to which I responded with an exasperated 'duh' and shoved his trays of shot glasses into his arms and took the remaining two.

Before we could leave and head straight for my station however, this... this weird person who had been all over Leroy Cox in the hallway earlier today appeared beside us and offered to help in this singsong voice that did not sit very well with me.

"No thanks, we're fine." I told him but White was a whole other story and *thanked* the guy who then picked up his portable induction cookers, wires and all, and tailed us to my station. Then, after transferring his stuff over to mine, did the same to my white chocolate shot glasses, the coolers, and my prep box.

"I really appreciate the help, Maple. It's really kind of you."

The pink-haired person beamed and said some stuff in return which I didn't really get but they were both really chummy and I, again, wanted to strangle White because obviously, this other guy wasn't from our school and that meant that he was *competition*.

"Why are you letting him help you?" I hissed when the other guy was out of earshot and all glasses boy does is look at me with that stupid calm face of his.

"Well, Miss Birchwood, as far as I can tell, I require the assistance."

"You're going to *owe* him, you idiot," I couldn't believe I had to lay it out for him word for word. "That's the last thing you should be doing at a tournament like this! I thought you had a brain. Where did it go?"

"Well... when the time comes, I shall be gracious and return the favor as well." He sounded like he was some philosopher in some ethical text I was never going to read.

"Oh my god, fine, whatever. I'm going."

"Thank you, by the way." Again, that god-awful, calm smile of his. "I suppose... I owe *you* one as well." Then I was starting to feel hot-headed and red, so I fled the scene and put my game face on for the next two hours of hell.

* * *

Apparently, the weather outside wasn't in its warmest state because the guests filtering into the function hall were warming their hands with the hot towels some facilitators were handing out and thanks to the turned-up air-conditioning, had no eyes on anything cold.

Myself, along with twenty other contestants stationed up front were left completely ignored save the one or two children who couldn't resist the temptation of white chocolate. My manual plate counter guy standing several feet away was as still as a statue and by god, was this embarrassing. I'd checked the weather app on my phone five minutes into the buffet and blanched at the snowflake symbols all over before wishing I'd done this earlier on and made a hot dessert instead.

In any case, Lee's plan to get the guests started on hot food instead of cold appetizers was working and people were flocking to things like chicken pot pie, soup shots and Cox's... ramen.

I've seen him done cuisines that were definitely *not* under his belt, but this honestly takes the cake. As a budding chef or culinary student, Cox had never crossed my mind as experimental or in any way revolutionary but his dish during the tag team content sort of said it all. He's been improving; just when instructors were handing him full marks on every one of his technique demonstrations and giving him credit for the flawless precision of his every move in the kitchen, he knew that sticking to familiar recipes wasn't going to cut it. Which is pretty hot. But also isn't an excuse to ignore or brush me aside, which means I'd have to stick it in his face eventually.

Either way, I don't know where he got the idea of Japanese cuisine or a spoonful of ramen, but bless his plating skills and the charred fragrance wafting from his station because, as much as I wouldn't like to admit it, he deserved that long line of guests.

His draw was number four I think, the Asian soup spoon, which I and many others would've tried to avoid but he'd made the correct choice of picking a sleek, matte black Japanese soup spoon that looked sort of like a ladle with how deep and sturdy it was and had a flat back that enabled the spoon to stand whilst holding up a generous portion of perfect-ratio ingredients on the inside.

Obviously, I hadn't had a taste of it but one could tell, right off the bat from the plating and all, that he'd created and served up what one would call the perfect spoon. I'd been to Japan a couple of times but only for PR events, so ramen wasn't exactly what I had over there and I was pretty sure they tasted drastically different depending on the prefecture but still, I was equipped with basic knowledge about the dish.

He'd gone for a fusion. *Spicy Yuzu Ramen* was what he'd listed down on the official floor map with every station's name and dish. On every spoon was a portion of traditional *temomi* noodles that were bouncier with a better chew than the thinner *gokuboso*, sitting atop a golden-red, smooth spicy broth, topped with salted seaweed and crisp, fresh greens that I couldn't quite identify but were definitely the texture he was going to need to cut through the rich, flame-charred slice of rich *chashu* pork.

The fragrance of the broth he had simmering atop the induction cooker and individual pork slices sizzling in their natural oils atop the grill he requested drew nearly every guest as soon as they'd made it past the door. It travelled far and was honestly so overpowering that he was nearly drowning out every other station around him. Kind of... unfair.

A couple who'd apparently stayed at his station for five portions had stopped by mine (finally) after a walk around and were talking about his ramen. In front of my white chocolate shot glasses filled with fresh strawberry mousse.

"I think it's really clever, reducing the portion of what's originally a main dish into a portion that... we'd usually get from an appetizer?

Because we're used to ramen being a huge bowl, right. So we'd auto-matically feel like having another spoon right after the first."

"Half the crowd's there to look at the boy's face up close, Mandy."

"You're so salty about it but you ended up having more spoons than me. Wonder what he'll look like five years down the road. He should just quit culinary school and become a model or something."

"That's a waste. He should be in the kitchen for the rest of his life with the skills he has. Yuzu in ramen broth... it's crazy how it works. Acidity cutting through all that heat and richness. The noodles were like... authentic, but different at the same time."

"... I can't tell if you're complimenting him or just dying *not* to see him on the front cover of magazines."

Obviously, I wasn't feeling very happy about guests talking about someone else's dish at *my* station when they were eating *my* dessert and so clearly enjoying it so I prompted them to speak about how it was while they were reaching for a second serving and they had the gall to give a generic 'it's good' and 'nice job' respectively before going back to talking about some girl from our school who made *Croustades Noix de St Jacques* aka Croustades with poached scallops in them. Wait. Wasn't that the girl who's always around White with the pixie cut?

Losing to a sophomore, fine. Losing to a first-year on the same team? Tragic and stupid, but I'll live. Losing to a straight-out competitor though?

"The guys we were talking to before coming in kept going on about this *laksa* station when I was getting drinks for the two of us. It's some... Peranakan cuisine or something. Never heard of it."

Oh my god, they were talking about noodle soup. *Again.* All because of the weather, spicy noodle soups were a hot pick and without an exact pinpoint target of frustration, I was the most unhappy Violet Birchwood I could ever be. When I die, I'm fucking... coming after the weather god or something. I bet their ugly hater asses that desserts weren't their thing.

Either way, I was pretty sure we didn't have anything close to Peranakan cuisine on our list of dishes, so naturally, this *laksa* thing had to be coming from CSS or LV. CSS, by the sound of it, since L'Assiette was a little too pretentious to be on Southeast Asian Cuisine because ha, they probably think everything European is superior and that's why they don't have any culinary classes on food from the rest of the world anyway, so.

I mean, most of their dishes made stars out of caviar, foie gras, wagyu, lobsters, bluefin tuna and the like. It's not a stupid idea because that's what people like at a buffet—to get their money's worth. Realistically speaking, they weren't going to fill their food capacity with cucumber appetizers or strawberries dipped in chocolate fondue. A single teaspoon of the kind of A grade caviar L'Assiette was serving would've cost at least twenty bucks. Two portions would've made their trip here worth the time. I wasn't sure if they actually paid for the meal though.

Overall, it wasn't easy trying to gauge how well everyone else was doing because the contestants who lost out initially to hot foods picked up near the end and I'd say this sort of happened across the board. Like, yeah, the chocolate fondue from L'Assiette caught some attention with the kids but the teen girls with *phones*, I mean, I was expecting this, but they were all over the dark-white chocolate marbled shot glasses that I made after the first batch ran out and the strawberry mousse gave the entire table a cute, pastel look which was exactly what most girls on Instagram at that age were going for.

My counter was at three-hundred-and-seventy-two five minutes before closing and shot up to more than four-hundred by the time everyone was out of the door because, clever me, the shot glasses were not returnable serve ware and the guests could take as many as they wanted on their way out.

"Students, I need you all to *remain* at your—no you're not going anywhere while I'm talking can't you hold your pee for a minute? Remain at your stations and start cleaning them up. Leave your left-over samples on a tray by the side and depending on how efficiently you guys clean up, we can consider giving you some time to try each other's dishes while the scores are being collated. Okay that's it. Five minutes bathroom break and girls, there's one down the hallway to your right and another to your left and one more upstairs near the library."

I didn't exactly need to go so I started packing up the coolers and washing out the moulds. I made the mistake of glancing over at White to check on his leftovers because we ended up making eye contact and he'd raised a hand in greeting which I was obviously not going to return because no one's ever going to catch me being all chummy with a nerd anyway, so.

"How was it?" Jael came over and I told him, immediately, not to take any photos of me (not looking my best after any tournament). "Okay, okay. Chill. You did well near the end."

"Of course. What else were you expecting?" I scoffed. "Who do you think is going?"

"Mostly cold food. That poor guy with the fruit salad... double digits. Not even fifty, I reckon."

"Know anything about the panko-crusted shrimp?" I asked on a side note. He seemed surprised I was interested in a dish other than my own.

"White? Uh... he was okay. I feel like he went for something easy because he knows he's not going to win or anything? I mean, for some people, surviving every round is good enough."

By the time bathroom break was over and we were given permission to roam around the hall to taste everyone else's dishes, Cox's station had a massive line which I *obviously* wasn't going to join. No one was going to catch me waiting for anything and joining the queue was only going to make it look like I was jumping on the bandwagon and giving in to whatever the status quo was. So I made for the croustades.

The pixie cut girl had an expression of surprise that I thought was clearly exaggerated when I came up to her station and picked the nicest-looking croustade. They were... quite expertly made. The garlic cream sauce was rich and thick, coating the sweet poached scallop in the middle and completing the mouthfeel of everything in a single bite.

I moved away without saying a word.

Chen's grilled lobster *mentaiko* in a cone sitting snug in a dessert glass was, begrudgingly, my top favorite. Apparently, he'd saved me a sample and produced one from under the table as soon as I arrived at his station.

"You're the number one *pastry chef*, you idiot." I told him. That was before I tasted the dish, by the way.

"I know." He winked. Ugh, I hate him.

Either way, I somehow ended up in front of Cox's station because the line had been reduced to three people which was within my definition of 'waiting' so I joined it as inconspicuously as I could but by the time it was my turn to be served, his display table was empty. I looked up at him.

"You're done?"

"Yeah... we're out." Then, after glancing over my shoulder for some reason, added an apology under his breath. I turned around. White was clearing his throat aggressively whilst adjusting his glasses and looking at the floor. Oh my god what a nerd.

I turned on my heel to walk away when, out of the corner of my eye, Cox pulled a brand new, untouched *bowl* of ramen with *extra toppings* out of the oven under the countertop and slid that towards a stunned White who was now standing in the exact position I stood a few moments earlier.

"It's hot." Cox warned him with what sounded like the gentlest I'd ever heard him speak (or, like, with any emotion at all) and good fucking god I hate them both.

"You saved him an entire *bowl*??" I nearly flipped his display table. And Cox had the gall to snort like I was stating something he'd so obviously do while glasses boy was offering to share his bowl of ramen with me. Share! Something a chef had made *for* him, specifically! No one was going to accept that.

Thank god I left the station to retain my sanity because soon, they were back with the results and needless to say, I wasn't one bit nervous. Like, I wasn't going to get eliminated. And I wasn't going to be bestseller but I could settle for top ten or something anyway.

I was honestly surprised. I think everyone else was, too.

We'd won by a thin margin. Like, fourteen points thin. CSS snagged runner-up thanks to some girl by the name of Juanita Castillo whose Singaporean laksa station lost to Cox's by thirty-something points. Which wasn't a lot since third individual was some guy in L'Assiette serving caviar canapés and was behind Castillo by a hundred and two. White also made it through. Either way, *obviously*, I won bestselling dessert, which was really all that mattered apart from the fact that we were placed first in overall score.

The narrow win had Chen giving the top thirteen a horrible pep talk which wasn't Layla Tenner's style since she wouldn't have... I don't know, she just wouldn't have panicked or anything like that. She always seemed to have things under control. Chen seemed pretty new to this, on the other hand.

"I'd like you all to have a good rest tonight and uh, be ready, okay? For round two. You guys were great in leading the discussion today back in the lecture theatre. I really need your help tomorrow. With all that kind of stuff. So... yeah. Rest up and I'll see you guys tomorrow." He dismissed us soon after and I headed to the bathroom to give my make-up a quick fix since the school was hosting a small celebration party for the participants who made it through to the second round and... and then when I was making my way to kitchen nine in the main building, I heard some voices down the hallway of the first floor.

I peered down, past the banister.

"—at the lodge, maybe? Liqin brought us some apple cider from the party she was at yesterday. You could join us for as long as you want."

The pink hair stood out at once and I know, I know, I'm a fan of pastel palettes but you don't understand. There's something about it on this L'Assiette boy that just, like, did not sit well with me at all. He was clinging onto Cox's upper arm like this was an open sea and he was about to drown or something.

"I have a shift in thirty minutes."

Cox did not look very keen but if I was being honest, that was his face twenty-four-seven anyways, so. No one's good enough to tell when he's happy or sad or, whatever.

"Aw. You always work so hard!" Pink boy was literally holding onto Cox and making it hard for him to walk past the ranking board towards the main entrance. He had a bag over his shoulder and didn't exactly look like he was lying about the shift thing. "Maybe it's time you relax a little. What time does your shift end? I can come pick you up. Where is it? We could maybe... spend some time together. After that."

From the second floor, I couldn't really see the expression on Cox's face but he stopped and turned to face pink-hair and everything sort of froze.

"I'm busy. And attached."

WHAT?! Leroy Cox is dating someone who isn't me?? Well then who the fuck is—okay, calm down Vi. Calm down. It doesn't matter. He's a disrespectful moron who's only good at cooking and has above-average looks. There's tons of better fish out there and... *oh my god, what's pink-hair doing?*

"That's okay. You can be attached and... still have some fun, right?" Drawing circles on his chest. *Circles. On his chest.* He did not just say that cheating is okay. He's so not implying what I think he's implying and why isn't Cox just punching him or slapping him or something for saying something like that? L'Assiette needs to have proper moral education or at least give this boy some private lessons I mean, what's he playing at a-and and and where's everyone? I can't look at this anymore someone put a leash on pink-hair oh my god he needs to be stopped someone just—

"Not if his girlfriend just heard your entire conversation, you little brat."

XI

⟨❦⟩

LEROY

I'd dropped him a text about not attending the party and telling him that he should, instead, because more than half the ramen recipe, he'd been the one to improvise and help me with. So if anyone was celebrating anything, he'd have to be there with seventy-percent credit. Knowing him, he wasn't going to claim a thing; and the fact that he wasn't felt like a wasted opportunity for everyone to recognize his abilities and admit that he was no fluke.

He gave in. Eventually. Then asked if there was any chance we could have a late-night supper together after my shift. The plan had been to surprise him with a take-home tub of ice cream from the parlor and drop by his room without telling but now that he'd asked, turning him down wasn't really an option. The catch: he'd be doing the cooking.

So we were texting, back and forth, and I was heading out of Roth after grabbing my things from the locker room when Pierson showed up. Out of nowhere, right by my shoulder; hugging my arm like this was an open fucking sea and he wasn't a swimmer. Initially, I thought it was some ghost hand reaching out to me but it wasn't, so I looked away in disappointment and continued down the hallway. He followed.

"—tulations on your win! You never said a thing about being so talented... you must be really humble. It's so nice to see a humble chef. I've never tasted ramen so refreshing and rich at the same time!"

"Guess you haven't been to Japan, then." I was counting the number of steps to the main entrance. *Twenty-three. Twenty-four.*

"Mmhm. Not yet. Have you? It'll be so nice to have travel companions. You seem like a very nice person to travel with, too. I'm always going out alone. It gets a little lonely sometimes," he said, gazing up at me the entire walking distance while I kept my eyes on the door that was less than a couple feet away. The rightmost corner of my vision was a pink ball and for some reason, the arm he was holding onto was feeling heavier by the second.

"Oh um, by the way. I was thinking... to celebrate a great first round and you winning. Would you like to join some of us from the other schools for a party tonight? At the lodge, maybe? Liqin brought us..." *Not again.* I tuned out as soon as he said something about hosting a party at the lodge and stopped in my tracks, turning to face him.

"I have a shift in thirty minutes," I laid out, serious.

"Aw, you always work so hard! Maybe it's time you relax a little," he was telling me what to do with my life and that wasn't exactly something anyone would like to hear from strangers. "What time does your shift end? I can come pick you up. Where is it? We could maybe... spend some time together. After that."

This made things clear. Although I wasn't the kind the sort things into black and white categories—his intentions hadn't been glaringly obvious, and it wasn't like I bothered observing him more than necessary—I made up my mind there and then to get straight to it.

"I'm busy. And attached."

Done. That was his signal to back off. I was about to turn back around and make my escape while he busied himself with shock or whatever emotion I was expecting him to feel when all of a sudden, he did my expectations a one-eighty and if anything, tightened his grip on my arm. With his other hand that was free, I was made into some art project of his. What in the fuck was I looking at?

"That's okay. You can be attached and... still have some fun, right?"

I backed up, struggling with rising flames and stamping them out before they were beyond my control. To be sure, I was holding Pierson at arm's length just in case he decided to get any closer. All he did was laugh sickly sweet and I thought he was out of his fucking mind to talk about cheating like it was the weather. Look, I don't want to—

"Not if his girlfriend just heard your entire conversation, you little brat."

In the span of just five seconds, I was experiencing three levels of *what in the fuck am I looking at* stemming from the general combination of Pierson mentally, Pierson physically, Birchwood descending the right side of the double stairs behind us, and whatever she just said out loud.

"O-oh. Violet? Um, I didn't mean to... so, um. We were just... talking about the party tonight."

Her face was table-salt white and unlike her usual irate self, had some other emotion written all over her face that looked pretty much like regret. I wanted out. You'd think a high-functioning introvert would know how. Not me. This level of social interaction should've been left to professionals.

"Yeah? Yeah you, you really think I'd *actually* buy that? Oh my god how stupid do you think people are? Your hands were—they were all over Co... Leroy, my boyfriend."

Hold my fucking chicken what in the holy fuck was I looking at?

I stared at her like she was mad and caught the brief tightening of her jaw followed by an instance of the usual glare she preferred to give. Which meant she hadn't completely lost it.

Pierson was trying to save himself. "Oh no, that was... w-well I stumbled and he was—"

"No you didn't!" Her jaw dropped and while I sure didn't know what to make of all this, I couldn't exactly deny the amusement either. "I saw the whole thing so you can stop your act, like, right now honestly. Show's over, okay? Go away. Shoo." She waved a hand downwards in short bursts, challenging Pierson to what seemed like a staring contest.

He gave her the auto-win, somewhat anxiously apologizing before leaving in the direction he came from—back down the hallway. I made for the main entrance.

"Hello?" *Just let me get to my shift already.* "I just saved your ass! You can't just leave, at least thank me or something you moron."

"Yeah?" I glanced over my shoulder. "I didn't ask for your help."

She followed me out the door. "That doesn't... you can't *ignore* my act of kindness, Leroy Cox oh my god why are you always ignoring people? You're a rude, ungrateful brat and I should never have thought of... god, why did I even... I don't even know how those words came out of my mouth! I saw the whole thing and my thoughts were just—they were running around and and I was supposed to be thinking and I didn't even realize I'd said those words until the two of your turned and oh my god I must have been mental."

I was crossing the plaza, past the fountain and down the steps to where the winery was at the bottom of the hill. A quick time check confirmed that I wasn't going to make it for the train I'd been planning to take so taking the bus was next in line on my option list. The bus stop was a little past the winery.

"I was just trying to save your ass, okay? The boyfriend thing doesn't matter. Pink-hair's not going to bother you if he thinks I'm your girlfriend. He knows the influence I hold over the school and is, like, one of my fourteen thousand followers so he's aware of my social media presence. He wouldn't dare."

I checked the bus app on my phone and saw that my ride was only going to arrive ten minutes later. Still better than the fifteen minutes for the train plus a little downtime since I was going to miss the other one before but the station's some ten minutes away too so I might end up missing another train. *Great.*

"So... not that I'm curious or anything. But since you owe me, I'd like a name. No questions. Just the name of whoever it is you're dating. Does Keith Tang know about this, by the way? Chief editor of the school press, magazine, social media thing?"

Torn between slowing down (standing still waiting for the bus wasn't my thing) and speeding up to put some distance between me and a voice droning on and on in my ear, I stopped to register how else I could rid of the latter only to actually start taking in what she was saying.

"Why?"

"I said no questions you moron. Were you even listening to me?"

"No."

"Oh my god Leroy Cox I swear by my chocolate tarts I'm never going to help you ever again even if Pink-hair starts rubbing himself all over you! Just tell me the name! What, don't tell me you're embarrassed or some stupid excuse like that."

Already, I could hear his ripples of a summer pool in my head saying something along the lines of 'if I knew a thing about politeness,' cute things like that. Still, we hadn't exactly had the talk just yet. The only person he'd told was Si Yin and I could see why he told her about us but he never really raised the topic about everything else and would only always go on about 'being in broad daylight' or a 'public space'. If I was going to make things clear, we needed to be on the same page and how was I going to know if we were, if we hadn't even had a proper discussion about it?

"Can't tell you. Don't have his approval."

Her reaction was immediate, but I didn't think much about it until repeating the sentence in my head and realizing that I'd sort of given it away. I mean, there was only one male companion I was so obviously—

"Wait *what*? You're dating *Chen*?!"

"Get your eyes checked."

VANILLA

The cocktail reception hosted by Chef Marseille had somehow turned into a meet-and-greet session with the guests we'd served earlier today and needless to say, Chen was the center of it all in Leroy's absence. There were several key players who did our school proud during the buffet, apart from those they'd expected it from—number one and two—Birchwood and Si Yin were among the few picked out by Chef Allan himself, our dean of culinary arts.

I, too, had intended to congratulate Birchwood in person but failed, for some reason, to spot her champagne-blonde hair amidst thirty other students joined by staff, facilitators and guests alike. When I finally saw her making her way across the room in a seemingly pleasant disposition with a wine glass of what seemed like apple juice between her fingers, I'd called out to her.

"Oh. It's you. Some people were talking about your shrimp. They're over there," she jerked a thumb over her shoulder, gaze not quite following the direction she had pointed me in. "My new fans are waiting to take a selfie with me, so. Bye."

"Hold on," I raised a hand, confused as to why she'd go out of her way to mention those people talking about my dish. "I wished to congratulate you on placing fifth. First, for desserts, of course. Naturally. The edible serve ware idea was ingenious!"

"Yeah well duh," she scoffed, a rather smug look on her face. Usually, it came with just the former, without the latter part. Someone must've put her in the best mood possible. "Are we done now?"

"Um... well technically, yes. But I see that you're in a rather pleasant mood this afternoon! Did, um, did you perhaps receive a stunning compliment from a famed or perhaps recognized guest? If so, I wouldn't be surprised."

Birchwood appeared mildly taken aback by my conversational approach to potential friendships and while I'd run at least seven simulations of probably content, this was in no way close to anything I had been anticipating. More practice was, um, therefore necessary. I made mental plans to bolster my knowledge of social interactions, perhaps by starting on the new text by L.O. Red, *The Art of Communicating in a Socially Destructive World*.

"Okay first of all," she was back to frowning and immediately I was afraid of ruining her decent mood. "What's this? Why are we talking? Why are *you* talking to me? Second of all, yes, I'm in a good mood. A sixty. What you're doing now is bringing it down to a fifty-six and I do not appreciate it. But you know what could bring it back up? I've been dying to tell someone but I can't because it's supposed to be a secret kind of thing but who cares, you practically have no one to tell, I mean, you don't have friends, so. Can you keep a secret?"

A-at once I was flustered and somewhat desperate to salvage the social mess I'd currently gotten myself into; remind me to never again attempt to start any friendship of mine with a seeming conversation because it has yet, to date, never worked out the way I'd hoped it would. What with Birchwood's act of kindness before the start of the first round—swapping stations with myself even though she knew it would've been incredibly risky had something gone wrong with the wiring of her coolers with two minutes left on the clock—I had, in me, harbored some hopes of establishing a new friendship.

I nodded quickly. "Yes. Yes of course."

"Leroy Cox is gay and *that's* why he showed no interest in me," unveiled Birchwood in a lowered voice. "It makes *perfect* sense, how he doesn't react to hair twirling or cutesy voices and short skirts. I haven't lost my game!"

Nervous, I blanked out for a good second or two before somehow forming a response. "Is that so? I mean... he's... he told you this? Personally?"

"Well he said something about having a boyfriend, so."

"Ah, so um, there wasn't a name?" I had to ensure, slightly relieved.

Birchwood rolled her eyes. "He wouldn't tell me no matter how many times I threatened him with... with threats. But who cares? I mean, point is: he's gay. Likes boys. Hooray!" Her hands did a mini dance in the air and I was careful to remind her of the apple juice.

* * *

I'd retired from the cocktail reception earlier than the others after feeling slightly drained from social interaction. Chef Marseille had come up to me in the middle of it to formally introduce Chef Allan, who only taught upper-level modules and wasn't familiar with first years like myself. She'd then very generously spoke of my apparent 'problem-solving abilities' and critical thinking, earning me a pat on the back from the dean himself. It had all felt quite surreal indeed.

So I was on my way back to the lodge for a quick shower (and to prep for the most important midnight-snack I, as terrible chef, was ever going to make) when I spotted my student buddy, Juanita Castillo, making her way back to the lodge with my other student buddy, Nia Williams.

Pleased to see that the two were getting along swimmingly, I'd waved them over and they spotted me at once, making their way across the plaza before joining me on my journey back to Cinnamon.

"Good work today. All of us made it, huh." Castillo was being far too humble with her words. I was quick to correct her understatement.

"I'm sure you more than just 'made it', Chef Castillo. Your Singaporean *laksa* was a hit among the guests! I'm surprised you didn't beat Leroy Cox from our school." This was not a lie. I'd had the privilege of tasting both and though a certain idiot had gone out of his way to save me a generous portion of ramen (and extra toppings), I had no doubt. Hers was better. "You made some stunning Sichuan dumplings the other night for everyone at the lodge, didn't you?"

"Global's her thing, y'all." Williams laughed, slapping Castillo on the back. "Or like, Asian...? Specifically, I mean."

"I have a passion for Asian cuisine, yeah. Vietnamese, Indonesian, Malaysian, Thai, Japanese, Filipino, Chinese, Korean, *Mongolian*. It's complex. Same region, but sort of like another world altogether. It's different from, like... us. Back home in the States."

"Honey, you right but you be roasting us on a stick and I'm not too sure how I be feeling about that." Williams was back at it and they both laughed before turning to me, somewhat anticipating a response.

I thought it was really nice of them to bother waiting for my opinion, having experienced such a dynamic for the first time with complete strangers. Let alone, in a group.

"Well, um. I think the food you have in the US isn't all that bad. It has some complexity, for sure. Especially down south! And Mexican food. Nothing beats a good understanding of spices and a love for local ingredients. Not everything's as one-dimensional as... as, um... goodness, I'm sorry, it appears that I'm having issues with my brain, um... I can't think of a hallmark dish that's representative of the States—hamburgers? Corndogs? Apple pie?"

"No shit sweetie, we can't either," Williams shrugged. "I mean, up North, at least. Your girl's from the city."

"But I like soul food. And you make some great hushpuppies, Nia. I saw your station had so many kids over. Oh yeah, did you make the cut for the... uh, the bonus round thing?"

"Nah. They got some others for that. What about you honey?" Williams redirected the question my way soon after, looping me back into the conversation. "Y'all go by the ranks?"

"Um, well the instructor overseeing us warned against fixing a team for the bonus round prior to the release of any additional information. So far, all we know is that a maximum of eight students per school are allowed to participate in the bonus round. At least that's what I've heard from a friend of mine," I added just in case. The last thing I wished to be doing was spreading false information.

"That's what we heard too," Castillo nodded. "Yeah maybe it's not a good thing to decide right off the bat... though I think they've got my name down already. Um... by the way. About your friend," she averted her gaze, awkward and stiff all of a sudden. "Is he the guy we saw on the porch the other time? With pink-hair boy."

I blinked—mildly taken aback. "Well um... yes, that is... I am familiar with him. Sorry I hadn't made this clear back then... I'd assumed it wouldn't matter very much."

"Aw hell no sweetie, don't apologize," Williams exchanged a look with Castillo before turning to me with an apologetic smile. "We been wondering about you all over dinner that night. Next time, hold me back, okay? Your girl's an insensitive bitch. Sometimes."

"You looked upset after seeing your friend with the other guy, but we didn't want to point it out just in case it wasn't related, but then I saw him serving you a bowl of his ramen and I told Nia," Castillo explained, a guilty look in her eyes. "So you guys were friends. Sorry I laughed back then..."

Immensely caught off guard by their kindness and lovely disposition, I felt a tight bitterness at the back of my throat threatening to surface. "No... no, you don't have to... it's not something to feel bad about," I tried to say, falling flat and instead ending up in a miserable, choked-up state. "I never knew I was one to wear emotions on my sleeve. I'm sorry I made you guys uncomfortable... Leroy's... well, we're dating. And I've never quite dated anyone. Though I understand how jealousy could very well be detrimental to any relationship, so... so I kept that to myself. And I trust him. Maple's... well, I don't know him very well. And I'm sure he's lovely but Leroy has his heart in the right place."

Castillo and Williams were the sweetest listeners, hanging out in the dining area while I'd prepped the ingredients for a nice platter of Thai lemongrass fried chicken—a sinful midnight delicacy for a certain idiot—and provided their very own versions of relationship advice that was both thoroughly amusing and insightful at the same time. Apparently, providing concrete answers to potential and existing issues was no fool-proof solution for Williams, but felt necessary to Castillo herself. Hugging someone else was a huge no-no for Castillo, but not for Williams.

Most importantly, neither of them acted strange or overly curious when Leroy finally appeared at the doorstep of our lodge, and had politely left the kitchen to ourselves once he was inside. Needless to say, I was quietly grateful. The next mental note I had made was to properly introduce them to Si Yin one day, and then the rest was quite difficult to remember since, well, you know how Leroy is with me a-and... well, me.

"The stringy bits," he'd noticed as soon as I'd served him at the table. The rest of the lodge had retired to their rooms. "You fried them? The lemongrass."

"Simply combined them with the pieces of chicken thigh and added to that a coriander garlic paste—there wasn't a pestle and mortar so I made do with a Ziplock bag and a rolling pin—and then tossed them into the deep fryer with some kaffir lime leaves," I'd said then, rather quickly. "How... um, how was your day?"

He'd looked up, after picking the juiciest-looking piece of fried chicken and holding it between his fingers. "Normal, I guess. Nothing much happened at work... was looking forward to this," he said, referring to the lemongrass chicken with a single glance. "You okay?"

"Oh," I'd filled the seat across, having expected him to say something about speaking to Birchwood. Leroy had his attention split between me and the piece of chicken he'd popped into this mouth whole. "Um... I wanted to tell you that I'd... told my student buddies about our... about us. They were very nice about it."

"The lemongrass... gives a nice texture. The crunch. And the flavor," he'd reached for another and I was at once given the impression that I had chosen the wrong time to be speaking about serious matters, but then he turned his attention back to the conversation. "You okay if I tell other people about us too?"

The rest of the night, too, had unfolded rather slow and calm. Leroy had made the choice of not making this a grave subject—agreeing or disagreeing in casual, ordinary tones that made it seem as though we were exchanging toothbrushing techniques but the effect of it was oddly miraculous. Instead of having a serious discussion over the dinner table after supper, we were aggressively kicking his bar of soap wrapped in plastic through the gap under the frosted glass that separated our bath stalls. This act had been appropriately accompanied by a conversation about making our relationship semi-public. That is, should someone ask, we would gladly provide an honest answer.

"Mind you, I wouldn't want you to be *provoking* others into asking the question. And do be sure to clarify their understanding of your sexual orientation... unless it doesn't matter to you." "Leroy-motherfucking-Cox is gay." "Calm down, we're in a common space." "Gay for Vanilla Julian White." "Good god, you're such an idiot." "Idiots are attracted to geniuses." "I'm trying to return the soap bar and you're just—you really want to play this game?" "I like embarrassing you." "Well, I don't like to be embarrassed." "I like that you don't like to be embarrassed." "I am not fond of where this is going. We're not going to have a war of double negatives in the shower, Leroy." "I'd war you." "There are at least three grammatical mistakes in that statement, and I shan't speak to you unless you somehow identify them and correct yourself." "You're speaking to me." "W-we're not speaking!"

The general consensus over a series of light-hearted, casual conversations was that we were oddly accepting of anything that either of us were personally comfortable with. As long as the other had made the decision of telling someone else, it was within both our zones of comfort to do so.

Before retiring to Leroy's bed while he stayed up listening to Chen and Layla Tenner exchanging feedback and an apparent blow-by-blow account of today's events, I'd come to the conclusion that I was, indeed, a very serious human being. *Uptight* was the word most people would have used and perhaps having a certain idiot around had its own merits that I'd so foolishly missed.

Nevertheless, I was careful not to be further influenced by said idiot's idiocy and double, triple-checked our ties before wearing my own and helping my sleepy companion with his. At present, the two of us were making our way down to the plaza for further instructions regarding the bonus round to be held first thing in the morning.

"You're wearing the wrong tie."

I'd glanced at my companion's, refusing to check my own at give away the multi-level insecurities I'd accumulated thanks to our previous escapade of swapped ties. Red. So, according to probability, which has never once failed my deductive abilities, I was wearing the correct—

"I have two ties."

Immediately, I was buying into his awful teasing and glanced down at my own, only to see that he'd done that just to annoy me and was at once sending a glare his way. Thankfully, Si Yin had arrived just in time to save me from the depths of the hellish flames he embodied and we parted ways, him heading down to the front where the 'C's were and me joining one of the rows at the back with my best friend.

"Is it me, or are you guys just wearing the correct tie? That's a huge problem," she snickered, and I nudged her in the side. She continued to laugh. "Oh and uh, remember how I told you about the uh the thing where I do incredibly well on individual segments when I'm *not* on my meds? Like, the—"

"The hyperfocus."

"—Kuroko no Basket 'zone' stuff, yeah hyperfocus, but 'zone' sounds cooler so I'm using that. Anyway... so uh... Birchwood came up to me after the party yesterday which, yeah, shocking, I know, and so she came up to me and was like 'Leroy Cox is GAY' and I was like 'Okay BEAUTIFUL' and she thought I called *her* beautiful...? Wait, is it okay that she's going around telling people that sort of thing? Should I be doing something about that? Not that being gay is bad but humans, you know. And, uh, is Leroy gay? I don't know, just because he fancies you doesn't mean he's gay but okay so back to Birchwood. She started going crazy and stammering and stuff so I thought *I'd* gone mad and then I started panicking too because that beautiful thing was *not* what I meant and then I somehow jumped ship—you know how I'm like when I panic—and started changing the topic and I ended up telling her about the not eating my meds thing and now she knows! Oh my god..."

I listened closely before placing both hands on both sides of Si Yin's shoulders in an attempt to calm her down. "And there is... nothing wrong with that, correct? Unless you're referring to the fact that she knows about your ADHD but that, too, isn't a problem, is it? There's nothing wrong with having ADHD."

"Yeah but what if she tells the captains when it's team picking time because round two is team picking time and no one's going to pick me if, you know... if I'm me."

I had proper reason and evidence to be disagreeing with Si Yin but most importantly, explained to her how her situation was not going to affect her placing in the competition. "You did amazing yesterday and no one's going to ignore concrete numbers. They loved your croustades! I've had guests talking about them in front of my station. Yes, the second round's going to feature teams, but I assure you... you will be picked for your talent."

We both paused, and in the middle of our silence, heard the sharp, unwelcome feedback of the open-air sound system. She finally smiled, seemingly relieved (for the moment) and I made a mental note to keep a lookout for related matters, especially during the second segment.

"Thanks, Einstein."

I returned her smile but soon registered the title and cleared my throat to correct her. "That is not a title I can live up to, unfortunately."

She squared her shoulders. "It's not a title. Just your half of the ship name."

I was about to ask her what the definition of 'ship name' was since, well, I'd always been an eager party in growing my mental dictionary when we were interrupted by Chef Allan's voice over the sound system. At once, all attention was drawn to the front of the stage, where they had a list of instructions similar to how they were presented in the previous round projected onto the screen.

Ingredient Identification
Type: Bonus

Style: Roulette
Participants: 8 x 3 = 24
Teams: 2 of 12
Scoring: Point per ingredient correctly identified

The explanation we'd received soon afterwards was unfortunately disorganized and overall confusing even for a meticulous, instruction-loving person like myself. The term 'roulette' had me thinking it would have something to do with a game of chance but according to Chef Allan's verbal explanation, was a turn-taking *Russian Roulette*, in which each team would have their members taking turns to identify the ingredients on the table according to the randomly-generated number.

"Each school is only allowed to send eight participants. Altogether, that's twenty-four which we will then split into red and blue team with an equal mix of all three schools. This is to enhance and assess your abilities to work as a team. Yesterday's opponents are today's..."

I caught several heads turning in the middle of Chef Allan's instructions and, well, naturally glanced over my shoulder to catch a glimpse of whatever it was at the back of the plaza. Nothing, however, seemed quite out of the ordinary, and so I returned my gaze back to the stage up front only to see more eyes on me.

"V. J. White?" A senior standing directly in front of me had asked.

I blinked. "Yes. That I am."

"—cooperate and thus assess each participant's ability to work with others and ultimately assign a private individual score that will be added to their team performance score. The participant with the highest score will provide their school with a huge advantage in this afternoon's..."

"They're calling for you to go up front." He jerked a thumb over his shoulder and I paused, turning to Si Yin to check if I'd heard him right and she very apparently gestured in the general direction of the stage as well.

"We might be playing a game of broken telephone here," I pointed out, trying to keep my attention equally split between the instructions and everything else happening around me.

"Get Vee White guy to the front!" "First-year Vee Jay White? Someone's looking for you." "Vay Je Wyatt?"

The sheer number of people getting my name wrong on purpose was not a matter of comfort and I, thoroughly embarrassed, was given no other choice but to quietly slip out of line and weave my way up front to avoid turned heads and stares. By the time I'd made my way past the 'C' and 'B' rows, I spotted what seemed like a non-alphabetical row at the very front of our school's third of the plaza. Chen did not just pick me to be one of the eight school representatives.

A familiar face appeared to be waving me over, whom I quickly identified as Leroy's senior from equestrian, Lee Jungwoo. Chen was standing beside him, apparently re-ordering the people up front according to whatever it was he deemed appropriate. He snapped his fingers in my direction upon spotting me from afar before pointing to his left. I made my way there.

"Missed me?"

I did not need to turn my head to identify the owner of an illegally attractive voice with the hint of a disarming smirk on his lips.

"We were barely apart for ten minutes. Of course not."

"Felt like an hour."

I was about to provide him a proper explanation of what seconds, minutes and hours were when Chen came by doing a headcount and stopped short between me and Leroy. He frowned. "Where's your friend? The Chinese girl."

"Si Yin?" I blinked. "She's... at the back. Did you call for her too?" I felt my spirits lift at the thought of someone else recognizing her abilities, but Chen seemed fairly impatient, what with Chef Allan's instructions coming to an end and teams about to be called on stage.

"Guess you can't even rely on teenagers to pass on a simple message. What's her row?" "X."

I watched him grab someone nearby and then after whispering something in his ear, propel him in the direction of the last row. Turning to the idiot beside me, I was surprised to see him so calm and casual about being picked for the deadly Russian Roulette. My first instinct was to assume that he had all his attention focused on Chef Allan's instructions but with his eyes insisting on following my every move, I could confirm that I was wrong.

"—reminded that participants demonstrating poor teamwork or attempting to cheat by giving the opposing team a deliberate advantage for the strategic purposes of the school they are representing, may be disqualified."

"Nervous?"

I met his sideway glance with a huff. "Naturally. This isn't on the same level as the cross-year we were in. Plus, having to work with complete strangers sounds especially daunting."

"Raul and the rest were strangers to you."

"They were *your* peers. Handpicked by you," I pointed out the obvious. "Of course I was sufficiently foolish enough to place my complete trust in your judgement."

He laughed, giving my forehead the usual and then nodding at something over my shoulder. I followed his gaze. Chen and Si Yin were apparently squabbling their way over to the front row in their native tongue, the former seemingly impatient, and the latter appearing thoroughly bewildered.

I couldn't understand what exactly it was they were going on about but her timely arrival was somehow also the cue for all participants to gather on stage for the sorting of teams. There was applause and cheers and Chef Palmer wildly gesturing for us to get ourselves on stage and Chef Marsielle snapping at Leroy to fix his tie (which I did) and then it was all eight of us, along with eight others from L'Assiette and eight from CSS up on stage, facing a sea of cheers coming from their respective schools.

From our point of vantage, I'd expected to see the judges for the second round lined up before us and had been anticipating guest judge Chef Yamazaki's radiant smile only to be disappointed by the three primary judges. Well, not that they weren't great people but... just relatively unfriendly. As most of the culinary world seemed to be.

"You're red. You're blue. You, red. Blue." Before the applause died down, Chef Allan had taken the liberty of getting started on the sorting, speaking through the mic as he did. He was going down the row, tapping each student on their shoulder whilst announcing the color of their team and in mere seconds, the rest of us were instantly aware of a single fact: that the people to our immediate left and right were not going to be on the same team.

Needless to say, I had resisted the immense urge to meet the flame of a candle for a grand total of three seconds before giving in—turning to him with an uncontrollable smile that he, too, seemed to wear. Only... well, only *bad* and *provocative* and borderline ban- and censorship-worthy. Almost at once, I knew what he was thinking.

"A stunning opportunity to reveal the list of things I have in mind for you to correct, starting with the unruly state of your room."

He raised a brow, holding my gaze sideways. "You think I'd let you win?"

"There's no 'letting' in ingredient identification, Leroy. I know what I'm doing."

"I have a list of my own for you."

"Well, let's hear it. It might be your only chance at mentioning it, even."

"Think I'd actually get arrested if I said the stuff I wanted you to do out loud."

Processing that gave me a headache and understanding it escalated things into an awful migraine that had me wondering how the authorities were allowing such outrage to walk the earth without being reported. I hid half my face with a hand.

The twenty-four of us were at once brought into what they called a 'waiting room', next door to the very same examination hall they had conducted my fifty-six-ingredient taste test in. I recognized the hallway as soon as we were making our way down to the very end in silence, led by a facilitator and Chef Marseille bringing up the rear. The embarrassing memories I had of misidentifying a banana species was enough to send shivers down my spine. I found myself no longer standing alongside Leroy and Si Yin, who had, by the power of fortune and authority, been placed in the red team while I and Chen, along with two other familiar faces, were placed in blue.

"Red will take the right half of the room and blue, the left," said the facilitator, reading out a chunk of text on her clipboard. "Each of you will be miked up before going into the room. Your performance as a team player will be assessed through your words and behavior during the ten-minute discussion. After which, you will all be proceeding into the examination hall. There should be no verbal or gestural exchanges between members of different teams."

I was among the first few to be miked up and made to test the volume of my voice. Each person took less than a minute to be done with the entire process and we soon gathered in teams—red and blue—on our respective sides of the room, awfully silent now that we were hyper-aware of someone else being able to listen in on our every word.

They called for our ten-minute time and started the clock as soon as the last participant entered the room, leaving the twelve of us on blue team staring at each other with blank looks on our faces.

"Let's start with introductions. Name, grade, course. How about that?" Chen was no different from his usual demeanor but with our leadership and teamwork abilities being assessed, I could sense an air of false confidence in his voice that, as much as I did not wish for to happen, could be picked up by the rest of blue team at once.

"Great idea. Then we could pick a leader and work from there," added an apparent senior from CSS. He, too, seemed rather keen on expressing his capabilities. "It'll also be good to know what everyone else is good at so that in the case we're asked to identify unfamiliar ingredients, we know who to go for feedback."

We went in a circle for self-introductions before jumping straight into making guesses at how we would be made to identify the ingredients.

"It's got to be taste. They'd blindfold us or something and who-ever guesses first gets the point?" "Or they'd put it in a dish. And then ask us to list every ingredient inside it." "They could also make it harder by eliminating taste and doing it purely according to touch." "I don't think it's going to be that complicated..." "Let's stick to the basics. We've got someone good with seafood. Yes, Mika, right? And then we have someone great with the cut of red meat—"

We had five people talking over one another, trying to establish a seeming confidence and attempt at bringing the team together to whoever was listening in and already, I could tell this was not going to work out. I'd kept my opinions to myself throughout the discussion since adding on would've only made the conversation extremely unhealthy. I was the only first-year on the team and telling everyone that too many cooks spoil the broth was not going to end very well.

"Times up. Can I get both teams lining up in a single file?"

This was the state in which we were made to enter the examination hall with an entire gallery filled with non-participating students watching us with their noses pressed up against the glass. The air was similar to my first time in the room. A long, empty table was set up in the middle of the floor and behind it, the primary judges.

My gaze drifted, on instinct, towards the person it always seemed to rest on, only to see that he was, already, looking my way. The candle in his eyes gave nothing away as our teams were told to stand in a row, facing each other down the empty space in front of the empty table.

"You will be taking turns to identify the ingredient labelled with the randomly-generated number presented on the digital screen behind me," Chef Allan began, and rest of the culinary deans stared us down as though weeding out our confidence was what they'd been told to do. "There will be no tasting. No touching. No smelling. This test is purely visual."

Almost at once, I could hear the mental shock gripping the room in its freezing skeletal fingers and our entire team exchanged a single look that did not bode very well. Somewhere from the several other entrances and exits in the examination hall, the wheeling of carts could be heard until finally, trays and baskets of ingredients, labeled one to twenty, began to fill the table. These were not everyday ingredients—they were aboriginal; Native Australian ingredients.

"There are four rounds in total. Your first challenge will be to identify these well-sourced, rare Native Australian ingredients. Can the first participant of each team step forward... we will now begin the exam."

19

The CSS girl from our team was up against a boy from our school and the panic on her face was written clear as day. None of us had expected to be identifying ingredients purely based on how they looked since, after all, the textures and taste of ingredients some-times mattered even more than their appearance. She turned over her shoulder, completely lost.

A separate screen showing a close-up of ingredient number nine-teen was presented to both the rest of the room and the gallery up-stairs.

"Dried peas." "I think it's... Garden Peas."

"It's Wattleseed," I said under my breath, and the four students, including Chen, standing in front of me turned almost at once, eyes wide.

"Unfortunately, nineteen is Wattleseed. Can we have the next two participants come forward?"

Chen was looking at me with a huge beam on his face and every-one in my immediate proximity had turned to follow his gaze. I was naïve enough not to get the message until our school's number one hissed under his breath. "What are you waiting for? What else do you know?"

And then before I could waste another precious second, I started naming all the ingredients that were large enough for me to identify from where I was standing, without the help of an additional close-up image.

2

"Two is Paperbark. Seven, Kakadu Plums. Nine, Muntries. Ten—"

In hushed tones, they told me to slow down, attempting to mem-orize them according to the numbers. On the other side of the room, the red team seemed to have notice our hushed whispers and were staring daggers down the space between us. Si Yin had on her face a wild look in her eyes, as though she was thriving on the adrenaline and loved the pressure. She'd given me a private thumbs-up from afar.

"Two is, indeed, Paperbark. Point goes to the blue team. Next!"

I wasn't the only one interested in Native Australian ingredients (albeit my interest began at the age of ten, after watching a documentary about bush tomatoes). Someone on the red team from CSS had apparently studied the ingredients as a part of their course and, um, according to their accent, was Australian. We were down half a point by the end of the first round due to a mispronounced word and before anyone could rejoice or feel the momentous relief of tension, assistants began to wheel in the next round of ingredients.

Traditional Chinese Medicinal Herbs.

Needless to say, I was no expert in this. And though Chen was Chinese, his face gave away every bit of his confusion, sealed by the private indecent finger he presented to the person behind. That's me.

Si Yin was whispering. She would be—it was likely the reason why Chen had wanted her to be on the team in the first place. Though I wasn't exactly too sure how much she knew about the ingredients on the table, she did mention about her grandmother's expertise in medicinal herbs just once.

Not to mention, Juanita Castillo, my student buddy who specialized in all things Asian, was on the red team too. Needless to say, we lost terribly during that round. Most ingredients were small too, and particularly difficult to identify from afar. This made most of us on our own, though it seemed as though red team had better luck.

Then it was an array of seafood and of course—this being something everyone was sufficiently familiar with (and also big enough for me to identify without looking at them up close) —our team emerged with six points more than red. This entire time, I had been resisting the urge to let my eyes wander and rest on a certain idiot.

And when they finally wheeled in the ingredients for the final round, I could resist no more.

"There are 7,500 known varieties of apples grown throughout the world," Chef Allan had the most brilliant smile on his face, sucking the life out of every other person in the room. "Here are thirty of them. All you need... is to send one person from each team to name as many as they can."

Admittedly, I'd once attributed the peak culinary experience of my lifetime to my travels with Uncle Al and our adventuring in every corner of the earth imaginable, tasting and understanding dishes ranging from pig's blood to pigeon hearts, deep-fried grasshoppers to century eggs. Never would I have considered the prospect of it all crumbling under the pressure of thirty baskets; baskets of whole, ripe fruit—some, the color of pale sunshine at daybreak and others, an angry crimson dusk.

Needless to say, the pulsing adrenaline at the back of my head was no illusion in the face of a challenge like no other. The temptation to start was unbearable. I couldn't quite understand the expression on everyone else's face the moment they had the baskets of apples wheeled in—quite the look of horror, which either meant that they'd mislabeled the genre of our current situation or... mislabeled the genre of our current situation.

"All you need is to send one person from each team to name as many as they can."

At once, heads were turning and the sheer number of collective smiles I'd witnessed in a single field of vision, in a grand total of five seconds, had the dual purpose of blinding *and* freezing human beings like myself.

I was about to tactfully remind them that I wasn't an all-knowing, omnipresent existence when they all but reshuffled themselves to have me stand at the very front of the group; stopping short only because the judge representing L'Assiette Vide was quick to reveal a critical catch—team leaders are given a choice to eliminate one person from the opposing team who must sit out for the *entirety* of the final round, banished to some fifty feet towards the back of the room.

"Pick wisely. Most of you at this age are fond of weeding out the weak but how well do you know the best of your enemies?"

The very first of logical instincts would have been to identify red team's leader from across the room and assess the probability of him knowing exactly who to eliminate (myself) and so already, I was scanning down the row, following the gazes of whoever it was most of them had their eyes on and in that very instant, ignoring the panic that had naturally seized my team, I met the heated gaze of a candle.

It was infuriating, how they'd done an amazing job at appointing the perfect idiot to lead and it was in situations like these that made it seem all the more incredibly obvious. Already, he was looking at me and by god, the flame was in the mood for serious play and legally speaking, it could not possibly be allowed to exist.

A single glance at the corners of his lips that were hiding the smirk of a challenge had my head shaking. I'd turned to the team with an odd inability to form any proper statement, account, sentence, *word*.

"Why are you smiling?" Our appointed captain was urgent for answers and most of them did appear as though they were hoping for my debut. I glanced at Chen, who had his jaw extremely tensed and looked quite as though this wasn't the kind of excitement he had in mind.

"He's going to pick me." I didn't see a point in lying, and everyone except our school's number one collapsed into chaos. The latter appeared genuinely surprised, glancing over at his culinary counterpart before turning back to me.

"Are you sure? He's just a schoolmate, though. Right? He can't know you're..." "He might let you off the hook. In the end, it's the winning school that matters." These certainly weren't poorly-made assumptions about any other participant that wasn't the idiot across the room but we were, quite unfortunately, talking about said idiot and of everyone else, only Chen came the closest to asking the clever questions.

"He'd do that to you?" The disbelief in his eyes was nearly amusing. "Even if this is your only chance to blow everyone away?"

Indeed, I'd run that by myself mere seconds ago, right after registering the look in Leroy's eyes but the answer was surprisingly short and simple. "Frankly speaking, this *isn't* my only chance to impress an audience. Certainly not my first and most definitely not my last. Further, I believe he's well aware of my priorities. Showing off isn't one of them. A challenge, however... is."

It was in that pause that I finally understood what exactly it was he was telling me to do, logic stemming primarily from the fact that it would've been in poor taste for a captain to pick himself as the final ace for a round as important as this one and thus severely affect his teamwork and leadership score. The only way the both of us could indulge in a sinful challenge—

"Pick him."

I had expected the double takes. "*What?*" "You sure?"

"Pick him too," I repeated, turning to the leader of our team. A senior from L'Assiette. "Unless you know someone else with a culinary background better than his. He's had an understanding of ingredient varieties since he was five or perhaps ever younger. I'm pretty sure thirty apples aren't going to be a problem for him."

"Yeah but..." he seemed hesitant. "Just because you've been a chef for long doesn't mean you know there's more than five kinds of apples in the world."

We noticed the silence that the rest of the room had fallen into and hastily returned to our former positions to avoid further conflict. Chef Allan had long covered the list of instructions he had to be giving and all three judges had paused to regain the attention the room.

"So... red team." They turned to first. "Your pick?"

No sentence; no phrase; not even a single word but the hint of a smirk on his lips, hands behind his back—likely clasped in fearless confidence—flames of a candle lit as they turned on a single target across the room. N-naturally, I was just. I. *I give up.*

"He means me."

I said to relieve the room of awful seconds, moments, centuries of silence and tension, a deliberate, intended effect he had hoped to enjoy, all whilst *knowing* I was the only one in the room who knew exactly what he'd meant by that look and and and just *criminally, illegally* using that to his advantage.

Not quite keen on wasting anyone's time, I made my way over to the far end of the room where a facilitator had marked out my position to stand and took my place.

"Ah." Chef Allan seemed momentarily stunned, turning to red team on his left for confirmation before moving on to the team on his right. "And blue?"

Mountainous embarrassed thoughts and much internal head burying later, I noticed the root cause of my concerns making his way over and resembling, for some reason, an advancing predator right out of the grand savannahs featured in National Geographic. The initial instinct had been to avert my gaze and spare myself the embarrassment inevitable blushing but I'd gathered every remaining once of courage to stand my ground, unblinking in the face of an illegal existence.

At some point in his leisure stroll before arriving at the banished square of participants, both Leroy and myself had given in to the irresistible urge—smiling to hide the uncontrollable laughter threatening to break the surface. Personally, I'd made it a point to *not* look like a fool in front of an audience. Naturally, my companion wasn't one to care very much about things like that. Neither of us said a word to the other.

11

Both teams had picked out replacements but barely a second's rest was given before the first number was drawn and the corresponding basket of apples projected on the screen for both participants and members of the audience.

The shade of rubies, dipped in a cauldron of simmering crimson blood and polished to jeweled perfection—"It's a Jonathan." "Jonathan."

I had to pause. Turning to the grand idiot standing an arm's length away with candles for eyes—still, lit with an awful intensity—I resisted a heinous smile and brushed aside the heat he practically radiated in a single glance. The flames were playful. Gaze flickering once; slightly downwards and then back up to meet mine.

Somewhere in the distance, Chef Allan's voice presented us with an awaited answer. "Unfortunately, it is neither a Fuji nor an Empire. This is a Jonathan apple."

A... a shockingly disarming smirk crossed the idiot's features and I was at once severely impaired. "One all."

It took me a moment to register that we were now very apparently counting scores and since sinful challenges were exactly what I had been expecting and Leroy had not the history of disappointing, I was quite honestly electric.

19

"Braeburn." "Well I think it's a Pacific Rose." *And it is!* I'd hummed in glee as soon as the judges removed the label to reveal the name of the apple, adding a point to the fingers behind my back.

Yes, we were counting scores with fingers by this point and though it would seem, to any passing outsider, an extreme version of insanity, I was feeling the adrenaline in the very *heels* of my feet.

10 was the shade of pale sunshine and honeyed goodness; a summer breeze weaving through cornfield shades.

"Opal," I'd named almost at once, delightfully confident. The very next second had Leroy turning to me with a look in his eyes that, in a single glance, had my mind re-wiring itself in an instant, coming to the frightening realization that I was wrong.

"Ginger Gold," he'd corrected. Eyes alit. And moments later, burning even brighter at the sound of Chef Allan giving blue team the point for identifying the Ginger Gold. Though I was glad that the team had managed to pull through with a couple of apples ahead, I had admittedly lost all sense of vocabulary at my mistake until a certain idiot had the gall to reach behind my back to increase the finger count on the hand that I used to keep his score.

He'd closed the distance to do so; an intimate gesture that had us side by side and needless to say, I was, if possible, rendered even more speechless than before. My companion's reaction to this was an after-laugh of amusement, visibly enjoying himself though admittedly, I, too, seemed to be having time of my life identifying... well, identifying apples. With him.

At present, both our teams were tied at three points to three while thrilled fingers behind our backs kept score at eight to Leroy and nine to myself.

"Twenty varieties to go," I counted, mildly upset. "Unfortunately, the difficult ones are out of the way but I suppose it was incredibly exciting while it lasted." The words slipped free before I could rein them in and catching the brief look of amusement courtesy of a flickering, hungry flame, I took to correcting myself at once. "I-I mean, this is. Moderately. Entertaining. A decent challenge—activity. That, um. I'm glad you didn't... oh, that one's a Rome. I'm glad you didn't consider abandoning your team by allowing myself to play. That said, I suppose we are playing. Now, I mean. Us."

I chanced a glimpse in his direction, peering up at him. "Which is a reasonable decision. We should be playing for our teams. Not our schools."

There was something else reflected in his eyes that did not seem quite characteristic of flames. It felt like waves; or ripples in the surface of a summer lake that he was in the middle of, in a boat, resisting the tempting invitation to skim his fingers across the waters. "Leroy?"

He seemed awfully serious. At least until English decided to give him away.

"I'm playing for you."

I struggled to comprehend the thickness of an idiot's skin and the sheer lack of proper sentence structure or meaning in his every word. "Y—that is, I don't... the grammar...? Clearly, you don't... ah, and it *is* a Rome. I'm at ten now. You best be catching up soon. Oh, and that one's a Cortland apple."

"Snap Dragon." He leaned in to whisper, as though this was a fatal mistake and he was somehow obliged to correct me, his currently blanked out, apple-red opponent, without letting the rest of the world know. Unfortunately, the heat on my cheeks intensified as soon as the answer was made clear.

"Cortland's... darker," he had the gall to run a finger u-under my earlobe as as as though it was an apple and he was observing it! "On the underside."

My hands had instinctively reached for the lavalier microphone attached to my collar, covering up the near-gasp I'd let slip in surprise. Needless to say, I had to take a step away from him after shivering at the sudden physical contact, sending a chilling glare in his direction as a firm warning. "Leroy Jeremy Cox. I... I do not appreciate the intimacy—the physical contact you are so willingly engaging in the middle of a very serious competition!"

"So..." He frowned in grave consideration, reaching over while I was distracted to raise his finger count behind my back. "*After* the competition? At yours?"

Immediately, I was lunging at the mic attached to *his* collar instead of mine, accidentally drawing the unwarranted attention of several onlookers in the gallery above. It was upon noticing this that I removed myself and resumed an arm's length's distance from the world's greatest idiot.

Said idiot had the audacity to be amused. "Was that a hug? Are we going public now?"

"No! No, you idiot," I hid my face in utter embarrassment. "I was reaching for your mic! Do you not realize that each and every one of our words are being transmitted to a facilitator transcribing everything for the judges to assess a-a-and possibly, a live broadcast? You're being highly inappropriate and I'd find myself in a hospital if I were listening to such... such criminal..."

I was halfway through reciting a compiled version of illegal activities listed under his name when all of a sudden, Leroy Cox (professional criminal, vocabulary terrorist, fire-starter, provoker, player of snow) had in him the nerve to pick up his mic and bring it closer to his lips before whispering, slowly, all whilst holding my gaze in an undisguised challenge: "Vanilla Julian White has the sexiest—"

* * *

Chen was perhaps the fourth person who had openly came up to me with a genuine disappointment regarding my individual score for the bonus round, which was, unsurprisingly, a mere point higher than Leroy who had placed *last*.

"Yes indeed. There is absolutely no explanation for our poor performance except that Leroy and I are a grave disappointment to the school. I s i m p l y cannot imagine how terrible the facilitators transcribing our words must have felt about our *awful* behavior." I'd made clear to the idiot seated across me at lunch, sending quite the murderous glare his way, only to receive an infuriatingly attractive wink in return. "W-well... at least Si Yin placed second with the red team's overall victory and that is worth some celebration."

I turned to the starving girl seated to my left on the very floor of the examination hall, where all twenty-four students who had participated in the bonus round were gathered and handed pre-ordered lunch packs. Most of us had sought the relative comfort of familiar faces; which meant that sitting in groups of eight, according to our schools, became the unspoken rule as soon as lunch was announced.

"I got lucky." Si Yin waved my compliment aside, stabbing her fork into a chunk of sweet and sour pork. "They don't tell you how you're graded, right? I mean. All I did was talk to people."

"Okay but L'Assiette landed the top individual scorer anyway, so." Chen was unusually uptight, dismissing optimistic remarks before stressing the bottom line he had been intending to put across. "The bonus goes to them."

"Why are you so worried?" Lee Jungwoo, seated across Chen and visibly proud of his team's victory, voiced an apparent distaste for our overall captain's increasing edge. "The bonus is only applicable to round two and the info isn't even out yet till after lunch. Could be some lame-ass extra time, for all we know. Oh hey, isn't that Birchwood?"

The first-year pastry chef had several additional lunch packs stacked atop one another in her arms and was making her way around the room asking if anyone else was up for seconds. She soon arrived at where we were seated, and instead of offering the last couple of lunch packs to everyone, pulled up a chair between Si Yin and Lee before casually inviting herself to lunch. The rest of us remained seated on the floor.

"Aren't you guys supposed to be having lunch at the commons?" Another senior by the name of Jean Mercier posed, staring up at Birchwood.

"I can have my lunch wherever I like. And you," she snapped my way, eyes ablaze. "What is with that stupid score? Are you *actually* trying to lower my expectations for you?"

I'd flashed her an apologetic smile and was about to admit that lowering her expectations of me would've been a superb long-term solution to avoiding disappointment when Chen came to my defense.

"I mean, he was rattling every answer aloud even when it wasn't his turn and they could obviously hear him, so they would've known he was correct eighty-percent of the time... but I guess that doesn't really count unless you perform exactly the same way when it's your turn to identify, so. According to the rules, we're graded by initiative and teamwork. They... probably think you're a bad leader or something."

Never in a million years would I find myself foolish enough to reveal the true reasoning behind my apparently shocking performance; and though Chen wasn't entirely wrong about my non-existent leadership skills and poor team spirit, that wouldn't have accounted for Leroy's ghastly score either since, well, since he wasn't as incompetent in that field of knowledge as myself.

The nine of us were nurturing private conversations to the side of the room, not particularly inviting anything out of the ordinary when several students from across the hall, having emptied their lunch packs, decided to leave by taking the oddly longer route to the side entrance several feet behind us. While one of the leading members—whom I could identify as the winning participant of the bonus round from L'Assiette—was distracted by a conversation of apparent humorous quality among themselves, he'd walked into Si Yin's shoulder and nearly caused her to drop her fork. By some miracle, I'd managed to catch it in mid-air before handing it back to her.

All nine of us had turned at once to glare but the student himself had not appeared to notice, strolling past the side entrance before anyone could call out to him and disappearing down the stairs with his group of friends.

"I'm *actually* concerned?" Birchwood scoffed, eyes following his back. "Like if someone's calves were so fat they couldn't help but shove into a seated person's shoulder, I mean... there's space? Everywhere else?"

This cascaded into a group conversation about general L'Assiette behavior and while Birchwood was thoroughly invested in the gossip (providing multiple accounts of her own), Leroy seemed surprisingly interested himself. He'd kept his eyes on her throughout the entire subject, which Birchwood appeared to notice and moments after describing several familiar characteristics of someone with pink hair, she re-directed her attention to Si Yin and asked if she was okay.

Needless to say, there was only one pink-haired person I was acquainted with and they'd coincidentally matched the physical description Miss Birchwood had so kindly provided us with. I was instantly reminded of Williams and what she'd heard of Maple, though she hadn't really spoken much about him ever since she found out about Leroy and myself. In fact, Birchwood seemed as though she had been on the verge of revealing some scandalous information... which unfortunately left me quite anxious.

The lot of us had re-joined with the rest of the remaining school participants after lunch to attend the briefing for round two of the W-interschool. This, unfortunately, was held once again on plaza grounds whilst wind speeds were at a grand twenty kilometers per hour. Thanks to the sixty eliminated in the previous round, there was overall less body heat going around and we were left to huddle in the square before the makeshift stage, where Chef Yamazaki himself ended up shivering into the mic.

"H-hello students. It is very cold and I am not enjoying this very much so h-how about we cooperate and make this quick? I am Yamazaki Shin. Your guest judge for round two. Elimination style. I mean, elimination... maybe you can just read the slides." My godfather's ex-student directed our attention to the instructions projected on the screen, which, too, wobbled in the wind.

Community Service New Year's Party
Type: Elimination
Style: Team
Participants: 30 x 3 = 90
Scoring: Point per rating (out of ten), Judge's grading

Without a doubt, we were all very excited about having culinary legend Chef Yamazaki as a guest judge. He was also apparently in the midst of shooting a TV series under a well-known production company keen on documenting the various aspects of his life, which meant that there were cameras left right center and, well, generally all around us.

Yet, what truly rattled the nerves and sent waves of chatter cruising among us participants were the three food baskets displayed on a table at the side of the stage, which seemed to have everything to do with our guests for the evening.

"So, each school will be organizing a belated, uh... new year's buffet dinner at either an elderly home, an orphanage, or a homeless shelter with your primary ideas stemming from key ingredients we've prepared for you in these three food baskets," managed Chef

Yamazaki without chattering teeth. "New year's is an important occasion across all cultures and yes, we celebrate it with our friends
and families but sometimes we take it all for granted, not knowing
or forgetting that... well, that there are people who do not have the
luxury of going to parties or... buying nice food and drinks, or even
spending it with the people they love."

Angels like my godfather would have been extremely moved by
the collaborative attempt of our schools at spreading kindness with
culinary warmth and love but immediately, I was narrowing in on
strategy. Organizing a new year's party for a specific profile we were
assigned to would explain the rationale behind the contents of the
food baskets; healthy and soft foods followed by hearty carbohy-
drates, and finally some... multi-colored... extremely vibrant-look-
ing basket containing packaging that were suspiciously similar to
the kind of food I'd disliked as a child.

"Can we have the top-scoring participant of the bonus round up
on stage please?" A facilitator said into the microphone and at the
same time, nodded at the school representatives waiting at the sides
to take their places in the center. Turns out, instead of drawing lots
to decide our guests for the night, the top-scoring participant not
only had first pick but also the choice to assign a basket to each of
the remaining two schools.

I was not surprised by the basket they went for at once; the one
that catered to the homeless shelter, filled with delightful, hearty ingredients for complex dishes that could both showcase their technical abilities and impress their guests without a doubt. As for the
rest of the participants having a hard time deciding if L'Assiette had
given us or CSS the better hell of the two, the answer was never
clear-cut.

Up on stage, Chen was staring down at the rainbow-colored basket he'd received whilst turning increasing pale thanks to the cold
or, well, the panic. He was looking for his team of consultants (and

by that, I mean everyone on the ranking board) as soon as he got off stage and Chef Allan took our guest judge's place to announce the timing of our bus arrivals. Each team had their buffet held at a different location that was about a fifteen-minute drive apart from one another.

"Alright we've got less than thirty minutes to come up with a menu," stressed our school's number one with a piece of chalk in his hands, ushering all thirty of us into an empty classroom as he spoke. "The ingredients in the basket are listed on the board and we need to somehow incorporate all of it. Adding extra stuff not in the list is apparently okay but only according to stock availability.

"We need two proteins, two mains, two veg-incorporated sides and two desserts as baseline for judging. Everything else is up to us." Chen had someone lay out the contents of our basket on the instructor's table for easy viewing but I was beginning to realize just how awfully out of my comfort zone I was at present.

Among the twenty-or-so ingredients, I could barely name *four*—and only because they were asparagus, Swiss brown mushrooms, cream cheese and pre-packaged buttercream frosting. The frosting had nearly slipped under my radar if not for the obvious bubble letters splayed across the packaging but everything else? Good heavens was I stunned to realize the existence of something by the name of *marshmallow fluff*. The red-capped, transparent jar with only one word on its label to describe itself (F-L-U-F-F) had been staring me straight in the face from the entrance to my seat and needless to say, I was rendered utterly speechless.

"... I agree. Mains should be done finger food style so that it's easy for the kids to pick up and go without a mess. So what do we have? Tacos. Fish tacos. Uh... yeah you. Pizza. Okay... I mean, kids like that but remember, we're working with a kitchen we don't know much about. I'm not sure if pizza's the right choice and it might be a little on the boring side."

Ideas were coming in left right center and nearly everyone had something to pitch. I'd turned to Si Yin seated beside me. "This is it. This is my elimination. I have absolutely no idea what children like to eat."

"Okay but you think you're alone?" She whispered in return, sliding a thumb across her neck. "Because you're not. At least you have god brothers and sisters. I have a *dog*. And Sebastian. And now that I think about it, I don't even know if Sebastian *eats* because I've never seen him do it."

At once, I was running through distant memories in an attempt to recall Miki's all-time favorite and Rory's go-to comfort food but all that surfaced was Chip's strawberry shortcake which did not exactly match the occasion or the menu. Interestingly, I never once thought of consulting distant memories of *myself* when I was a child because really, was I ever keen on adopting the diet of an ordinary five-year-old?

Well, no.

"Do pizza pockets with a waffle iron," Leroy was standing before the blackboard, alongside his fellow peers up on the ladder. He'd given the ingredients in the basket a brief scan before instantly coming up with something. "Panko-crusted for the fish in the tacos so you cheat them into thinking it's not all veg. Then fried chicken three ways for the protein. Thigh chunks so they don't have to deal with bones."

Needless to say, he was... exceling. And though I had, myself, never been familiar with his personal tastes as a child, I had been certain of his exceptional culinary skills and knowledge, adopted from his father at a young age. The possibility of his personal tastes and skills being entirely different or belonging to a completely separate culinary realm had never really crossed my mind and now that I'd thought of it, Leroy had never once made something overly fancy for me or himself. When he was in a private space.

I spent most of the discussion listening in and avoiding the prying gaze of Chen, who'd more often than so looked to me for an opinion which I was unfortunately not versed enough in the subject to provide. Even Birchwood herself had raised several suggestions about a chocolate fountain only to be rejected by number one after deeming most of it 'too unhealthy' for extra points since they would not be able to balance out the heavy richness of the fried and salty mains.

"You okay?"

I'd set my eyes on an empty double seat on the bus after Rosi had waved Si Yin to join her at the back when a certain idiot decided to slide in after myself, casually handing me a bottle of mineral water after drinking from it.

"Aren't you going to sit up front?" I'd posed to him, quietly happy regardless. "I did the triple checking of the ingredients before they were loaded onto the truck but I'm sure Chen would like to run the list by you before showtime."

"They're kids," he turned to me with an after-laugh on his lips. "We have it easy."

"Well I guess we know who's taking care of the children ten years down the road," I put forth lightly, not quite expecting him to respond with an expression of surprise. "I-I mean. This isn't... that was not a... I meant hypothetically and figuratively. I'm glad you were more of a child than I ever was. Not that I never thought of you as a child, back then. You were, but. Of course, that's with you being different from all the kids I've ever met."

He reached over as the bus turned out of its lot and started down the hill towards the front gate of the school, brushing the side of my cheek. "They'll like you." He said. "I mean, I did."

XII

VANILLA

If the question was whether I'd somehow considered an alternate, parallel universe in which Uncle Al had never decided to take me in and become my legal guardian, the answer would be no. There were better things to be thinking about. And while I do, indeed, subscribe to the astronomical theory of the multiverse, there simply wasn't any practical use in entertaining a different story I could have lived.

Pulling up outside the orphanage did nothing to jolt the memories I'd long discarded. Realistically speaking, no two-year-old was going to remember the exact details of the kind of infant lives they used to lead and the apparent week I'd spent at a baby adoption center before Uncle Al returned from the other side of the world to cradle me in his arms was... well, quite forgettable.

"So the head welfare officer wants to remind us about the no-swearing rule and that conversation topics should steer clear of anything regarding past or ex-families. Remember—be nice. Smile like you're at Disneyland, and uh... yeah." Lee Jungwoo raised a thumbs-up to conclude before disappearing down the front exit of the bus.

Most of us had decided to alight from the back instead, where boxes of craft and equipment were stacked atop one another and required our assistance to transport. Half of it was filled with vibrant origami paper, ice cream sticks and rolls of felt, materials that were to be used during the hour's-worth of activity time while the party was being set up.

"Hello everyone. It's so nice to see you all and so kind of you to be thinking about our children despite your busy schedules," a bespectacled, dark-skinned woman greeted us as we gathered in a semi-circle around the front gate of the facility. "I'm Tiana, welfare officer here at Sunbeam. The kids call me Mrs. Tea, which I do like, so I hope you have something tea-flavored on your menu today." In mere sentences, she had managed to lift the dual nerves of meeting new people and competing in a foreign environment, all whilst putting smiles on our faces at the same time.

"We'll start with a quick tour of the orphanage—just the dorm, the living space, where we have our pre-school classes and activities, then we'll show you guys the kitchen so that we can get started on the party."

After leaving the boxes of materials with a pair of friendly teacher volunteers, we were shown around the facility and given a brief explanation of their daily schedule. The main building housed an activity center, where the younger kids of kindergarten age had their morning classes before joining after-school care with the elementary school children.

The garden was a mere vegetable patch with cherry tomato plants in their flowering stages and a small lemon tree. In contrast, the backyard was large enough to include several outdoor swing sets, an elephant slide, a sandpit, and a seesaw—apart from mismatched outdoor furniture lining the fence that were likely donated.

"What's on the other side?" Si Yin posed to Mrs. Tea while we were about to leave the playground and head through the back to the center's meal kitchen. "Behind the fence, I mean. There's like cones and stuff, so it looks like an obstacle course."

Mrs. Tea nodded. "You're not far off! There's an animal shelter next door and the kids have a weekly duty roster, taking turns to help out with small stuff like feeding and cleaning or just spending time with them. It gives them a sense of purpose and helps in giving back to the community too."

What a sustainable model! I couldn't help but think, albeit certain that the main reason for having the kids help out next door had to be the healing properties of dogs and cats as company and vice versa.

"So this is it," Mrs. Tea showed the lot of us into a double station kitchen with a decent island and two additional fold-out tables in the middle for extra workspace. In total, there were six stoves. "I'll leave you guys to split into the teams you came up with and if you need any help, I'm with the kids. It's not the biggest kitchen, for sure, and I'm really sorry about that but if you need any extra tables, we can always bring them in from the classrooms. Unfortunately, one of our ceramic pots were chipped so we're left with two non-stick pans, one skillet and just one other pot..."

Chen was quick to reassure the welfare officer that we were prepared to make do and that we'd brought our own necessary equipment like crockery, tableware and coolers. As soon as we were left to our own devices, the thirty of us organized ourselves into the three separate teams we were assigned to on the bus ride here—the kitchen team led by Chen, the entertainment team led by Lee, and the set-up team by Birchwood. The facilitators keeping a close watch on us stood by with minimal intervention, only reaching out whenever a staff member of the orphanage had questions to ask.

"That kitchen's for dwarves," was all my team captain had to say, squinting past the doorway we'd come from and eventually spotting our boxes of party décor and tablecloths. "How's this fair? The elderly home CSS got has, like, three floors. Wait no don't open those you moron, I obviously haven't decided where we're setting up." The sophomore who'd reached for the opening of a box retreated at once, opting to stand aside with a guilty look on her face instead.

"Do you have something in mind?" I posed, giving our surroundings a quick survey. Judging by the corner they'd left our boxes in, the teacher volunteers had assumed we were setting up in the activity room where space was abundant. "Lee's team should be starting on the craft activities very soon. We should do as much as we can to avoid distracting the children from their tasks."

There were only five of us on set-up and whoever put me here must have been hoping that I'd make up for the lack of members but alas, that was not to be. Leroy, Si Yin, Raul and Rosi were assigned to individual items on the menu so at present, I was on my own. Technically with Miss Birchwood on something relatively behind-the-scenes which therefore meant a certain extent of relief, but still.

"Why don't you guys take the area behind that bamboo room divider thing? Mrs. Tea said they use it during nap time for the nursery and kindergarten kids," suggested Lee upon our consulting, simultaneously unpacking rolls of felt and stacks of origami paper and passing them to members of his team waiting in a line. "We're starting in five minutes so you can pull up the dividers while we're handing out the craft materials."

Birchwood had been slightly hesitant on picking up the idea but eventually started dishing out instructions on the number of tables we were using and walking us through the ideal timing and direction the children should be taking to go down the buffet line.

"So they'll start here, with the plates and utensils," she held up her hands in an imaginary table form before leading us farther down. "Separated by the centerpiece right down here, and walk down from here—main one, protein one, main two, veg one, protein two, veg two, then drinks and then dessert on a separate table..."

Immediately, I was envisioning a professional catering team meant for wedding receptions and cocktail parties at the mention of centerpieces. As surprising as it might sound, I was human enough to comprehend and therefore predict the basic behavior of most children under ten; and the one thing I knew for sure was that lining up and going down a buffet line in an orderly, polished manner was the least of child-like behavior.

"Um," I tapped Birchwood on the shoulder. "Sorry. I was just wondering... have you ever organized a birthday party for a sibling? Or perhaps a cousin or some distant relative. Commissioned to, maybe? Considering that you're highly sought after as a pastry chef," I'd added for extra measure.

"No of course not," she said rather frankly. "Children don't know how to appreciate high quality desserts. I mean, they're happy with gummy bears and boring vanilla ice cream."

I nodded, testing the waters for something along those lines. "Exactly. Well, you see. It might very well be that the children will end up skipping the line, heading straight for the desserts or, well, skipping the vegetables and then getting reprimanded by the teacher volunteers for not respecting us when, in fact, it honestly doesn't matter if they're behaving themselves or not as long as they like the food. If we set the buffet up in a line, we're establishing an unspoken rule that, well, this is first and that comes second and then this comes last and I don't think that is what children will be fond of. Should we somehow find a way to eliminate this restriction and allow them to decide freely what it is they want to eat without the adults thinking that they are being rude, that would be ideal."

Observing a grand total of four blank stares, I summed up at once: "So um the bottom line is that I'd hire you to organize my—I mean *a* wedding reception, yes, but, not, let's say, my nephew's birthday party."

Still, blank.

Desperate, I made a split-second decision to adopt a certain idiot's vocabulary. "This set-up is 'adulty' and far too polished for a children's party. It might suck."

The light in their eyes returned by some miraculous feat. "Well, why didn't you say that from the start?" Birchwood had scoffed at once, rolling her eyes. "Yeah, okay. I get it. Does anyone have other ideas then?"

I could tell from the silence that everyone else either did not wish to voice ideas of their own for fear that either one of us would pick it apart or had run out of creative straws to draw from. The bouts of laughter coming from the other side of the activity room beyond the bamboo partition were full of joy and delight. Lee and his team were working their magic.

The environment was conducive, for sure. Standing in a corner, by the window, away from the laughter and happy noise—this was the kind of environment I was wholly familiar with. What, even now, felt beyond my zone of comfort was the Everest of a sandpit; the earthquake of a swing; the avalanche of a slide; the impossibility of joining something or fitting in and only in the comfort of a see-saw was...

I chanced a glimpse out of the window, up at the sky. Clear. The view from the window we were standing next to felt oddly similar to the view from that window I'd often found myself sitting by back in Evergreen Kindergarten for Future Leaders and this, this was where I would listen to the sound.

The creak of a seesaw.

* * *

It was after consulting Mrs. Tea about setting up in the backyard that we finally settled on a circular, six-station floor plan that both utilized and factored in every surrounding outdoor dining bench and playground equipment to create the most fun and dynamic eating experience a boringly programmed mind like my own could possibly think of.

With the help of two volunteer teachers, the five of us were able to rearrange the outdoor furniture and decorate each station differently to exemplify the dish they were serving. The waffle iron pizza station would have a classic tartan tablecloth while the dessert station would be two tables combined with a thicker waterproof material draped over it and the letters 'D-E-S-S-E-R-T' stuck to the side in craft paper.

While our team captain handled most of the aesthetics and décor, she'd left the preparation and arrangement of basic serve ware up to me. I had been mildly confused; with most of the stations ready to go, the only remaining task would have been to stack and arrange the party plates. The forks and knives were perfectly fanned out in respective fancy tumblers so apart from getting the plates out from their boxes and transferring the juice dispenser to the beverage station, there wasn't much else to be doing.

"Oh my god, you are so dense," was all Birchwood had to say upon my questioning of her decision. She hadn't once looked up from her glitter glue signboard for the 'Princess Toast' dessert. "They'll come looking for you in, like, five minutes or something. Most of the food should be done by now."

"Ah, but I'm not exactly an expert in this field of..." As though on cue, Chen had emerged from the backdoor of the main building and, upon spotting the lot of us dealing with the décor, came over for a quick time check. "Twenty minutes to party. White, I need you in the kitchen as soon as possible. Taste everything—make sure it's good."

I'd given Birchwood a surprised glance to which she'd rolled her eyes and squinted as though I was a puny little speck of dust that did not even deserve the words 'I told you so.' After assuring Chen that I'd be with him in five minutes, I took to the activity room in search for the box of party plates whilst entrusting the setting up of the juice dispenser to a sophomore nutritionist.

As I was picking up the box and getting ready to leave the activity room without being noticed by the kids having fun with craftwork, I noticed a girl seated in the corner of the room with a book on her lap. There hadn't been a chair, let alone a girl seated in it, when we first left the room to set up in the backyard.

While she did seem old enough to find the arts and craft entertainment mildly boring to sit out on, the book in her lap was closed and pretty much untouched from the direction of her gaze—out past window and towards the front garden. The next thing I knew, she'd noticed my awful staring and hastily opened the book to hide her face behind it.

Needless to say, I was both embarrassed and extremely guilty for scaring her off, leaving her overly conscious about whatever she was doing and overall causing discomfort. As most would know, I hadn't the radiant, cheerful face of an angel like my godfather did and the closest inanimate thing I probably resembled was the face of an ice cube.

After arranging the party plates and ensuring that the juice dispensers were washed and working, I made my way to the kitchen for tasting at once. Needless to say, it was a fair bit chaotic in the back, as it tends to be in every production kitchen, professional or not—providing a perfect juxtaposition to the quiet outdoors.

There was, however, the fragrance of something oddly nostalgic. Just, wafting in the air and all of a sudden, coursing through my veins.

"Right, you can start with the mains," Chen had attacked me

with as soon as I was through the door, nearly shouting over the noise. "Taco's here. Pizza's there. Sides are on that table over there. Chicken. Asparagus. Potatoes. Nutjammers. I know you're a fan of perfect balance but it's kids we're serving so go light on the criticism and turn the sensitivity down a notch. They like it a little sweeter than you do, and maybe a little saltier too. Oh and make sure you taste all three flavors of the chicken, by the way. Then it's dessert but we're running late on that, yeah I know, I'm the number one pastry chef, but I'm also the one overseeing everything and I'm still not used to it."

I was about to assure him that I had nothing against a one-off occasion of poor time management when someone else pulled him aside to discuss kitchen matters that thankfully did not concern my kitchen-less self. Wary about his earlier remark on the sweet and saltiness of the food however, I pulled up an unofficial scoring rubric (dug up from past archives thanks to Keith granting me access for a 'splendid' job on the school festival article).

While it was important to cater to the tastes and preferences of our guests, we were, inevitably, going to be assessed by a judging panel of professionals. Additionally, I was highly aware and familiar with the heightened sensitivity of children's' taste buds (unfortunately, unlike others, mine did not decrease over time or maturity) and had to factor that into my tasting.

It was upon taking a single glance at the tray of perfectly crisp, fried chicken bites that I was able to identify the familiar fragrance, electric in the air and almost sizzling in my mind that could, at once, pull up the visual memory of walking into Annie's diner and the countless number of times I was led up the stairs and into his room.

I didn't need to taste it to know exactly who the chef was and by god, did that infuriate me immensely. They were done in Annie's three signature ways: southern, garlic butter and sweet soy. Fresh

out of the fryer, I had to pick them up carefully before quickly sending one of the smaller portions into my mouth; hearing the first
crunch at the back of my teeth and each subsequent bite ringing its
way to the top of my head, giving way to well-seasoned, perfectly
juicy chunks of chicken thigh infused with spices that wholly reminded me of racing on Peach Beach as fictional characters in tiny
karts.

By this point, you'd think I could no longer be surprised by the
cooking of someone I had become so helplessly intimate with and
indeed, I'd thought so myself. Yet, here I was, standing in the middle
of a bustling, noisy kitchen, recalling a childhood I had, moments
earlier, unconsciously categorized as... well, as non-existent.

I *was* a child. One whose spirits could be invariably lifted by the
scent of fried chicken and familiar company and games and having
someone else to sit with on the other end of the seesaw; I had so
foolishly put myself on a high horse, as though being childlike was
something I was never young enough to experience with an older
mind when, in fact, it had existed all along.

Trust an idiot to come waltzing by with some awfully delicious
chunks of fried chicken, topped with his signature criminal looks
and embarrassingly provocative words I could already hear in my
mind whilst tasting the rest of the chicken flavors.

It was obvious by the sound, texture and bite of the crunch that
he'd not only double dipped the chicken in buttermilk but actually
went on to double fry it for the science and secret to a perfect, crisp
exterior. Other compliments like the glazes being of perfect consistency to evenly coat the chicken but at the same time not too oily
and thick to be seeping through the crust were, well, applicable but
I wasn't going to waste any time giving him mental praise.

There was one thing I did not quite like about the sweet soy version, which most likely involved brown sugar judging by its defini-
tive caramelized flavor and consistency. While it was, indeed, clever

of him to be using brown sugar instead of the pure carbohydrate that white was and the often-healthier association of the former, I'd unfortunately found it a tad too sweet for my liking.

I did, however, remind myself about Chen's earlier warning about laying off the criticism since it wasn't as though Leroy's every dish was *meant* for my consumption, so I'd merely noted it down after concluding that it was just the right sweetness for every other six-year-old.

The asparagus were done cleverly similar to what we did over at Chip's for thanksgiving—wrapped up bacon and puff pastry strips and baked, ultimately paired with a refreshing garlic and herb veggie dip that was both healthy and sinfully delicious at the same time. Perfect for the children and a brilliant way to be hiding those vegetables.

The fish tacos were packed with heat, citrus and herbs, chock full of cilantro lime slaw, avocado, red onions and smoky, crisp, panko-baked cod bits that could have tricked any adult into thinking they were unhealthily fried.

Hm. Si Yin must have been on this one. I couldn't quite tell which others she would have been on, and the cilantro lime slaw tasted vaguely similar to that sauce she made me try the other day.

Raul's job on the waffle iron pizzas, assisted by two others, was in simple terms every child's dream breakfast, lunch and dinner in one dish. Cheesy, toasted to perfection, but also sufficiently soft and fluffy on the inside to compliment the crunch and texture of crispy bacon, peperoni, olives, mushrooms and grilled cherry tomatoes double-sealed by the cheese and the waffle press so as to prevent the fillings from falling out.

While they were, indeed, a sad violation of pizza rules, I wasn't going to further offend an Italian by, um, claiming that his waffle iron pizzas were offensive since they did taste exceptionally suitable for children and would most likely be the biggest hit among the other dishes. Those were the hardest to figure out since, well, I wasn't too sure if the judges were the conservative kind. Especially L'Assiette's culinary dean, Chef Henri Pierre.

I mean, he *was* the one who took jabs at Leroy's phad thai during the tag team contest we did during the school festival.

Moving on to dessert, I set the nutjammers made by Chen aside—perfectly fine, no comments required—and inspected the slices of watermelon and cantaloupe we were using for the interactive activity station. Initially, we hadn't a clue how the obligatory fruits were supposed to be included in the menu since, well, no typical child under the age of ten would jump on the idea of having *cantaloupe* for dessert but it was after contacting Layla Tenner as a last resort that she'd come up with allowing the kids to cookie-cut their names using alphabet shapes and slices of fruit.

All I had to do was to ensure the slices were of similar thickness. Already, including an interactive food station in a children's party buffet was ingenious and would most definitely land us a favorable spot on the 'Organization and Planning' rubric—taking pictures of the kids with their cut-out names arranged neatly on a bamboo skewer to form a pegged polaroid photo display would've made the experience much more memorable than any other catered food party they'd had in the past.

The other interactive station that stemmed from Tenner's idea was letting them have a go at making their own colorful buttercream toast. Naturally, several of us (including myself) had been thoroughly against the idea of 'Princess Toast', which was the mere spreading of pastel, multi-colored buttercream on toast and allowing the children to sprinkle as much edible glitter, chocolate rice and M&Ms on top of it as they liked. Just the thought of it sent unholy sugars coursing through my veins.

To increase the technicality of the dish and not make it seem as though the pastry chefs on the team were skiving off, I'd suggested pumpkin bread instead of the white bread they were intending to use in the first place, toasted with a hint of honey and also adding natural flavoring to the pre-made, store-bought buttercream.

The pastel shades were mostly the work of strawberry compote (pink) and blueberry jam (purple) and according to the recipe, should've been properly balanced in terms of sweetness to acidity, which shouldn't taste all too bad even if store bought buttercream was enough to make me shudder at... *good god.*

Immediately, I was searching for some water and thank goodness for the dispenser nearby or I might have had trouble swallowing.

"Chen?" I called out to him but barely made it over the noise. Most of the kitchen were rushing to get their dishes out of the door and into the backyard with about seven minutes left on the clock.

Glancing down at the bowl of pink buttercream in front of me had the effect of triggering an acid reflux but for the sake of competition, I had no choice but to taste the other bowl of purple buttercream—only to reach for a second cup of water.

There was no telling if the store-bought version had, before alterations, been sweetened to an unpalatable extent and needling out whoever was responsible for the diabetic concoction was not the solution at hand. Everyone else in the kitchen did not seem to have the time or the capacity to entertain my concerns so when Violet Birchwood walked in to demand those on dessert to speed up their process, I had instantly pulled her aside to taste the buttercream.

Needless to say, a second opinion was necessary for things like these and considering the fact that I, specifically, was not a fan of (most) junk food or candy, perhaps someone else might find the buttercream to their liking.

This was unfortunately not the case for Birchwood. Almost at once, she'd spat the thing out on a kitchen towel. "What's this shit?"

"It's far too sweet, even for children," I proposed and she looked at me as though I was stating the obvious. "Is there anything we can do to save this? There's simply too much buttercream and the color's the entire reason this Princess Toast thing might appeal to the kids."

"We're tossing this out, for sure. Like, no one's going to eat this and not go to the hospital."

"What happens if we leave out a compulsory ingredient from the basket though?"

"We're allowed to leave out three. Which we've done already," Birchwood drummed her fingers on the table. Impatient. "Oh my god think of something."

Glancing at the basket of ingredients we'd received earlier today, I noticed the jar of marshmallow fluff I hadn't known existed on earth till three hours ago. "We have five more minutes. And the main course might buy us some time—"

"Hello? Are you forgetting something? Like, you literally just told me that the kids are going to be all over the dessert table first. *That's* why I've been rushing the dessert team. Why is fruit slicing taking so long?" She glanced over my shoulder at the two juniors rapidly slicing watermelons and cantaloupes.

By this point, most of the kitchen was empty since everyone else had to be setting up outside and ensuring that the trays of food were well kept and manned by the assigned chefs. There was no one else we could immediately consult.

"What do you think of simply replacing the buttercream with marshmallow fluff? Do you think we'd have any strawberries and blueberries left for the flavoring? The color and acidity is crucial in balancing out the sweetness. We could just split the jar into three portions and that's pink, purple and white."

Already, Birchwood was demanding for mixing bowls and a double boiler. The kitchen was unfortunately empty. "If it's a compote, all I need is five minutes. Leave the balancing to me but you're out on the dessert station alone."

I nodded, wholly surprised and grateful that she hadn't thought of pushing the blame on the person who made the buttercream but had decided instead to prioritize resolving the crisis before anything else. "I'll try my best not to disappoint you."

Leaving the fixing of dessert to Birchwood, I made my way out of the kitchen through the back, running into self-proclaimed chicken professional Leroy Cox. Initially, the idea had been to report the slip-ups to Chen whilst giving him a quick summary of what I thought about the other dishes but upon, quite literally, having some sense knocked into me (how, exactly, can a human body possibly feel like a wall?), I realized that Birchwood had not factored in the absence of a blast chiller and that the compote might not even cool in time for her to add it to the fluff. Five minutes was most definitely not going to be enough.

"I need your help," I'd established in the heat of the moment, not quite yet thinking through exactly what it was I needed help with. "Um. Are you... sorry. You're probably busy with the..."

"Go on." He waited, reaching for a pair of tongs lying somewhere on a table behind me.

"We don't exactly have an appetizer, which is the only thing I can think of that would distract the kids from dessert," I tried to explain. "Something that would catch the eye of any child in a heartbeat like... potato chips. Or, something along those lines. We have to buy Birchwood some time. Could you make an appetizer? Anything that takes less than five minutes would be ideal."

The first thing he suggested off the top of his head was lotus root chips.

Needless to say, I had to first check if I'd heard him right. "You brought *lotus root* here."

His smile was criminal. "Was what I ate as a kid all the time," he said, squaring his shoulders. "Chen rejected it last minute."

Without a doubt, it was a brilliant idea. Lotus root was not only higher in mineral and overall vitamin percentage, it also averaged four percent less calories than potatoes. "And how long will you be needing?"

"How long do you think I need?"

Knowing him, the most probable estimate had to be a maximum of three to four minutes but deliberately provoking him into proving me wrong was likely to achieve the effect of speeding up his process in an attempt to, well, either rise up to the challenge or impress me. "Oh, well... maybe five—"

"Three." He saw through my words, smirking and reaching for my forehead. I let him.

"This is the only reward you're getting," I said beforehand. He responded with a grand total of two indecent fingers.

* * *

Moments before the start of the dinner party, Chen was back inside the activity room with Lee and the entertainment team for a short new year's resolution speech while the rest of us were on standby at our assigned stations.

Birchwood was in the kitchen with Rosi, trying their best to cool the strawberry and blueberry compote by rapidly stirring it in the coolers we brought along. Thankfully, Leroy had arrived just in time with three bowls of lotus root chips seconds before the children emerged from the activity room, hand in hand with several team members. To say they flocked to the potato-chip-looking appetizer like a hoard of enthused pigeons felt like an understatement, so I'd left it there and merely given the chef at his station a nod of approval. The look he gave in return was mildly illicit and so I'd turned away and resumed my minding of fruit skewers.

"They put him on fruit." *Oh. Hm.* "Yeah I mean. It's the only logical option..." *Ah. It appears that I am the subject of a casual conversation! Likely among two or three members of the entertainment team who were seeing the set up for the first time. What an achievement.* "You think Chen did it on purpose?" "How are they going to grade him if all he's done is taste the food?"

Oh, was all I could think then. Ultimately, they'd raised a valid point about the scoring system and taking into consideration the fact that this *was* an elimination round, I, too, hadn't quite an idea how the elimination would come into play. Still. I could hear them.

"I don't think Chen's like that. Anyway, what else can he put him on?" *Ah.* "Critics huh. But he can't plate too, right?" *Not wrong.* "I don't know. Fruit punch?"

Admittedly, I had been sort of prioritizing the state of us as a team rather than focusing on the individual aspect of elimination like I did in the first round. The nature of organizing a buffet party for a specific group of people was somehow different and had close to nothing to do with our individual performances as culinary learners. In fact, how was one to grade the entertainment team who'd done arts and craft with the children instead of the cooking?

Well. If this was going to be my last participating round, I suppose I might as well enjoy it. A tad bit disappointing, but I should at the very least ensure our guests a good time.

"Hey, uh." *Ah. Someone part of the conversation I'd overheard.* "Should we encourage some kids to come over to your station? Like, call them over or something?"

I'd blinked in response. Significantly surprised. "Oh! No, don't worry about that. It's part of the plan, you see. Birchwood isn't done with the Princess Toast half of the dessert station we're manning, so I told Leroy to distract them with an appetizer instead. It's working, as you can see."

"Leroy?" They seemed confused.

"Cox, I meant." Clearing my throat and inwardly accusing myself of letting my guard down, I then politely suggested they help the kids out with introducing the food instead of standing around. That way, some form of culinary knowledge, too, would be required.

This was sadly rather hypocritical of myself since, ultimately, I was left to sit alone in a tiny plastic chair, watching cling-wrapped bowls of sliced fruit and a jar of alphabet cookie cutters next to a container of bamboo skewers.

Waving to the kids did not help. Their faces scrunched up at the sight of fruit and it did not take long for them to notice a general trend of their peers avoiding the sad station. I crossed my fingers for Birchwood to be on her way or I'd be spending more lonely minutes staring at floral tablecloth.

On the other hand, a certain idiot appeared to be thriving in his natural habitat of fried chicken; entertaining an enthused line of tiny fans returning for a second or third serving of crispy, fragrant chicken chunks. The southern style was a surprising hit amongst the younger kids despite the heat it packed and as expected, no sane human being, young or not, could have settled with *one* serving.

Even with the judges, it had received countless praise and repeated orders. Minutes after the start of the dinner party, Chef Allan and Chef Yamazaki were making their rounds. They were scheduled to be starting with ours before heading to CSS's elderly home some fifteen minutes away while the other judges started first at L'Assiette's homeless shelter.

For some reason, the chefs themselves had gravitated to Leroy's station upon their arrival, much like the children themselves. Specifically, the garlic butter fried chicken.

"It was a good idea to double fry the chicken for the ones with glaze," I'd heard him note, reaching for his third chicken chunk. "The garlic butter glaze coating the crunch on the chicken doesn't compromise the crispiness of it. It's rich without being too heavy. Ah. The sweet soy isn't doing too bad either but... it's not to my liking."

Chef Yamazaki had laughed, nodding. "I know what you mean. But I remember you, from the paella stall at the school festival. The sugar in this... was intended, no?" He said, referring to the sweet soy glaze I had, myself, tasted earlier and doubted for a second.

"It's brown sugar," the chef clarified and instantly, I was having a private 'aha!' moment with myself, having guessed earlier on. "More flavour and moistness without the pure carbs. Was thinking they'd like it sweet."

The exact term was caramel sweet but, yes, taking into consideration who it was he had in mind whilst frying up the chicken, there was some justification in him going heavy-handed on the sugar. How someone so oddly magnetic to adults and children alike despite his apparent stoic exterior had something to do with a keen sense of taste—apt at identifying and reproducing food that suited one's exact preferences. Simply put: his ability to adapt.

While he did, on the surface, appear stubborn and uninterested in the tastes of people other than himself (and, um, me, I suppose), he, in actuality, possessed an aptitude for service and empathy. I on the other hand, did not. Occasional glances in Si Yin's direction also proved herself of similar species; paling at the sight of four children holding out their bare hands for another fish taco with 'extra crisp' and not quite understanding what they'd meant by that.

"Ooh alphabet cookie cutters," Chef Yamazaki noted on sight. He was, I think, my third visitor. Most kids had flocked to Birchwood's Princess Toast as soon as she'd emerged with the bowls of pastel-colored marshmallow fluff. It certainly helped that she herself looked the part and soon attracted an entire table of girls seated at her station sprinkling edible glitter over their pastel marshmallow fluff layer spread on top of a slice of honey pumpkin toast. I spent most of the time watching until one of the girls asked if she could borrow a heart-shaped cookie cutter and a slice of watermelon.

"Well, um. It's unfortunately dead simple," I conveyed to the judges before me, who were picking out slices of cantaloupe for themselves. "They pick the fruit, choose the cookie cutters to spell out their name and slide them onto the bamboo skewer. There's also a picture involved at the end of it." I held up a polaroid camera. Si Yin's.

"I mean, it's effective." Chef Yamazaki had laughed, punching out an 'S'. "And an innovative way of incorporating fruits into a children's buffet. I can't get my girl to eat her fruits unless its strawberries we have."

"O-oh. I think my uh... Chip mentioned that." I did not want to seem overly affectionate with Chef Allan still around, since, well, Chef Yamazaki was here as a judge and certainly not my godfather's ex-student. "Your daughter might be a fan of what we have next door, then. Fruit-flavored marshmallow fluff on a slice of honey pumpkin bread. Toasted. The glitter's edible, by the way."

The pair 'oohed' and proceeded to shuffle on with their slices of cantaloupe. Birchwood seemed a tad too busy with the kids to accommodate the judges, so I helped hand out a slice of freshly toasted pumpkin bread. They tore it in half and shared the piece.

"Mm! What kind of honey is that?" Chef Allan nodded. "It goes amazingly well with the pumpkin. Doesn't overpower. Are we supposed to... dip it in the..." he gestured towards the bowls of marshmallow fluff. I provided a sheepish laugh in response.

"Um. Well, you tell Miss Birchwood over there which color you'd like—or a mix, if that's what you wish—and she'll spread an even layer on your toast for you. Then, you decorate it with M&Ms or chocolate rice or... the edible glitter."

Chef Yamazaki was about to say something about the final station they were assessing when, from a distance behind us, someone called out to our school's culinary dean.

"Allan. You're still here?"

It was L'Assiette's representative. The one who had been extremely critical of Leroy's phad thai and had publicly claimed that should his dish be the standard of our school, L'Assiette would have no issue at all with this year's W-interschool. I had wholly understood where he was coming from at that point in time with the gimmicky, color-changing food but he'd said something about Michelin star restaurants and put Leroy in the worst mood imaginable that I had to call him an idiot three times before he eventually returned to his original state of indecent fingers.

"Oh. Well... yes. We still have ten more minutes," Chef Allan checked the time, appearing rather confused. "You're done with the shelter?"

"We finished pretty quickly," said the culinary dean of CSS, flashing a quick but oddly uncertain smile as she tailed Chef Henri Pierre. "Ah. This is your last station?"

"Yes. It's—"

"You call this dessert?"

Chef Pierre had taken one long look at the kids sprinkling glitter over their Princess Toast before striding over and scoffing at the bowls of marshmallow fluff. Right in front of Birchwood and the children. "Miss Birchwood. What happened to extravagance? Weeks ago, you were walking up to the table with a stunning black forest chocolate *tree*. What is this?"

At once, the pair of judges who had been harmlessly making their proper rounds according to the schedule were stunned into silence. The facilitators who'd arrived together with Chef Pierre and the culinary dean of CSS, too, appeared speechless, unable to act in an instant. I, myself, hadn't expected this level of sheer... *insensitiv-*

ity. At once, I was feeling embarrassed, outraged and bewildered by his absurd behavior.

"Firstly, this was not my idea."

Birchwood was in the middle of preparing a nice bed of marsh-mallow fluff for another girl's Princess Toast and had stood up as soon as she'd slid it in front of her guest to decorate but every child at the table was looking up at the silly culinary dean going red-faced at some toast. It was downright embarrassing, to say the least.

"I didn't come up with any of this. Second of all, I colored the marshmallow fluff with strawberry and blueberry compote—all natural—and you haven't even tasted it! Third, do you really think kids are going to like the desserts I usually do? Sorry, but I'm here to win, so... and by the way, I'm telling my dad about this... PMS of yours. Your mood swings are waaay worse than anything I've ever seen, so. Go away. We're full here. You'll have to wait till it's your turn to sprinkle some glitter."

Needless to say, I was blown away by the sheer embodiment of royalty in her very words but even then, I could not help but worry for her scores and subsequent status. While she was the daughter of our school's headmaster, I wasn't too sure if this warranted immunity from elimination since, well... that would most certainly be cause for concern. Chef Allan, a close friend of both L'Assiette's culinary dean and Birchwood's father, had sought to diffuse the situation while some kids, including boys, were already abandoning their Princess Toasts and running off to tell Mrs. Tea at the fish taco station.

"Henri. I understand where you're coming from but this isn't the right time or place to be speaking like that. You're embarrassing a student in front of her guests. Who are very, *very* young. You have to be sensitive... we're representing our schools out here."

"Allan," Chef Pierre nearly laughed. "Don't tell me you don't faint at the sight of one-dimensional, gimmicky garbage like this. Nothing about it is refined or technically challenging. You're expecting me to grade a dish anyone else can make by slapping some store-bought—"

"Sorry to interrupt, but I believe the nice student over here has made her point. She'd re-calibrated the taste of the marshmallow fluff knowing that it would be one-dimensional, adding natural flavors to it using fruit compotes, which I'm sure she is familiar with." Chef Yamazaki was a guest judge and had thus appeared unfamiliar with most of the primary judges. It was after stepping in that Chef Pierre actually registered his presence. "Not to mention, the pumpkin bread was handmade and toasted to perfection. I wouldn't say boulangerie isn't 'technically challenging'.

"Either way, if my daughter were here, I'm pretty sure she would, um, unfortunately be staying at this station throughout the entire party," he'd added light-heartedly, flashing a gentle smile. "I think... it's important to know our guests, above everything else. What I cook at home will always be different from what I cook in my restaurant."

Birchwood and I exchanged a look of relief but neither of us made a move to continue whatever it was we were doing until the judges decided to dissolve the impromptu meeting of seeming aggression held over a table of desserts and allow the kids to return.

On the bright side, most of them seemed to have noticed the commotion and had, after hearing about what had happened from their peers, decided to drop by my fruit-cutting station. It eased the two of us back into our duties and soon, I was finding myself swarmed with children digging for alphabets in their names and slicing them into watermelons and cantaloupes. Some had decided to go for just stars and hearts but that, too, was entirely fine since the fruit did end up going in their systems. Leftovers were put aside for blending purposes after clean-up.

"Hello. Do you need any help?" I said to a girl who'd come by without company, recognizing her as the one I'd seen gazing out of the window with a book on her lap earlier this afternoon. Not quite participating in the activities that the other children were enjoying together. In fact, I'd seen Mrs. Tea propel her in the direction of our interactive dessert station in what I assumed was an attempt to get her involved.

"So um. Do you prefer watermelons or cantaloupes? If you haven't had these, I guarantee they are the sweetest slices of fruit," I pushed the trays of fruit her way for some form of a reaction. After pausing, she'd pointed at the cantaloupes. *Ah! An adventurer.* Most of the kids had gone for the familiar watermelons.

After selecting a nice big slice of the pale orange fruit, I let her pick the cookie cutters. At this, she appeared visibly hesitant.

"Um," I sat beside her. Mildly anxious. "Is... is something the matter?"

"I don't like my name."

"Oh! And... well," I'd managed without sounding too surprised. Inside, I was experiencing quite the earthquake, hearing something I'd most likely said so myself when I was a lot younger. "Why not?"

"It's embarrassing."

"Brilliant!" I told her, refusing to give in despite her sour mood. "We have something in common. I assure you; no one has ever beaten me in the game of 'I have the most embarrassing name in the world.'"

Enthused, I'd proceeded to search for cookie cutters of my own and cut the treacherous word out of beautiful cantaloupe, skewering each piece as I sliced. Once finished, I'd held it up for her to see. "Imagine having this as your name! And as a male species of the human race."

Thank the gods of rolling pins—she actually laughed.

"Okay... that's totally embarrassing."

Humored by her reaction, we partook in a short conversation

about our ages (she was ten, and much older than the other kids here) and hobbies while she spelt out her name in cantaloupe. *L-O-T-U-S.*

"That's a flower!" I'd exclaimed, thoroughly offended by her prior embarrassment. "It's a beautiful name."

"No," she'd rolled her eyes and huffed. "The root has so many holes in them and it's so ugly... and... my acne... just makes it worse. School sucks."

I paused; oddly speechless. The look in her eyes felt almost familiar in that instant and I, afraid to dwell in waters close to the heart, channeled a furious wave towards dry shores. "Wait here."

Most of the lotus chips were gone by the time I'd made my way over but I was certain a handful of them would make my point so I brought them over to the dessert station and placed them right in front of her. "These were what all of them were scrambling for as soon as the party started. Try it."

She had blinked at the form of lotus root she never seemed to have witnessed in her entire life, gingerly picking up a chip before nibbling at a corner and then sending it into her jaws whole. "It's... really good. I thought they were slimy and... weird. But this tastes totally different!"

I nodded in perfect agreement, arms folded, proud of a certain idiot's work. "And you're not the only one who thinks so! They're almost out. How about I get the chef to make an extra portion for you to bring to school? Share them with your classmates and they, too, will come to realize how delicious lotus roots are. And how beautiful your name is!"

In the time I'd disappeared to return the bowl of lotus root chips to their rightful station, someone extremely additional and unnecessary had the audacity to take over my station *a-a-and* my precious conversational guest. The intention had been to send him back to his fried chicken place but Lotus had, in a lovely and excitable disposition, waved as I neared and mouthed the word 'chef' whilst pointing at the lotus root chips on a napkin by her cantaloupe.

Leroy, apparently free from his shift, had raised a skewer in his hand with a criminal smirk of his. 'Impress me.' It spelt. The nerve of him to add a watermelon heart behind it! And and and *hand* it to me as though this was... this was a—

* * *

By the time we'd cleaned up and ended the new year's party with sparklers for wish-making and resolution setting, Chen had gathered the thirty of us before a laptop broadcasting a livestream of the results. Some of the kids, curious and all, had joined us in hopes of celebrating a nice little victory.

The announcement began on a long and confusing note of elimination rubrics before finally revealing the overall ranking of each school and the subsequent members who'd passed the round on each team. According to the system, only fifteen participants from each school could make it to the next round.

The team had neither burst into shrieks of despair or cries of joy upon registering the number 'two' beside our school's name but instead, had fallen into an uncanny silence as soon as the elimination board came up onto the screen. The first couple of names were uninteresting, if not expected. Chen, Leroy and Si Yin had all made it through to the third round. At number fifteen, however... was an odd arrangement that had some of us thoroughly confused.

V. J. White / V. Birchwood

The power of a single, oblique slanting line—the slash—a likely representation of exclusivity between that which was on the left of the separation and the right. It hadn't struck me then, in that instance, what exactly it was the results had meant but the case was different for Birchwood, who, amidst the groans of frustration of those who hadn't made the cut, up and left the backyard moments after taking in the rankings displayed on the screen.

Chef Allan, the host of the live broadcast, had went on to give a brief explanation of the rubrics before moving on to the schedule for tomorrow and just like that, they'd ended the announcement.

The first thing I heard was Chen cursing under his breath, raising his gaze to Jean Mercier, the school's number five, before nodding in the direction Birchwood had left in. Sighing loud. Though even a fool would have understood that as a cue for non-conversation, I was anxious enough to go up to him despite the sour, heavy mood that had descended upon most of us.

"Sorry, um. I know you must be troubled and all... I mean, most of us are. Half of us didn't make it through, of course, but, um... what does the...? Does the number fifteen thing with both our names means that we're safe? As in, that our scores were tied and that we passed, together?"

"Yeah it's a tie but," Chen was having a hard time directing everyone back to packing up the place. "Ultimately, it's an either-or. Either you advance, or Birchwood does and honestly, it's not something very rare... last year we had three people tied for finals and the drama... man. All because the officials leave the final decision up to you guys. Some people host private one to one's for fair play. Others either back down or talk it out."

Needless to say, I had reason to suspect a dysfunctional grading system the interschool hadn't made transparent even up till this point in time. As a matter of fact, how was anyone to believe that I, a mere tasting spoon stationed at a *fruit-cutting* dessert table, was given scores equal to that of someone else who'd led the entire set-up team *and* saved the children from a nightmare of diabetic butter-cream?

Albeit the requirement of some additional prompting by myself, I hadn't personally fixed the princess toast or had the interpersonal and leadership skills to ensure that everyone else was on task and assigned something adequate. This was a team segment, very much unlike the previous individually-focused round one and I couldn't help but attribute her lowered scores to the childish opinion of a certain overly-conservative judge.

And if so, this was nothing short of injustice.

"I should go talk to her."

"No." Chen's hand was on my shoulder before I could go after Mercier and speak to Birchwood on his behalf. "I've never seen her walk off like that without a word so I don't think she's going to be in the mood to talk about anything. Leave her to us. There's time after the bonus round tomorrow so you guys can talk then."

What he said was, indeed, nothing short of the truth. And upon further consideration, several texts I'd read about social convention had also mentioned the importance of not speaking to someone at the right time, which was apparently *as* important as choosing the right time to actually speak. In fact, I too, did not recall ever witnessing Miss Birchwood leave a scene without some snarky remark or arrogant comeback, apart from our short conversation at the waterfall during the cross-year segment.

At the same time, I had the strangest feeling that even if I were to frankly and politely reason her through the weighed possibilities of the pros and cons each of us could bring to the third and final rounds of the interschool and arrive at the rational conclusion that *she* would be the better pick to stay since everything was only going to involve challenging and complex culinary techniques I wouldn't be able to execute, her spirits would remain the same.

"Vanilla?"

I started at my name, turning to see Lotus with a jar of freshly-made chips and a small, handicraft picture frame made out of colored ice cream sticks with a polaroid photograph of us in the middle. "You can have this," she said, handing it to me whilst cradling her previous snack jar.

Incredibly moved, I'd reached out to accept it with a bow of my head but instead, she'd leapt forth with open arms for my torso and for the first time in my life, I was hugging a child who wasn't Miki. Somewhere in the distance, I spotted a certain idiot watching us from afar and had the vaguest impression he'd perhaps encouraged her to do so just to prove something I knew not what. As though I'd magically turn into a sentimental darling!

We bid Mrs. Tea and the teacher volunteers goodbye before some of the kids started emerging from the dormitory side of the orphanage (some in their pyjamas) and waving at us as we were making our way to the front gate. To many, it was a heartwarming farewell and perhaps one day, a possible return that would transform what was supposedly a mere crossing of paths into something more.

After loading most of the equipment back onto the storage truck making its rounds, the facilitators dismissed us on the spot and listed several transport options of which included a complimentary bus ride back to the campus. Mentally and physically drained from a day's worth of competitive spirit, I was prepared for a short fifteen-minute nap on the ride back when Leroy handed me his phone with Google Maps running and my *address* input in the search bar.

"Just two streets down," was all he had to say, gaze lowered directly into mine before I practically combusted. Needless to say, several key questions arose.

"How is that you know the exact details of my address? A-and you did not, just, extend an invitation to me, to *my* house wh—uaegh iit simply doesn't... it's *almost* eight o'clock and... and I mean, if two hours is enough... not that it isn't because two hours in the presence of an idiot like yourself can be highly taxing, for all I know."

"What about ten?" He suggested criminally, bag over his shoulder whilst holding out mine. "Or twenty hours."

I huffed, relieving him of my book bag and starting in the direction stated on his phone after returning Si Yin's star jump wave. "Are we talking about your term of imprisonment? If so, I believe the authorities are having a discussion about extending it at every illegal second of your existence. But... well I suppose they've authorized a momentary self-invitation to dinner, so." He fell into step, close enough for me to actually *feel* the hint of a smirk on his face without even looking.

Neither of us spoke about the elimination or our general sentiments towards the second round in the next minute or so we spent in absolute silence—oddly transfixed on the way our steps sounded so incredibly distinct despite being at the exact same pace, listening to the gentle hush of a chill winter evening. Dwelling in the comfortable presence of each other.

Several hundred feet down the street was a nursery of the animal shelter Mrs. Tea had told us about earlier this afternoon. The fairly decent-sized facility had a nursery out front that appeared to double up as a pet supply store where adopting families could make their purchases of pet food and toys. Display windows into the play areas of several puppies and kittens up for adoption was a fail-proof strategy to attract the attention of those strolling along the sidewalk.

Indeed, I was never really one to be distracted or swayed by marketing tactics appealing to one's sympathy and emotional engagement; as, after all, once identified, most were able to build a surprising immunity towards it. Unless one possessed the soft, gentle heart of an angel that was my godfather, the eyes of puppies and kittens were... they were...

I slowed and came to a stop, staring past the display glass and meeting the eyes of a small, harmless puppy that bore a striking resemblance to Berry—a stunning Siberian husky I remembered playing with in the park back when I was a child, often accompanied by Giselle, Xander's sister. "Oh."

My companion, now several feet ahead, had slowed before glancing over his shoulder at the involuntary sound I'd made upon making eye contact with the grey-white puppy. Embarrassed, I pretended to be observing a notice on the outside of the store. *No knocking on the glass.*

"So you do feel."

He was facing me now; eyes disarmingly soft against the light of a setting sun. I cleared my throat.

"Well yes of course. Unfortunately, I, too, am part of the human race and would therefore be as susceptible to emotions as any other human being would be. But if it's now you're referring to, then I'm afraid you're mistaken. I don't feel anything for them," was all I had established, eyes unconsciously drifting toward the display case that had caught my attention mere moments before. Then, continuing down the street.

Leroy waited till we were side by side before falling into step, glancing sideways. "Even pity?"

I held my breath. It was, by this point, fairly evident how we had our thoughts on the exact same page, hinting at a subject I had hardly explored on my own. The afternoon spent at the orphanage and interacting with the kids had entreated upon creatures deep, unstirred by the currents above, hiding in the dark.

"Pity," I repeated after him. Buying a second's worth of thinking. "Well there's nothing directly pitiful about not having any parents or an owner. Nothing about being an orphan should warrant any pity. I'd pity a victim of abuse or neglect and that applies to both animals and children but not a parentless young. One can have no

parents and grow up perfectly fine as long as they receive a sufficient amount of care and concern. Vice versa—meaning, one can
have parents but grow up utterly destroyed because of it. In any
case, the term 'parent' itself is vague and ambiguous. To me, Uncle
Al and Aunt Julie are as good as any parent there is, regardless of
our biological status. Does that answer your underlying concern?"

I'd peered up at him upon finishing only to flinch at the heart of
a hand blocking half my vision. Bracing myself for the usual forehead treatment, eyes scrunched shut and feet coming to a standstill,
my expectations were wholly subverted by the touch of fingers in
my hair. Gentle.

He was reaching over with the most unusual look in his eye. A
small, softened flame that nearly resembled a tear.

It was in that moment that I realized Leroy might have been referring to himself all along; that he was, at this point in his life, the
farthest away from anything related to a family and possibly even
asking if pity played any part in the affection I had for him.

"Just so you know, I don't think you're worth pitying. That sort of
emotion is reserved for the weak. And, well, I have reason to believe
that you are not. Weak."

The flame in his eyes flickered once. A smile.

"Overestimating my abilities again?" "Unfortunately, yes. Ah, the
crossroad. Should we head to the grocery store for some ingredients
first or, um, would you be alright with microwaved ready meals?"
"You still have that chicken korma?" "Well, I've been saving it for
an occasion." "Is this the occasion?" "W-well, maybe. Yes. There's also
creamy garlic chicken tagliatelle, if you'd like. And butter chicken.
Oh, and a chicken risotto. Brilliant. You must be exhausted. This
way, neither of us have to worry about cooking or cleaning the
dishes. H-hold on, you're not staying the night, are you?" "I'm leaving
if we don't do something sexy tonight." "Ah. You may leave now." "I
was kidding." "I know," I couldn't help but laugh. "Me too."

We stopped at a light, waiting for the green man and Leroy turned to me at once, as though significantly surprised by my honesty. "... about the leaving or that we're not doing anything exciting?"

Should there be a grade for conversational aptitude on the report cards I had, over the years, grown increasingly unimpressed by, it would have at least made my younger self invested in pursuing improvement in the fail grade I would have otherwise been assigned. As such, having had years of experience avoiding difficult conversations, I'd made a deft escape from embarrassment by deliberately proposing something else for his attention to narrow in on.

"If it's something exciting you wish to be doing, I have board games," I offered, clearing my throat to dispel the heat on my ears. "Classic Monopoly and chess. Whichever it is you prefer. I'm pretty sure I've already established the fact that I do not possess any form of entertainment in my apartment."

"You can entertain me."

"I am unfortunately the least entertaining person to ever exist," this, I was fairly serious about. "I don't quite know how I am supposed to do that."

Leroy was the kind of culinary expert with a strange, shocking capacity for mediocrity; producing stunningly fragrant, impeccable dishes one minute and settling for microwaved pizza in the next.

Thanks to the handy microwave Aunt Julie had sent over, we had a private feast of chicken. The chicken korma he'd apparently been eyeing since the last time he came by had been dubbed 'a steal' and the biryani rice I'd heated up to go with the butter chicken, too, he'd ingested without question. Dinner was palatable; or so I'd often settled for, alone in my humble abode without an ounce of culinary skill.

We spoke about the qualms of treading carefully around Chen whenever he was in the kitchen ever since he'd been under pressure to perform as well as Tenner did; Si Yin's efforts to become a better team player, and Birchwood's apparently-regained confidence upon learning about Leroy's attraction to a member of the male species. Otherwise known as myself.

"She thought it was Chen," he'd laughed, amidst generous chunks of butter chicken.

"Well," I'd sipped at some water to hide my amusement. "He *is* fairly good-looking according to the standard conventions set by both Western and Eastern societies alike. You two would've made a decent match."

His response was to select a non-verbal form of communication from his fortunately limited vocabulary and thus present the indecent finger, accompanied by another one of his criminal smiles. "Who tops?"

Ah, my reaction had been a tad slower than I'd expected it to be, *an encounter with a familiar term!* I'd read about this somewhere, online, and assessed its decently sound reasoning although overall iffy about citations and altogether a tertiary source that hadn't a clue what proper justification and evidencing meant.

"Just to be sure you understand: one's sexual position has absolutely no relation to their identity and no human being should be caught up in labels or stereotypical roles," I had to establish. Before opting for a dashing tease. "That said—him, of course!"

Leroy had altogether stood up, the legs of his chair scraping across the floor before advancing with the look of absolute, unlawful, i-illicit, behind-bars possible amusement unimaginable for entertain, I escape must and so cleared the table and and and dismissed, banished him to the bathroom for a shower whilst searching for something he could wear.

Alas, the results were unfortunate. He was out in a minute and the only options I was able to present him were three oversized, stretched T-shirts I could no longer wear without them slipping off my shoulders at every miniscule movement I made. Lo and behold, the idiot's first instinct was to hold them up close to his *face*, bunched up in his hands.

"What are you doing?"

"They smell good."

I was flabbergasted into infinity. "W-what does that..." I watched him settle for the darkest shirt, slipping into that before dropping his towel and thank goodness he was clothed under that.

He was quiet for the next minute or two, despite my repeated attempts to extract a full explanation of himself. As I was gathering my toiletries and pyjamas into a basket, I caught him bunching up the neckline of my shirt he was wearing and raising it to his nose. The next thing I knew, we were staring right at each other and he, unembarrassed and completely unfazed, proceeded to lower his gaze.

I followed it before experiencing quite the fright of my life. Whatever that was in his underwear, I could not comprehend.

"Wha—! *How?*"

Leroy poured himself glass of water as though having a substantial erection in someone else's apartment was all part and parcel of mother nature. I was having a hard time maintaining eye contact without combusting into ashes of embarrassment.

"It has your scent," he said, as matter-of-factly and casual no human being could manage in a situation like this. "The shirt."

"Asfdghl!" I hastened in the direction of the bathroom and spent some time reflecting on life decisions in the shower before emerging refreshed, rejuvenated, and naïve enough to believe in a Leroy Cox who'd reflected on his words and actions. Instead, he was standing right outside the door with the spare toothbrush I had (after purchasing a set of three that were on sale), comfortably joining me in the bathroom where the hair dryer was.

Alas, a single, sweeping glance over the general lower half of his body ensured that a certain part of him had remained unfortunately active throughout the fifteen or so minutes I'd spent in the shower. Brushing our teeth over the same basin; staring at each other in the same mirror, I nearly shriveled up from the deadly combination of second-hand embarrassment and otherwise romantic tension.

We climbed into bed in silence and, after setting my alarm for seven in the morning, switched off the lights. I'd left this to Leroy who'd slid in after me and was closer to the bedside lamp than I was. He remained seated up on the bed while I made myself comfortable under the covers, not quite reaching for the lamp as I'd instructed him to be doing.

"Is everything alright? The switch is right by the—"

"Can we kiss," his gaze lowered to mine, tone shockingly neutral and calm despite the bold nature of his request.

I'd paused. "Do you hear yourself?" Then, after a sigh and straightening up in bed, "fine, here." I leaned over to plant a fleeting one on his lips.

His response was to groan, visibly irate. "Tease."

"What is it now?"

"How long has it been since we had a kiss like our first?" Leroy held my gaze; a still display of a candle flame. "Or the previous time we were in your bed."

Almost immediately, I knew what he meant because there was simply no effective way I could banish the detailed, burning image of our first time by the pool and at once, I was red under the light. "W-well. Indeed, we haven't... though it isn't that we've necessarily had the time nor the place to be indulging in such frivolous activity although, yes, I do admit a certain degree of... desiring that extent of physical contact, which isn't, not, desirable."

I could see the gears turning into his head come to a stop before rebooting its function and then somewhat coming to an under-standing of my roundabout, embarrassed way of saying that I, too, shared similar sentiments. The next thing he did was offer to let me initiate.

"Ah," was all I could say in response, startled. "Well it's not that I won't. Or that I haven't thought of doing so. But I was hoping to observe subsequent instances since, um, clearly there appears to be some technique to all this and, despite scouring the internet, I have absolutely no clue how extended, long-period kissing works. What I'm saying is that I'll learn from you. By paying attention, of course."

He laughed. Low and amused. "Observing?"

I felt his fingers on the back of my neck, stroking down from the hairline of my nape to the bare skin before coming back up in a circular motion. He leaned in; head angled to the right and as always, the proximity made me freeze.

"You go the other way," he explained, guiding with the fingers he had on the back of my neck. "So if I'm left, you go right. Vice versa."

"Oh! How convenient," was all I could rejoice before he closed in completely. Quite underhandedly, he'd used the fingers supporting the back of my neck to m-massage the acupressure points below the base of my skull and illegally so, I was momentarily *liquified* into... into a... goodness, he must have studied this.

There was simply no other explanation.

I was somewhat eased into a state of relief and had unconsciously, like our first, allowed him to part my lips with his tongue. "You're weak here," he brushed the back of my neck, "and here." His tongue slipped in and, angling upwards, brushed the roof of my mouth. I nearly yelped and bit down on instinct but resisting the urge had instead reduced all that into an embarrassing whimper and by god, was I done.

"Wh—alright, al... that's enough," I told him, catching my breath. "We have school tomorrow and should this continue, or... or escalate further, well. I'm sure we'd be losing a little more than an hour's worth of sleep."

The idiot's laugh was criminally attractive even without the kiss and now, after he'd seemingly had his fill, the willingness to let it rest somewhat returned. He turned to switch off the bedside lamp. "I'll be in the bathroom."

I nodded under the covers and heard him make his way across the room before shutting the door behind him. Oddly enough, I didn't need to reach under my quilt to register my all-natural reaction to the kiss we shared but knowing that we had much to be doing tomorrow, I scrunched up and thought about that awful cover letter I'd written to the Baker's Times for an internship application—tragically destroyed by the presence of a single typo.

* * *

It was barely two in the morning when I heard the constant, never-ending vibration of a phone and sitting up in bed, I'd spotted Leroy's—balanced precariously on the edge of my bedside table, seconds close to death. I caught it before it fell from vibrating in silent mode and squinted at the screen for a caller ID.

"Leroy... someone's... Leroy," I shook him awake. He sat up, hair resembling quite the lion's mane. "It's seven missed calls from the same number. You didn't save it."

The half-eyed idiot took the phone I was holding out to him and, after glancing at the unsaved caller ID, accepted it at once. "Yeah. Sorry, I was asleep. She okay?"

Someone was speaking rather urgently on the other side of the call but Leroy seemed relatively calm. It didn't look like he was going back to sleep any moment, so I felt for the lamp switch and sat on the edge of the bed beside him. Waiting.

"Yeah, I'll go. The first train's in three hours," he said, glancing at the digital clock on my desk, then, meeting my gaze. "Does he know?"

I paused, taking this in. *He's going somewhere?* But—before school, and the interschool, but, everyone would be wondering where he was. The first train... that would be five in the morning. Something must have happened to Annie. But the look on his face... it was practically unreadable.

"He said that?" It was at this that his eyes narrowed. "Right. I won't. Yeah... thanks. See you."

Handing him a glass of water as he ended the call, I waited for him to explain.

"She woke up," Leroy placed his phone back on the bedside table, taking a gulp of water. "But she's in shock, so they sent her to emergency... if she makes it, she gets transferred to ICU."

"Wh—" I could barely speak. "Shock? Would that be cardiogenic? Obstructive? O-or distributive?"

"Uh..."

"Oh, um." I saw a need to rephrase. "Does it have to do with her heart?"

"Yeah I think it's like a heart attack."

"A cardiac arrest, then..." I swallowed, increasingly anxious. "But she's in the emergency room now?"

He nodded, staring into space; then, sighing. The first thing he did after was to reassure me that he'd be back in time for the bonus round but having heard just how serious this could be, I asked if he would be alright if I went with him instead. That, surely, the team would understand.

He advised me not to, primarily because the nurse who'd called him had informed his father beforehand who, apparently, said he'd fly over and arrive in less than two hours. For some reason, Leroy did not appear very convinced by his own words but even upon further attempts at persuasion, he'd remained adamant on my absence.

We fell in and out of sleep in the next two hours before officially waking up at four in the morning. Leroy got dressed while I stood by the stove with a pot of water, boiling him two eggs for breakfast. Knowing him, he wasn't going to be in the mood to feed himself for at least the first half of the day. Then, after handing them to him at the doorstep, watched as he took the stairs and waved.

Leroy Cox had arrived at the hospital moments after daybreak, finding his way to the ICU with the head nurse while she kept him updated on his mother's unstable condition. Siegfried sat alone on an empty bench outside the room, staring at the red light, lit, above the main door.

His son did not look at him as he stood, the farthest he could, from the well-clothed man. It was only approximately thirty minutes later, when someone finally emerged from the room, that the two came side by side to attention. They listened, and, after confirming that Annie's condition, though officially diagnosed as post-coma, would most likely remain unstable for the next five hours or so, Leroy could not help but ask.

"Could she move?" He managed. "Did she say anything?"

The nurse appeared mildly uncomfortable, as though put on a spot to say something grand and moving to put the family at ease. After all, they were just words to her.

"Little lion." She turned to leave with a bow of her head. "That's all she said, I'm afraid."

XIII

LEROY

"We're looking at the next ten hours in ICU... and depending on her condition within this period, psychological and physical assessments for post-coma treatment. Unfortunately, the heart attack caused a cardiogenic shock, then worsened into a cardiac arrest... we're in the middle of assessing any heart damage, but for now, her monitor is beeping."

The hospital was in the middle of a small town. It had been the only one I could afford. Monthly fees were basically ninety-percent of whatever it was my part-time job could cover. The emergency doctor on duty who'd come out to greet us, I'd recognized as the weekend doctor I would see making his rounds when I dropped by for Annie. In the end, I couldn't think of anything to say.

She'd pull through. She has to. I'd be left alone; she knows that. Permanent breathing and nutrient support had brought the numbers up to seven hundred a week but that was already hundreds less than half the price of the one closer to school and not once did I miss an opportunity to tell her 'wake the fuck up I want fried chicken.' She had to open her eyes eventually. She wasn't going to leave me behind.

"Is there anything else I can help you with?" The doctor was familiar and it made the whole process a lot more bearable. The real stranger was the one standing beside me. He asked if he could speak in private with the doctor, who turned my way.

"Yes but I think the patient's son has the right to hear everything. He's the one who has been picking up the patient's bill for the past year and visiting every week."

This had made the other parent pause—likely speechless—before going on to ask about the chances of Annie recovering completely and her being able to live as a normal person post-coma, during and after therapy.

The doctor explained. "Our nurses identified her as minimally conscious before the heart attack, which means that she wasn't in a vegetative state when she woke. Could speak, and move her fingers and eyelids. Whether or not she is capable of complete recovery would depend on the presence or absence of brain damage, and if positive, the extent of it. With the heart attack, like I said earlier, we're still in the middle of assessing the damage.

"If it's a concrete answer you want, it's... unlikely. Full recovery is unlikely. Judging from the immediate shock her body was in seconds after waking up, I'd say that her condition is generally unstable. As soon as things are looking on the brighter side, we will be doing the necessary assessments but... yes we're looking at months or even years of physiotherapy, occupational therapy and psychological assessment. The period of rehabilitation ranges from five months to the rest of the patient's lives."

"When's it gonna start?"

The doctor looked uneasy when I asked. He and the head nurse were the only ones aware of my problem with the bills. So they knew I wasn't going to be able to afford it. His smile was sorry.

"Leroy. I can't confirm if her condition will or will not destabilize. Her heart is weak and we're giving her all the support we can, but should her condition worsen, and further medical assistance be required... I might even have to advise transferring her to a bigger, better-equipped hospital." And we were to square one.

I thanked him as he left, starting to think about the numbers and summing without a calculator was honestly kind of hard so I mostly did them rounded up to as many zeroes as possible, avoiding headaches at seven in the morning. The worst part was trying to subtract that out of our savings before realizing that that the digits in the savings was overall two numbers less than the one on the imaginary bill and going into the negatives was just not helping.

I dropped my bag on the bench and started doing it proper. With a calculator and the back of a receipt I found in the front pocket of my jeans. The stranger turned to me. I stayed busy.

"Don't you have school, Leroy?"

There wasn't a need to look at him. He wasn't a calculator, or the receipt that could at least provide some use to whatever problem I was facing at present; a concrete solution to solving a problem he wouldn't even acknowledge.

"You can go back now. I'll call you when she wakes." *Not forgetting the tax. Multiply after that. One-off cost for emergency. Then ICU for at least a week... what's the tax on that?* "It's the interschool now, isn't it?"

I usually sleep great after jerking off. And I did, for two hours before the phone call. Every minute after that was just silent in's and out's, trying not to wake him breathing soundly under the covers, which somehow resulted in a very bad neck and eyes that just pretty much couldn't be bothered with taking things in visually. I closed them; leaning against the back of the bench.

"You can't go into a tournament half-hearted, son. Nothing should bring you down. Us chefs, we stand the—"

"There's no us." I told him. Eyes closed. "I'm not competing." Lips dry. Hungry.

I heard him sigh like this was five years ago and he was about to give another lecture on the spirit of a chef; that all I was doing now was wasting his time being a rebel. "Leroy. I know you think you're not in the best state of mind to be thinking about the interschool, but this is *important*. You have centerstage. All eyes are on you and that's only going to snowball into something better than you can ever imagine. I'm not letting you throw this opportunity out of the window. Again. Like you did last year."

The kettle was on the stove.

Someone had put it there; cranked up the heat and left it on high.

He said something about this all coming together at the wrong time. That I'd given up the final round of last year's W-interschool for Annie over some stroke of hers. That now was the time for me to regain the acknowledgement I had from all tigers of the industry. Something like that... it was hard to get. Like always. He was hard to get.

"Look... I'll settle the money."

I heard him sit. Again, he sighed and I could feel the knob on the gas stove turning. The fire, rising—bottom of the kettle glowing a hot metal red. It was very much like him, wanting to put the gas on low but ironically unfamiliar with the direction he should be turning the knob in so that he ended up with flames on high. Humiliation was the kind of feeling that boiled.

"All the therapy, all the rehab. I'll pay for it, okay? If she needs to be sent to a better hospital, I'll find one."

So I turned to him. For the first time in three years. Looked him straight in the eye. "That's what you're *supposed* to do. It's what you haven't been doing."

He seemed to have some sort of excuse. "Leroy... your mother and I have been unofficially divorced for—"

"Yeah," I snorted. Laughing. "Afraid signing some papers will make you look bad on TV?"

There it was again. That look. That tone. In his eyes, I was the same medal; same token; same trophy child that he needed to have in his pocket, on his shelf. Just a little polishing, from time to time. Otherwise, kept on private display behind a glass. Shown to once visitors came round.

"Leroy, please."

Gotta admit, though. I could understand how he managed to sway thousands of people in front of cameras and screens. Sometimes, he sounded desperate enough; even for me.

"I don't want to think talking to you is like talking to Annie all over again."

The kettle on the stove. It was whistling.

"Yeah?" I felt it needling in. The sound, the heat, the steam all up in my ears, at the front and back of my head. In my eyes. "Right. Because I definitely had a choice to be your kid, huh."

I fought the knob. *Turn it off.* It was hard to get close; the water inside, bubbling, boiling over, spilling out and foaming at the mouth, shrill, sharp, shriek. Whistling, whistling, whistling while I waited, waited for it to still, for someone to turn it off, to be dropped into the cold, a freeze; to be submerged in the silence of a frozen lake. Eyes closed.

Medical carts. Monitors. Beeping. Wheels. Footsteps. Doors. Opening and closing.

"I love you." The pungent, nauseating smell of something falsely clean. As though disinfectant was enough. "And I'm tired of... of the misunderstandings we have. It shouldn't have to be like this."

Giving up isn't as hard as people make it out to be sometimes. There's no great struggle against the current; no swimming, no staying afloat; no battle against a storm—not even a boat. Some storms... some storms just aren't worth the swim.

"You love my talent." I told him before I left. "Without that, I'm nothing. To you. To a lot of people. I'm nothing outside the kitchen.

"So, no. It's not me you love."

VANILLA

I had been waiting for him at the train station with a perfectly pressed set of uniform for the past fifteen minutes out in the snow. Admittedly, I'd arrived a tad too early even after receiving the text he'd sent some time ago about arriving in approximately an hour's time. If you're wondering how I could have possibly gotten my hands on a full set of reds, this was Leroy's, from yesterday. Having sent that straight into the washer before hanging it up to dry and then carefully ironing out every crease just this morning, I was pleased with my sudden inclination to household chores I never really enjoyed. Oddly enough, doing it for someone else had changed its nature almost entirely.

"Hey."

I heard his voice over my shoulder despite the pair of eyes I'd fixed on the fare gates by the station's exit. How he'd magically appeared there without my noticing him felt like part of the magic trick. "Good heavens. I thought you were... never mind. Here's your uniform. And I brought you some freshly brewed tea in a thermos. The snow doesn't look like it's going to let up anytime soon."

Leroy hadn't so much as taken a glance at the thermos—he had, for some reason, fixed his eyes on mine without warning—before reaching straight for it and in the midst of doing so, casually leaning in for a kiss on the cheek. It was in the middle of this sequenced interaction that I noticed how dark his eyes were. Much more than usual.

"I'll be out in three," he said, taking the pressed clothes and heading to the men's room.

Three minutes later, we were on our way up the hill to the school's main gate, seconds away from the supposed start of the bonus round briefing. Leroy hadn't raised a word about his mother or anything regarding his visit to the hospital, for the matter. Our journey, approximately ten minutes long, had been characterized by the gentle hush of falling snow and our hands, held, stuffed in the pocket of Leroy's down parka.

Needless to say, I was unwilling to pry. Finding my way around personal boundaries in a romantic relationship was not something I was decently familiar with and the last thing I wanted to be doing was subconsciously pressuring Leroy to say things he preferred to keep to himself. *That said, aren't couples supposed to be sharing the most private of emotions—unafraid of judgement, ridicule, or insecurity?*

I couldn't be sure.

Instead of the god-forsaken, freezing tundra of a flatland that Anton plaza was, the briefing for today's bonus round was held, instead, in the institute's main lecture theatre where sufficient space and heating resources came hand in hand apart from the presence of presentation equipment. Guest judge Chef Yamazaki was unfortunately no longer part of the assembly.

Production Kitchen: Stamina
Type: Bonus round
Style: Individual, plate to plate
Participants: 4 x 3 = 12
Scoring: Plate count after five hours / Last one standing

"It's a five-hour shift," I'd said first to Si Yin, who'd narrowed in on the 'individual' aspect almost at once and proceeded to clasp her hands together in glee; and then turned to Leroy a row away, seated beside Chen. The latter was already standing—counting heads, assessing his options as soon as the details were projected onto the screen.

"What are the chances you, me and your man get a spot in

the four?" Si Yin was in her world on fantasies, floating above the clouds. I reminded her about this being a purely skill-based round, since working in a production kitchen meant recipes to recreate and rules to follow. Being fast and consistent was essential. "Well... yeah I guess but... yeah. Hey, have you seen Birchwood around? We're missing so many people. She wasn't looking too good yesterday too even though she had that cool princess hairstyle going on yesterday."

"Three, four and five are taking a day off before round three tomorrow and some of us don't have the skills to frontline a production kitchen, so..." Chen pre-empted to less than fifteen of us. "Unless anyone has any objections, we're going with common sense and sending one and two, and then I need Julia Kingsley? Number eleven. Yeah, you were great with switching up the pace yesterday even with the minor mess-ups down the line. And... I'm giving the fourth spot to Xu Si Yin."

Heads turned at speeds and angles I didn't quite imagine the human neck was capable of doing; snapping in the direction Chen was looking at and staring down the seeming first-year student he was talking about. Someone was insensitive enough to voice that characteristic, to which Si Yin actually nodded like she agreed and would've liked an explanation but judging from the way her feet wouldn't stop tapping each other in anticipation, I knew she wanted the part.

"Yeah well, Cox was a first-timer when he joined us in the last interschool too," number one laid out without a moment's hesitation. "Doesn't matter what year you're in. As long as you're good enough to win us that trophy, you're up. I'd pick anyone able to crank out a good cilantro lime slaw *and* panko-crusted fish at the speed she did yesterday."

It was at this that the smile on Si Yin's face turned radiant with glee and she sort of stood up, as though trying to relieve some of that sizzling energy in her, before sitting down when participants from other schools started staring.

"I'm assigning each of you the four dishes they have. We're all given the same options across the schools, so bear in mind you have two other people next door making the same dish," Chen spoke directly to the three others he'd picked but with everyone sitting around, his instructions weren't exactly out of earshot.

"Cox, this is a no brainer. You're doing the lobster ravioli. Technical nightmare, so we're leaving that to you. Xu you're on the wok-fried vermicelli and I'm not giving that to you just because you're Chinese. Be precise. Timing is key. Kingsley you're on the pan-seared scallops. Should be easy for someone your caliber... and that leaves me with the gnocchi."

Five hours, I couldn't help but think—knowing how, in truth, this was no out-of-the-ordinary bubbling hell others would have made it out to be. In fact, it was nearly a typical shift in every other bustling restaurant. Five hours without rest was an everyday occurrence for professionals and should be of no issue to those aiming for the top of the industry after graduation.

Chef Marseille was the emcee for the day. Oddly enough, Chef Allan and the rest of the judges were seated quietly on stage, barely exchanging a word among themselves despite the buzzing excitement going around in the room. Apparently, the rest of us were allowed in the restaurant as immediate guests!

"Everyone is allowed a choice of two items from the menu of four. You won't be told which school the plates are taken from, which means even if you ordered a lobster ravioli in hopes of giving a falsely high rating for your schoolmate, you might end up giving those five stars to someone from another school. Once you're done with your meal, we have other invited guests on visit, so we'll be assigning each and every one of you to service for different tables."

Waitering service? Thank goodness this wasn't part of a competitive round. Restaurant practice was a second semester course and I had unfortunately minimal background in any form of waitering.

Before the participants were separated into chefs and guests, we were escorted to the school's famous, established, open-to-public fine dining experience: The Golden Eagle. Needless to say, this was the only restaurant on campus that could refuse guests based on their attire and their method of payment. Only gold credits were accepted. Otherwise, credit cards were usually required since cash was apparently not an option.

I myself had never witnessed the interior of the classic French pavilion, walls in the shade of pale vanilla and drawing room blue, accented by golds. The open-air kitchen and dining space was separated by glass, allowing guests to catch a glimpse of the head chef and whoever it was they might wish to thank for their meal.

Before we were seated, I'd held back and sifted through the crowds for Si Yin before pulling her aside for an urgent request.

"You have to win," I told her. She did a double take, nearly stumbling. "Do not, for anyone's sake, give anything that isn't your best because I'm highly certain that your best is enough to rival that of everyone else in the kitchen."

"Okayokayokayokay," she raised both hands in surrender. "Where's this coming from? Am I supposed to be worried? I mean, not that you and your man are fighting or anything, because I'm pretty sure you think my best can't possibly win *his* best but uh... yeah can you explain because I'm not really getting all this. I'm hungry by the way. Do you think I might end up eating the stuff I make?"

"This is all I have on me," I handed her an energy bar from my pocket. Raspberry yoghurt flavored. "So, um. Leroy's not in the best condition. Something private happened this morning and he's clearly not in the mood or the state to compete, and after some logical deducing, I figured that I'm currently *not* the solution to his immediate issues. Leroy doesn't care about winning. Not now, he doesn't. I can't explain how I know this, and how terrible it is to have a conclusion without proper premises, but there are times when it comes to him, that I... that I just seem to *know*. Without reason. Alright, I am derailing. My point is: everyone is expecting Leroy to carry us to victory but I need you to take that load off his shoulders. If you can, by some of your magic, relieve just that bit of his burden, I would be very, *very* grateful. Although, well, admittedly. I'm quite already indebted to you for being my friend."

Si Yin had paused with her mouth open, about to take her very first bite of energy-bar-goodness when she stopped and lowered her hand, processing all this within five seconds.

"I'm not sure if you realize this but you tend to confess your feelings for your man without knowing and it's?? Cute?? And I feel?? Lonely?? Just kidding. I'm happy for you oh and uh yeah of course! Yes to the winning. I mean, I didn't eat my meds today. Again. But I mean, yeah," she somewhat squealed in glee. "I'm super excited. I wanna win too. I love you."

Perfectly stunned into oblivion by her candid, innocent expression of platonic affection, I'd nearly felt my heart pause and entertain the urgent question marks flying around in my head before resuming activity.

"I-I. Well... I." Summoning every bit of worldly courage and channeling all that into my mental dictionary, I willed myself to return her words of affection. "Yes, I love you too."

By some fortunate miracle, I had been assigned a random table and a random seat number *within* that table that so happened to be in the presence of five other L'Assiette students and Raul Dalto, who had been fawning over the scented napkins for the past five minutes. To my left was a gold-plated centerpiece of the restaurant's second floor dining area—an eagle with her wings spread wide, ready for take-off, labeled 'Victoria' and overlooking the open-air kitchen down below.

Our table had called for service nearly five minutes ago and already, papers were flying around left right center, down the line and ready for the chefs to start preparing. Raul and I had ended up ordering the exact same dishes (uncoordinated, purely by coincidence) without realizing that we could very well have combined our orders and been able to at least taste every dish once.

Alas, our stupidity had left us with two portions of lobster ravioli and two portions of wok-fried vermicelli.

"Because Leroy's on them, or...?" His lodge mate had teased under his breath as soon as our orders were taken and I took the opportunity to politely corrected him on his opinion.

"What I'm doing is opting for the most technically challenging dish to gauge the tournament's level of professionalism, since it is likely that most schools will be having their most skilled culinary students on the lobster ravioli. Knowing who we're going up against is as critical as knowing ourselves. The vermicelli is interesting—I'm wondering how something wok-fried makes it to fine dining without a fuss. I'd like to see how they are thinking of elevating that. That is my thought process," I explained before reverting the question back to him. As most books for conversation dummies recommended doing.

Raul laughed. Seemingly nervous. "They sound yummy."

"Ah," I nodded. "Indeed."

And then we were silent for quite some time, finding ourselves within earshot of L'Assiette conversations despite not quite wanting to be a part of it. One of my student buddies, Juanita Castillo from CSS, had been selected to participate in the bonus round and, according to table gossip, was going up against Si Yin and a Vietnamese girl from L'Assiette on the wok-fried vermicelli.

I wasn't one bit surprised, to say the least. Castillo's *laksa* noodle soup had been the absolute star of round one and it was a wonder how Leroy had managed to emerge as champion with his spoonfuls of ramen back then. To see her hard work and talent being acknowledged by others was indeed heartwarmingly pleasant.

Most importantly, her passion and love for Asian cuisine despite being of Hispanic descent had translated into incredibly delicious forms of traditional Asian recipes. She wasn't at all fazed by those discouraging her from the kind of food she liked to cook and eat on the basis of her not being Asian. It was chefs like her that made the industry recall the humble roots of food and its universal quality.

"Lobster ravioli for four?"

Impossible, was what I'd thought at first before raising my gaze to register the rushed waiter serving us the dishes we'd ordered off the top of his head. Whoever did these portions... no doubt, they were fast.

Either way, we were barely a tenth into the grueling five-hour clock, which meant that most of the kitchen were still in their best condition. Picking up my knife and fork, I went straight for the one in the middle and right off the bat, at, perhaps, the first chew, I could tell it wasn't his.

It wasn't *bad*, per se. Just... well. Not good enough. The consistency of the lobster cream, made out of the stock that would supposedly be what the ravioli was poached in, wasn't thick enough. The chef hadn't reduced it for long, resulting in a thin, less concentrated burst of flavor. The technique of making a perfect ravioli itself, though immaculate, had made for compromises in the dish's filling. No doubt, the ingredients, especially the lobster meat, were incredibly fresh and decently sized. Still, a mouthful felt almost less-than; lacking in wholeness from the imbalance created by a gap in the flavour wheel, losing out in texture without the thicker consistency and coating of the sauce on chunks of lobster meat.

"Do you mind if I swapped out one of yours for an equal number of mine?" I asked Raul, who seemed to be enjoying his plate and hadn't so much as said a word of complaint or praise.

"Oh, yeah. Sure!" He transferred a single pillow onto my plate. I did the same for him before diving straight into the one he sent over.

Halving it was enough to give me a completely different impression from the first and almost at once, I could hear myself curse the realm of idiots down below. Good god.

Fresh basil gently perfuming every ounce of rich, creamy lobster meat finished on a tangy bed of fresh tomato chutney cutting through the heaviness and then completed by something extra. A mild, delicate sweetness of honey in the sauce reduction. It was very much like him to toy with any recipe and this was his mark.

Well. Wouldn't be long before someone catches him doing so and perhaps penalize him for breaking the rules of every conservative, traditional kitchen, so. The thick texture of the honey he used had been a tad too rich for working with lobster. I would've pulled him aside to advise on something thinner, or, perhaps, including it in the chutney instead of individual drops into the sauce.

Right above the grand modern clock on the biggest wall of the kitchen guests were able to see into were twelve mini digital displays of plate counters. One each for every chef. At present, Leroy was in the lead. Castillo and Si Yin were two and three portions behind respectively and then a draw between Chen and three other participants from other schools.

I had to constantly remind myself that he was a pastry chef, competing against others who were most likely trained in a real production kitchen unlike himself. Fortunate enough to have landed myself a first-class seat with a bird's eye view of the kitchen, I was able to make out the speed and focus at which Si Yin was going, caught up in the passionate flame and heat of the kitchen she at present considered hers. Though I wasn't sure whether the plate of vermicelli I'd been served was made by her, general sentiments around the table were equally good. As long as she kept up the pace...

Clang. Down below, someone had dropped a tray onto the kitchen floor and the sound, nearly thunderous in an enclosed space, had every head turning. I could not recognize the person standing over the aluminium tray but he seemed to have his hands held up, momentarily frozen by the sound and the fact that he'd ran into someone else. Leroy.

"Who the fuck runs in a kitchen?" Everyone up on the second floor heard him say. I wasn't too sure about the first since they had an insulating glass between the dining area and the kitchen, but heads had continued to turn in both curiosity and confusion.

Something else was on the floor that did not appear to belong to the tray or the person who had dropped it. Squinting was enough to make out a mound of pasta dough. Goodness! He was going to have to make it again.

A single glance at Leroy's face in this very instant could frighten any brave and courageous soul foolish enough to provoke a starving lion; and there was something else, something wrong about the way he'd turned back to his station to redo the pasta dough and ignore the frozen figure to his right. The kitchen resumed its pace as quickly as it was distracted and soon, guests returned their eyes to the table.

Nearly done with my meal, I decided to time him. It was only a matter of using the stopwatch on my phone and averaging out the time he needed to prepare the number of dishes he could do at once. I was familiar enough with his usual speed to put a number to his condition and alas, my conjecture had been proven true. I'd seen him churn out complex dishes at a much better rate than he was going at present, albeit continuing to average above most of the people he was competing against. Leroy was...

He was tired.

In fact, minutes later was the moment Castillo's plate counter overtook his to an eruption of cheers by CSS students and then it was Si Yin and then Chen and Leroy was... he was falling behind.

Good god.

I didn't know what to think. Or feel. In that instant, I felt the dread that he was feeling down below and the horrid, bitter taste of being left in the dust despite having been the first. This wasn't—it couldn't be—the first time he felt immense pressure to win on behalf of a team. He'd participated in events and tournaments a-and and live cooking in front of cameras and I was so sure he'd been through things far worse and so the only explanation, the only anomaly present, was that phone call and his visit to the hospital.

"It's all because of that dude running into him. Throwing him off his pace," Raul had kept his eyes on the kitchen the entire time, fingers bunched up in a heated gesture. "That's just low. He should just... what is that word. Repute... repalt... report him."

The conflict was between what he desired as a person and what others desired of him. It was in times like these—when his wellbeing should be prioritized over something as insignificant as a bonus round in some minimal interschool tournament—that he still could not afford to drop out or give anything less than his best because to those, to the others on his team, this was much, much more.

"Oh good god, I can't watch this," I told Raul, rising from my seat and leaving my napkin on the table, to the left of my place setting. "Stay here and keep an eye on Leroy. I'm running to the infirmary."

"W-woah, wait, the infirma...? Why? Dude, come on I'm just a—"

Minutes after I'd left The Golden Eagle was when Rosi sent me a text about participants being dismissed to allow the next batch of invited guests to dine. Supposedly, the rating of the dishes we had was to be done upon leaving the restaurant but I honestly couldn't be bothered. The instructors and facilitators had also called for student volunteers as table escorts two hours into the five and just to keep an eye on him, I had willingly offered my assistance.

There are times when I do not wish I was right about things. Leroy wasn't just falling behind—I'd catch him with his head hung, hands braced against the countertop as though trying to dispel a headache before snapping back to work. While he wasn't the only one increasingly fazed by pressure (even the others on simpler dishes were struggling to keep their heads on the task at hand three, four hours in), the fact that this was completely uncharacteristic of him began to show and soon, after a participant from L'Assiette and CSS had dropped out, he'd stopped completely to lean against his station. Hand on his head.

A facilitator had come by to check on his condition and that was when I saw the look on his face. Needless to say, they called for medical assistance from the infirmary at once, which was really what I had run off to do before even volunteering as a table escort. Miss Samantha, the school nurse, had readied a wheel stretcher and several ice bags right outside the restaurant and even the facilitators themselves were surprised by how fast she had arrived.

Apparently, Leroy had insisted he was fine and was going to walk all the way back to the administration building where the infirmary was, but Chef Marseille shut him up with an ice bag to his face and he ended up being forced onto the wheel stretcher but stubbornly remained up in a seated position instead of lying down.

I wasn't proud to have abandoned my post as a table escort, mostly leaving without a word and still dressed in the waiter's uniform they'd handed out to volunteers earlier on. With absolutely no clue if and whether I was allowed in the infirmary in the first place, I'd hurried after the stretcher and, together with Miss Samantha and two other facilitators, wheeled a certain idiot to rest.

"Please lie down. I would prefer not to have you falling over with your head unprotected."

He'd taken longer than usual to register my words, ice bag lazily held over his forehead so that it really seemed to be cooling just his right eye. The other one scanned the top of my head to the bottom of my feet.

"... if I get a picture with you in that. Sure."

"Ma'am? Half this man's brain cells appear dysfunctional. I'm afraid he is dire need of some medication and rest."

We passed the entrance of the administration building while one of the facilitators held the door open. The infirmary was to the right and at once, they'd wheeled the stretcher and the malfunctioned idiot on it into the room. And the nerve of him to have the energy to send a flirtatious wink my way before disappearing past the doorway—!

"It's probably a combination of mental and physical exhaustion. Mostly mental. I'm having him rest in the infirmary for the next fifteen minutes before he goes anywhere. Oh yes, did he tell you the only thing he's had all day were two eggs at five in the morning?"

Oh good god to think I was right down till the very details of his eating habits! I'd blanched the color of the floor, thinking at once of portable food options to serve him before his condition could worsen.

"I'll be back with some bananas. Or an energy bar. Ah, but I don't think he'd be able to stomach that. What about—"

"No, you're not allowed to see him yet and I have the stuff he needs to eat for sugar level regulation inside. Wait out here and I'll call you when he's ready to go," she instructed, pointing towards the bench positioned right outside the infirmary. "Don't look at me like that. I'm not the one who thought relying on two eggs for an entire day would be a good idea. He knows about the bonus round and didn't bother eating something before that? What was he doing all morning anyway?" Her question was rhetoric from the way she'd simply turned and walked off into the infirmary as the facilitators emerged, not quite waiting for my response.

Taking a seat with a sigh, I was about to let my mind bury itself in conjectures and guilt for not having noticed the extent of his exhaustion when the sound of familiar footsteps came from the doorway of the administrative building.

"Wow, you actually look ugly when you're sad," Birchwood observed with a snort, nodding in the direction of an exit to the gardens. "We need to talk."

I stood, slightly dazed. "Oh. Yes... well I do have fifteen minutes to spare."

"It's going to be short."

"Ah, I see," was all I could say in return, tailing her past glass doors and down to the benches surrounding a marble statue of the school's first headmaster. I stood around while she made herself comfortable, opening my mouth to speak but as though having sensed an oncoming storm, Birchwood held up a hand. "No, don't talk yet. If you go first, I'd only sound stupid afterwards, so I'm going first.

"Anyway, you probably know this already but I'm not giving up my spot to *anyone* without good reason. You, being a critic without technical skills, is not good enough reason," she established with a grounded stare before lowering the hand she'd raised. "That's it. Okay, now you."

My initial reaction had been to blink. "Oh. Well. I think you've pretty much said it all!"

Her eyes narrowed at once. "I don't like it when you agree with me. Makes me think something's wrong."

"Well, I'm not going to disagree with a perfectly sound argument, Miss Birchwood," I began. "Every valid argument or claim has equally sound premises, supported by logical reasoning. Premise one, I cannot julienne carrots. Premise two, I cannot dice an onion in less than thirty seconds. Premise three, I have zero foundation in plating techniques. Premise four, this is a tournament based on culinary skills. Premises one, two and three lead to a logical inference: I cannot cook. This is inference one. Inference one, in relation to premise four, leads to conclusion one: I will fair poorly in the tournament. What amazes me should be the fact that I've come this far without an ounce of assistance! It is quite the feat of a first-year critic, if I do say so myself. Oh. Would you like me to continue with premises five, six, seven, inferences two, three, four, and conclusion two?"

Her gaze was blank as I came to a momentary pause, the universal non-verbal sign of needing to rephrase my words.

"What I'm trying to say is, that, well. Winning is important. Both to me and yourself. That is undeniably, the truth. However, there is a difference between idealistic dreams and practical, rational reality and here lies the difference between you and me. Winning a culinary competition as a critic is idealistic. But for you, less so.

"You having a higher chance of winning also therefore means our school has a higher chance of winning the overall, thereby making us all very happy. Not to mention, as we head into rounds three and four, four being the final round, there will inevitably be more complex, professional culinary techniques to be executed and I'm fairly *certain* that having someone who is more familiar with these techniques on the team would provide greater overall use and support."

I finished with a slight bow of my head, quietly proud of myself for the perfect explanation of my thought process without scaring away a conversation partner who wasn't Leroy Cox. Si Yin herself had never heard me in my final form.

"Well?"

Birchwood was quiet. And... and *frowning*, which got me severely anxious. The moment she folded her arms was the moment I knew she didn't exactly agree and this was what set me on the path of sheer bewilderment.

"You cannot possibly disagree with my professionally-formed argument," even to myself, I sounded appalled. "I'd spent fifteen minutes in the shower this morning *including* the walk to school, crafting, bolstering it to perfection! It is flawless."

"Wow, you are *such* a nerd." The first thing she said was thankfully within my expectations. Then, she stood—as though to leave—before frowning more and resuming her seated position.

"Can't you... I mean, can't you for once be a little bit *dreamy* and, I don't know, shoot for the stars like every other main character does and not stick to whatever's boringly realistic? Like, *that's* why people are interesting, you know. They... they try and they fail and they realize that they're wrong because they thought they could do it or something but it makes them so much more human because we all dream about, I don't know, being famous and successful and shit."

"W-well." I stared in return, back to being bewildered and generally disarmed. By my calculations and relative inferences, Violet Birchwood was criticizing me for being correct all the time and to be honest, I wasn't quite sure what to think about that.

"I... I suppose I could, but..." Inching towards the bench she was seated on, I tested the waters before finally filling the space beside her. "I *am* boring. That is something I cannot deny."

And to that, we sat in silence. Her, tapping her fingers on the side of her elbow in her permanent state of impatience. Moments later, I decided to call for a truce.

"Miss Birchwood. If what you're disliking is the fact that I'm agreeing with you, then, should I perhaps disagree with you for the sake of ending this conver—"

"Stop with the 'Birchwood' thing!" She burst out all of a sudden, startling me, the bench, the bushes, the marble statue of our first headmaster. "It's, like, creepy. Why can't you just call me Violet or something?"

"Ah."

Stunned. I could practically hear the creak of an un-oiled joint as I turned my head away out of embarrassment. "Duly noted. I shall call you Violet. From now on."

"Okay I'm leaving this conversation before it gets any worse than it already is. Bye nerd."

* * *

I was able to somehow transport Leroy back to Cayenne lodge without the help of a wheeled stretcher and no, it did not involve any form of bridal carrying, or so Leroy had attempted to trick me into doing, thinking I was some foolish lovestruck idiot of the 90s, charmed by the suave requests of a smooth criminal.

Tucking him into bed was the easy part. Asking if there was anything he wanted to have for dinner was the difficult one. Telling him that L'Assiette had won the bonus round advantage was surprisingly neutral. He appeared mostly unfazed until his phone started vibrating and the caller ID was 'Chen'. I'd left them to speak to one another and made my way down to Cayenne's kitchen in search for spare ingredients in Leroy's labelled food box.

The idea of pan-seared salmon on a bed of mustard herb butter lentils sounded perfectly delicious whilst also doubling up as a good source of nutrition for his current condition. The prime issue was if I could execute it... or at the very least not undercook the salmon. I was bringing the lentils to a boil after making a quick phone call to the ice cream parlor for some changes to Leroy's shift schedule when a familiar shade of pink popped out from behind the front door.

"Maple," I'd greeted from the kitchen as he removed his shoes and changed into house slippers. "Good evening."

He waved, removing his Bluetooth earphones before toddling over. "Oh! Vanilla! That smells very nice. How have you been? Did you make it into the third round? I wasn't too sure if I saw your name on the list..."

I told him that I'd unfortunately been eliminated, skipping the part about having tied with Bir—Violet, since he was technically a supportive fan of hers and the last thing I wanted to do was hurt his feelings. I was, however, aware that he'd advanced to the third round in seventh position. Needless to say, that certainly meant he had a fair bit of talent. "Congratulations."

"Haha!" He dismissed my compliments with a wave of his hand. "We were just having fun! I'm not all that good.... by the way, what are you doing in Cayenne? Have you moved here?"

"Ah. Well..." I paused. Hesitant. Before recalling the conversation I had with Leroy in neighboring shower stalls, fooling around with a bar of soap. "Leroy is unwell and I am making him dinner. And then maybe some dessert. For a little pick-me-up."

Almost at once, Maple appeared immensely concerned.

"What! Oh no. Is he resting in his room? Should I go check on him? What... was it a fever?" He stood right by my shoulder in the kitchen. "Why don't you rest, I'll take over and make some nice pumpkin soup to cheer him up. And then some banana pudding for dessert."

I reassured Maple that I was quite alright with doing it on my own, and wouldn't like to bother him during his free time in the evening. "I have it covered. Thank you for offering."

"I really don't mind!" He insisted. "I'm good at taking care of others. But I wonder why Violet isn't here to look after him... I had an idea it would be like this. Leroy's always alone in his room and some-times, I'd like to keep him company, you know?" He laughed, sur-prisingly suggestive. I had to pause. "But he's really loyal and doesn't budge at all... and look, she doesn't even come by to make sure he's okay. I mean, as his girlfriend, shouldn't she... I don't know, be com-forting him in times like these?"

I had to turn away from my lentils. "So... um. Violet. You think her and Leroy...?"

Maple nodded, sighing. "She said it herself. Leroy was there too. He didn't deny it."

Being a rational human being was something I had always been extremely proud of, and it was in times like these that logical thought processes were perhaps even more important than the problems themselves. I'd lasted all evening without saying a thing about Violet or Maple to Leroy, mostly because I knew she must have had her reasons for saying whatever she did back then.

While I was, indeed, extremely concerned about his familial sit-uation, I at the same time did not wish to pressure him any further than the cliff he was already standing upon. He'd turned in at eight in the evening and slept throughout, waking up at seven for the round three's briefing at another lecture theatre. Though the color on his face had returned and he seemed well enough to give me a knee-buckling, rule-breaking, *liquifying* kiss, I insisted on following him to the meeting point in Roth hall, just in case he felt unwell on the way downhill.

We were five minutes late by the time we arrived at our destina-tion, greeted by an anxious-looking Chen who thanked the gods we were *both* present.

"Is something wrong?" I asked, mildly confused. I'd told him just last night about my discussion with Violet.

"Birchwood," he said. "She's not turning up."

XIV

VIOLET

"Okay I'm leaving this conversation before it gets any worse than it already is," I had to leave before the onset of a migraine. Talking to him always required more brain cells than necessary and I couldn't afford to spend more than the remaining amount I had from hours of fuming over Pierre's lack of common sense last evening. "Bye nerd."

I made a quick time check just in case, but one of the things I actually liked about talking to him was the speed at which it would end. Like, at a proper conclusion. Some people take forever to decide on something and, hours into the discussion, wouldn't stop going back and forth on something we thought we'd decided upon in the first minute. *Three-thirty.* Dad should be in his office by now.

Pierre was a bitch but I could not get him out of my mind the entire evening after yesterday's elimination list fiasco, knowing that I'd been unfairly marked down over some stupid little opinion of his. So with the ranking stuff settled and my path to receiving an invitation to the spring bake-off cleared, I headed straight for the headmaster's office on the third floor of the administrative building.

Being the youngest of the family *and* the only daughter was like, a free ticket to making as many complaints as I wished. Dad had never refused me five minutes of his time in his office, usually stopping his paperwork just to give me his full attention and then reverting back to it once I was done.

Like, I've always warned him about the so-called 'friends' he invites to evening dinner parties because he's honestly too damn *nice* all the time to see their little back-stabbing eyes actively looking out for some material they could blackmail our family with. Kind of like mom, but less hysterical? Thank god she moved out. Lindy's a lot less dramatic but Dad and her got remarried only a year after the divorce so obviously, we weren't all that keen on the wedding. Five months later and we're still keeping an eye on her bank account. Just in case the numbers go up too much, too fast.

Honestly though, the thought of Pierre taking advantage of dad's kind nature got to me just as I took a turn down to the end of the corridor, where the double doors to the headmaster's office were. *How dare he embarrass me in front of—oh.* I paused right outside the door. *Someone's in there.*

The voices inside didn't sound like they were coming to an end anytime soon so I was about to turn back with a worse mood than before when they started becoming a little clearer and louder. *Yes! He's sending them out, which means the guest is leaving.*

I waited outside by a corner, three feet away from the double doors. Dad's voice, I could easily recognize as they got closer and I think he's got to be, like, a foot away from the door when the two of them decided to stop. It was painful, waiting for one of them to reach for the knob or something because, lol, I needed to vent about Pierre, like, *now*—

"Henri. There is a limit to my influence..." *That's dad.* "I cannot... increase the number of plates... is a... number for that. Things like leadership and teamwork... yes. The rubrics are vague."

Henri? I was still waiting for their exit. It took me horrifying moments to realize who it was he was talking to. *Henri Pierre?*

I couldn't make out what he said in response but could, however, tell from his tone the kind of face he was making. Tldr; he wasn't happy. And somewhere in his agitation, there was Cox and Chen in it. Just their names.

"If you would just put some faith in your students... I can't afford to tamper with anything else." Dad sounded even closer than he was before. "Imagine if we haven't gotten rid of the previous number one—if you're having trouble dealing with these two... things could have been far worse."

I felt it. A creeping dread; an emptiness at the back of my throat and my entire mouth that went dry, like I was moments away from throwing up and my system was preparing for it to happen.

"Remember what you owe me." This was Pierre. "Do you... how *much* I had to do to keep... critics quiet about you buying your daughter... convention in Paris?"

He was harder to decipher. Not just because of his accent but because he was practically a stranger whose verbal habits threw me off and because this wasn't what I wanted to hear. Already, I could hear my heart in my ears. Deafening.

Dad was quiet.

"Henri. Trust me, I know... I know how you must be feeling and that is precisely why we've agreed on a deal like this. I am doing the best I can—opaque judging criteria, indirectly forcing our top student into quitting school... just to make this victory of yours a little more believable. You can't expect more than that. The other judges aren't fools, you know."

"You know what... promised." He had us cornered and I so wanted to punch him through the wall. "You know the pressure I'm under. Winning bonus... not enough an advantage when you continue to... others before us."

Frustration. Anger. I couldn't and yet *could* understand every word they were saying and I was never boiling like I was now—bubbling and spilling over in rage and disappointment. Everything pooled behind my eyes and, when they paused for some silence, I hear something trickle onto the carpet floor. *Oh my god, Violet. You know better than to cry.*

Something else was happening in the room. It was quiet for way too long and I was about to put my ear against the door out of concern for dad when there were footsteps and the I bolted behind a nearby pillar *just* as the door burst open. Nothing came out.

And then, it was Pierre reminding dad about the deal. Then his footsteps down the hallway and me waiting until they were no more; then heading for the stairs down to the first floor, away from the headmaster's office with the worst, bitter, sour taste in my mouth.

* * *

"Miss Birchwood? You're... are you alright?"

I ended up in the staff room and quite honestly, I didn't even recall ever passing the corridor it was on—which meant that I'd somehow wandered there without actual thinking and by this point, I wasn't going to bother with the specifics. All I needed was someone to scream at. The receptionist would've done the trick, but it wasn't really appropriate and I couldn't find a single thing on her to nitpick on! Even the Swarovski rhinestone on the second ring of her middle finger was a perfect shade of Montana. *Fuck.*

"I want to see Lindy."

Her face turned from shock to understanding and then stiff,

half-sheepish fear. "Yes. Yes of course. Ah, but Chef Lindy is in a board meeting with the rest of the instructors at present and... it only just started. Perhaps you could come back in an hour...?"

I was about to *scream*. The weight on my shoulders was unbearable and I didn't even know what the hell was making it so heavy and hard to breathe except the fact that literally *everything?? Was?? Wrong??*

Dad bought me a spot on the Summer patisserie convention in Paris even though I *so* didn't need it; Chef Pierre for some fucking reason knows about this and had the guts to use this as leverage to, what, get his school a win so that, what, he can get promoted from his stupid-ass position when he doesn't even have the skillset to do that without blackmail; Dad had to cook up lies to get Layla Tenner to leave school so that it would be *believable* that we didn't win; and we might *still* end up losing *anyway*, all, because, of *me*?

I wasn't going to stand around for an hour.

The big ass 'fuck you' I gave to the receptionist was uncalled for but the shock on her face made it so that I could get past her without her chasing me down for the next five seconds within which I was able to spot the main conference room that was in use and headed straight for that. I actually liked bursting doors open; the dramatic effect suited my taste and once, I even thought of making it my official hobby.

Heads turned, eyes refocused and I was just standing in the doorway, heaving while staring at the presenter up on the podium, who'd stopped mid-sentence to follow everyone else's attention. Her eyes went wide.

Chef Romanov was the first one to speak. "Miss Birchwood. Is there a fire? What is the emergency?" He seemed confused but also genuinely frightened. I'd say no one in the room had ever seen me in tears. It's mostly just screaming and throwing a tantrum—that's how I roll. *Not* tears.

Lindy met my eye and at the very least, she had the common sense to know that something was wrong. She didn't say anything. Just breathed, standing there and waiting for me to say something like I was capable to say anything in my current state before finally getting the message and excusing herself with a sigh.

"One minute. Christian? Could you take over just a moment on the part about the additional course units. I'll be right back."

She gestured to the door and I moved out of the way, letting her pass and then following her as she led the way past several other empty meeting rooms down the hallway and then to a staff pantry at the end. She was about to open the door to the balcony so that we could speak in private but then noticed how cold it was outside so instead, she just closed the one to the pantry before crossing her arms and waiting for me to speak.

"Well? We have a minute. And this better be good because it's definitely one of the worst tantrums you've thrown so far."

I was so mad, I even let this slide. Technically speaking, I was already mad enough to instinctively turn to my stepmother of all people but she also happened to be the only other adult who wasn't dad that I could actually look to for help. *Alright Violet, time to do what you hate doing—confiding in others.*

"Dad messed up. Really bad. Oh my god this is the stupidest thing he's done so far."

"Yes, yes. Did he forget your first word anniversary or something?"

"Oh my god shut up you are so mean!" I snapped back and I think something in my throat broke because my voice died and for some reason, they were replaced by this ugly bawling I never knew I was capable of executing. If this blows up and I never get to be a pastry chef, I guess I'll settle for an Oscars. The look on Lindy's face was priceless. The shock value was out the roof.

I told her the whole damn thing. Some parts were hard to get out because it wasn't as though coming to terms with the fact that my hard work for the past two rounds plus placing first in the cross-year and rising up the ranks to ninth place could very well all just be a complete *ruse* was an easy thing to do. Every cent of effort. Down the train. Discredited by a single, foolish act.

Better yet, we basically had no chance of winning and still, people like that nerd and Cox and Chen and Xu were working their asses off, giving up their spots for *me*.

Lindy handed me a glass of water in the middle of my rant and I gulped the entire thing down in less than three seconds before continuing my rage and confusion. Obviously, this meant that dad played some part in my rise to fame and and and exposing the truth of what he and Pierre were up to would have meant to some extent destroying myself too and I wasn't too sure how I felt about that.

After all, truth was never the priority. It was the confusion and frustration that got to me in the first place that had me cornered enough to turn to *Lindy* of all people, and by the time I ended my grand speech, she was looking at me like I literally had no marbles left to lose.

"I know you're not going to believe me," I finished into balls of tissue paper. "But I heard Dad and Chef Pierre in his office."

The look on her face was just unreadable. She didn't say a word for the next couple of seconds while I was blowing my nose as loudly as I could to fill the silence but she did seem like she was thinking hard; only, all those thinking apparently made her speechless. After what seemed like years later, she finally asked if I'd told anyone else.

"No, of course not. Who am I even going to tell? They'll lose all respect for my accomplishments when, obviously, I don't need *any* help from *anyone* in the first place! Why did Dad even have to do that? I can get invited to conventions *by my own efforts*. Why doesn't he get that?"

"Did you record them?" Lindy went as far as to ask. For a moment, I froze.

"No... I was... I was too... oh my god I should have done that oh my god I've caught someone else's stupidity."

She refilled my glass of water and that, too, I gulped down in three seconds while she talked. "This is a serious matter, and I can tell from your... behavior that you know it is. You'll have to keep it to yourself for next couple of hours or so, okay? Leave the snooping around to me and no one else can know that you are involved in this or Pierre or whoever it is might hold something against you.

"And I'm glad that you decided to confide in me," she finished with a rare smile. One that she'd already given to glasses during our first practical class and never, never to me. I'd always wanted to punch her for that.

I didn't say much in response because I was feeling very moody and PMS and just overall tired from all the emotional burden so I listened to her explain that she was going to have a talk with Chef Allan and maybe the other judges before looking into the matter. I on the other hand, was to do nothing and keep quiet and *obviously* I couldn't just do that because then I'd just never be able to sleep at night with all those residue thoughts in my heads running around being all jittery and whatnot.

"Okay fine," she gave in eventually. "No one's going to hear you out if you don't have any proof, so I want you to get Tenner's phone number, contact, anything. Call her, and ask her for some form of evidence. Something we could use to prove that they pressured her into..."

* * *

Today needs to end. Like, right now. It needs to go.

The sun needs to set; the sky needs to dark, the birds need to stop chirping like happy little things because no one else is allowed to be when I'm tired and *done.*

Lindy's solution was to send me back to Hudson where my spare room was so that I wouldn't bump into the others spending their time socializing at the cocktail party in Roth Hall after the bonus round and accidentally spill my overflowing cup of piping hot tea. Either way, my makeup was ruined and I had nothing on me to touch it up so retreating into some cave was actually a proper solution. I wasn't in the mood to entertain anyone bragging about their experience and the exposure they got from The Golden Eagle's kitchen.

I was like, a hundred feet away from Hudson residences with the reception in sight and my student pass out and ready for scanning when someone else came into view as soon as we made it onto the part where two roads converged into one.

Xu had her hands stuffed in the pockets of her bright red windbreaker that, by the way, I was *not* a fan of and her eyes fixed on the road ahead without even noticing that we were practically five feet apart on the same pace to likely the same destination. It was a one-way road.

She skipped the cocktail party? I thought, surprised. *Must have lost pretty bad, then...*

It was the only explanation for her not wanting attending the party and, well, making her way back to the residence alone. Wait. She's in Hudson too?

"If I soaked it in hot water and *then* transferred it into the cold to stop the process I could've saved minutes." She was talking to herself. Loud and clear. "But then it would take longer to fry in the wok... but it's on high, and the heat's enough, isn't it?"

I cleared my throat, waiting for her to notice me but all she did was continue to speak to herself so I sped up till I was directly in front of her. Still, no response. That conversation she was having with herself basically had all her attention. Mad that I was grasping for straws of the attention of someone clearly insignificant, I maximized my walking speed the rest of the way to the reception, tapped my card on the scanner, made my way to my block and stopped to wait for the elevator. It took forever.

"... using a meat fork for the twirl but would the vermicelli stick? It's not like pasta so the..."

Oh my god you cannot be serious, I thought, jamming the call button five times. *She's in my block!*

She came into the lobby and stood right beside me, still lost in her thoughts and absorbed in the dumbass conversation with herself that clearly wasn't as important as I was. Not a single glance my way was made and I was furious with both her and that stupid vermicelli thing she was so concentrated on. *Fuck* vermicelli. I'm sad! My eyes are puffed! My makeup's ruined! It's *so* obvious!

The elevator arrived with a ding and when the doors slid open, she was the first to go straight in and that was the exact moment she raised her head and our eyes met in the full-length mirror that spanned the inside of the lift.

She froze.

I froze.

The elevator doors closed behind us on auto. The ventilation fans stopped functioning because neither of us went for the operating panel with the floor buttons.

"Uhhh hi." Xu had the gall to say through the mirror. I hadn't recovered enough to even fumble with the buttons. "You're... crying. Cried. Past tense."

Looking at myself in the mirror made the whole makeup situation a lot worse than I imagined it to be. I looked like *shit*.

"Yeah well, what else do you think I did? Seasoned my eyeballs with salt for red eyes?" I went for the operating panel and pressed the button for 'six'. Xu made no move to do the same and I was further shocked into thinking that her room was on the same floor as mine.

"Maybe? I don't know. Who made you cry?"

"No one. It's none of your business."

Thank goodness the ventilation returned, and the fans came back to life or I probably wouldn't be able to stand the awkwardness riding an elevator up six floors with nerd's best friend who has now apparently seen me in my ugliest state. Luckily, her phone was nowhere in sight and she didn't seem to be thinking about sneaking a photo of me in ruined makeup. That kind of photo, I'd never allow on any social media platform. Twitter being the worst.

"Is it just me, or you're super cold all of a sudden. You were all cute and embarrassed that time during the cocktail party after round one. Where'd all that go?"

I had to calm myself before looking in the mirror and registering the pink in my cheeks. God, was this not an ideal elevator ride. She followed me out onto the sixth floor and again, I tapped my student ID against the scanning device to the right of another glass door and headed straight for the suites. First years weren't eligible for one so Xu would have to be in the other direc—*oh my god she's... is she following me??*

"What are you doing," I spun around to ask, stopping short in the middle of the hallway. She gave me a look like *I* was the one asking the obvious.

"You're obviously sad, so why don't you just tell me what happened," she said as I brisk-walked all the way to my room number and fumbled for my key fob. "Your room's a studio suite, right? What about some real good spicy stuff for dinner so that you can cry your heart out? Sounds good right?"

"W-what?!" I dropped my keys and had to pick them up, scanning the fob over the lock, and as soon as I managed to unlock my door, Xu had the nerve to put her iron grip on the handle while I was pushing it open—refusing me entrance into my *own* room.

I looked at her like she was crazy. "I don't need you? Like—"

"Yeah well, who else is gonna listen to you, huh? You don't have any friends."

Lightning struck; thunder boomed, I felt that hard and fell to my doom. *Oh my fucking god.* How dare she... how dare she say the truth in my face without batting an eyelash? Doesn't she have the tact to, I don't know, please me, the literal goddess in a school of brats? Can't she tell I was having the worst day of my life and that the truth was *not* going to help?

Apparently, I actually broke down crying in front of my door, in the middle of the hallway, crouched down, hugging my knees as though my life depended on it. "I have *fans*, okay? I don't need any friends! Like, who needs friends when you're popular and like, have fourteen thousand followers on Instagram?"

Her face did not have a single streak of emotion whatsoever and I was, quite frankly, shocked by her response. Usually, I had people panicking in milliseconds of my tantrums—and that didn't even involve a single teardrop—because they were mostly afraid I'd go around badmouthing them (not wrong) so they'd at least show some kind of redeeming pity but this... this Xu girl was just! She just!

I watched her pry the key fob out of my hand and unlock the door to my room before grabbing me by the back of my collar and, like, literally hoisting me into my room. *What? Where did that—how does she have that much strength??*

She had the nerve to sit me at my own dining table and search the rest of the living for the tissue box before coming back with a bunch of them in her hand and stuffing that right in my face. The next thing I knew, she was scanning the contents of my fridge. I was, like, offended? Upset? Shocked? Stupefied?

"What do you feel like eating? Oh, and how hot can your tongue handle?"

W-WHAT?! How hot can my... j—what was she thinking of doing to me? Oh my god should I say something? What do I say? Do I words? I felt my face burn like it was on fire while Xu continued to ransack my fridge, spouting a whole load of nonsense. The embarrassment worsened my runny nose and I was sniffling, blowing my nose, and sniffling again. Just, dying.

"Ooh, you have kimchi. I'll make you some really hot kimchi fried rice. Like, level eight-out-of-ten spicy. You're okay with that, right?"

It took me a good long moment to actually realize that her previous question about the heat and my tongue and handling or whatnot was actually referring to the level of spice she was going to add to the dinner she was all of a sudden making for me in my own kitchen and of course, I had to slap myself awake.

"Well... yeah, but. Aren't you, like... didn't you just spend five hours in the kitchen on a wok?" I couldn't understand where her energy was coming from and was quite frankly in awe. Also just generally annoyed and felt like pointing out everything wrong with her.

"Five hours, yeah. But I didn't win," she sighed, magically producing a non-stick pan of mine that I was pretty sure I hadn't been able to find for the past month or so. "Second place. Tied with another girl from CSS, she's really good, so... it's like I'm not satisfied or something, you know? And I didn't eat my meds all day so... I'm just feeling jittery from not winning. Hidden energy, you know."

I reached for more tissues, watching her set the pan on the induction cooker before prepping the ingredients. Kimchi was something I secretly indulged in and I wasn't going to let anyone, let alone her, know that I was *actually* craving some kimchi fried rice. It better be good, because the only other time I had it was in Seoul, at a Michelin star restaurant celebrating traditional South Korean cuisine.

I wasn't in the mood to converse but for some reason, the words were kind of automatic. I wasn't required to use a 101% of my brain like when I was talking to nerd boy (and still not understand half of the things he's saying) and didn't need to be thinking twice about what I was actually saying. Kind of like if I were talking to someone who didn't care about my image at all.

"Oh. Wasn't it you who talked about taking meds the last time? What was that all about? Are you sick or something?"

She glanced over her shoulder with wide eyes and then burst out with a huge 'Whaaaat?' like I'd said something that blew her mind. "You forgot about the whole thing? Oh my god, you made me so worried about letting it slip and now you're telling me I was basically anxious over nothing."

Then she got to prepping and wasn't very good at having conversations while doing all that so I sort of just let her do her thing and slipped away for a quick shower. Which was weird because I've never really had anyone over, let alone to *cook* for me 'cuz, well, most people know that I have tastes and lol not just *anyone* can satisfy my preferences, so. Also, people can't take criticism. I think we've fired, like, maybe ten chefs in the household since dad was appointed the headmaster and stopped having time to cook for us. Now that I think of it, no one outside the family except our personal chefs have, ever, cooked for us.

"Okay, try this." She set a plate of kimchi fried rice before me at the table, topped with a perfect sunny side up (runny yolk) and seaweed strips as garnish. It was moments before my first spoonful that I realized I pretty much hadn't eaten all day except for some rolled oats in the morning, mouthwatering at the garlicky, spicy fragrance even before tasting.

Obviously, presentation wise, it was far from the first-class stuff my brothers served in their restaurants and what I was used to back home with our house chefs and premium ingredients making up most of our meals. This was literally thrown together in minutes from whatever I had in the fridge and yet... tasted absurdly, unfairly good.

I didn't say a word; just cleaned my plate while Xu finished her own.

"So... you gonna tell me who made you cry?" She said halfway through our silence, just when I thought she was going to settle with making me dinner and seeing me without my makeup on.

I made her promise to keep whatever I was about to tell her to herself before confirming that, well, it wasn't as though she had many friends any way and even if she told her only friend, aka nerd boy, he wasn't the kind to tell anyone else either. So... unfortunate or not, I ended up spilling the tea.

Compared to Lindy who was technically both my stepmother and one of my culinary instructors, Xu was, like... a nobody. Which oddly made it easier to delve a little deeper on how I was actually feeling about the situation with dad, and the fact that I was entrusted the fifteenth place in the second round in order to advance to the next.

I mean, clearly, now that I knew what was going on and that the truth was no matter how hard we worked to win the interschool, we wouldn't be able to unless dad gets exposed and I get discredited for everything I did up till this point. So obviously, I wasn't feeling too good on whether or not I actually deserved the advancement to round three. Like, I was kind of, sort of the main reason everyone was going to lose. Then nerd boy can take my place anyway, so that meanwhile, I could at least set my mind on dad and Layla Tenner before Pierre gets ahead of himself and causes more trouble. At least I had Lindy on my side.

Xu was surprisingly quiet while I let her in on the details, only reacting in terms of facial expressions and gasping and stuff. Even though there were times she clearly had something to say but would cover her mouth with both her hands to stop herself from interrupting me. Which was kind of nice.

"Wait, so," she uncovered her mouth after I done. "The thing with Layla Tenner quitting school and all—that... that had to do with Headmaster Birchwood? Wait, but, so then, but wasn't he...? Didn't the judges for the cross-year say anything or... did he somehow convince them?"

Already, I was being the most clear-headed I could be about this whole fiasco. "I don't know, okay? He somehow got them to forfeit whatever she did but that's *so* not like my dad, I just know it. He wouldn't do something like that... Tenner was our ticket to winning the interschool but not only that, like, he wouldn't... sabotage a student, I. I don't know..."

Xu slumped onto the table. Her pixie cut was actually a very good decision for her face shape. "Maybe he's desperate. Like, Sasuke-angst desperate. The Pierre guy threatened him with the uh, the buying you into the convention thing... and uh, stuff happened... sorry, I can't connect the dots like how Vanilla does it, so like I'm kinda useless here. Plus, if you're looking for someone to expose your dad and Pierre in an objective...? Manner? Vanilla's, like, the best writer I know of. I mean, you and I basically know *one* writer from the Chronicle."

I paused. Re-wiring.

"What's Vanilla?"

"Uhhh." She was back to doing that weird sound whenever she had to fill the silence and search for words, jumping from thought to thought and I could *literally* see it happening in her brain. Her awkward and stiff face muscles gave everything away and almost at once, I could tell that this wasn't free information and then, I made the connection. Told you I was a genius.

"So *that's* what 'V' stands for?"

Xu sat up and rubbed her hands together like she was praying and pleading. "I don't think you're supposed to know this oh my god can we redo the past two minutes like I promise I'll do better just forget everything I said like please my life depends on it and I can't have you making fun of my best friend on social media or laughing in his face."

This got me frowning. "Huh? What are you talking about? I don't have time to do all that. I'm just surprised 'cuz like... what? I thought it stood for Viktor or Vincent or, or Vladimir or Vaughn or something evil along those lines."

"Wait *what*?" She burst out laughing. "Does he *look* like a Vincent?"

I scoffed, rolling my eyes. "I don't know, don't most villains have names that start with a 'V'? He's like, a know-it-all villain so I wasn't surprised when he had a 'V' in his name but to think it was something all *soft* and *cutesy* like Vanilla. Ew. I'm stealing his birth certificate and changing it to Vladimir."

Xu literally cackled and it was oddly contagious. But then she dropped the next sentence that made me double, triple-think about my life. "Okay, but, like, your name starts with a 'V' too."

We were silent. Then I stood up to do the dishes and she joined me at the sink, still thinking about the name thing before I somewhat arrived at the miraculous conclusion that maybe people whose names started with 'V's were somewhat destined to be at the frontline of a battle against everything that we stood for.

XV

VANILLA

"She's not turning up?" I struggled to understand this, wondering if I had, by some malfunctioning of my ears, made a mistake. "Are you sure that's what Birchwood, herself, said? What are your sources?"

The look on Chen's face made me question the memory I had of speaking to Violet by the administrative building just yesterday and for a moment, I even entertained the prospect of it being all part of a very long dream. Si Yin was the one who came by to confirm that the supposed contestant had, in fact, changed her mind last evening and because the decision did not seem to bother anyone else in the room, we started at once towards the lecture room where further instructions were going to be briefed.

How no one else appeared to notice Si Yin's blatant anxiety of hiding something more than she let on, I could not comprehend. Needless to say, the urge to pull her aside and ask what exactly it was bothering her seized half of my brain as we took our seats in the front, but she was clearly avoiding my gaze. Something she couldn't tell me, then.

Fine Dining (Lunch) Service
Type: Elimination
Style: Kitchen Crew, Service Crew
Participants: 23 Red + 22 Blue = 45
Scoring: Guest ratings, teamwork, role competency

The organizers had done away with the suspense speeches present in every other briefing prior to this one and had, instead, decided to cut to the chase by having the details of round three up on the screen before even starting. And there it was again. Vague, non-transparent forms of assessment without concrete rubrics for proper judgement. How was one supposed to put a score to teamwork? They couldn't possibly mic them up on a production line.

Red and blue teams were assigned members across all three schools by a computerized balloting system, which sorted us into red or blue on a fifty-fifty chance. I was put on blue and in an instant, I saw his name directly below mine as though by some miracle, the computer was a wish-granting fairy in disguise.

My gaze would rest on the entrance of the lecture theatre every now and then in the middle of Chef Allan's further instructions, somewhat expecting a rejuvenated, confident Violet to burst through those double doors with perfect curls and flawless makeup. Fifteen minutes passed; the forty-five of us were split into our respective teams and led to separate dining areas.

"We're not gonna win." Leroy and I were walking alongside one another, somewhat apart from the rest of the team up front with our primary facilitator. A pointed look was all he got in return.

"Yes," I admitted, recalculating our chances of placing higher than anyone else on the team and my personal chances of elimination. "We're missing Violet, who should be walking in my very shoes this—"

"We're not gonna win," the idiot repeated, as though I hadn't already heard and understood four simple words, "because you are distracting in a waiter's uniform."

I nearly rolled down the stairs on purpose for a grand concussion, unable to conceive the sheer embarrassment and cheesy romantics of someone I almost hoped to spend the rest of my life with. Clearly, he was a mistake.

"Chef's whites or not, Leroy, your existence is impossible to look at. Please reflect," I adjusted my glasses that had gone askew from nonsense. "Without Violet, you'd have to work doubly hard to make up for my technical insufficiencies. That is, we don't know if either of us are on the kitchen or service crew just yet. I'm assuming it's another ballot, and should that be the case... well. Good luck."

It was not a ballot.

L'Assiette's representative, Hugo Nicolas Hall, also the one who'd won the champion spot for both bonus rounds one and two, was given the advantage of *assigning* his team the roles he deemed them suitable for. For the students of L'Assiette, this was indeed, an easy way to excel at their task but as competition, people like Leroy and I were at risk of being assigned a role that was completely out of comfort zone, such as—

"Head chef, then? Who are you picking for that?"

Hall was standing right beside the facilitator with an iPad, keying in the names of the crew members for each separate role. Naturally, he'd started off with giving himself the one he was apparently most comfortable with. Menu Design and overall staff management. Then came the other big names.

It was strangely naïve for anyone to expect the name Leroy Cox beside every leading culinary role in tournaments like these but I had, myself, unconsciously done the same. In fact, the person himself had been waiting in a visibly indifferent manner; watching Hall as the latter swept the room before then resting an unexpected gaze on my own.

"Him."

He'd pointed, directly in my face and naturally, my first instinct was to dodge the invisible line and shimmy aside for Leroy beside me to fill the space since, clearly, he'd made a terrible mistake of mis-pointing his index. "V. J. White."

Good god! Good heavens, he must be out of his mind. I turned to Leroy at once, blanching the color of my ivory dress shirt and quite frankly, feeling faint. "No. I-I mean, I appreciate the acknowledgement but as you can see, I'm dressed in blue accents. It means I'm a critic, not a—"

"Yeah, I know that," Hall finished with a cold, ghostly smile that frightened every streak of common sense I had in me. "And the guy beside you. He's on waitering."

All at once, the entire room seemed to understand exactly what he was doing and though no one had spoken a word since he started the assigning of roles, the silence only seemed to deafen upon comprehension. At present, I couldn't help but wish upon any reckless, magical star void of realism that could in some way or another, summon Violet Birchwood from the skies.

Leroy's face said it all. I could hear the fire in his gaze, the crackle and the spit; feel it radiating in waves of intense, livid heat. Hall ignored this and went on down the list in a casual tone of indifference, giving every competitor the same treatment of 'shock factor' by assigning them something completely out of their comfort zone, miles apart from their forte. Needless to say, not a single person could protest against such a vile strategy that would, perhaps quite certainly, give L'Assiette an upper hand while leaving everyone else in the dust.

As soon as he was done with every role, the facilitator spared no time in getting us to the changing rooms and ignoring faces of reluctance and concern. Not because this was plain, open sabotage and, quite frankly, a stellar example of the student's complete lack of

sportsmanship, but because the majority of us could not see a functioning kitchen, let alone a proper fine dining service.

"Coward."

Leroy had nothing else to say, rudely snatching up a uniform set
in his size on our way to the changing rooms. The sole chef's whites
with the title 'H.C' embroidered to its breast pocket was in a one-
size only and after receiving it from the facilitator, I could, already,
feel its weight in my arms.

"This is punishment, in a way. We were thinking too highly of
others as though their grand priority would be the noble act of ensuring every guest a premium experience. We were wrong."

"Yeah?" He snorted. Frustration in the very tone of his voice.
"He should sign up for Hell's Kitchen, if that's what he wants. Little
fucker's too scared for fair competition."

He picked the locker beside mine and, after jerking the door
open with full force, chucked his belongings inside before reaching
for the top-most button of his dress shirt. I turned away whilst reminding him to keep his volume down. Everyone else on the team
filtered in.

"Now I know you're upset. It wasn't responsible or appropriate
of him to deliberately sabotage his own team to make himself look
better and at the same time, compromise the comfort of our guests
but Leroy, what you're doing now—this is exactly what he intends
to achieve." I pointed out in a lowered voice. "Do not let people like
that get to you."

I changed out of my uniform into chef's whites just as Leroy was
done changing into his. He'd glanced over, noticing the wide, open
sleeves before reaching down to help me with them. I did the left
while he folded the right.

"And you?" He said out of nowhere, gaze still fixed on the sleeve
he was working on. "He getting in your head?"

"Well, quite frankly, I'd say he got me," I had the nerve to laugh, albeit nervous and letting slip a crack that, to others, would have otherwise gone undetected. Leroy met my gaze with what seemed like amusement in his eyes. "Head chef? Absolutely unthinkable. I don't know a thing about working in the kitchen, let alone heading one and leading several other culinary experts far more experienced in technique than I would ever be. So, yes. If anything, he most certainly played a strategic wild card I never thought of anticipating!"

My companion snorted. "Choosing not to play fair just to weed out others who could have competed against him on equal standing... that's being a coward, not strategic."

We made our way to the production kitchen of Hyatt Ballroom which the organizers had transformed into a fine-dining area (chandeliers, velvet seats, white tablecloths) with an adjacent practice kitchen hall. There were lines marked out for waiters and a steel tabletop with heating bridges doubling up as the pass where dishes that were ready to be served would be placed for pick up. Each station had a label to it—Rotisseur; Entremetier; Pastry; Sauté; Hors d'oeuvre—and by god, was I completely buried in information.

The terms, albeit familiar, swam in the reality of an *actual* production line when I realized I would have to be calling the wheel or expediting and that, while incredibly exciting for a select few up to the challenge of stress and pressure, was not what I ever imagined myself to be doing. At least not after traumatizing video clips of executive chefs hollering down the line and chaining expletives when they didn't get an echo in return.

At once, we were split into servers and kitchen crew for further instructions and I, together with the self-appointed menu designer, came together with the rest of the Line for a quick run down of what he had in mind.

"We're giving the guests two choices for each course," he started off with. "Hors d'oeuvre will be doing a thinly-sliced seared Wagyu with yuzu ponzu and a cucumber cream cheese smoked salmon canapé *a la minute.*"

"Ah..." I offered to speak with a raise of my hand. "But should a table have four people and three of them order the Wagyu while one of them prefers the canapé, we'd be having the latter on the pass, waiting for the three of them that would take five to ten minutes longer, especially in the case of there being three orders."

Hall snorted. "Yeah but the cucumbers are cold, no?" He turned this into something completely different from what I had meant. "We have good cooks. They can handle a bit of pressure... unless you don't trust them?"

I had to prevent my thoughts from showing and it certainly wasn't as easy as I had thought it would be, given the circumstance. Nonsense was not my forte and Hall had, seconds ago, gestured at those he'd put on starters—two girls from CSS who had, earlier on, declared themselves students of the patisserie course—whilst having the gall to twist this into something personal. "You're mistaken. That was not what I meant—"

"Okay, then do we still have a problem?"

The urge to challenge him to a duel of logic then and there had me by my throat but reminding myself that this was, precisely, his intention all along was enough to rein in every desire of winning over some awful nonsense in the kitchen. Smirking at my hesitance to answer him, Hall moved on to the next course, which, to my surprise and confusion, was soup.

"Hold on. Soup? Is this not a three-course we're doing?"

He had the audacity to look at me like my question was the silliest thing he'd ever heard, goading the rest of the Line from L'Assiette to do the same. "Hello? Head chef? Three-course in a competition? We'll lose if that's all we're doing."

"No, I don't think you understand—you just said we're going to give the guests two options for each course. Already, we are a person short with twenty-two of us against red team's twenty-three. You're forgetting that doubling the dishes on the menu doesn't mean we can afford to have more courses because that would quite frankly be insane." I could hear the panic in my voice and had to pause. "Please, listen to yourself. I promise, you will not regret re-considering your decision. A three-course can be superior to any other fine-dining option and it is fundamental that we prioritize quality over quantity. We'd only be giving the servers a hard time with the guests when the Line gets buried in orders."

Thankfully, the kitchen crew had the sense to agree for the sake of their own sanity and Hall, upon cleverly noticing the shifting tides, settled for a five-course instead of the seven he had in mind. That meant a soup, appetizer, salad, entrée and dessert. Two options for each meant ten dishes in total and by god, there were only twelve of us on the Line, including myself. Everyone else, however, seemed to think it was an average idea and did not voice a word of protest. I was stunned into oblivion.

"We'll have a traditional French onion and wild mushroom with white truffles."

Yet again, another dish that was *a la minute* with a variation that would take much longer than its counterpart! Already, the Line was going to be stretched and he was leaving it to me, the expeditor, to rush those who couldn't match the timing of the dishes on the same table. While the wild mushroom could be prepped ahead of time and plated in less than a minute (which was what the term *a la minute* meant, which, clearly, Hall had no understanding of), the French onion would take some time in the oven.

"For the salad, we'll go with a nice summer salad, cooked and raw, Mandoline-sliced so that we get the paper-thin texture. The other option's going to be a charred citrus salad with an Aperol vinaigrette.

"Entrée. Some nice pan-seared scallops on a bed of miso asparagus and a Mediterranean-style herb baked firm white fish... striped bass, maybe, on some lime cilantro rice with panko in it for texture."

Strictly speaking, he had his flavor profiles perfected and quite frankly, the dishes, by themselves, sounded perfectly delicious. The main concern, however, came down to it being a curation for the planning of a fine-dining menu fit for realistic production. Hall's dishes were extravagant, elevated and professionally conceptualized but already, I could feel the pressure on the Line to perform against technically challenging dishes.

Unfortunately, most of the crew had yet to comprehend the extent of sheer torture they were in for, blinded by the mouth-watering dishes they were hopefully about to produce. Hall got to crafting recipes after laying out the menu for dessert in less than a minute before any word of protest could be made by anyone including myself. I was, quite literally, brushed aside. Made irrelevant in the span of fifteen minutes.

By god, half of us in the kitchen were going to be eliminated and I was most definitely the first person on that list to go down.

LEROY

I was laying out fucking *plates*. Eight years of professional training and prior to that, culinary education from the age of two, now reduced to some dumbass shit that, guess what, was probably the exact thing that was going to get me eliminated.

If you don't already know, service doesn't like me. It doesn't like introverts. And people who don't give out smiles like they were grapes or something. Even for smiles, those needed to be practiced. Doesn't take a genius to know I don't have any.

"... H.C so that we'd mess up too. If the kitchen's buried, guests start complaining about the food, the waiting and... the stress we're under? Dude's out for all our throats." "Wait, you mean the restriction's removed? Aren't they... eliminate... equal number from each school?" "Doesn't apply in the second half of the competition, buddy... hey Cox."

I grabbed the plates they hadn't finished laying out to send a message ('stop talking because it's making you lag behind') and they somewhat stopped to drag me into the conversation.

"You okay? Man, he got you hard... I don't think I've ever seen you not in the kitchen... like, even during the service course last year, you were the ticket guy back there."

"Expediter," I corrected. Eight years of professional training. And without that role being part of the roster, head chefs were expected to do the expediting. Shouting. Expletives. Calling tickets. Making sure the Line doesn't crash and burn. Timing. Efficiency. More shouting. More expletives.

"Yeah, that." The guy moved on. "So... you okay with all this? No offence but I honestly thought you were gonna beat some sense into Hall or something."

I snorted. "Do I look happy to you?"

"Uh." He backed off. "I mean. Can't tell, honestly."

I told him to cut the crap and that we should be getting back to laying tables before Hall was done with the menu design and decided to micro-manage everyone else in the dining area. They listened, but mostly because we'd worked together prior to this—most of the student union had, since they seemed to need me all the time—and were used to how I roll.

We had some briefing by the facilitators on service and spent some time memorizing table numbers, familiarizing ourselves with the window and the pass (where ready dishes were called for service), where to stand in the receiving area and walking through the vestibule. I'd like to say that these were all 'coming back to me' but they honestly weren't. Even the exercises servers did to facilitate smooth transitions in and out of the kitchen... I'd mostly watched others do.

At least doing it myself sort of made me respect the servers I usually take for granted. I always thought they had it easy outside of the kitchen. Anything's easy outside the kitchen.

But an hour into training and minutes away from opening hours, I was part done with dish recommendations and practicing how to properly apologize for a bad dish. See, problem is, it wouldn't *be* a bad dish or subpar quality if I *was* in the kitchen, so, why am I apologizing in the first place? Because if you're raging about your dish, I'd probably stand on your side since, yeah, wouldn't mind the manager being called out on this.

Either way, I knew where exactly they'd put the blame on subpar quality and food being sent back into the kitchen. This was where head chefs did not have it easy, so either I eat that shit up, try to be a decent server, or feed the kitchen crew to the wolves.

Minutes into service and tickets flying up the window, the kitchen was the quietest I've ever heard anything in a restaurant setting. I was in for pick up table three's deuce for hors d'oeuvre, one of the first few tables seated, when, through the doors, I thought I was in a fucking library.

He was out of his comfort zone.

"Ordering table four: three French onion; one mushroom. Plating table three: one Wagyu; one cucumber."

He forgot to call for an all-day. There were probably ten starters by now. He's got three tickets before that on the board and no one's on the plating counter.

Not a single echo. No 'heard'. Nothing. They weren't responding to him and I couldn't even tell if it was his voice or just the Line collapsing in the first ten fucking minutes of service. Sauté wasn't even done with her mise—she wasn't going to make it in time for assembly and service was only going to pick up while she's off mincing *parsley*.

"Pick up, table three." I told him. He turned to the pass and, yeah, it was empty. Thunderstorm waves weren't supposed to be part of frozen lakes and yet, I could see them.

"Yes—hors d'oeuvre two, Adams? Could you please start on the plating?"

Hors d'oeuvre two, or whoever it was on the latter part of starters and doing all the plating, looked up across the kitchen and nodded before fucking standing there, continuing the slicing Wagyu when that was supposed to be hors d'oeuvre one's job. They hadn't been properly assigned.

"No please," I told him, keeping a firm grip on his arm. He was trembling. "Tell him to get his ass over to the plating station and make sure they hear you. Shouting is allowed here, y'know."

The last bit made him relax just a little so I turned back through the vestibule and out into the dining to appease table three just in case they were getting a little impatient, only to be slammed with another table for seating, and then, another that was ready to order.

Hall on the other hand, was having a good time walking around the damn place, chatting away with guests, and not bothering to check in on the kitchen crew that was basically falling apart. The menu he designed was a blatant 'fuck you' to everyone trying to stay afloat and the best part? Not a word from the organizers.

Fucking rigged.

"Waiter?" Table one. Rim bowls empty, which means they're done with soup and salad needs to be up. I cleared the table whilst mentally preparing to fuck whoever was assigned here. "Thanks. Could you also help us check on the salad? We ordered this, uh... charred citrus salad and it's been ten minutes since we finished the soup."

They could've been exaggerating—a lot of guests do that—but having one waiter to three tables should mean less than a five minutes interval between guests finishing a course and a cleared table, at the very least. I tried to look apologetic. "I'll check on it for you."

Into the kitchen, I spotted table one's server in the receiving area past the vestibule and I was about to wake him up when they called for pick up table one, salads and I connected the dots. He'd been standing here, waiting for pick up. Great. The other two tables he was assigned to must have been neglected beyond belief by this point.

I looked over at the pass. Okay, table three starters finally plated. He wasn't losing; and I wasn't surprised. If anything, the strongest part of him was up there and, under any sort of pressure, it was going to be the last one standing. A first timer, but decently on track with the timing of every table's service... he had one ticket in his hand that wasn't clipped up on the board.

I picked up table three and glanced at the ticket. "What's that?"

"A special request by table five for wagyu without yuzu but with orange zest and then cucumber canape but for the salmon seared.

All for hors d'oeuvre who are clearly under their production limit, so I'm holding this ticket before calling it a few minutes later."

I blinked, surprised. "Okay. Good call."

It's better to drag a table with special requests and wait out a couple more plates than bury a station that's cracking under pressure. I was out for service table three before doing nine's drinks and fifteen's order.

Someone had to remind me about some extra fork they needed because they dropped it. I got that, and then was met with another one for ice water. Then table one stopped me again and asked for top up. Problem was, I didn't know which wine they had. Only their server did.

I spotted the guy at his other table, apologizing for the wait so I went in to check on the status of soup for table three and send in orders for table fifteen before running into the guy and telling him about the wine. By this point, there were at least five hots on the pass—all mushroom soup—just sitting there, out in the cold.

He saw me coming in, eyes going to the line of mushroom soups in the window as soon as he did before going back to the tickets on his board and calling out for the re-firing of table two's French onion soup. *Table two.* Soup was falling behind.

"Re-fire?"

"The cheese clumped up," he explained. "Grease forming a layer on top of the soup. I can't possibly send that out." It was on instinct that we turned to the bowls of mushroom soup just resting on the counter. Timing was off. "I shouldn't have called for the mushroom soups."

"Maybe if they had a little common sense to drag the prep of *a la minute*, you could." I gave him the benefit of doubt. Cool phrase. Learnt it from him. "They don't think under pressure. You have to do the thinking for them."

Luck wasn't on our side without anyone else familiar on the

team. Chen, Raul. Rosi, Si Yin. They were in red, probably popping off on their own regardless of whatever tricks L'Assiette had up their sleeve.

If dishes for the same table weren't coming out the pass at the same time, sitting around out in the cold, there'd only be more complaints out in the front and, if you haven't guessed, I wasn't the best at mediating anger or frustration. I suggested using the heating bridge on the left end of the kitchen for sauté if he needed it, but to re-plate the rest of the mushroom soups. The look on his face.

He'd nodded firmly but behind those glasses, it was easy to tell the presence of something else. And here I was, reining all of it in, trying to keep my kitchen senses in check so that I wasn't overpowering his status as H.C. and also *actually* having to watch him struggle in the very slow burn of hell that was the heat of the kitchen. I left through the vestibule, not in the best of moods or thinking conditions; still trying to keep it together, still wondering how long it was till the end of service.

"Waiter."

I responded to the call. It was, again, table one without their assigned server. "Yes. Your wine's on its—"

"Oh no, it's not about that." The male guest dismissed, glancing down at his entrée and without even looking at it, I knew what he was about to say. "I ordered the fish and... as you can see, it's not cooked through. On the other hand, my wife's dish—the scallops—they're overcooked. They've gone rubbery." *Ah, fuck.*

I cleared their table, again, trying to look apologetic. "I'm so sorry. We'll get these replaced. Is there anything else I can do for you?"

"It's all students like you at the back, isn't it?" The other guest smiled. "Must be tough. Take your time."

I thanked them, honestly surprised. Guests like that, you don't get them every day.

Out in the back, the soups for table three were ready and I was just going to leave the returned plates on the rack without telling the head chef who was worrying over the multiple tickets he was keeping track of but he saw right through me, even though his entire back hadn't so much as moved or turned an inch.

"You're forgetting something," he said as soon I passed him on the way out, thinking I'd gotten away with slipping in and out for pick up. Freezing up was the initial reaction I had. He wasn't frozen lakes for nothing. Sharp as always, no matter the circumstance.

"Table one. Scallops overcooked, fish under," I told him, tight-lipped. He actually cursed under his breath. I was stunned. And knowing him, he would've known the consequences of having two entrée varieties that had way too different cooking times. Amateurs weren't going to nail the timing on their first day on the Line, let alone the first hour. This menu was wiping out more than half the kitchen.

"On the rail: one scallop, one fish." He called. *Highest priority?*

I told him that table one wasn't rushing and that they were nice. He needn't put them above everything else. "Service for those who haven't gotten their food comes first. Put them two tickets behind."

"Are you mad?" Vanilla was the most frank and blunt version of himself I'd ever seen. It stopped me short. "All the more reason to fire their items first! Sending back food is as good as not having put the plates on their table in the first place. Even *worse*, they're being nice about it! Common sense: would you prefer serving nice, understanding guests so that they'd come back for more or silly adults throwing a fit over one meal of their lives?"

I backed off. He was too far focused to remember this was a three-hour service part of some dumbass tournament and he was *right*. I had been this close to stepping over a guest being nice like they were a carpet when they should be on a higher priority list than fuming idiots picking on a restaurant's choice of tablecloth. I didn't even stop to think about it when something like that made perfect sense.

"Fuck, you're right."

I stuck the ticket before the first one on his board and picked up table three soups before heading out front, serving, and then checking on the rest of my tables. Fifteen's deuce had both of them leaving the table. I had to make sure they weren't leaving for good.

"Oh no, just out for a smoke. Could you hold off the starters maybe? Ten minutes."

I told him we were a smoke-free campus and offered twenty minutes instead, since they had to spend some time walking to the gate and back. They agreed on that, so I headed back into the kitchen, just barely through the doors.

"Hors d'oeuvre, drag table nine twenty minutes. Out for a smoke." He made the subsequent call and moved their ticket down a couple others. This time though, he got the call back from Hors d'oeuvre, which was a good sign. They were waking up.

I was out front with table one's re-fired entrée and only just served them when a facilitator with a pass came up to me. Just as I was about to head back to my tables for clearing.

"Cox, right? You have an emergency call from the administrative office," she said, handing me a weirdly gigantic phone and already, I was fucking up non-existent heavens for throwing all this shit my way. If she'd left without saying goodbye, I was—

"*Leroy? It's head nurse McCartney.*"

"Please don't tell me she's gone."

"*Annie's in a stable condition and she's awake—*"

"Oh thank fucks."

"*We have her transferred to another room for further monitoring but as of now, she's just had her first meal of soft foods and we have nurses with her around the clock, so don't you worry. I know you have school.*"

"I'll be there." Already, I thought of forfeiting by simply choosing to leave. "My phone's in the locker, but ask her what she feels like having for dinner. Leave me a text."

"Sure thing. She said not to tell you because she knew you'd be in school, though. Yes, and as for the ICU charges, Mr. Cox has already paid in full."

This was where the 'I'll be there' sort of paused and looked over my shoulder, like it was having second thoughts. He wasn't even giving me a choice by this point, paying in full. He *expected* me to win.

I couldn't leave.

Doesn't take a genius to figure out I haven't got the patience to continue watching kitchens crash and burn before my eyes—not when he's right in the middle of that heat, cracking under all that and still trying to keep his waves in check. The head nurse dropped our call and I handed the phone back to its owner and, on my way back, was already loosening the black tie, ready for chef whites.

Past the vestibule, back into the heat. Our eyes met and he threw the ticket he had on hand onto the board. I was already moving. Past sauté, rotisseur, drying racks and out through the back door, up the stairs, unbuttoning the black vest, through the first door; undressing.

"Table nine's drag is down to fourteen minutes," he started, unbuttoning the tunic. Then the pants. "Table two has a citrus salad on the rail which I was about to call. Table five needs a re-firing of wagyu. It was overcooked."

I tossed the dress shirt his way. He caught it and slapped the chef's whites in my face.

"Three. Nine. Fifteen. Those are mine," I buttoned up. "Three has some attitude, but rest are okay. Someone asked for water but I forgot who... yeah we both know I can't serve." He laughed.

"Sauté's reaching their production limit in two orders. For the love of anything, please help them." He did his tie, slipped into the vest. It was in my size, so, definitely too big but still hot. "Salad's mise en place was a terrifying mess. He ran out of Mandoline-sliced cucumbers thirty minutes into service and had to start slicing them up *again*. Help them too."

"Serve me something in this," I played, lowering my gaze. Holding the door. "And I'll consider."

He rolled his eyes, cheeks dusting pink and heading down the stairs first. "I want Hall destroyed. He's an unintelligent idiot. A brainless fool. Just... vapid! *Pea-brained! Absolutely idiotic."

I laughed. "No one's stealing my title."

He glanced over his shoulder, a wry smile on his lips. One that I could definitely get used to. It was very sexy.

"Then earn it back. I'm waiting."

He pushed through the back door and we were back in the heat. I took a moment while he headed for the front, just scanning. Someone looked up; saw the chef's whites on me and froze. He watched me take over the wheel, jumping at my first word.

"Salad: rail a citrus in two. Starter: re-fire one Wagyu. Kill it again and you're paying. Five cucumbers all day, four Wagyu all day. Ordering: fire one mushroom soup, one French onion. Soup: six mushroom all day, three French onion all day—table eight pick up—Sauté two, Mandoline cucumbers at salad. I'll take over for ten or until you wake the fuck up. Heard?"

They better not be fucking idiots and disqualify the people saving this ship. *They better not.*

"Yes chef!"

See? Only place you can get away with shouting.

VANILLA

"You have a really nice smile."

I glanced up from my notepad, pen hovering over table twenty-one's ticket. The mother and daughter deuce were beaming up at me throughout my pause to register a compliment received. The only response I could come up with was an appreciative nod. "Ah. Do you really think so? I suppose you could say it is well-practiced." They laughed as soon as I said this—leaving myself moderately confused since I hadn't identified my diction as particularly humorous. "And, for your entrée?"

Their eyes lowered back to the menu before them and the words I had been crossing my fingers to hear made their grand appearance as though on cue. "I can't decide... Lily, what are you getting?" The younger of the two then re-directed the question, glancing briefly at the silver name tag pinned to above my breast pocket. "What do you recommend? Mr. um, Mr. Cox?"

It was the only item we forgot to switch.

"Well, the scallops we have this afternoon are the freshest of the season," I started off with. "The miso asparagus it comes with is a great introduction to fusion dishes rising in popularity. I'd say the flavors and textures make a splendid pair."

Both mother and daughter seemed notably swayed by a swift but precise nudge in the right direction and decided upon the scallops soon after before moving on to dessert. I took my leave after repeating their order in full and then got straight to adding it behind the mental checklist I was in the middle of working through; a habit I'd developed ever since Uncle Al first introduced it to me at the age of seven.

Table three's entrée should be served in two minutes. Table nine's salad,

*cleared in one. Fifteen should be coming back from their smoke in less than
five. Water for tables six and eight. Table eighteen and twenty-one just ordered—*

"Waiter." I passed table eight on my way back to the kitchen and
he made a brief gesture for attention. I exercised the same well-practiced smile. "Hey, think you could make some changes to my ticket?
I ordered the panna cotta for dessert but, uh, I'd like whatever that
first table's having. Saw them enjoying it on my way back from the
bathroom. Is that possible? To change my order."

I glanced over at table one. "The caramel meringue in pate su-
cree crust?" Glancing down at the rim bowl of mushroom soup he
had in front of him, I was relatively certain about the possibility
of an order change. Nevertheless, I knew better than to make any
promises. "I'll see what I can do and get back to you with a glass of
water and hopefully some good news. Is there anything else I could
help you with?"

The guest shook his head and I took my leave from his table
with a polite bow before continuing on to the kitchen, once again,
going through the mental check list and adding his request to the
back. Once in the back, I put up eighteen and twenty-one's orders
on the board before searching for table eight's ticket and checking
the progress of his course dinner. *Still on salad prep.* I cancelled the
panna cotta he ordered and replaced it with the hazelnut chocolate
dome cake, also verbally conveying this to the head chef while doing
so.

Within minutes of our switch, he'd cleared at least seven late orders that had bottlenecked the Sauté station and at present, had
not a single order on the rail to fire, which meant that he'd also
cleared all urgent requests in a matter of minutes. Rationally speaking, I couldn't be giving him full credit since he clearly didn't possess
eight limbs and had to have the assistance of the Line in order to
have carried out such a feat in such a short span of time. Admit-

tedly however, he'd transformed the buzz of the kitchen into the sound of a well-oiled machine that wasn't falling apart by helping out whichever station that was close to their production limit. At present, there were none.

"Must've seen table one's serving," acknowledged Leroy, cleaning the edges of a plate for spotless presentation.

I hummed in surprise. "He did. And we have dessert to thank. A minute to table three's entrée, I hope? It's right before clearing table nine on my list of things."

He glanced at the magnetic kitchen timers stuck to the bar above the board of tickets. One for each ticket. How they had appeared out of nowhere was another mystery. "Forty-five seconds, if Sauté doesn't mess up." He sent the plate out the window, calling for table eleven's pick up before taking a glimpse at the two additional tickets I put up on the board. "You took eighty percent of the orders since we swapped. Makes me think what the rest of them are doing."

"It is simply a matter of efficiency. Timing is key. I wouldn't hesitate to send tickets into the kitchen when the head chef has everything under control."

He raised a brow, glancing sideways with a smirk. "Scallops also magically becoming a thing on all your tickets. Just when we're stretching on the herbs for the fish."

As much as I did not wish to appear smug, it was extremely difficult to suppress the smile threatening to surface. "Someone has to do all the work."

The next hour or so before the end of service was an adrenaline rush doing the very things we were suited for, and I myself, had found an unlikely way to satisfy my penchant for organization. Mentally assembling every order, pick up, request, and clear timings in my head painted a clear overall picture of both the front and the back of the restaurant and having it all under control felt immensely rewarding. Needless to say, Leroy was in his element. No one in the kitchen crew seemed to care about the switched roles, which goes so far as to say that I was the most terrible head chef they'd ever had the misfortune of encountering that having me out of the kitchen was a blessing regardless.

Throughout service, I was entering the kitchen for pick up whilst dropping compliments from guests up front every single time I returned. "Compliments from table two. Scallops were perfectly cooked and buttery." "Compliments from table six. They like the French onion soup."

Everyone seemed perfectly content with the arrangement we had and though the facilitators had stopped to speak among themselves for a short moment upon noticing the switch, they never once approached myself or Leroy for further instructions. In fact, the only person who confronted me directly was Hall himself.

He'd stopped me as I was coming out of the kitchen with desserts for table three, pulling me aside with narrowed eyes. "What do you think you're doing?"

The composure of his smile wasn't enough to hide the hiss in his tone. I'd brushed him off, requesting him not to speak in front of the food since, logically (as he so lacked), guests would not wish the berry sauce topping their panna cotta to have his spit as an added ingredient. Hall, a fuming little git, had intended to leave me brooding over certain disqualification.

I had merely snorted in response, brushing past his irrational existence and moving on to table three. "Correction, I've already been eliminated. I simply adore the look of madness on your face. Like it is now."

* * *

"Two points," laughed the idiot, shoulders relaxing as we headed past the main entrance of Roth Hall and out onto the plaza. "Imagine the look on Chen's face."

"He'd be surprised you weren't put on head chef for the first half, naturally," I said, redoing my tie. I'd done it up in a hurry as we were changing out of our uniforms for the round. The tallied scores were right outside the dining areas, in an adjoining room between red and blue team. "Neither he nor Si Yin were at the post-round briefing. Their team didn't look very happy with the scores either."

"Cuz we were this close to beating them?" He motioned with an indecent finger and I calmly censored it with my bag. "Even though we were that far in the weeds?"

"I'm not sure about you, but the rest of the kitchen crew you were leading seemed somewhat converted to the worship of Leroy Cox as soon as service came to an end. They must have expounded the miracles of making such a comeback to their peers on the other team... after all, it's not every day that we get to see a bunch of competitors protest against a sole participant's disqualification. They must find you very charming."

He glanced sideways with a softer flame. As expected, I hadn't made the cut for top fifteen overall, comprising of six students from L'Assiette, four from CSS and the remaining five—Leroy, Chen, Si Yin, Lee Jungwoo and a girl in her final year. Rosi and Raul, like myself, had been on the elimination list. Unlike their names, however, mine had been relegated to a special position at the very bottom, and in red. For disqualification.

"They don't know who to thank."

"Frankly speaking, I need a break. I'd give all this chaos a pass any day. It's exhausting at times." I'd been waiting for Violet to show up after the round to fume at my disappointing elimination, but she never came.

The decision had been rash and mildly insane; switching roles despite acknowledging the possibility of being disqualified and having our efforts to salvage whatever that was left of the Line go down the drain. Yet again, Leroy had proven his point: I was fond of taking risks. Calculated ones.

The probability of Leroy rising to the occasion in his element was nearly certain and while I couldn't be sure if I could do sufficiently well to be noticed as a server, I'd made a fifty-fifty gamble at him winning over the rest of the kitchen as their captain and had we not taken the risk of switching halfway through, Leroy would never have had the chance to shine and might have therefore been eliminated along with myself.

To factor faith and trust into any mathematical equation was a fatal error for most. A gamble, at best. Yet, for some reason, the orderly spirit in me was up of a thrill and this was one of many.

"Guess you're picking the location for our first official date." He reached over to pick something out of my hair. Fluff, I assumed. "Promise. No vetoes."

Amused, I turned to him as we headed up the hill to Cayenne. "Alright then. The Hudson Museum of Arts and Natural Sciences. I'm sure we'd enjoy a day of education in the presence of superbly curated exhibitions."

His reaction was priceless. I'd imagined an indecent finger or two but he'd altogether went for my sides with tickles which quite unfortunately snowballed into an uphill chase. It was unsightly—completely irrelevant and downright cheesy! As though lifted right out of some boring romantic novella.

He'd even suggested alternatives to persuade me like I wasn't at all joking in the first place (which I wasn't, quite frankly, but of course I'd never decide on something without his consent) whilst packing his bag for a visit to the hospital. Minutes before he left the lodge however, he seemed to pause at the bottom of the stairs, reading something on the screen of his phone and then glancing back up to me a couple of steps behind.

"She's awake. You can come," he offered, as though moderately uncertain of how I was going to respond. "If you like."

Needless to say, I was reduced to a bewildered animal scrambling for words to fill the multiple blinks I managed in the next five seconds of silence. I'd slept poorly the evening before from a heavy grey cloud of unnecessary thunderstorm thoughts, centering around the seeming reservations Leroy had about opening up to me, especially regarding his family.

"W-why, yes! Of course. I mean, why wouldn't I? It is a surprise to *me* that you're, well, inviting me in the first place. Which I gladly accept." Giving my uniform a quick fix was the very next thing I thought of doing; first impressions were key and if Mrs. Cox was going to see myself shabbily dressed and looking quite the disaster after three hours of service hell, I would most probably be the primary cause of her relapsing back into a coma. "Do you mind if I, maybe, took ten minutes to look presentable? In some manner."

He snorted. "You don't need it, but okay. I'll take ten too. Meet me at the front porch when you're done."

I wasn't too sure if I actually acknowledged whatever he said before zipping off (well, the fastest I could manage) to Cinnamon next door and bolting up the stairs to arrive at my door—fumbling with the keys thanks to jittery fingers sizzling with the rush of adrenaline. Multiple notifications buzzing in my back pocket did not stop me from thinking of what to wear. Scanning the rows of casual clothing I'd bothered to bring along for our three-week-stay on campus, I had a grand total of three variations. All of which happened to include an old-fashioned Argyle sweater vest: the only 'statement piece' my wardrobe could afford to cough up in a timely crisis.

It was either that, or the suspenders gifted to me by a certain idiot with surprisingly good taste. Still, I had, admittedly, been reserv-

ing that for something more romantic and I wasn't too sure what
Mrs. Cox would think of a fifteen-year-old in suspenders, so. I even
made sure to pack extra tea bags and cash just in case we ran into a
florist along the way. After all, I couldn't possibly be going empty-
handed.

At the very least, I was hoping not to leave a disappointing first
impression on Mrs. Cox; not when Leroy himself had invited me to
see her the very day her condition had stabilized.

As agreed, we convened at the front porch of Cayenne in exactly
ten minutes, me, attempting to assess what Leroy thought of my
outfit, if it was presentable to his mother, and him, illegally reaching
under my vest to run his hands along the material of my dress shirt.
While T.M. Lewin was understandably irresistible in terms of quality material, I'd pointed out, red-faced and bewildered, that he could
have done the same with my entire arm of fabric. He then reasoned
that I was wearing a coat, and therefore had my arms covered.

Upon arriving at the main station after a bus ride of Googling
for 'florists near me' (and also ignoring the multiple notifications
that I was, again, receiving on my personal email account), Leroy
and I made a short detour to fetch a bouquet of blush pink carnations adorned with stems of baby's breath. Satisfied with the pur-
chase, I was about to hand them to my companion since it would
perhaps be more appropriate for *him* to be presenting Mrs. Cox
with the flowers and me, an outsider, quietly supporting somewhere
behind when I noticed he'd produced what looked like a Japanese-
style lunch bag (the kind that was really just layers of cloth secured
by a bow at the top) and was holding onto that instead. And thus, I
was once again left on flower duty.

We boarded the train headed further out into the suburbs and
found it relatively empty—which, again, allowed for a cozy little
spot in the middle and the luxury of presenting the window seat to
one another. I finally resolved the issue by proposing a turn-based

system, which seemed to both ease his concerns and leave the semblance of a troubled smile on his lips. Realizing my mistake, I hastily corrected myself.

"What I meant was that, um. That should we travel anywhere at all, just the two of us, then this turn-based system would apply for effortless decision-making. It is not that I believe more visits to the hospital is necessary—I mean, should it be, then of course, I would be honored to come along—but in the case that your mother recovers, which I hope is the case, then, well... oh you know what I mean."

He laughed, shaking his head and stuffing his coat in the compartment under his seat. "I'm just tired. Aren't you?"

This, I admitted to. "Head chef is certainly not a role I am suited for. Barely an hour in the kitchen and I already feel as though I've aged a grand total of thirty years." I watched him laugh, once more. Relaxing into his seat with his eyes closed. "The more time I spend with you, the more I see why your father sees you as an investment. Your culinary talent is undeniably... endless."

He'd glanced my way then, a single eye open. "Guess what he said to me yesterday. While Annie was in emergency." I'd paused, unsure. He rested the side of his head against the glass just as our train began to depart from the station. "He told me to get my ass back in school. To win the damn thing.

"Which was what I let him down on last time, by the way. Annie's stroke before the coma... right in the middle of the final round."

I listened closely, tired but not nearly as exhausted as Leroy must have been. The hour-long ride he'd usually spend catching up with sleep, he spent instead letting me in. I couldn't tell if it was for his benefit or my own or possibly both; the issues he faced within his family was something that had always been beyond my knowledge or understanding and hence, part of my insecurities regarding the truth of him. Hanging onto every word and waiting for him to finish before settling for a moment of hand-holding in silence instead of more questions, more needling at his father's intentions. He'd mentioned something purposefully vague, which I think he was afraid to acknowledge or consider the prospect of happening; that should his mother require special attention or post-coma treatment that the hospital could not provide, they'd have to find her one with better facilities.

The underlying implications of that... I myself found rather hard to digest, and hence decided not to consider them until time required me to do so. This, without a doubt, was a rare occurrence. I was never the kind of person to allow for exceptions when it came to rational predictions or the anticipation of a near future.

Against the words of someone who gave them out sparingly however, I was in no place to disagree.

In the face of death; of certain issues beyond our comprehension of its magnitude, how was Leroy to feel the weight of a mere *interschool tournament* that mattered not in the face of a life?

"Like Pierson," he gave a surprising example. "Crying because he hadn't seen his friends for a day. Yeah, sure. Okay." He somewhat laughed. "Or... no offence. Those who treat exams like it's their whole world? Like there's nothing more important than getting that grade? Yeah, maybe it's for a scholarship. Or some college entrance thing. But you know. Grand scale of things... when you put it in perspective. Would you miss your parent's death for an 'A'?"

The initial surprise and chill of his words had worn off and given way to a new form of guilt I'd never before experienced. Being a complete beginner at reading and comprehending certain emotions, I hadn't even been able to tell that Leroy had been struggling with such personal concerns of his; things that didn't quite show on his face, or even, the flame in his eyes. Which, now that I come to think of it, was how quiet candles were.

Back then, he'd sounded so calm receiving that call in the middle of the night. I-in fact, I myself had mostly regarded him as someone relatively in control of his condition.

The crevice between his world and mine appeared wider and far deeper than I'd first imagined it to be. At present, I knew not how to feel. Examinations and grades were, like he said, extremely important to me all my life and were among my top list of priorities without having to encounter something as heavy as what Leroy was currently experiencing in my fifteen years of living.

In simple terms, I was sheltered; while he, a single flame, had been bracing against the wind.

The unread emails from this afternoon were beginning to accumulate with every buzz I could feel from the inner pocket of my coat. I'd chanced a quick, unwilling glimpse at the lock screen for a short preview but they were mostly notifications from WordPress about comments on my dashboard, pending for approval. Recalling that I'd recently published a recipe of the lemongrass fried chicken I made for Leroy a week ago, it did not cross my mind to pay the comments any mind since, well, there were far more important things to be attending to.

Seconds after arriving at the front entrance of the hospital and heading right in, the head nurse, whom I recognized from my previous visit, came up to Leroy at once to inform him about his mother's condition.

"She's in the middle of a visual assessment. It should be ending soon, before dinner is served at six-thirty, but I did tell her that you'd be late since, I told you over the call, she insisted on keeping you busy in school."

Her and Leroy walked slightly ahead, speeding past the waiting area and towards the lift lobby. I followed behind with the bunch of carnations in hand, unsure whether the extreme palpitations I was feeling were the result of anxiety and nervousness over meeting someone of such great importance or excitement and anticipation of being able to confirm that she was in good health after an extended time of uncertainty.

The head nurse had left Leroy and I to take the elevator up ourselves after giving him a rundown of the past couple of hours; and while we were standing in the lobby, waiting for any of the three elevators to arrive, I caught a glimpse of his fingers—now out of his pocket—itching towards the 'up' button despite knowing that pressing it a second, third time would not miraculously speed up its arrival. His grip on the lunch bag was tighter than necessary; shoulders tensed and his steps, like a wound-up spring he was trying hard not to let go of.

It was after arriving at her designated floor and emerging from the elevator that I noticed the strained weight in his feet. How he was trying so very hard not to run. To match my pace. I tried to speed up, fazed by the physical manifestation of his control over all-too-powerful feelings but required his guidance around the hallways nonetheless.

Then, it was stopping outside a room with a special label and, even before looking past the open door, hearing a voice from the many dreams, many distant, fond memories that brought as much joy as pain from resurfacing, time to time. I had recognized it at once; how it sounded exactly the same as I remembered it to be and should a cold stranger like myself be feeling such an extent of emotions, then surely Leroy would not be able to keep himself together for long.

He'd glanced at me then, as though asking.

"Go." I said.

And he did; off he went, right past the door and into the room while I stood out in the hallway, forgetting about the flowers and learning against the wall in a blind spot, gazing past the open door into the room and hearing his footsteps as he walked in and then, coming into view by her bedside as her conversation with a nurse came to a gradual stop and the latter stepped outside to give the pair some privacy but neither—neither of them said a word.

I heard her laugh. Feebly. And there was no hug. No kiss. No nothing. Not until Leroy started to unpack the lunch bag he'd brought along and the fragrant scent of crispy fried chicken fresh out of the deep fryer in a small, quiet diner wedged between a hair-dresser's and a florist, came wafting out into the hallway.

He pulled up a chair by her bed while watching her eat, helping her with the fork and holding a napkin under her chin as she bit into a chunk of the one thing they never failed to share. It was then that I wondered how it was like for someone like Leroy to have tears running down the sides of his face or to even have them in his eyes, red.

For some reason, I imagined them to sting. Like heated droplets of wax; running down the sides of a candle, lit.

* * *

"You ready?" He came out to say after several minutes of speaking to doctors and nurses, and that was after a very brief, quiet exchange of words with his mother who had been continually glancing at the doorway which thankfully had me out of sight for the entire dura-tion. I was listening in on the nurses speaking aside about her con-dition, relieved to hear that the upper half of her body was in a state of recovery. She could also speak—which was honestly the best news of all time.

"Quite frankly, no," I admitted behind pink flowers, looking at him through the stems and fancy bouquet paper. "I think you should give her the flowers and tell her that I came. Now that I've thought things through, it's been barely five months since we last met and she would be in quite the shock and and and I think you're forgetting about my uncle being part of the entire reason your mother's diner was under scrutiny in the first place! I-I can't possibly... the nerve of me to walk right in—"

"She wants to see you." He cut to the chase. Candle flames amused.

This, I could not possibly argue with. Swallowing once, I breathed to calm thunderstorm thoughts and then let him lead me past the door and into the room whilst having the bouquet act as part of my natural habitat. I chanced a glimpse at his mother's face but she'd picked up a hand mirror at the exact time I'd chosen to look and could merely be seen fixing her hair.

"Told you he looks the same."

I heard Mrs. Cox's laugh in response to her son's illegally false statement and felt the very tips of my fingers warm with nostalgia. "Sweet boy. Ten times smarter than you will ever be, Leroy. Are those for me, dear?"

I'd lowered the bouquet to allow my eyes some leeway and saw that she was gesturing to the very flowers in my hands. Immediately, I was fumbling.

"Y-yes. Carnations, they are. A mother's love, they represent." *Disaster, I am.* "Oh good god I did not just speak like that."

Both had their ways of displaying amusement and I, an embarrassed thing, hadn't even felt the hand on my lower back propelling me closer to the bed. Before I knew it, I was handing Mrs. Cox the flowers and then realizing that she wouldn't be able to put them in the vase herself, hurriedly offered to help her with the arrangement. Her smile was as sweet as I had remembered it to be.

"Please do. One look at the flowers by my bed the minute I woke up—I knew it had to be some unruly little lion who put them right in without thinking twice. It's probably what gave me the heart attack," she added in a whisper and I nearly burst out laughing. Leroy had rolled his eyes then and presented his mother with the indecent finger of his and before I could splutter words of shock and demand he put it away, Mrs. Cox responded with one of her own.

That was the moment I realized I had been wrong about the idiot picking up *all* of his indecencies from the kitchen or his father. Mrs. Cox, herself, was a professional!

"Alright, shoo. Run along."

I nodded at once, not quite pausing to register the exact implications of her words. "Yes of course. Certainly." I hastily removed the carnation stems from the wrapping when she stopped me with a hand.

"No, no. Not you dear," she then turned to her son at the portable bed table, dismissing him with a wave. "Sweetie, what are you doing? Go! Get something from the store or the cafeteria downstairs or, I don't know. The bathroom. Don't you ever pee? It's not good to hold it in you know."

Leroy had been popping chicken bites into his mouth when she said this and, well, I wasn't sure about him or, well, myself, since I'd never been on the receiving end of the kind of parental embarrassment techniques (an apparently worldwide phenomena) I recalled reading about in fictional forms but this was very apparently a perfect example of it, unfolding right before my very eyes. Needless to say, I was somewhat glad that it remained beyond my comprehension or understanding.

"I'm not leaving him with you," Leroy had the audacity to challenge despite the obvious victory his mother proudly had over him. He slid one of the boxes my way and nodded at the fried chicken chunks.

Gingerly, I reached for one. Just to avoid standing still like a pebble wedged between a lion cub and his parent. For some reason, he'd made it exactly like how he did back at the orphanage in round two of the interschool. I made no comment, knowing that it wasn't the time or the place to be—

"I can't believe you have the nerve to claim the title of fried chicken king when your sweet soy flavor tastes ten times worse than the ones I make. I'm still better." Mrs. Cox did not hesitate to inject, and Leroy was back to rolling his eyes and blocking his mother's view with a glass of water. He was thoughtful enough to include a straw.

"Stop fucking embarrassing me. You're doing it on purpose and I know it."

"Alright, then shoo! I told you, go pee or something," the supposed patient who'd spent hours in the emergency room was as fiery as her son was, but perhaps a hundred times more on the outside. "I want to speak to him alone."

Needless to say, this got me nervous at once and Leroy being, well, being him, he'd approached me with a look in his eyes that I was used to reading as a question of whether I was going to be alright. I ended up nodding. He too that as a green, grabbed his phone and wallet, and left the room but not before glancing over his shoulder with a non-verbal warning gaze directed at his very own mother. Again, she dismissed him with a wave.

"Come, sit down," she gestured to the chair by her bed as soon as her son was out of earshot. I did, fixing my tie and smoothing out my vest before clearing my throat and turning to her, bracing myself for a conversation. I'd expected nearly everything, but again, she surprised.

"I heard what you said, you know. That time you came to visit."

Naturally, I was a block of ice. Now staring at the floor and the state of my shoes, I was beyond recovery. "I am so terribly sorry to have put you through such torture. Th-there is no excuse. I am frightful at conversations."

"Vanilla," she warned and I immediately felt as though I was being lectured by an aggressive version of Aunt Julie. "You are not. I've always liked that you were around the little lion. He'd probably be an idiot without you helping him with homework or using complex vocabulary around him. I still don't get why you wanted to be friends with him back then. And truth to be told, I don't get what it is you like about him now." Her laugh was contagious, and I found myself easing into her words that were kind and characteristic. "But he's hot isn't he? Takes after me, of course."

I did a double take. "W-well! He... he *is* very attractive..."

"So?" She went on. "Is it the food? People always fall in love with a good cook."

I gave that some thought; finding it oddly easy to be honest despite our past. "I can't deny that he is professionally trained and extremely skillful at what he does. And talented at every culinary aspect thinkable. Yet... well. I'd hesitate to attribute my feelings to that. I mean, it should play a part, but... he could be a plumber, a driver, a teacher—though god forbid he'd be able to teach anything with that sort of patience—and I will perhaps never arrive at any concrete reasoning to my feelings for him.

"He is important to me. That much, I know and have come to understand."

I looked up to finish and was at once fazed by her smile, trembling at the bottom lip and the wavering in her eyes as she attempted to recover. She had a moment and we were quiet in that time. This was how long it took for me to realize that this was the social cue for being on the verge of tears.

"Oh. Oh dear," I scrambled for tissues. "This must be the seventh time I've made someone cry from having a conversation with myself. Including the previous time with you, that would be eight."

She laughed. "Sweetheart. I'm crying because I'm happy! Don't be silly. Come here," her arms opened weakly, still feeble despite the strength in her voice. I had paused in shock, unfamiliar with the arms of any other adult who wasn't a part of the family who had brought me up. We embraced.

"I'm glad you were here for him when I couldn't be," she said into my shoulder. "Sometimes, it scares me. How I dream about the wind just snuffing him out."

To hear someone else apart from myself speak the truth of the candle flame as how I had come to understand him felt almost therapeutic. Yet, to hear it aloud was... was concrete. It made the image seem so much more than it was inside my head and the reality of it—the reality of the flame he'd reduced himself into—seemed almost painful to digest.

There were times that I, myself, had made the mistake that everyone else had fallen for, and regarded him as the strong, grounded person he seemed to be when it was really just difficult, sometimes, to tell what exactly it was he was feeling. Thinking. Hiding.

"So?" Mrs. Cox recovered moments after blowing her nose and wiping stray tears, leaning away from the hug. "Is he a good kisser?"

I nearly stumbled back into my chair and missed the seat entirely. Needless to say, I was starting to flush.

"You don't have to say yes. I wouldn't be surprised. All that little lion does is talk about your adventures and—while it is, of course, very nice to hear about you—imagine having to lie still, unable to close my ears when all he ever talks about is how good he is at kissing. Ears should really have the same function as eyes. Earlids. You'd think we'd have the common sense to evolve. Who knows? He may very well be the one who is terrible at it and you are simply the one with more experience!"

Clearly, this was not a subject within my expertise or simulated conversations and I was not in the proper state to respond but thankfully, Leroy returned with a can of coke and green tea from, presumably, the vending machine downstairs and was glaring at his mother as though he knew exactly what she had been talking about.

They soon got back to bantering and after listening to them and sipping on the green tea he handed me for a couple of minutes in a daze, I decided to check the time.

That was when I registered the exact number of notifications I'd amassed in the span of the last four hours. A hundred-and-fifty-six. All notifications from WordPress about comments and, naturally, I was no longer going to reasonably assume that my godfather and Miki had left that many comments on my blog about the lemongrass chicken recipe.

Three was the usual. Five per post was a stretch and ten was almost impossible with the kind of scarce readership I had. A hundred-and-fifty-six in four hours.

Confused and anxious, I had a finger hovering over the preview of the emails, unable to decide if opening and looking at them now was the right decision but scrolling further down the lock screen seemed to provide more information on the matter at hand. There were text messages from Si Yin and mentions from Keith in the Chronicle's group chat. The last preview-able text from Si Yin was a cause for concern.

IGNORE THEM

XVI

⚭

VANILLA

It was not until Leroy's mother had fallen asleep after her meal and medication that we left the room a minute before the end of visiting hours and boarded the train back home. My repeated attempts to lend a listening ear to the details of her medical condition and plans for post-coma treatment suggested by the emergency medical specialist fell flat by the end of our two hours spent in the hospital.

With every added buzz of the phone in my pocket, heavy grey clouds began to gather for thunderstorm thoughts. The urge to relieve anxiety and read everything on the spot while Leroy was speaking to his mother lasted for the rest of the evening even after I'd switched off my mobile device entirely. On our way to the station, my companion seemed to have noticed the slight (or drastic) change in my disposition and had asked, for his sake or mine, I couldn't tell, if he could stay the night.

"Of course," I'd said simply; watching the clouds gather. He seemed shortly surprised by my lack of resistance to the idea and had the audacity to remind me that he hadn't brought along extra clothes of his to which I'd resolved by mentioning that he could, once again, borrow one of my stretched shirts. The next two days were the only luxury of a break for those participating in all of W-interschool, meant for final preparations before the bonus round and then, subsequently, the round that determined the ultimate rank of the top fifteen participants.

Neither of us spoke any more than that and while I could most certainly tell Leroy had much to be processing—his mother's recovery and the cost of therapy or even the feasibility of it all, how long it would take—I had selfishly chosen to indulge in personal issues gnawing at my chest, shortening every breath in a night that was cold. By the time we'd settled into an empty carriage on the train and Leroy had fallen asleep resting his head against my shoulder, I was resisting the urge no more and going through every notification, every email, every word in the comment sections of every blog post.

The system had a safety function of automatically filtering out hate words and sending them directly into the approval box, which had, in the span of two to three hours, amounted to a grand total of three hundred and seventy-two. That did not include the ones that were equally hurtful but without the presence of indecent language.

Reading feedback was one thing. I've read countless essay feedback and advice from writing professionals or school counsellors that had me under their radar for being the youngest of students back in the private high school I'd attended but this was a whole other world of social convention that had me immensely bewildered and quite frankly—afraid.

Indeed, my writing was made public for all to see but with my, well, relatively low profile, I hadn't quite thought of traffic going beyond two per hour. At present, the number was hovering at seventy-five.

Some of them had bothered to leave irrelevant remarks on every blog post about my apparently lackluster appearance, which were the easiest to ignore. The bulk of it had turned out to be a massive disapproval of me having 'displaced' Violet for the entirety of the third round and landed myself the idealized position of 'head chef' when I clearly did not 'deserve it'.

Well, anonymous human being, I find no fault in your opinion! In fact, I'd found this so terribly amusing after scrolling through a bunch of vulgar indecencies narrowing in on my lack of experience and 'scheming ass', that I was snorting the entire way down the filtered comments. Then came the longer ones speculating my supposed involvement in blackmailing Violet for a spot in the third round, essentially stealing her place, and then *somehow* threatening the student from L'Assiette to appoint myself as head chef and then have 'karma shoved up' my rear by messing up and needing Leroy to save myself from embarrassment.

They were grand, really, such comments were. To think they thought so highly of my social capabilities and even came up with such elaborate strategies I myself would've been thoroughly impressed by.

And there were those who laughed. Others that had things to say regarding my writing and my personal enjoyment of tasting and writing about the culinary world; well, to put things simply, they weren't being very encouraging.

Thinking back, Uncle Al did say he hadn't the easiest time starting out as one. For some reason, everyone liked chefs. But no one seemed to bear the same kind of revere; hold the same kind of respect; give the same sort of attention to critics.

I had to search up some of the derogatory terms they'd used. 'Clout' was one of them. What odd vocabulary people these days resort to using and how strangely emotional they can get behind their screens, with anonymity as shields and their keyboards as weapons into the heart of someone they barely understood.

But it was reading about what strangers thought about my personality that, oddly, had the greatest effect. They were a bunch of roundabout sentences claiming they knew the reason I was writing at all and even going as far as to conclude that I'd joined the inter-school (as though it was a choice) to 'stay relevant'.

Essentially, I was not needed. Fundamentally, I was, to these people... boring.

Needless to say, I knew perfectly well the futility of such words. That these were digital receipts I shouldn't be spending the time and energy brooding over or caring about since, strictly speaking, none of them were logical, reasonable criticisms that had the intellectual power to break a protective layer of ice.

But to be misunderstood in such a manner had no doubt, chiseled cracks in the surface. I was, quite frankly, a fair bit more exhausted than I would have usually been on a day like this.

We were back home in more than an hour or so; Leroy had fallen asleep on the armchair waiting for me while I was in the shower and if that wasn't enough to show what exactly it was we needed in that instant, I wasn't sure what else would have. I'd forgone all thoughts of confiding in him about the minuscule issue I had the moment I emerged from the bathroom and saw that the lights were low; him, unmistakably knocked out on the chair, seated upright without a stir.

Admittedly, I wasn't all-too-eager to be sharing what seemed, against the comparative extent of worldly problems, to be petty concerns regarding anonymous human beings who clearly had no logic whatsoever in their actions. The idea was to fill him in on the truth since, well, should I decide not to tell him, that would be obscuring it and leaving a partner out of a whole in which I was experiencing did not seem like the best thing to do. Regardless, even a fool without an ounce of emotional intelligence would have the conscience to comprehend the extent of Leroy's exhaustion and hence refrained from adding to that burden in which he had been shouldering all morning.

I had, of course, intended to share my experience the next day since we had the entirety of it to spend alone, together (preferably in a museum) but as soon as we'd made plans for a quaint, peaceful walk along the Hudson river, I received a call from Chef Marseille who then requested to see me in school at once.

"Ah, I... yes, I understand. Should I be concerned? I am aware about the extent of my poor performance in the third round and I am deeply sorry if I disappointed you in any manner but... I'm certain I put my best foot forward and eventually got eliminated. Still, it's a two-day break we're allowed to enjoy, no?"

Chef Marseille had kindly reassured that this had nothing to do with the results of the third round and apologized for requesting my presence in school despite it technically being a holiday.

"I'll get dressed if you're going," said Leroy, sliding a mug of café au lait my way before taking a sip of his own and then adding an unworldly amount of sugar in it. I'd pointed that out and flagged the possibility of diabetes when he had the audacity to wink behind his mug and respond with a criminal "I like sweet things."

Brushing that aside after privately calming my malfunctioned brain, I assured him that we were going to take a proper day off. He then told me about Chen texting him minutes ago about an emergency strategy meeting in the student union room, which he'd apparently responded to by sending what appeared to be, at first glance, a picture of two coffee mugs, but upon closer inspection, included me in the background speaking to Chef Marseille on the phone. Chen's reply had been a dashing emoji of an indecent finger.

Eventually, however, since both Leroy and I had reason to be heading back to school, we did. And I ended up missing the opportunity to have a meaningful, detailed conversation about yesterday's events. He seemed to notice something off about my disposition while we were headed to the station, which I was thankful for, and offered to spend some time together after his closing shift in the evening. That, I had agreed to.

After parting ways on campus—him, making his way to the student union lounge and myself, to the staff room to see Chef Marseille at the arranged timing—I was oddly overcome by the urge to see him again seconds into the opposite direction and had, involuntarily, glanced over my shoulder in hopes of catching a glimpse of his back.

He was standing at the very end of the hallway, nearing the turn that would have otherwise removed him from my line of sight; he had been standing there, watching, waiting for me to turn. He flickered like a candle when I did. Though there was no telling the exact expression on his face, the passing moment felt very much intimate despite the complete lack of physical proximity.

Leroy raised a hand. I stopped, providing a small wave in response.

How odd. Had I brushed aside the urge to turn, I would have missed this entirely; had he not been staring at my back he would not have seen me turn and how odd—how odd it was to realize that he, too, watched people go.

I arrived outside the staff room in the strangest of thoughtful dispositions, as though my mind was housed in a basement without any indication of the weather outside and left wondering if the sounds coming from above were the result of a man-made commotion or thundering of an imminent storm.

"Come in," Chef Marseille was at the door as soon as I'd notified her by text, leading me past the reception, down rows of office cubicles to a private conference room filled with familiar faces.

"Mr. White," Chef Lindy acknowledged as soon as I entered the room and closed the door behind me. To her right was Violet and Si Yin. Seated across them with a deceptively positive smile on her face was Layla Tenner. "Have a seat. This will be long."

My first thoughts came straight from the bottom of a lake and needless to say, it showed on my face. Si Yin was struggling to catch my attention, brows furrowed and lips thin from attempting to keep her words sealed behind bars. Her constant fidgeting gave away the clear signs of discomfort she was experiencing.

"We have reason to believe that the interschool you are currently a part of has been a... is under suspicion. Of foul play."

I paused. "Pardon? You mean... you mean to say the W-interschool? But who, exactly? You can't be referring to..." My thoughts strayed into the awry path of vile comments. "I would never do something like that. I assure you; I did not mean to participate in the third round at all! Had Vi—"

"That is not what we are referring to." Chef Marseille could wait no further. She slid a folder across the table and, nodding as I received it, filled the seat across me. "What we are about to share, you must keep to yourself until the release of the article. Do you understand? And the information that we require you to withhold, these, too, you must not divulge. You are smart enough to understand the importance of information in court, I believe. We are dealing with a potential lawsuit."

Scanning through the contents of the folder, I first came across what appeared to be a transcript of a private interview with Tenner and then a voice recording of something about her meeting with the headmaster before she decided to leave school. Then it was a seeming testimony from Violet against... against her very own father. And then emails and emails and documents regarding the interschool and something about a convention in Paris during the previous summer.

All this, I took in whilst listening to the allegations, summarized by Chef Marseille and backed by Violet herself, who seemed both eager, anxious, and angered enough to speak all at once. Tenner did not provide a personal account. She had listened closely and nodded at certain points with a smile that was most certainly a mask. Si Yin was apparently not directly involved but had helped in the tracking down of Tenner and persuading her to testify.

"This is very private information," I began after a long, tepid silence. "I don't... I don't see why you're telling me all this."

"We were thinking of taking a journalistic approach on this. And as it stands, you are the only writer of the school's press who has actively participated in the W-interschool," Chef Marseille explained. "It is clear that you are level-headed and critical enough to have perhaps, along the way, identified certain aspects of the competition that may have seemed oddly subjective. Otherwise, you would be better able to put into words the experiences that Miss Birchwood and Miss Tenner have been through."

"Wait, but I'm... as in, it'll be anonymous, right?" The headmaster's daughter appeared to have her doubts regarding the matter, and it was clear as day how recent this all had been conceptualized. "I can't have my dad and brothers finding out that I... I mean, like, they'll disown me or something."

"Your name will not be mentioned," I assured her on instinct, before realizing that I hadn't quite agreed to this matter and then, stumbling over my words for the next couple of seconds, tried to envision a piece. "You should hand this information over to the media. I'm sure they'll do a better job. Additionally, the final bonus round is less than two days away. What of those who have worked hard to... well, to clinch that victory? Writing the article and publishing it by tomorrow would necessarily deem all results null and and and... should we really be denouncing the hard work of all the other students? Further, is the timing of it all not suspicious enough to warrant some sort of prejudice against the writer? After all, I was most certainly *just* eliminated yesterday."

"The idea is that by getting this out sooner and through a medium of a smaller scale, the headmaster and Miss Birchwood's reputation will not suffer an impact as heavy as should it be sent directly to mass media. That was Miss Birchwood's concern. Should we be able to settle this privately outside of court by returning Miss Tenner to school and give justice to the prior mistreatment she had experienced as an innocent party in the whole situation, it would be ideal. Or so Miss Tenner herself has expressed.

"And if you agree to this," Chef Marseille emphasized. "I will be appointing you as a store assistant without dating records. Which means you will be regarded as having had insider information all along and had a part to play in the interschool regardless of elimination. That should reduce suspicion of someone tipping you off."

The room returned to silence.

Needless to say, I had my reservations. Was Violet really alright with her father coming under fire and being scrutinized by his students and the public alike, potentially (or most certainly) losing his status as a culinary expert and headmaster of a prestigious school? What of her own reputation as an online celebrity and her thousands of supporters? The consequences were endless.

"But uh, you know," Si Yin was talking for the first time since I'd entered the room and knowing her, she must have drained a huge chunk of her energy by simply sitting still and not expressing her immediate and direct thoughts. "This might not really be a good idea too because yeah now that I think of it, uh, don't people who write stuff like this, like, journalists in general, don't they also end up being... you know, being under fire for calling people out or 'exposing' others too? Like, some people really like Violet and uh... look I know I said this was a good idea but last night, some shitty idiots were commenting some shit about—"

"Y-yes well the um," I interjected without proper thinking, which was not a good idea considering the fact that most of everything I said aloud were simulated. Only to a certain idiot, this does not apply. "The bottom line is that uh, yes, there is a risk to all of this which all writers do have to take when they um when they undertake this sort of... task. Covering a beat of um, such nature. The primary concern would be for Violet. Miss Birchwood. If she is alright with all this and if she has, wholly, agreed to the writing."

Si Yin was glaring at me for interrupting her and I, too, shot her non-verbal warnings. Violet on the other hand, sighed three times. It was mildly amusing.

"I mean... we'll be reading your first draft, so..."

"Keith Tang, the chief editor, reads my first draft and then you, and then minor corrections are made, and we should be good to go," I explained. "I rarely do third drafts. Signs of inefficiency, really."

Tenner had straight out laughed and slapped me on the back before presenting me with a thumbs-up. Chef Marseille appeared mildly surprised but with a smile. "Yes, we have discussed this with the chief editor as well. About potentially releasing a controversial article. But unlike him, you will be given all the details and evidence you need to write a good piece. He will merely be reading it. The fact-checking will be done on our side."

I paused, staring down at the documents spilling out of the folder. They were sufficient. Perhaps a little time to run them through the original sources themselves and specific questions... and some close reading. But then there would also be the underlying risk of *what if it all turns out to be false?* It was on me to assess and ensure that it remained as low as possible.

After all, writers had to be taking full responsibility of their every word and being relegated to an inferior group of nosy, gossip journalist desperately hungry for scoops was simply not my cup of tea.

"I'll have the first draft ready before sundown."

Si Yin had been the one to push right past the door for a shoulder-to-shoulder conversation about something I had brushed aside for the sake of clearing my mind; a necessary step of good journalistic writing. Objectivity was key and clouded thoughts were never an advantage in conveying truth in words. We were walking down the hallway of the staff room, out of earshot, when she burst into a series of flustered questions. It was unfortunate how contagious some emotions can be. Things like anxiety and irritation often leeched upon creatures in their cages and I was no different.

"If you need anyone to track those people down by their IP addresses, I've got a guy. Also, I got another guy who can probably program something to ban or glitch out comments like these on your blog in the future. Oh, and if you need any legal back up or stuff like that, my mom knows tons of people. You really don't have to do this, you know that, right? Are you sure?" She fired away without stopping to breathe and by the time she'd tailed me all the way to the entrance of the school library, she had both hands in her hair, scratching at her scalp. "You're so calm you're scaring me."

I stopped before the glass doors, student card hovering over the electronic gate for checking in while she fumbled for her own. She hadn't brought it along. "You don't have to worry about me."

She seemed to pause, stunned, and most likely confused. I went on to explain that I would prefer some time alone in the library to focus entirely on the article, which she then took as her cue to leave after a moment of hesitation. I'd gone right past the doors and headed for the quietest seat in the quietest corner of the quietest floor and there, cranked up my thinking capacity to its maximum for the churning out of draft one.

It was one document, multiple corrections by Keith and a single instance of reviewing that all amounted to two-and-a-half-hours later that the entire process came to an end. And as promised, all before sundown. I'd contacted Keith for a final quality check and the exact time of publishing and he'd gotten back to me with an instant response, suggesting it be put up on the site and publicized on social media the next morning to catch commuting demographics and have the impact last throughout the day instead of having it fade into the night. This, he had consulted with Chef Marseille and Chef Lindy, who both thought it had decent reasoning and agreed upon it.

I was left on the third floor of the library, gazing out of the window at the setting sun and realizing how much of the day had gone by without so much as a sliver of personal, intimate emotion from myself.

Alas, they returned; like they always did after a day's worth of leaving them aside, untouched and unstirred. It was the bottom of the lake that I had the heaviest rocks placed without a disturbance but it was the shaking, or the crashing of a wave that would sometimes have them rise to the surface in bits that clouded the waters that were otherwise clear. Perhaps one could never truly avoid having to face the deepest and the darkest. Distractions in the form of truth and its pursuit for objectivity was ironically ignoring the truth that was sediment at the bottom of a lake. Eventually, they had to be cleared.

Realizing how cold I must have been moments earlier, I reached for my phone to send a text.

To: Si Yin
About earlier, I'm sorry.
I know I can be cold.

Exhausted and altogether drained from the influx of weighted decisions all day, I'd retired from the library whilst composing a text to Leroy for his location when, as though right on cue, I received one from him with a photo attached. It was a beautifully plated dish comprising of elements that seemed all-too-dainty and elegant for his culinary style. The background was what appeared to be kitchen nine of Roth Hall and at the very corner of the picture, most certainly not looking his best, was Chen in a tracksuit.

It was upon arriving at the kitchen to pick him up in anticipation of some time together and a hearty dinner that I encountered
an experimental mess that Chen and Leroy were in the middle of
cleaning up.

"I had no part to play in this," professed Chen, hands raised in
defeat while his companion threw a rag in his face which he had,
moments before, been using to wipe spills on the countertop. "He
was the one who suggested we swap signature dishes for a challenge
even though I already told him they did that last year for the third
bonus round."

"Time's ticking," Leroy had the audacity to remind the school's
current number one, who appeared to be adding the finishing the
touches to his dish. *Ah, so the picture of that braised chicken dish had indeed belonged to Chen.* Over at the idiot's station was a stunning purple sweet potato Mont Blanc in the richest shade of lavender that
was most certainly a favorite of Chen's.

"I'll wait outside—"

"We're moving on to tasting in a minute though," Chen elabo-
rated whilst adding artful droplets of sauce on the Scandinavian-
style ceramic plate he'd chosen to present his dish on. I paused at the
door. "Feeling hungry?"

"Ah," was all I managed in that moment. "Well... I'd assumed this
was a... sort of, private discussion about the um, interschool matters
and," apart from the fact that I wasn't in the best state of mind to
be thinking about anything related to the competition, "seeing that
I am no longer exactly involved in the issue, I should really leave you
two to yourselves. Oh and don't forget to clean up."

Chen was somehow able to prevent me from increasing the distance between their stations and myself with a single question.

"Have you ever tasted a dessert he made?"

Needless to say, hesitation came in the form of troubled thoughts
that had, at once, sided with Chen. True enough, I had not.

Making an embarrassing U-turn, I drew closer to their stations before ultimately deciding to banish myself to the wide window sill of one of the floor-to-ceiling gothic style windows lining the room, seated patiently in waiting.

It was apparent to both Chen and I that Leroy had had his Mont Blanc ready minutes before I'd even entered the room, which therefore explained his calm demeanor and his moving on to station cleaning. The digital kitchen timer went off just as Chen wiped the last unwanted speck off his plate and the pair of rivals looked up at each other before presenting their dishes on a tea trolley placed between their stations.

"You're fast for someone who doesn't make desserts very often," the school's number one had to say, handing out forks and knives for tasting whilst calling me over, eyes fixed on the dish that was finished first. "It looks... good. The bird-nest piping takes practice but for a first attempt, I'm impressed."

Leroy had a characteristic smirk on his face that conveyed, in a single glance, an unmatched confidence of *knowing* the standards of his dish. He then suggested we start with his Mont Blanc, since, as in most traditional culinary tournaments and competitions, they had the habit of calling up those who'd finished their dishes first.

His opponent had provided a brief roll of his eyes before scoffing in response, sinking his knife into the tart and checking for texture. The cross-section was just as impressive as its exterior plating and already, pre-tasting from the faint notes of sweet potato aroma and the complexity of its design.

Chen made sure to have a little bit of everything on his fork (the crust, the Chantilly crème, the sweet potato cream, chocolate balls) before sending it into his mouth. Both Leroy and I waited. Initially, I had thoughts of tasting it at the same time in order not to influence my thoughts on the dessert after Chen had said his but having missed the beat, I decided to be respectful and let him have the spotlight first.

His face was blank.

It wasn't clear to me if he'd always been the kind of person to take his time with reactions especially with regards to culinary tasting. Needless to say, this was nerve-wracking behavior for both the chef and the audience watching him, waiting for some form of response. It took so long for him to actually react that by the time we were at the limit of our silence, he was done chewing and had swallowed.

The first thing he did was point at the Mont Blanc and move over, reaching for a glass of water behind him on his station. I filled the space he had created after a moment's hesitation, hovering my fork over the dessert. "Should I wait for you to say something?" I asked Chen but his expression was hidden behind the glass of water he was drinking from.

"Just try it."

This made Leroy snort. I was guessing at Chen pretending there was something wrong with the dish since, well, he'd always been the kind to take unnecessary jabs at number two whenever the context did not involve some form of culinary seriousness. The latter seemed to think the same. "You just love to fuck around."

I sent an approximately similar section of the tart with every aspect of it on the fork into my mouth and about a second after taste transformed into flavor, I could feel the sweat on my palms and the sudden, disturbing flow of saliva reacting to the sickly sweetness of the Chantilly crème and sweet potato cream combined.

Certain that I was pale by this point from trying not to spit it out, I placed the fork down and searched for a paper towel in an attempt to hide the expression on my face. Eventually, I swallowed.

"Did you taste it?" I was numb without water and amazed at how

Chen managed not to let a single streak of emotion show up on his face. *He made mistakes too.* "Did you taste the filling?"

Leroy was staring at both of us with an expression that was now blank. "Yeah. I did."

I paused. "You mean to say you tasted it before you added some additional sweeteners, correct?" The laugh that escaped my lips was nervous and uncharacteristic. Drawing towards his station, I searched for the ingredients. It was during this exchange that Leroy had picked up a fork and, after cutting a section out of his Mont Blanc, tasted it.

His chewed slowly. And then swallowed; turning to us with an expression that was not the face of someone who'd had the sweetest forkful of Mont Blanc in their whole entire lives. It had been a mouth of sugar.

I must have staggered. Chen and I exchanged a glance and Leroy, out of the picture, seemed increasingly vexed by that which we could not word. The gears turned and the puzzle pieces converged to form something I should have realized from the very first of signs. *Chip's pumpkin pie.* When was the last time he had something sweet?

Questions. "Did you use honey in your lobster ravioli?"

He stared. "Yes."

It was him. "And—and your sweet soy chicken at the orphanage. And for Annie. Did you taste them?" And the coffee this morning. And... oh god.

"Yes." It came out urgent.

I went up to him, quiet and close. "Did you taste the buttercream for the dessert toast that we ended up throwing away at the orphanage?"

The light in his eyes were strangled and dim. It was the strangest look on him and it was then that I realized I'd never seen him so visibly lost in information; stunned into silence. "I made that."

No.

It was him? But what was he doing on dessert and how long had it been since he had something sweet without realizing that it was bland but that must have something to do with him not having a consistent dessert or sweet dish that would have acted as a control for the past couple of months to have him not even realize that his taste buds were changing and that, that they were abnormal but there was nothing wrong with the savory dishes from yesterday or the day before that and the ramen during the first round so when? *When did it all start?*

"Leroy."

It, cracked and hollow, was all I could manage. Chen had made the decision to leave us alone, exiting the room from the left and slamming the door behind him while Leroy and I kept our eyes on each other. Waiting and, just, momentarily coming to a standstill. The sound, the creak of company on the other end of the seesaw seemed to stop. "Leroy."

"Your tart is inedible."

Through the glass, he seemed to distort in the lens and they blurred and focused and blurred and focused and I waited for the words to come right after but they did not and so I had to compose.

"It is far too sweet."

His gaze did not falter; nor did it move away from my own. And not a word, not a single word was said while we struggled to breathe. I staggered again, holding onto his sleeve for balance but he did not move to reciprocate. Rational thoughts. Rational thoughts; premises for a conclusion. There had to be a reason.

"If you are on some kind of medication, please tell me now."

It was simple, the shake of a head was, but for some reason they provided more confusion, desperate than ever. I shut down after a while and was quite unable to think of anything else. "Taste it again, and please tell me that this is a—"

He took off, grabbing his bag without warning and crossing the room towards the door and left, in his wake, the darkness of soot and burns and in the air, the scent of a candle

extinguished.

The darkness followed at his feet, shadows falling asleep at the setting of the sun to gather under streetlamps, lit; flickering as he passed and, a few hundred feet before the parlor, stopped at a convenience store in mindless smoke. A fried chicken thigh, he bought and bit into even before leaving the counter and felt a burst of salty, spicy flavor that matched the aroma and fragrance of crisp, seasoned batter. It was not bland.

He looked small against the wide, empty street, standing outside a well-lit corner store facing the shadows and chewing. Just chewing. And moments after he could finally convince himself that he hadn't lost it all, started farther down the street for the ice cream parlor. The palm-sized snack was gone by the time he arrived and the other staff member he was supposed to be taking over had done a double take as soon as he entered through the back.

"Leroy? Um, you okay?"

He punched in and had the other girl do her own, not quite answering her question. Making his way to the front and then going up the stairs to where the staff lockers were located, he checked the duty list and noticed that he'd been placed out front instead of the back.

Come to think of it, Leroy had spent most of his shifts serving customers at the counter or cleaning up even during closing shifts when previously, he'd always been made to prepare the batches of ice cream bases for the next day. Especially vanilla.

In fact, it had been nearly five months since he'd sat down in private for his usual fix in some corner at the back of the store. Just a cup. The exact same recipe they had been using since he joined the team. And as for the reason why, Leroy could not find it in himself to turn the gears and work things out.

The cravings, they seemed to disappear upon the reflection of a summer pool or the chill of a frozen lake. For the times they'd spent together, there seemed to him, little need for the comfort of something cold against the heat that had been growing within. Simply put; there was no longer a need for a fix. He was whole.

Had things been a little different, he may have, perhaps, discovered his deteriorating sensitivity to the taste of sweetness at the very back of the store, in the process of making the very same ice cream base every week or so. After all, it was his only constant; the only control; the only flavor he was so familiar with that he would, at once, know when it was wrong.

He changed out of his clothes and into the staff uniform, making his way down and ignoring those out front trying to get his attention, heading straight for the back and spotting the only other guy on base duty before taking over without a single word or question.

"Hey, Leroy. Aren't you supposed to be out front? I'll handle the base. Don't worry, I've done it a couple of times—"

All he had to do was insist. The other guy, he'd never heard Leroy say a single word outside of serving customers, let alone insisting on something that was otherwise considered by everyone else to be the most tedious role on the list and the one that would have to clock in an extra couple of hours just to make sure things were right.

He got to work. Cream, liquid sweeteners, salt, prepping of vanilla beans; they were part of his routine and usually, they'd all sit in the chiller over night before going into the machine the next morning for overnight aging that was what really made the texture of it all so smooth and scoopable. Today was different. Today, he'd got a quarter of it into the machine and had that running for thirty minutes.

And though the texture wasn't the perfect, smooth, airy, light cream he was used to having, he forced it out of the canister and into a desperate mixing bowl he'd found and out of that, he ate.

It was an entire spoonful he'd sent into his mouth. A life-sized mound of frozen cream that fell right apart on his tongue but nothing—nothing. Nothing. No crunch of leaves under his feet, no crashing waves over his head for a good drowning chill, no creak that was the sound of company. Nothing to soothe the burn of his flame that felt, at present, so beautifully close to being snuffed out by the wind.

XVII

⚭

VANILLA

"Good evening."

He shoved the key straight up the lock in a jump. "Fucking—"

Turning made him stop and squint in the darkness in which I was standing in, at the bottom of the steps up to the back door of the ice cream parlor. Frankly speaking, I would have found his face mildly amusing had it not been for the seriousness of our circumstance and the string of tension, pulled taut between us, ready to snap.

The accurate term was *ambush*. Leroy had no intention to be seeing me so soon after an ugly escalation of matters in which he'd quite literally run away from, and to be confronted so soon was perhaps an underhanded but necessary manner for the issue to be resolved.

He appeared speechless, standing at the top of the steps with the keys dangling off a hooked index. The flicker in his eyes warranted some form of explanation in countering disbelief.

"I can see you're surprised," I sighed, wisps of mist escaping from behind my scarf. "'How did he know I was coming out from the back door?' Well, most stores lock their front doors after opening hours, and this being an ice cream parlor, I was certain that preparations for the next day's batch of ice cream had to be done, which meant that someone had to be in the store itself for the next hour or so even after closing and the only exit would be from the back. Judging from the timing of your shift, I deduced two possibilities. One, cleaning duty, and two, you being in charge of the ice cream base. Factoring in your personality and the way you ran off a few hours ago, I thought the chances of you opting for the latter were higher. Nevertheless, I'd eliminated all chances of not being able to see you by coming early and waiting out in the cold just in case you were the anomaly and somehow chose cleaning over making ice cream bases and would leave right after locking up the front. Though now, I see that my initial prediction had been spot on. And 'how did he know where the back door was?' Google Maps. So. With that out of the way," I paused, having provided a clear and detailed account. "How was it? Your ice cream."

His reaction, delayed and oddly tame, was to finally start descending the steps to level our eyes and then, saying nothing, remove his wine knitted scarf and add that to whatever garment that was already around my neck. I could barely speak, wrapped up like an unwieldy dumpling-burrito-thing, and struggled to make myself heard in a flurry of blushing embarrassment.

"I—Leroy! I-if this is your way of asking whether or not I'm cold from standing out here, it does not work. Take back your scarf. I don't need it."

This idiot had the nerve to roll his eyes before unwrapping the piece of clothing and relieving me of my dumpling-ness. In return, I was able to reach into my tote bag and produce single-use hand warmers which I then slipped into his pockets.

"I had these prepared. They must make a lot of money from producing these things, especially since they practically run out of steam every twenty minutes or so. I've used five in the past hour sticking them all over the insides of my coat. Not including the ones in my pockets."

He laughed, and the sound itself made it seem like he was nearing the end of a three-day triathlon. Which probably did not exist.

I met his gaze and it was a small, flickering flame. Constantly. Struggling against the wind. The very tug on his lips made for a smile that was sad and at no point in my knowing of Leroy had I ever identified, in a single glance, that fearfully simple emotion. He'd been upset, disappointed and at times aggrieved but *sad* was... sad was a slow burning flame. Dying.

"It was bland," he said eventually.

And I registered this at my own pace, unconsciously huddling a little closer for warmth. Breathing in. "When you came over for thanksgiving and had Chip's pumpkin pie. Was that bland too?"

"Not as much," he admitted. We drew closer towards a streetlamp, away from the shadows directly outside the back door of the ice cream parlor, and stood under the orange beam out in the January bite. "It's hard to compare. They have different flavor profiles, you know that. But the pie... I remember it was sweet, at least. Now..."

"Alright." I nodded, pleasantly surprised by the direction he was going in and hoping that he'd continue down the rest of my mental flow chart after giving answers to the primary question I had. "So we've established that this is a gradual thing. Okay. And this um, lack of sensitivity... it has only applied to the tasting of sweetness? Of sweet things?"

"Don't know," he frowned. Honest. "I got through the three rounds plus all the bonus ones, so. And we did okay back in SOY."

"But back then... well, I know you weren't necessarily in charge of the dessert, that was Rosi, but when you tasted it..."

"It was fine."

"Exactly," I emphasized, glad that we'd arrived at another form of evidence to support the gradual change. The more justification we had for a premise, the closer we were to having a valid, sound conclusion. This was the hard part.

"And do you... I mean, are you sure you haven't been... well, you do know that, between us, it is completely acceptable for you to tell me *anything*, right? Anything at all. The chemotherapy drug bleomycin is an antitumor antibiotic that might result in a lack of—"

"I don't have cancer."

"Okay thank god." I'd breathed in relief while he snorted, laughing at my incredible overthinking skills with a shake of his head. "Well if you were on such medication yourself, the doctor *would* have warned you about it and you couldn't have been so oblivious or surprised about this whole thing either. Oh stop laughing. You know I had to confirm. I mean, I'd prefer for us to spend the rest of our lives together in the living world."

His laugh subsided and left traces of a genuine smile on his lips. It softened his eyes and it was then that I'd realized we'd huddled a lot closer than before. Then it was leaning in and and and embracing, for want of a better word; a much-needed relief from the hours we'd spent apart brooding over a matter of such weight.

"Think it's genetic," he said into my hair, slightly above my ear. "Annie was losing hers too. I might end up losing it all."

I looked up at him. Or more precisely, at his jawline since that was all I could see in our current position.

"Sorry to burst your bubble Leroy, but what you're experiencing is most likely hypogeusia and the percentage of it being genetic is incredibly low beyond belief. Additionally, your mother losing her sense of taste, which I presume is one of the factors that had her sell the diner, could have been due to the medication she was taking since, as you mentioned some time ago, she was in poor health. We don't know if *all* your taste receptors are going to be affected until we consult an expert but until then, the only thing we're *certain* about is that your ability to taste sweet things have been, well... have diminished."

The idiot did not take this lying down. "Pretty sure it's genetic," he insisted, and I could practically hear the frown in his voice. "Says I'm likely going to end up losing all five basic tastes too."

"Says?" I'd blinked in response, stepping slightly out of the hug. "Says who?"

"Google."

I stared up at him, calmly waiting for more. "Alright." I nodded. "And did you check your sources?"

This made him pause. "What's that."

"Well, it's where the knowledge or information you attain stems from. Most of information on the net is secondary information, made easy to digest relative to proper scientific research that they either cite or refer to, so we should always check their sources. Sometimes, they source secondary information, which makes them tertiary, and so on so forth. Information is lost. Misinterpreted, paraphrased to no end. I refer to *primary* sources—research papers written by proper nutritionists, doctors and researchers. And I will have you know that hypogeusia refers to diminished sensitivity to detect a specific taste quality or class of compounds.

"While, admittedly, the study of clinical abnormalities in taste perception in pediatric populations has received little scientific attention, in part because, the clinical assessment of taste is not well developed, most information regarding your symptoms point towards hypogeusia. Most importantly, distortions of normal gustatory perception may occur with isolated injury to any one of your major nerve pathways even when you, the patient, do not recognize the problem. Which is precisely your issue.

"Of course, there will be a need for psychophysical taste and smell testing for proper diagnosis because gustatory dysfunction can possibly signify a number of systemic or neurological disorders. And we don't know for sure if it is merely a symptom of a bigger issue or if this could possibly lead to much distress."

I paused to check for understanding. Which was what I'd learnt to do over the years; allow others some time to digest the uncontrollably large amount of information I tend to dish out in a short span of time. Information per second was the term.

My companion's processing face was, as usual, unfairly attractive and I was forced to stare at it for the next couple of seconds until he was done and his attention had returned. He seemed moderately surprised.

"How long did you..."

"One can tell just how many research papers I'd gone through for the past couple of hours you were gone," I sniffled, noting the onset of a runny nose. "It's past ten o'clock in the evening and I haven't had an ounce of rest at the rate my heart is going. It doesn't help that I haven't had the greatest morning or afternoon either and today has just been a complete mess and all I had been hoping for was a peaceful, quiet evening preferably without your absence. Clearly, this did not turn out to be the case.

"What I'm trying to say is that I'd very much like for us to head home," I summarized. "And cuddle. If that is alright with you."

The pause that ensued had been, oddly enough, the perfect moment for a gentle, quiet cloaking of the land. Snow started to fall in whispers and I sneezed, breaking the silence. This time, Leroy made no attempt to bother about the protests I had voiced while he, again, removed his scarf and once again, transformed me into a dumpling.

"Love you too."

Under the fabric, I was cooked to no end in juices of embarrassment.

Later in the evening, it was in our respective sleepwear that we gathered around the coffee table with a pot of instant ramen and a serving bowl each, expertly enjoying a piping hot supper at eleven in the evening over further conversation and pooling of information or findings that would help the two of us form a general, preliminary assessment of Leroy's condition.

"You could have the hospital refer you to a specialist as soon as possible. What about tomorrow, when you give your mother a call?"

"I don't want her to worry. She's got enough on her hands," he said, serving himself a huge portion of springy noodles and spicy soup. "I'll look for numbers up on the internet."

"Well, I've already done that." Pulling up a memo note saved on my phone, I slid it across the table. "Reliable experts, doctors and specialists with at least a hundred or so positive reviews. Depending on what sort of medical help it is you are seeking, that is. I... understand that you and your father... well. The situation unfortunately requires the necessary presence of an adult."

He listened as I explained the importance of having someone else older to rely on, preferably for financial stability which in his case, he desperately needed. A mere consultation could cost him hundreds in the case of a specialist. He needed an adult to be there for him at every step of the way, help him digest the loads of information he was probably going to receive and, most importantly, find out about the likelihood of there being a cure.

"He's not that kind of guy," was all Leroy said in return and quite frankly, it shocked me.

Indeed, he hadn't made a single mention about how exactly he'd spoken to his father several days ago while his mother was in emergency and so to an outsider like myself, their relationship seemed murky and vague.

"I'll think about it. But these contacts," he scrolled through the names, clinics, email addresses and phone numbers accompanied with additional information like price points and expertise in bullet points. "They help a lot. Don't think anyone's ever... done something like that. For me. Know what I need without asking and actually being able to do it."

I paused with a chopstick of noodles midway between the bowl and my lips. "Well, you aren't the easiest of human beings to read either, you know. I can hardly tell what you're thinking, sometimes. And I'm sure your mother wouldn't like it if you were hiding such an important issue from her... though I suppose I'm... I suppose I would like to, perhaps, become accustomed to knowing what you need or... knowing you. At the very least, I would like to be someone you can rely on in times like these. When you feel like you have no one else."

He laughed quietly. "You are."

I had steam from the noodles fogging up my glasses for a moment of sheer embarrassment before registering the casual romanticism he himself did not seem to have noticed, merely continuing to slurp the noodles in his bowl without a care for the struggles of bespectacled beans across the world.

* * *

We had spent so much of the previous evening thinking of logical explanations for Leroy's gradual loss of sweet sensitivity that I, once again, hadn't a single window of opportunity to be thinking of troubles of my own. The idiot and I were mapping out a brief history of anything sweet he could recall having over the past couple of months all the way back to the summer holidays before the start of school, considering the involvement of psychology that may have very well played a part in his current state and had ended up sleeping at two in the morning without being quite able to identify a concrete independent variable.

Needless to say, Leroy and I were so mentally exhausted by the end of the day that I'd nearly forgotten about worries of my own and had seemingly brushed them aside as petty in comparison to every single problem my companion was facing.

In fact, by the very next morning, I had woken up to yet another wave of anxiety after realizing that Chef Marseille and the team had, along with Keith, decided to go along with Keith's suggested publishing time of 9AM, mere thirty minutes after I'd brushed my teeth and checked my messages.

Leroy had the habit of lying in bed even after he was awake either in an attempt to get back to sleep or simply because this was not a day he was willing to start and I'd left him there to, um, burn some toast and overcook scrambled eggs because high and low heat was the vaguest concept I'd ever come across unless I somehow had a stove that presented everything in accurate numbers (measurements of thermal units). Hovering a hand above a pan was, to me, the silliest way to gauge heat levels but Leroy was the kind of chef that would do that and go 'yeah its ready' and I'd never be able to understand such miraculous phenomena.

I'd excused myself to speak to Keith on the phone, who had the article on scheduled publishing and every other medium of publicity on the same mode. Comments were turned off for the Facebook, Twitter and Instagram publicity and the Chronicle's site itself in which the article would be published had all remarks and comments filtered for approval.

I made up an excuse to return to school and Leroy had offered to send me to the station which, of course, I had declined and encouraged him to, instead, start making the necessary calls to his mother, the hospital, and some contacts on the list I provided him last evening for a referral as soon as possible. Tomorrow was the day of the final bonus round and though despite the whole conspiracy with Chef Pierre and Headmaster Birchwood going on, one could never be sure if the interschool would even continue in the first place, I needed to at least ensure that Leroy wasn't going to be left behind in the mess.

At exactly 9AM, the article was published and I had been on my way past Anton plaza to Roth Hall when the private messages starting flooding in on social media. Of course, I had been afraid to even look at them and had thought of deactivating my accounts and temporarily disabling access to my blog but I soon realized that... well, some people were coming forward with their experiences of prejudice and injustice both in the current interschool and previous ones as well. Especially among those who'd gotten eliminated earlier on in the competition.

I wasn't sure if Leroy was an active reader of the Chronicle (as much as he liked to claim that he'd read anything I write) or if he was on social media often enough to be knowing what was trending or being shared among his peers on their feed. Either way, he'd texted me about lunch, even providing a picture of whatever it was he made in my apartment and consequently, the dish I was missing out on, but nothing about the article. So I assumed he hadn't read or seen anything related to foul play.

"Don't pick that up." Chef Marseille had received me as soon as I was in the building and she saw me reaching for my vibrating phone. The caller ID was unknown. "Do not speak to anyone. They might be related to the headmaster. Or Pierre. You don't want to be giving away information before the lawsuit... yes, you are very smart and extremely intelligent, but you are also highly defenseless about some things in your pursuit of truth and people could easily use that against you, so. But good job on the article. It was... more objective than I'd imagined it to be. Just the mere presentation of facts but done so skillfully. I don't know what you're doing here in culinary school when you should be a lawyer."

I'd stopped short, thanking her before quietly slipping my phone back into my tote bag and then following her into a room that had Keith, Violet, Layla Tenner, Chef Lindy and even Chef Allan in it, with documents all over the conference table and laptops open. Some of them were on phone calls. Out of nowhere, a superior force struck me square in the chest and I was soon able to register it as Si Yin.

"Oh my god you actually did it you are so smart but so stupid because I don't understand how you're brave enough to do this and oh my god people are actually coming forward and Layla might?? Get a chance?? To come back to school??" I'd hugged her back while she spewed words into my shoulder. "They're trying to negotiate for settlement outside of court so so so part of the deal we're like thinking of offering is that Layla gets to compete in the interschool?? Replace someone?? I don't know but like I think we're getting somewhere and it's so cool how you did it."

I could see Violet pacing the room while Si Yin continued to crush me in her arms, glancing over occasionally. Keith was trying to speak to her but she did not seem to be listening. Chef Marseille was only able to provide me with details on my store keeping duties after Si Yin had filled me in on what had happened.

Apparently, they were receiving good publicity on the article because the previous winner of the interschool from CSS had retweeted it and added her take on the entire thing. Headmaster Birchwood had only just made a call to his lawyer and Chef Lindy was the first one to know. Chef Pierre was the only one who had gone completely bonkers about the situation and threatened to sue me, the writer, for defamation. And everyone else behind it.

Still, nothing was a match for Si Yin's um, apparent wealth and connections. Or her family, to be precise. So either way, I had on my side three well-known professionals apart from the fact that Chef Marseille had promised to ensure that I was not going to be implicated in any form of malicious intent since technically, I had none.

"These are the instructions for the store keeping. As long as you do them before ten o'clock in the evening, should be fine. But make sure they have your records of your student pass going into the inventory and whatnot, so we can prove that you're part of the team as a logistics member. This is the list of ingredients you'll be checking for. That aside... well done. We'll take over from here on out."

I stayed for a little while longer until the afternoon was over, running through stories from past and current participants of the W-interschool and their words that could potentially discredit the entire system. Needless to say, they were unexpectedly encouraging in light of the wholly precarious situation and the risk I'd taken. At the very least, there was a certain extent of truth beyond our own experience. And while Violet was most certainly conflicted about this all, she'd thanked me.

"It's not like I'm surprised or anything. I knew you were a nerd from the beginning." Yes, that was her thanking me.

Layla Tenner had, of course, been the most emotional one. It was weeks and months of bottling it all in, possibly being the scapegoat of several instances including having placed last in the cross-year segment and being shamed by most of the school for 'quitting' at her worst.

"How are you and Royroy doing, by the way? Last I heard, you guys were obviously hooking up," she'd laughed amidst tears and I had turned to Si Yin, who had pretended not to see, hear, or notice our existence. "I... thought I'd never get to do what I love again, you know. I let everyone down. Like, the team. And poor baby En." I had to pause to register that she had been referring to Chen. "You barely even know me... and you're putting yourself out there. I just really want to say thanks."

I told her that it had nothing to do with taking sides or, well, doing something for someone I necessarily 'knew' since ultimately, journalism was about the truth and nothing more or less. She'd smiled and told me that this was certainly not the case for most of the world, and that sometimes, people simply preferred an entertaining lie.

* * *

Somewhere along the way, days had become much shorter than nights and here I was, emerging from the conference room having bid Chef Marseille and the team a brief farewell before entertaining thoughts of retiring to Cinnamon instead of my apartment. Meditations of Leroy waiting in the latter with a simmering pot of chicken soup and the image of it steaming in a bowl—glistening clear broth, onions, carrots and all—was enough to imbue a sense of purpose in my feet despite the cold.

I was midway down the steps of Anton plaza, headed towards the front gate when the buzz of a text caught my attention. Leroy had returned to Cayenne and appeared to have been, indeed, in the process of testing out an old creation of his which was what we established as a decent way of figuring out the extent of his condition.

It was in receiving this text that I recalled the list of ingredients Chef Marseille had entrusted me with, meant for the bonus round that was to be held in less than twelve hours. I responded to Leroy's text before making a U-turn and going back up the stairs into Roth hall, informing him that I was to be giving the ingredients in the storage room a quick check. He'd given a quick show of disappointment in the form of an :(which I'd found myself laughing at.

Pulling out the list and attaching it to a handy clipboard I preferred to bring around, I made my way down to the basement of the building where the storage and freezer rooms were, apart from the wine cellar. They weren't very hard to identify and the food safety foundation course taken by every first-year student helped in that we had been showed around and taught exactly how food should be stored in a proper manner.

The logistic checklist had in one of the columns, checkboxes for valid expiry dates beside the name of each ingredient and while there were a mere forty or fifty items in total, I could tell that I was going to take some time.

"Hey, you're kinda late."

I'd scanned my student ID by the entrance to the cellar just as Chef Marseille had reminded me to and rounded the corner to see a small group of three other assistants with checklists in their hands. "Oh, um. My apologies. I was... well. I have no excuses. Should we get started then?"

One of them snorted. "Too busy partaking in cancel culture?"

I'd paused, stunned into confusion. "Um. Sorry. I don't quite under—"

"Here, take this," one of the storekeepers swapped his checklist with mine, snatching it out of my hands and removing it from the clipboard before handing the latter back to me with his attached. "Marseille claims you're pretty fast on things so guess you wouldn't mind taking the meats instead. Can't waste your amazing brain on stuff like canned food, can we?"

I gaped, incensed and highly disturbed. "I'm sorry but I don't think that's how it works. I apologize for not being on time but, well, I was handed a specific checklist and I'd prefer if—"

"Yeah exactly, you were late, so. The least you could is make up for it by doing the harder ones. We all want to get this over done with. You're that way," the seeming leader of the group jerked a thumb over his shoulder and I stared past it down the hallway.

None of them appeared bothered by whatever had just happened, occupied with checklists of their own and were heading towards their specified, allocated storage rooms before I could protest. I thought of giving Chef Marseille a call but a single glance at the screen of my phone confirmed either poor or a lack of reception.

I sighed.

At the top of the list were dry-cured smoked meats stored in low-light conditions and as though spending the entire morning and afternoon staring at a computer screen wasn't enough, the next fifteen minutes in a dimly-lit store room squinting at tiny words on paper took the cake.

Naturally, I was physically fazed by the end of the section and was near aghast to learn that next on the list were red and white meats in the freezer room. Once those were out of the way, I would be spending the rest of the evening in Leroy's room with a bowl of piping hot chicken soup, listening to the music he liked.

It was on my way to the freezers further down on basement two when I had the idea of collecting samples for Leroy and drafting up yet another list of dishes and ingredients that we could run through. The point was to narrow down the exact level of severity and per-haps give his taste buds a quick test on the level of sweetness he seemed desensitized to. After all, more information was always go-ing to give a better and more accurate diagnosis once he'd made an appointment with an expert. What had started out as an idea rip-pled into decisive waves and soon, I was hastening towards the stor-age rooms in an attempt to finish the remaining items on the list and collect some samples on my way back up to the ground floor.

There being less than ten ingredients remaining made things much more optimistic than I'd first put them out to be and so the initial plan had been to run through everything as quickly as possi-ble and be out of the walk-in freezer room in less than five.

The first blast of frigid air that hit me in the face was perhaps the best of signs that I wasn't going to last any longer than three minutes in the life-sized refrigerator; searching for labels under fluorescent lights and breathing out wisps of air every now and then—turning over packages and counting, checking their conditions for tomorrow's use.

I was on the different cuts of poultry when I heard something clicking against the door of the freezer room. The scratching of metal against metal and the clink of what sounded like a hasp or a lock. Mildly confused, I checked the safety light I'd switched on that would have alerted those outside the room that it was not empty and indeed, the bulb *was* red.

I pushed against the door.

And then, with all my weight.

"You can't be this much of an idiot," I breathed, heading for the other side of the door where the safety bell was located and pushing the button twice. Once short and then again, for long. Whoever locked up couldn't have gone far.

But when nothing seemed to be happening on the outside in the next fifteen seconds or so, I simply opted for the safety release handle that, by the very definition of the term, would allow the freezer to be opened from the inside and thus reasonably prevent against moronic situations like these from happening but lo and behold. Something was keeping it jammed.

I pushed the safety bell three times, again, before staring at the malfunctioned release, but also stepping away from the door that was directly under a vent spilling out blasts of chilled air.

"You must be the silliest person on earth to—good god, can't they hear the bell?" I seethed in white, quickly driven to madness by the extent of their atrocious attitude and careless behavior, whoever was in charge of locking up the rooms. I glanced at the screen of my phone. Nothing. No reception whatsoever. "What complete morons."

This was no ordinary situation, at least according to what various safety classes had prepared us for. No other contraption should override the safety release on the inside and unless the other side of the door had a hasp that someone could have put a padlock over but this was usually the case for chiller rooms that were not in normal use, which would explain the need for a security lock to prevent against theft, but... but goodness, for whoever it was to do that, it must somehow mean that the safety light was not in proper working condition on the outside of the room.

It was at the first shiver that I began to realize how much unnecessary time I'd spent in refrigeration. I was standing the closest I could do the safety bell, ringing it every few seconds or so whilst taking the deepest breath I could, and exhaling to rid of the adrenaline that would only cause the further depletion of somewhat limited oxygen in the room.

Three vents. Negative ten degrees Celsius, according to the wall thermometer. The floor had to be some kind of galvanized steel; that or aluminium or stainless, which might be what the ceiling and walls were made of, four to six inches thick but with some kind of insulating foam underneath the steel sheets but were they soundproof? The lighting was not going to provide an ounce of heat. The doorway had a row of thick plastic curtain sheets flapping in the continuous blast of numbing air and was by rational deducing, the worst place to be positioned at.

I moved away from it. Needless to say, the first of logical concerns should have been, in chronological order, the fear of hypothermia. Then frostbite, and then air supply. But reasonably speaking, or at least within my current state of disbelief, someone *had* to have heard the safety bell and would either be running off to inform the person-in-charge or done something about it themselves. Judging by the time it took for me to arrive at basement two and the last text I'd sent to Leroy, he would have... he would most *certainly* have noticed the abnormally long time I was taking down here in the storage rooms.

I was in a dress shirt, a blazer, tie and muffler. No extra padding. No coat. No thermal underwear.

Process of elimination; banging on the door like an idiot for attention just in case the safety bell wasn't at all in working condition—no, because breathing quickens with energy and energy is lost with further exertion in addition to the location of the door, plastic curtains and air blast; shouting was as stupid, a waste of breath, unclear if the room was soundproof and, again, unnecessary heavy breathing; vent one, two and three leave northeast, northwest and southeast corners free of indirect air blasts but northeast was shelves of frozen food and northwest was empty metal flooring which I wasn't going to sit on because that would only mean more rapid loss of heat but I wasn't going to stand either because conserving heat meant conserving energy and I needed all the energy I could afford at present. Perspiring and breathing had to be kept at a minimum level or more heat was going to be lost.

"Good god, why didn't I think of wearing the coat inside."

Shivering was keeping me warmer than I would've been without it but the mere boosting of heat production by tenfold was in simple terms a major source of energy depletion and perhaps the ultimate cause of exhaustion.

I needed insulation. Some thick plastic sheets layered between stacks of products caught my eye and it was after calculating the opportunity cost of the heat energy I'd exert trying to get them that I decided to do so, dragging them to the southeast corner nearest to the safety bell and sandwiching myself between some cardboard boxes and the sheets that I proceeded to lay on top of me to reduce as much areas of exposed skin as I could, since they radiated the most heat.

I was also careful not to be sitting on the metal floor that was scientifically speaking a decent conductor of energy and possibly the coldest surface in the room. My best bet was a foam cooler box.

With most of this set up, I curled further into myself, only reaching out every second or so for the safety bell. Focusing on constant intervals. And the flame of a candle that seemed to be the only semblance of heat left remaining. Trying not to lose consciousness.

LEROY

It was after getting off the call with a general practitioner stationed in the hospital that I got a gist of the funding I needed to be getting anywhere with the current state of my taste buds. Every single step of the way from the initial consultation to the referral to the *specialist's* consultation and then the diagnosis, the treatment, the post-treatment required a thick wad of cash.

Didn't help that my only source of heavy loans was the very person I couldn't afford to let in. He'd do onto me exactly what he'd done to Annie and then pull out every resource he'd initially thought of investing in the prodigy he thought I was going to be. Including Annie's treatment charges.

I was striking out the practitioner's number on the sticky note I'd copied the original list of contacts onto whilst finishing up a bowl of chicken soup that tasted a little off when I gave the clock on the quick check. Fifty-two minutes. Any time now.

The front door opened, and my first thought was to tease him about punctuality but the figure at the door turned out to be Raul.

"Oh. Hey man," he nodded, removing his muffler and then, his coat. "Uh, why do you look like that?"

I turned back to the clock. "I'm waiting for someone."

"Playdate, you mean?" He laughed shortly, then did something weird with eyes. "So uh... you know what happened, right? Like the whole Pierre fiasco and everything and Headmaster Birchwood being in on it. Hey you think his daughter knew?"

I stared. "What fiasco." His eyes popped.

"Dude you're kidding. Don't you ever read the Chronicle? I thought playdate writing for them would, I don't know, make you do stuff. Go read it."

I reached for my phone, checking the lock screen for text notifications but there was none. He was taking a little long.

"I read his blog," offering an alternative wasn't much of an excuse but it was at the very least, true. I spent five seconds thinking about it before sort of realizing that it had been a week since I last checked in on his posts. The interschool hadn't exactly given us the luxury of time.

"No man, it's different. This stuff's serious. He didn't tell you about it? Birchwood's probably going on trial. Pierre might have it bad too. The whole competition's rigged or something and, like, it's probably going to affect our scores. Might even end up cancelling the whole thing."

I frowned. He'd said nothing about that. "You sure about this?"

"I mean, playdate's the one who wrote the article. Pretty sure he's legit I mean, he's not the kind to be spreading shit for no reason, right."

Clearing the table and dropping him a quick text for his location, I tapped the shortcut I'd saved in the browser of my phone and scrolled through his blog for some kind of pre-emptive information.

"Heard some of the organizers were in on this. Like, exposing Birchwood I mean. Playdate couldn't have gotten all that info on his own, right? So. I mean, some people hate on things for no reason anyway... you okay man?"

He had a comment section at the bottom of every post that was usually filled with encouragement from his godfather's end. Sometimes the kid. That was not what I was looking at.

"You seen him today?"

Raul paused at the bottom of the stairs. "Er, no but I saw his friend, the Chinese girl, come out of the conference room an hour ago or something. Thought he should be here by now if you're expecting him."

The usual had been pushed to the very bottom of the comment section by a bunch of anonymous shits with less than a brain cell hiding behind technology on the majority of his recent posts. Most of them were censored, meaning they hadn't any profanities, but I had the common sense to assume the ones that *did* would've ended up in his inbox pending for approval or something.

But he hadn't said a thing to me.

"You should call him, man."

I was on it. His number was on dial before Raul had even said anything, but it was seconds later that it came back with a dead line. The call was not going through; he's either turned off his phone or in the middle of another call. Both were unlikely.

"He mentioned store keeping."

"Yeah, there's no reception down there. We did that in our first year too, remember?"

I knew him. He wasn't the kind of person to dive in and out of focus, tempted by distractions or by anything irrelevant. His work was fast and that applied to just about any task he was entrusted with. I tried his number again and ended up with the exact same result.

"People usually take fifteen minutes max."

Raul shrugged. "Maybe they gave him a longer list. He's probably done it many times." Haven't heard him mention it even once.

I left the dishes in the sink and I don't think I've ever done that but there was something—something off about the way things were and I was reaching for my coat, scarf and shoes before thinking twice, ringing him all the way down hill, past the plaza and into Roth hall. The building was near empty.

It was pretty much silent all the way down to where the store-keeping area was and it had been a good couple of months since I made any visits so I was stuck outside the gate for a minute wondering how the hell I was going to get past it when I recalled the student ID requirement and realized I hadn't thought of bringing it along. *Ah, fuck.*

I was searching my pockets when I heard it.

The ring of a bell.

It sounded like it was coming from two or three floors down into the cellar, travelling its way upwards and almost inaudible past the closed gate. It rang, shrill. Twice. And then stopped.

I paused, hovering between reality and mere imagination—then, footsteps. Someone was in a hurry, making for the gate and he all but froze the moment we met. A stiff smile surfaced. "Hey. Uh, think something's broken downstairs. Gonna head to the staff room for some help."

He tapped his ID on the card reader and the gates opened for him to slip past. I swapped places with him while they were. He didn't look very happy about that.

"Wait, you're not supposed to go down there without permi—dude. Hey!"

The hallway was dimly lit, looking like how it usually would minutes before locking up the place but the fluorescents at the end down south past the dry-cured meats were bright, leading down to the second basement where the freezers were. Still no bell.

I turned the corner and farther down the cellar was another door. It was ajar. Yanking it open made hushed voices clear about a hundred feet to the right end of the hallway. Two or three people. Whispering. The second door was opened and the light from the inside of the storage was turned on, filtering into the narrow corridor.

Initially, I thought it was him. Possibly giving out final instructions or finishing up the last of storekeeping duties that he for some reason was entrusted to a day before the final bonus round but it was nearing the voices that I could tell none of the three belonged to him. I wasn't quiet. They heard my footsteps and stopped completely.

"You seen Julian White?" I asked at the doorway before registering the people standing just beyond it, huddled in a group and nearly jumping at my voice. His classmates. They seemed to know exactly what I was thinking—that something was up. Something was wrong.

"No, we're just locking up." It was the guy I threw a frying pan at. The girl had a phone in her hand and but it wasn't clear what she was doing. There wasn't any reception down here.

The other guy turned to the one who spoke; glaring, but nervous. Tight-lipped.

"So you're standing around for fuck?"

They shut up further. The girl looked down at her phone and the guy with a bruise on his face had his hands behind his back. He said something about wrapping up last minute checks but there was no list, no documents, no nothing they had on them. With what happened a couple of weeks back, I wasn't in the mood for talk, let alone anything more than two sentences with mindless shits like them but it was clear that they knew something and wasn't telling.

I looked around. Nothing out of the ordinary. The dry storage was in place. The entrance to the cold storage to the right was closed. Their faces, though, paled by the second and just from the look in their eyes, any fool could've sworn they were hiding something. One of them gave it away with their eyes.

A glance towards the freezer. The slow, almost feeble ring of what was otherwise the safety bell inside the room was back. Twice. Then stopped.

I turned on them.

"You've got to be fucking kidding me."

"I-it was supposed to be a prank!" The girl had the nerve to be defending. She snatched something out of the other guy's grasp and it turned out to be a key. Rusty with the end of it broken off. "Like, just five minutes and we were going to let him out. It was just to teach him a lesson not to mess with us and if he'd *apologized* or something, like, or asked us to let him out we would totally have done that but he's just staying in there all quiet and—"

"Oh my god Brianna can't you just shut up?" The guy who had been holding onto the rusted thing was a hissing fit. I was looking around. Before, I hadn't noticed the padlock attached to the hasp that was overriding the safety release on the inside. "The key broke, okay? It's not our fault. We were gonna let him out forty minutes ago."

I shoved them aside, inspecting the padlock for a second. It was old but the shackle was the short type—thick, durable brass. The hardest kind to break. For no reason, I tried jerking the door open with a foot on it. The hasp did not budge. To see if he could hear me from the inside, I balled up a fist and slammed it against the door twice.

There was a moment of silence where the three of them stood idly by the side like a bunch of useless fuckers, waiting for a response like I was while the fire inside burned with rage and the fumes and smoke, black with poison, torched everything within reach.

Then it returned; the ring of the bell. Three times now and the last one, longer than usual. He noticed. He knew I was here.

The kettle's boil died down to a simmer and it was then that I recalled the dangers of burning over in the white of rage, blind and the consequences of it all. I wasn't going to add to the list of things I was hiding from him. The least I could do was learn.

"Get an instructor," I said to one of them. Meyers or Li, I didn't know which. Whoever it was, they didn't look very keen which was full of bullshit. "Move it? What the fuck."

"Yeah but if we get the school involved, then we're going to end up in real shit for—"

"Okay, so you prefer spending ten years in jail for a fucking murder attempt?" I shouted, on the verge of beating some sense into him. I decided it was a waste of my time and moved on. The girl panicked at *jail* and said she'd go up to get someone before running off.

It wasn't like I trusted her, but that I had no other choice. I looked around for something hard and heavy enough to break the padlock. The other half of the rusted key was jammed into the hole and there was no saving it. A fire extinguisher hung by the corner of the dry storage, protected by a metal case. That, I opened up and grabbed.

"Call the fire department?" The guy I tried to talk some sense into earlier on was apparently the biggest disappointment of the human race. His brain, if it even existed, shut down completely and hadn't even thought of a solution that he could translate into action. Standing still was the only thing he could do.

"Uh, yeah. I... gotta get reception." He snapped out of it, glancing down at his phone. "Fuck." Then ran off.

"You, get here." I told the last of them, needing to know what exactly they'd done to the lock and what the hell it was doing there in the first place. Smashing the bottom of the extinguisher against the padlock produced an unholy clank, scratching against the inside of the hasp that the shackle was put through. It swung around and then, back to the same position. It was hard to get an accurate hit. "Where the fuck did you get this?"

"Just... it was in the utility room upstairs," he explained, standing around. Useless. He shook his head. "Dude, we tried with a hammer. Don't think it's going to work... honestly, we were only going to have him in there for a minute. He keeps messing around with people he should be keeping quiet about. We just heard he was gonna be here so, like... it was just a prank."

The hasp wouldn't budge and the padlock was just stubborn as fuck. But the hasp, depending on the design or how they'd added it onto the door, there'd be something like a wing screw that had its end on the other side of the door. *The freezers Siegfried had in his restaurants all had one, and the screw would connect to the hasp on the outside. Meaning, if he unscrews the wing nut on the inside, the hasp could drop, and he'd be able to open the door regardless of the padlock.*

But there was no way to let him know; and he wouldn't be inside for the past god knows how long in the negatives if he did.

"Someone should lock you up in there dressed in whatever it is you're wearing now," I said to the guy, who came back with a hammer while I continued to slam the bottom of the fire extinguisher against the corner of the padlock, hoping to break the shackle's catch on the inside of the lock.

Footsteps. The one who left to give the fire department a call was back—phone in his hand, jittery from the nerves. "Five minutes, they said."

I turned back to the padlock and continued hacking away at it. The next of options was to increase the force by raising it above my head and possibly smashing it hard on the shackle by nearly throwing it against the hasp. I gave them the cue to step back, ready for a god-forsaken screech and possibly creating a huge dent in the extinguisher with the impact I was about to—

Clink.

I had it over my head when the sound, clear as day, slowed things to a stop. The hasp fell to one side, dropping an inch and then, all the way to the ground with a clang as soon as it was unfastened.

He'd unscrewed the wing nut on the inside.

I dropped the extinguisher and made a break for the door, yanking on the hinge and swinging it full open to the blast of cold fucking air and saw his body, limp and kneeling against the metal, fall forward towards me. He wasn't even shivering by this point. There was little energy in him remaining.

"Oh shit. Oh shit oh shit is he oka—"

"Get the fuck upstairs and show the medics down as soon as they come."

I had my coat, blazer, muffler wrapped around him in seconds, cupping his face and then, his hands. Then ordering the other guy to hand over his jacket whilst moving him away from the freezer room and kicking the door shut. He was cold. Freezing. Ice. His eyes were closed and his breathing, laboured.

"Vanilla?" I held the sides of his face, massaging the area below his eyes. "You're out. You're fine. Don't sleep. Just stay with me."

His ears were bitten stiff and most of his body remained limp as he leaned against me for support, legs on the ground and not quite working as much as I'd liked.

"Leroy?" He breathed into my muffler, moments after I started warming his face and stuffed his hands in the pockets of my coat.

"I'm here."

He laughed once, weak. "Could have really used... a candle."

* * *

"My god," Marseille came through with something in her arms, heels clicking down the hallway before appearing at the door with the girl by her side. Anxious. "Oh my god! What have you—" She was up in flames and nearly lost for words; rare for an instructor like herself.

She came over, pushing past the other two standing around and unfolding the emergency foil blanket used in cases of hypothermia. "Whoever is responsible for this, individual or collective, you're all explaining this to Chef Allan when he arrives and do not expect a single word of help from me."

Marseille pried the layers of clothing off her student and tossed them my way, laying the reflective sheet over him and wrapping the excess around his body. She held out a hand for the muffler and had the bottom half of his face and his entire neck bundled up before ordering me to tie the coats and blazers around his torso and then the rest of his body.

"How did he get like this?" She directed to no one in particular, feeling his face in her hands. "The boy's freezing! Cox, are you done? Hurry up, we need to get him near a heater upstairs since there's none down here and if anything, it's oxygen he needs." Marseille gathered the remaining pieces of clothing we'd swapped the blanket for and helped Vanilla onto my back. He was limp.

"What are you three standing around for?" She snapped at the idle motherfuckers. "Help him!"

One of them got round to supporting him on my back, just in case his arm slipped, or he decided to fall backwards while we were going up the stairs. Someone else held doors open. His weight wasn't unmanageable in any way; still, I'd be lying if I said going against gravity with an additional fifty kilos or so wasn't tough. He was heavier now, compared to the previous time I had him on my back, mostly due to the additional layers of clothing.

I was spending most of my energy focusing on the next stable step upwards. Even I had any left to spare, I wasn't exactly in the right state of mind to be thinking straight—lost in adrenaline and the god-awful sinking in my chest.

"I have the heating pads." Someone arrived at the top of the stairs, just beyond the electronic gates leading down to the storage cellar. I couldn't afford to look up, with him on my back and knowing that off-setting any form of balance was probably going to send him slipping down. "What happened to the boy?"

"He's been in the freezer," Marseille went ahead, scanning her ID and holding the gates open for us to pass through. "For at least thirty minutes."

"What! You're kidding."

I had one of them lay out a parka coat on the floor by a pillar for support before setting him down on it and whoever it was coming through proceeded to arm the coats and blankets with heating pads without directly applying the heat to his skin. It was only after taking a step back that I recognized her as the school nurse. She shooed me aside, checking his pulse and then his pupils.

"Where's the bloody medics? Are they coming or not?"

"They said five minutes some time ago..."

I looked up. The one who'd made the call was several feet down the hallway, pacing at the end of it right before the entrance of Roth hall. His head was lowered; somewhat preventing a clear view of his face which may or may not have given away his culpability. If remorse was an emotion he'd ever feel.

The girl spoke to Marseille while the nurse attended to Vanilla and though I was aware of exactly whom I should be keeping my eyes on, flames could be fanned and the danger was in forgetting to be a candle. Tolerating a bunch of idiots was one thing. Having to deal with them fooling around with life-threatening situations was another.

"Madame, we really didn't mean to do anything." She looked anxious. Scared, but not enough. "It was a—"

"Save it for later," Marseille wasn't in the mood. She held up a hand. "Not a single word until we separate you all into rooms. We can't have one person giving the whole account and everyone else nodding along or we'd be taken for idiots. Shut up and go direct the medics here when they come. One of you, get Chef Allan before I blow your brains out for adding to my plate because as you can see, I've got enough on my hands without you morons fooling around."

I watched the girl run off, hesitant. The other guy joined the one further up front in waiting for the medics, who'd most likely be pulling up right in front of the plaza where the fire access was. Then turned back to the bundle on the floor that was now shivering. A sign of recovery.

"Hello? Can you hear me? Nod if you can," the nurse addressed him, tapping the side of his face. He nodded. "I want you to take long, deep breaths. Okay? Count with me."

She started counting.

I did nothing but feel like a useless fuck for the entire duration. Even minutes ago down in the cellar, right outside the walk-in freezer. Nothing. For the past hour, I'd done no shit but fail to realize something was up, to do anything about the situation, to get him out, to do *something*. He'd ended up saving himself. Probably figured out the presence of a hasp and linked that to the wing screw and the nut on the other side of the door.

Now, looking at him closely, trying his best to even breathe at the pace set by the nurse, I felt like shit. The rise and fall of his chest was feeble. The ends of his fingers barely stuck out from underneath all those layers but I brushed against them to let him know I wasn't leaving anytime soon.

"Alright, is there any pain in your chest? And which part of your body feels the coldest?"

The nurse was keeping him awake and alert, feeding his mind some form of activity while the wait turned into painful seconds of dread.

I heard Marseille sigh, coming over to him and sitting by the pillar where he was. She seemed genuinely worried, and it wasn't the kind of obligatory emotion instructors often had under the responsibility of student lives. "It was foolish of me to think it alright to involve you in something like this. I don't know what I was thinking, approving that idea. The storage keeping was completely on me and... I should have been more careful. Goodness. Please be okay."

It honestly didn't feel like it was enough. Personally. Since I hadn't a clue what exactly it was she was talking about and that it probably had something to do with whatever Raul was trying to tell me. Something that Vanilla couldn't even tell me about.

I was glaring before I knew it and the only time I realized this was when both Marseille and the nurse averted their eyes, lips drawn into a line as though they had nothing more to say.

It was sirens first in the distance, growing in intensity and volume, accompanied by flashes of red before it was shouts and footwork and the slamming of doors. Those at the entrance were directing the first couple of them over; a mix of the fire department and a medical team with the former heading down the hallway with what looked like a sledgehammer but with a pointed end, presumably for lock-breaking.

By the time they were filled in and realized that a stretcher and portable space heater was going to be of better use, Allan had arrived on the scene and spoke to Marseille in a heartbeat.

They set him up on a stretcher with a raised backrest, supported by multiple pillow cushions and blankets. The man who'd picked up him looked as though he'd done the exact same thing to people four times his weight and the school nurse got to reporting his condition to one of the medics before the team requested some breathing space. Then it was placing a mask over his nose and lips, asking for his name, and talking to keep his focus grounded.

The girl tailing one of the medics around refused to back away. "Does he need to go to the hospital or something?" They ignored her.

"How are you feeling Mr. White? Any discomfort in the chest area?" He nodded once. "Right now, we're administering some direct humidified oxygen to warm your airways. This will help with the tightness in your chest, okay? Don't worry, we're not going anywhere near the cold until your body temperature's fully recovered indoors. Think you'll be able to drink something?"

He nodded again.

"He needs something warm to drink," said the medic to Marseille. Allan gestured for her to leave while he kept an eye on the situation in her place. She appeared hesitant, glancing between the medics and those involved in the incident before heading for the stairs in broad strides.

"The nurse and I will stay with White." She concluded. "You four—Chef Allan's office. Now. No excuses. I'll be there as soon as I can."

I watched her go. Turning back to where he was, under the care of those who actually proved to be of some use, unsure of what it meant to be a candle burning in a house on fire—of drowning in flames that weren't my own.

* * *

"You do know that the three of them have given vastly different accounts from your own, Mr. Cox?" Allan had fingers pressed against his temples. I was the last to give the story a go. "It doesn't help your case that you were the last of everyone to arrive on the scene. You can't be sure what happened beforehand."

"Just check the cameras." I was done.

"Yes, and we will. But I'm telling you that the cameras are *in* the freezer room. The one outside has its view obstructed by a stack of boxes," he sighed. Glanced down at the papers. "Are you even listening? I'd really appreciate it if you were a little more cooperative sometimes."

I ignored his comment. Staring at a spot on his office desk. "Yeah but did the three of them give the exact same story? 'Cuz I'm pretty sure they aren't capable of telling the truth."

"No Cox, I'm asking *you* what happened—"

"And I told you everything."

"In very loaded language filled with profanities that I can never translate into a legitimate report," Allan stressed. "If you're not going to calm down and explain, objectively, what happened, it is only going to make the case for you and Mr. White much harder to resolve. It doesn't make any sense. I've never seen you so emotionally charged against three students you've barely met. Who aren't even in your academic year!"

I said fuck it.

"This isn't the first time."

He paused, looking up. "Sorry?"

"It's not the first time they've done something to him." I'd let slip, and the rest of it was a slope. "The festival? They sabotaged the booth décor."

Allan frowned. "Cox, they're in the same class—"

"I have proof."

"Why would they do that? And even if this really is the case, why didn't you say something about this before?"

I stared at his pen. In too deep. There really wasn't much of an option, by this point; and if I was going to make things work, some form of a trade was at least necessary. I told him about the frying pan and how Li or Meyers got that bruise on the side of his face that hadn't exactly recovered completely. I showed him the nasty things people have been putting up on his blog for reasoning. That, and photos of the décor remnants Chen had salvaged from the barn and kept in a storage room. Allan did not take this well.

"... Leroy. You're a... a talented chef and as your mentor and dean, I have always regarded you as a model student we haven't had in a long time." His looked away. It was hard to tell exactly what he meant. "And here you are, admitting to... something I must necessarily punish you for and I wasn't even sure if I could handle the expulsion of three students, let alone four and one being the most skilled in culinary arts across the school."

He was quiet for a while. I let him think. It was hard to do that, in my case.

"For now, I will be suspending your involvement in the W-interschool. Which, by this point, I'm not even sure is going to continue at the rate things are escalating with Chef Pierre and the headmaster." Again, he massaged his temples. "You may leave. I will discuss this with Chef Marseille, regarding your case, and review the camera footage before arriving at a conclusion. If the three of them are indeed found guilty of inflicting physical and mental abuse on a classmate, they will face expulsion. Take care."

Ten minutes to midnight.

I was outside the infirmary, where Marseille said he was going to be put under close watch till the next morning. The hallway was empty and I was alone, seated outside on a bench. Waiting. Listening to muffled voices inside the room before the click of an open door and footsteps.

Someone from the fire department, accompanied by a medic, walked out with a duffel bag and a clipboard, which the nurse was asked to sign at the doorway. They were nearing the end of a conversation that did not seem to register in my head; filled with thick black smoke, rising from ruins. It was hard to think.

"Can I go in?"

They turned to give me a look. As though not exactly noticing I was there in the first place. The fire guy and his medic partner gave a brief rundown of his condition before looking away in seconds and, after retrieving the signed document, nodded my way and took their leave. I stared down the school nurse. "They said he's awake."

She sighed. "You're *not* seeing him. It's nearly midnight, boy. Go back to your lodge and enjoy the luxury of sleep while you can."

"Are you keeping him warm?"

Her jaw dropped. "I am the school *nurse* you moron. Of course I'm taking good care of him," she had the door half-closed. I jammed a foot in the gap and had another hand on the edge. She glared. "What are you doing?"

"I brought him tea." It was in a vacuum flask. Chamomile.

"Do you not understand what the word 'no' me—"

"I can't sleep if I don't see him," I finished. Final.

The nurse was looking at me with eyes that deemed none of this any of her business but, after glancing at the clock on the inside of the room, rolled her eyes and left the door ajar. "Midnight and you're out. No talking for more than five minutes. *Both* of you need all the rest you can get."

I headed past the doorway and straight for the curtains, parting them to reveal the first sick bed at the end of the room. He was seated up straight, back propped against three pillows stacked atop one another. Two quilts keeping him warm as he hugged his knees and looked up at the sound.

His cheeks were tinged red. "You know, I can hear you." *So... not from the cold, at least.*

"All planned." I shrugged, stopping by the side of his bed, un-capping the flask. Using the top as a cup for his chamomile fix. He peered up, reaction slow.

"Oh. That smells..." He paused while accepting it. I brushed against his fingers. They were trembling. "Good. Thank you." He somewhat laughed—short and breathless.

I sat on the edge and he leaned closer, resting his head against my shoulder. Something I never expected him to do without warning but was pleased that he did. I waited for him to recover. Listening to his quiet breathing. His sips were soundless.

"I heard it, you know." He wasn't speaking at his usual speed or breath intake. Everything was much, much slower than usual. Dazed. "Someone trying to break in from the outside and... well I assumed it was a malfunctioned lock. Which it had to be, of course. I mean... the rational conclusion was that they'd noticed the safety bell and... tried to open up but found that, well, it wasn't working. Of course... I unfortunately do not possess a photographic memory and hadn't exactly noticed the type of lock they had on the other side of the door so... I wasn't too sure what kind it was. But then... when I heard the impact of the force—it was you, wasn't it?—trying to break the overriding lock system on the outside, it felt... it *sounded* like a sledgehammer. Which meant that it *couldn't* be an electronic or a master key and so then... I had to consider the presence of a padlock. Which meant that there would've been a hasp to hold it there. So... so then I saw the wing screw on the inside and made the connection."

He breathed, leaning further into me and I caught the side of his head. Refilling his cup. Letting him take his time.

He peered up. "Thank goodness for the sound of the impact. I wouldn't have noticed the wing screw, otherwise... it was... it was really cold in there."

Ah, fuck.

I was leaning down, into his shoulder. Hiding there.

"Leroy?" He sounded shocked. "I-I um. Are you... are you alright? Is there a... it's warm." He must've felt the tears on his neck, but figured it wasn't exactly the smartest thing to be pointing out. I held him in my arms and he froze for a bit; before sinking into my chest and holding onto the fabric at the back of my blazer. "Well, I don't really know what to... um."

"Stop talking, dumbass." I pulled the back of his head closer to the flames. Where it was the warmest. He was somehow able to angle his head otherwise and plant a kiss on my jawline.

"Sorry if I... caused you any concern. Or worry. Or... well, you know what I mean."

"No shit you did."

"I'd like to remind you of your extreme worry-inducing tendencies as well and as such, we are," he stopped to catch his breath, cough once, and then sink further into the hug. "Even."

XVIII

LEROY

"Hey, what's going on?" Chen. "You look like shit."

I couldn't even find the will to turn so I just looked straight ahead at whatever it was they had up on the screen, projected for the briefing. "Feel like shit too."

He sighed, sliding into my peripherals and waving a hand several inches away from my face. "Hello, don't mean to break it to you or anything, but the entire thing nearly got cancelled and all our efforts would have gone to waste if not for the deal Tenner came through with. We can't afford having half-hearted chefs on the team..."

I gave no response. A tell-tale sign I was deliberately dishing out. Against the last-minute instructions they were dishing out over the sound system and people filtering in and out of the waiting room, he finally pulled me aside. Somewhere over his shoulder, I saw Tenner's heard turn.

"So are you going to spit out what happened to White or not?"

I gave him a look. "Those fucking brainless kids."

"What," he frowned, gaze hardening into something briefly unrecognizable. "The same few from his class? Weren't they taken care of?"

"I thought you read his articles," I snorted. "Isn't that what nearly got the interschool called off? Birchwood's die-hard simps getting defensive and gunning after people who have anything bad to say about her. They tried to play a prank and ended up almost freezing him to death in the cellar."

Don't think Chen took this very well but I wasn't going to be the judge of that since my own reaction the night before was nothing short of irrational fear. I'd left the infirmary to let him get the rest he needed but back at the lodge, I was having problems drifting off. If it wasn't fretting over Annie, it was him and having to control the house on fire—rage and hatred directed at a couple of blind idiots—and then the possibility of losing everything with disappearing taste. Of being left behind. Alone.

And again.

"You're kidding." Chen glanced over his shoulder. Tenner was waving him over. "I was wondering why he hadn't walked you down here or something. Even though he was technically disqualified."

The bonus round was a duo-style back-to-back relay of five dishes. Cuisine of choice. Chen had insisted on placing my name next to Tenner's, even though I specifically emphasized zero capability of desserts. Tenner was a red too. Worst case was necessarily producing a dessert course. Neither of us were good enough to cover the other, especially in my current condition.

All I could think about was ending things fast and running off to see him in the infirmary. And then Annie at the hospital. And in the process, try not to crash and burn.

"I need all remaining students to make your way next door and, according to the numbers beside your names, take your places at the assigned stations. Do not touch anything on the countertop. Just stand beside your stations. Everyone else, head up to the gallery."

Chef Pierre was in the room. He had eyes on Marseille, who'd left most of the administrative duties she'd been in charge of to Allan, now leading the organizing committee instead of her. His students from L'Assiette had headed out first to the practical exam hall and for most of the duration, he'd been either glaring at Tenner or sneering at anyone else who looked his way.

"Royroy," she liked to call. Since day one. "If this is you being ungrateful that your magic tongue boy got me back into business then you're being very childish right now."

I gave her a look; then raised a brow. "You think I'm intimidated by an ex-number one?"

"No, but you sure aren't the usual lion king I know."

We passed the doorway and were handed numbered aprons without names on for 'fair judgement'. I told her what happened. Asked if it was worth it now that she got what she wanted.

I wasn't even going to deny it if someone called me out for blaming everyone left right center for consequences a single pair of shoulders had to bear as a result of 'truth' and 'justice'. No one would be in the right mind to think I was angel enough to be objective all the time. In a way, if Tenner hadn't agreed to using an individual writer for an article on the entire controversy, he would have been left alone.

"You're right," she admitted, tight-lipped after getting over a minute of shock from the news. "Yes, we should have been careful. One person shouldn't have had to suffer the brunt of all that but this, we've discussed and... and Vanilla bravely agreed to it—only, none of us knew about the issue with his classmates. If we'd known, there would have been..."

And that was it.

I shut off, not exactly in the mood to be listening to explanations and 'what if's since neither seemed to add any value to a concrete solution. That, and I was aching, itching to end all five rounds, get out of the hall, and make a break for his side.

"... all the more reason we have to make this count. He did so much to make this happen so we can't just let it all go to waste. Imagine how disappointed he'd be if you let him down now." Tenner wasn't letting me off. Most of the stations had their occupants standing along the middle aisle and on our right were two girls from CSS; one of them, I recognized as his student buddy from Cinnamon. A Latino girl. "If this is what he worked hard for, you're winning the whole thing. Got it?"

I said nothing. They announced the first dish. A hummus variation. In fifteen minutes.

The collective whispers and groans across the room put me in a mood that was worse than before. Hummus. What the fuck. I was prepared to shut down and reach for the chickpeas at the start of the clock but Tenner stopped me with a hand.

"Let's do fusion. An *edamame* hummus. We need something crazy for it to be paired with. Go get the pestle and mortar. I need sesame seeds, seaweed, bonito flakes and miso powder from the pantry for a *furikake* topping. Could you do toasted baguette chips?"

"I'll make them curry-flavored," I settled, somehow glad that I wasn't given the role of thinking things through with a mind that was already full. She made things easy.

People were grabbing bags of chickpeas off their countertops left right center and I was back in the pantry tossing *edamame* into the cart, along with the other ingredients Tenner had laid out. Then I was back at the station, grinding up sesame seeds and sticking them into the oven for some toasting. And then slicing up baguette thins and brushing both sides with a layer of curry mix, chopped parsley sprinkled on the tray before switching with the seeds in the oven.

Someone came around. It wasn't Pierre or Allan, so probably

the representative from CSS. "Layla Tenner! Good to see you again. You're always the one with surprises."

She laughed. "Hey chef. No, I'm probably just... here to win the school some reputation and whatnot, you know?" There was a pause on the other end of the room, like people were looking over. Listening in on the open conversation.

"Well, you're not wrong," CSS's culinary dean nodded stiffly. "People expect a lot from you, judging from your performance last year. Hope to see you in the final round."

"If I'm allowed to participate, then yes," Tenner popped half the *edamame* into the food processor. "I'll see you then."

I wasn't paying them much attention, if any at all. Whatever I caught had something to do with the terms of the deal Tenner had made with the headmaster and Pierre; though nothing was completely transparent up till this point and I really couldn't care less as long as it had nothing to do with him, resting under the covers with a cup of chamomile tea.

There was hardly any leeway of faring poorly at this point, or producing subpar dishes that weren't up to a competing standard. They weighed heavy on my shoulders but it was odd; I wasn't feeling a thing.

Not a single cell in my body felt like giving a fuck.

"Roy? The chips." Fingers snapped. Pointed at the oven. The slices at the rear end were unevenly toasted. Edges, black.

I threw on a mitten and got the out to a blast of heat and an unpleasant bitterness in the air. Half the batch was ruined. I counted the ones that were decent. Six.

"Do a new one," Tenner said without looking up, adding herbs to the blender. "Fast, or else you're not going to have the time to rest them."

"The *furikake*?" I hadn't started on that.

"I'll do that." She was already moving on to the mortar and pestle whilst letting the processor run on its own—a nice, smooth mixture on its way. I knew she was fast so none of this really came as a surprise but the truth laid bare on the table at every passing second.

I was cracking under pressure.

"Four minutes."

"It's done."

"Tasted it?" She picked up a chip, broke half and bit off a quarter. "Perfect. It's spicy too. This will go great with the *edamame*."

Tenner did most of the plating over the couple of minutes and neither of us really talked. I'd taken a back seat, falling into the role of assistant and merely handing her whatever she asked for.

Do fires crack?

I might as well have been picked up and put on Tenner's back the entire duration, carried endlessly into the next round of soup, then a protein salad, and then the appetizer, which in this case, had to be a small-portioned risotto dish. The complete lack of energy and will to attend to anything beyond the thoughts burning inside kept most of everything running on dry fumes. Tenner was the one telling me exactly what to do.

"Just a classic parmesan risotto with roasted shrimp," she got to work as soon as the clock started ticking. It was by this point that most of the room were at the peak of their performance level. The remaining two rounds had to be more of an uphill battle than before. "No gimmicks, no twists whatsoever. Your head's elsewhere and I don't really appreciate that but it's not like you'd snap out of it if I tell you to."

Tenner had rinsed, seasoned, and marinated the shrimp whilst prepping a saucepan of chicken broth. I was melting butter in a sauté pan.

The layer of ice atop a frozen lake is brittle.
It cracks.

"Chop the onions and mince the garlic. The station beside us is way ahead y'know. And it looks like they have more fusion up their sleeves, so. You need to be faster than this." I looked over. His student buddy, the Latino girl, had the ingredients for Thai red curry on their countertop. She and her partner were going big.

Turning back to the chopping board, I diced up the onions, minced the garlic and tossed that into the pan of melted butter. Tenner was still dishing out instructions. The most basic kind like 'cook till soft' 'add the rice' 'make sure it's all coated' that I would have supposedly known without her nagging but it was clear as day—I wasn't in the right state of mind to be thinking.

The last thing I remembered was sliding the tray of roasted shrimp out of the oven without knowing how the fuck it even got in there. The seasoning, too, didn't look a mere combination of paprika, salt and pepper. Tenner must have added something. Jerk seasoning, maybe.

Then it was the usual. The three instructors making their rounds for tasting and it was times like these that you could see the effect of a true number one—seasoned and versed under time constraints, no compromises on quality and taste.

Even Pierre who'd went around with an unreasonably harsh palate had nothing to say about our dishes for the past couple of rounds. This was *with* the prejudice he had against Tenner. Still, speechless. He tended to have a lot to say about people's choice of cuisine, apart from their 'lack of technicality'.

It was hard to give a fuck.

"Telling Layla Tenner that her shrimp is perfectly cooked is like telling Michael Jordan that he's got dribbling nailed." Allan was the first to arrive at our station and though I wasn't exactly paying them much attention whilst cleaning up, pretty sure he didn't look my way when he said all that.

Him saying something to lighten the mood did not seem to sit very well with Pierre. It was after tasting the risotto that he left our station, without a word. Tenner didn't even bat an eyelash. It was our third five-stars.

"What is this?"

We hadn't so much as looked away from our plate, still in the midst of clearing up the second after the judges moved on from our station to the next when Pierre, a couple of steps ahead of the other two, stopped short several feet away from the two girls from CSS.

He had his back towards us but the stance he took was clear as day even from a distance. The room could tell, without so much as a glimpse of his face, that he was offended.

From where I was standing, the Latino girl's face gave the only indication of whatever the fuck Pierre had going on in his mind. She somehow managed to freeze the smile on her face in place. It was stiff.

"You keep pulling the Asian card."

She was looking up at Pierre who was speaking to her. Specifically. Not even giving her partner a single glance of acknowledgement.

"Um, yeah. We did. I mean, I do too." She was the one who made the *laksa* that should've topped the individuals for best dish. Vanilla had been a fan of it. He talked about her excelling in multiple Asian cuisines despite a lack of Asian heritage. Which didn't matter. Really.

"Indian, Filipino and now Thai cuisine," she went on proudly, watching Pierre pick up a spoon and pick her risotto apart. "Um, slowly making our way 'round the world map. This is a Thai red curry risotto. Rich, creamy—"

"Maybe skip Asia next time."

I watched her face fall.

It wasn't even a subtle drop; she could hardly control her expression. The rest of the room was dead quiet, turning to stare at her and Pierre while the latter's spoon scraped the bottom of the plate every now and then. He wasn't even eating.

"Sorry, um... I'm not quite sure what you mean..." "It is as I said. You don't understand? Skip Asia. You said it yourself girl. Vietnamese, Asian. Filipino, Asian. Thai, Asian." "Yeah but—"

He dropped the spoon and was about to walk away without listening to what she had to say. All he had then was less than a spoonful of the risotto. I couldn't even understand what the fuck he was going on about, sounding as though he'd grouped all the cuisines under 'Asian' and dubbed them as the same kind of food.

Which was a mistake only novice chefs would make.

"Pierre, there's nothing wrong with her risotto. What are you going on about?" The culinary dean of CSS quickly tasted her students' dish and called after the man already making his way to the next station. He snorted. No further comments.

Do fires crack?

"Skip Asia next time." He repeated. The girl was already in tears. Her partner at her shoulder with tissues and blood drained from her face.

"Pierre," Allan. "You're saying this as though one could group French, Italian and Spanish cuisines under the same umbrel—"

No.
They crash and burn.

"You sound like a fucking joke."

Paused. Turned. "I dare you to repeat that."

"A mother-fucking three-year-old going around
screaming about things you clearly don't know a thing about."

"Leroy."

"Should have known you had students like these, Allan.
Boy, you are disqualified from—"

"A judge should be versed in cuisine diversity.
You're acting like a kid."

"Ha! You don't even know what you're talking about right now.
Boy, I suggest you calm down and leave the room
before you embarrass yourself any further."

"The cuisines and dishes she made were nothing alike in technicality and taste. You're fucking delusional."

"Leroy!"

"Are you challenging me to bring this up to your father?"

"Don't think he'd even defend someone that stupid but you
could try."

"Enough!"

Allan was on Pierre, standing between us; blocking each other from our line of sight. Tenner got in mine. I nearly shoved her aside easy. "People like him need a fucking—"

"Leroy, no!" She held something in my face. A ladle right out of the saucepan. I stared. She was breathing hard, eyes wide. In my peripherals that had narrowed, I paused and it seemed to expand. Eyes. All eyes. "Please. Calm down."

"He's shit, Layla."

"And it's obvious," she hissed under her breath. "You don't need to do a thing. He's being stupid and he'll pay for it, don't you see? I know you're upset and under a lot of stress but taking it out on anything is only going to give you more... Roy? Leroy, where are you go—"

Ah, fuck.

They called out to me. Multiple times, from somewhere behind, but I wasn't about to turn or slow to a stop when the energy inside was ablaze; and I was out the double doors, slamming, open, closed, open again and footsteps. Calling. Chen. He had someone after *him*, too, I could hear them and they were loud and demanding because they were 'in the middle of it all' and going after me would mean getting kicked from the round. And I could hear him arguing with them.

But I was done and staying any longer was only steps closer to being unhinged.

The hallway down to the main entrance, out where the plaza was, had an air that was cold. Outside, it was colder. Biting. I was in chef's whites and pretty much nothing else but I wasn't about to turn and head back for the lockers, so. The track it was.

Insulation was minimal but I'd live. There was straw all around inside the barn and Caspian looked decently appreciative of apple and oat treats I always had hidden away in the club room so that kept me distracted for some time. Straying every now and then.

It wasn't until the thirty- or forty-minute mark that things started to sink in and daytime, now shorter than ever, began to wash and fade.

Initially, I thought I'd turned off my phone for good measure but it was at wanting to give the time a check that I realized I'd left that back in the lockers, too. The clocktower was a little too far in the distance for an exact telling of the time and was slightly blocked by the shades at the grandstand. I nudged Caspian for a ride out on the tracks, but he wasn't looking all that keen. Glancing back out, I understood why.

It started snowing.

"What do you want me to do, make a quilt out of straw?"

The stallion grunted, chewing on a treat while his tail swung freely. I gazed out into the open, the gap between the barn doors and where fresh air could filter in. They had those portable electric heating fans over in the clubroom that they put out on the grandstands whenever things got a little chilly. Those were a hot favorite of the horses.

I got out the spare key from a pot outside the room adjacent to the barn and retrieved one of them for Caspian; knowing that I'd eventually have to return and that sometime soon, I wasn't going to be able to look away from everything that had accumulated till this point.

He'd come, too. And I wouldn't be able to refuse.

But just a little longer, while he's still resting in the infirma—

"What an absolute fool you are, Leroy Cox."

I had the device hooked on my index with the heating grills faced outwards away from me so hearing a voice that wasn't too far away made me pull back on instinct, thinking I'd been a little too close.

There was really no point even registering who it was because identifying him was like an instinct. No thoughts required. The only issue was what to do *after*, and presently, I wasn't going to sugar-coat the deep shit I had to be in.

"You must be mad, even to *entertain* the very idea of riding out in such weather!"

I said nothing; placed the heating fan on the ground and undid whatever part of my chef's whites I could offer and adding that to his minimal layers. He was out in the cold less than a day after being in the negatives for minutes too long, barely back in his original condition but here he was, shoving aside every piece of clothing I sent his way and rolling his eyes as he did.

"I'm not a matchstick, Leroy. I don't need unnecessary shielding from the wind. There is none, by the way. I've checked the weather forecast and wind speeds aren't going anywhere above two miles per hour until morning. Oh, and just in case you were wondering, this is the first location I decided to drop by after hearing about you from Chen. Who's fairly enraged, just like Layla is, and Chef Marseille. And many others. They said you'd run off right in the middle of third tasting without a word, *and* with three five stars to boot." He picked up the portable heater and needed both hands on the handle to actually lift it. "You're telling me what happened, even if you weren't intending on doing so in the first place. I'm not leaving until I hear it."

I sighed, reaching over to take the heater out of his hands, starting towards the barn together with him. "There's a lot."

It did not faze him. "That is precisely what I am here for."

"It's cold out. You should be resting in the infirmary."

"Now you're just making excuses," he challenged. "We're on our way back into the barn with a portable heating fan. There's tons of straw for insulation. And may I remind you that I am perfectly capable of acknowledging the limits to my mortality."

"You nearly died in a freezer."

"Yes but thanks to my superior intellect and your subpar rescue skills that ended up being significantly useful, I did not."

I re-entered the barn, holding the door open for him while the horses looked over and went back to minding their own business after a moment of disinterest. "Dumbass," I laughed.

He stopped right in front of me at the door and seemed to pause in thought; then held out his arms and made an awkward attempt at a hug, wrapping his arms around my torso. I held the heater farther away from him, just in case it burned.

He was waiting for something. For me to return the hug, was what I assumed, but it turned out he had other plans on his mind. I'd relaxed—not much, just some relieving of tension that was barely noticeable—and that was his cue to let go.

I faced the heat towards a stack of hay and we sat in front of that, on a single crate. It wasn't much, considering the fact that neither of us could fit on it let alone together, but the general mood sort of made for a casual settling of things. Expectations of everything else was low, priming the air for something heavy.

"It's a lot to take in," I told him, staring at the glowing red grills of heat. He was quiet, I saw him turn a little. Towards me.

"Is this about your mother?"

"Kind of... everything."

He waited for me to continue. I was gazing out into the dark, watching flakes of white fall and collect on the tracks, the grass, the gap in the door. The soft whir of the heating fan; rustling of hay; breathing. There was much to burn and lighting a single end of the forest was only going to be the start of an island in flames.

"What if... I don't ever get it back. If I can never make anything taste like how it used to." I turned to him for a glimpse of his eyes. Checking the waves. "Nothing from me. None of it. No chicken, no soup, no eggs, not even lotus chips." He didn't look very different. "You're not disappointed? You not... gonna leave or something?"

His face stayed exactly the same for a good fifteen seconds or so until the chill in the air hardened and then altogether disappeared in an instant. Behind the glass, his eyes were heated waves. Bubbling.

"Leave?" He sounded like I was absurd. "And, disappoint—well firstly, Leroy, my feelings for you have nothing to do with whether or not I will be able to taste your food so I am inclined to believe the presence of some great, magnificent misunderstanding between you and I.

"Tasting your food is strictly speaking, well, the job of a food critic, assessing the head chef of a restaurant you seem to think you will have in the future, or some sort. The job of the *me*, that is, as myself, is to eat the food made *by* you, for *me*. And not anyone else *but* me. Just, me, as a matter fact. In a private space... preferably a nice little apartment. I say preferably but should we be somehow unable to afford an apartment, then a rented, shabby little hut would do just as good.

"And second of all, just as I have mentioned multiple times over the course of the last couple of months, I am fond of you—not because of your cooking, let alone the fact that you are extremely good at it, but, because, w-well... because of reasons other *than* your ability to produce palatable dishes.

"Rationally speaking, if you'd be so much of an idiot to assume that I'd fallen for you because of your superior culinary skills, then, perhaps, you'd be horrified to know that I've had much better tasting dishes in the past fifteen years of my life than yours! Uncle Al is not a critic for no proper reason, and I have, indeed, paid several visits to Michelin-star restaurants and had had spectacular home-cooked food alike. Should culinary aptitude have some miraculous part to play in my reasons for love, then I might as well have swooned over the head chefs of those restaurants o-or or or said silly romantic things to them as I am currently saying to you! Well? Do I do that? No!

"I like you for... for reasons that are... rather private. Like the fact that you understand me on a level that no one else has. And that you listen to me. My rambling. Like so." He gestured to the now. "And that you are stubborn, and that makes you awfully determined. That you are willing to sacrifice bits of yourself for the good of the people that you love. Things like that. I-it also doesn't help that you have an incredibly attractive face and a... rather... decent torso that, um, happens to resemble bread rolls.

"But even without these features, should you question my motivations for being so affectively moved by someone by the name of Leroy Cox, I'd like you to know that... reasons for love can very well be... be strangely incoherent and sound perfectly nonsensical at times, especially in the case where rational thought and unexplainable phenomena cross paths and that is precisely where feelings seem to stand, at times. Not even between reason and instinct—elevated to a point whereby... well, whereby I, a walking dictionary, cannot put into words."

He came to a stop, breathing hard and under the white lights filtering in from the window of the racetrack, the gentle spark of flowing water in a creak. He looked away, needing some time to regain his composure. I wasn't in a state to respond either. His words were big. Heavy. Much more than I ever thought they could weigh.

No way in hell could I ever wrap my head around deserving the person that he was.

"This... this isn't very like you at all," he said, removing his glasses and passing the back of his hand over his eyes. I reached over to help. "Words like 'leaving' and, and *disappointment*. Maybe your father said something to you the time you rushed off to the hospital. Something you aren't quite keen on revealing to me either.

"Perhaps it was whatever happened last night that might've

caused you to somehow make an insane leap in logic to arrive at a conclusion for the necessary blaming of yourself." He sniffed, removing my hand from his face and staring at the glowing grills of heat. "That, and perhaps something else, too, occurred during the bonus round which furthered your concerns. Although judging from your apparent omitting of the truth in several past occasions, I'm inclined to believe that this isn't the kind of truth you'd be keen on telling me either."

"Vanilla."

I had him face me, but his gaze remained low. The chill was different this time around. I'd never really seen the surface of a frozen lake so indifferent and unreflective of the person staring into it. I hadn't been very honest. The gaps in our knowledge of each other were finally showing.

"Sometimes... I'm weak, too." I told him. "Just like everyone else. Sometimes, I can't be like you. Brave enough to always be telling the truth, 'cuz I'm not."

The moment I'd said this, it sounded wrong. It wasn't exactly what I'd thought it would sound like. Or what I thought it was going to be, to him. He looked up. Lips pale and dry. Something in him was shivering. I put the chef's jacket on him but still, he trembled.

"W-well I... I mean I thought we were fairly unafraid of being honest with each other. I'm sorry if I gave you the impression that—"

"It's not that." I had to clarify off the bat. He wasn't the problem. "I wasn't kidding when I said that you overestimate me, or whatever I am." *Wait.* "No, not you, overestimating. I'm the one not meeting the... never mind. It's okay to have ideals, like that I'm always going to be honest—"

"Ideals?" *Fuck.* His eyes were wide. "Of all people, Leroy, you should know that I am the most realistic, most practical robot to ever exist! You being honest isn't an *ideal*, it's... you *are* sincere and truthful—"

"Yeah but that doesn't mean I don't ever lie," I tried, quietly. Restrained. Flickering fast. "Or that I don't ever decide not to tell you something." This wasn't the crash; wasn't the burn I wanted it to be.

Kill the flame

"Well if you're doing that because you wish to protect my feelings, then I believe I've made clear to you that you are allowed to hurt me with the truth and that I will never hold it against you if you do because I—"

"Don't want to." *Kill it now.* "I don't want to hurt you even if you say it's okay. I hurt when you hurt. It's the one thing I wish you would get sometimes."

It was forest fires all around. Flames and ash, smoke and smog, rising into the night sky against the falling snow and turning flakes into rain that could, at least, put out the glowing waves of heat, red and fiery, furthered by the wind.

"I fucked up. And I'm fucking up now. Too. Like I do with pretty much everything," I think I laughed. "I nearly killed some classmate of yours with a frying pan. I lied about it so that I wouldn't get expelled. I told Chen to hide it from you. I don't tell you about my dad because he's the whole reason I blamed your uncle in the first place. I couldn't forget about you. I basically made you think that coming here was your voluntary choice, but I told your uncle to get you here. I practically told Pierre to go fuck himself. Allan found out about the thing with your classmates. I'm probably going to get expelled. I don't like cooking. I like *you*. I don't even want to be a chef. Just, *your* chef."

C A N D L E

Can I run
Should I burn

I've always thought it was a bad idea; the kind that was good to have. People should be allowed bad ideas sometimes, because knowing they are bad—that they should remain as ideas and not some part of reality—must mean some good. But I wasn't good.

Felt, sometimes, like I was only pretending to be. Like I was only doing that for the sake of everyone else I kept close. But too close to the flame was a heat that no ordinary thing could stand and even against frozen lakes and snow, they begin to melt. That would mean I had to burn alone.

It started out as a thought. A bad idea.

Like I knew it wouldn't have to happen. Being alone. But I considered it anyway. Kinda like a form of entertainment. Like being allowed some bit of the future and laughing at it not because it sounded stupid but because you weren't all that keen on believing something you knew was possible.

SNOW

Can I stay
Should I freeze

What a pleasant idea it might sound to the majority; the act of slowing time or perhaps the notion of stopping it completely. To have things preserved in its pristine, original state of preferable bliss—where times were pleasant and at their peak of joy and all things good. Was I good?

It seemed to be the case that the art of ethical goodness had its own color of extremes, in which the wholeness and seeming purity of white (a multitude of shades) was up against the precise absence of everything. Of a dark, abysmal void I, for one, would never be able to understand.

For all intents and purposes, whiteness was the color of the lens I'd often see the world through. It is comparable to looking up at the sky from the bottom of a lake, through a sheet of ice on the surface of it all, the only thing that separated deep waters from the above. White is not an ideal, contrary to what many others may think.

It is a shade of indifference and objectivity; of having all colors and none at the same time.

It wasn't the bad kind of lonely. Just, alone. Singular. Like, with two dogs and three rooms. Bed, dogs, and a gym. The gym's the living. Or the kitchen. Or something. Maybe I don't even need a kitchen. Take-outs for days. Weeks. Years. Yeah I could get with that. Working at some gas station, making average, scraping through, not living the life 'cuz that wasn't what I needed anyway, and definitely not anything close to busting my ass off to get by. Maybe move on to a farm or something. Get a barn. Buy Caspian. Or steal him, whatever. So Caspian and two dogs, then. Fifteen years in a gas station, thirty years in a barn. Buy a cornfield or something. Make scarecrows and shit. Die alone.

Sounded like a plan.

But they better come for me at fifty or something since anything beyond that was just way too long. Now that I think of it, the whole thing didn't even sound like a bad idea. It was a neutral thing. Not bad in any way, but not good either, not anywhere near the kind of happiness that the rest of the world seemed to be searching for, but also not the summary of some tragic life story that was honestly kind of boring. Just a little...

Empty.

These lenses provide nothing more than truth and fairness to all that I could experience, and even in times like these, there would be a struggle to determine what was right and wrong, the truth of it all.

Flames stemming from a single spark of life, could it somehow have been the fault of the cold? Was it wrong to desire warmth in the presence of winter? Was it selfish to burn in the face of snow? Would he have struggled to contain his flame had I not returned in a season's change?

It is not a terrible idea to think about 'what if's, prospective futures, endless possibilities of simulated alternative realities, parallel universes in which candles would burn freely without having to mind the melting of snow.

To be the object of such love and affection, dedication and loyalty, was of unspeakable, tremendous honor and responsibility. To be reasons for one's motivations—him wanting to become a chef, years of struggle and suffering, every emotional trigger and perhaps even played a part in his current condition of his taste—was to sit on the other end of the seesaw. To be granted that access, to be given one's all, to be weighed. On equal grounds.

I don't think people really get what I mean by empty; and what thinking about things like these at the age of sixteen really mean, and what thoughts could really do. Dark ones. The kinds born out of an abyss, because there really isn't anything down there. Just a hole. Not a sad hole; not wet, not dry, not uncomfortable, just, a hole.

It's there, sometimes. Like I see it up ahead, that sort of thing, but when something's in front of me I just forget about it for a moment and then when they leave, I see it again. Up ahead.

I started seeing it back in the guy's apartment in New York. He was at the restaurant and I was making lunch according to the menu he fixed. Tortellini. Mushroom and ricotta filling, I think. And I was doing that by muscle memory, not exactly thinking about anything in particular, just doing my thing in the kitchen to the whir of the fan with the radio on. The weather forecast was up and they were talking about a snowstorm next week upstate.

I didn't even know what I was doing next week. Probably cooking. And... spelling. Maybe one or two practical sessions in the restaurant. Then... if he had some time, a five-course dinner at some place he liked. It had been two years since KFC, by the way. The uncertainty was probably my only hope at hanging on to a nice bucket to myself. Wasn't going to happen, but back then, I was a little more hopeful.

That was the thing about homeschool. Bad homeschooling, at least. Or maybe he did good in comparison, I'd never know. I never knew what was going to come. Could never really see what I was... going to do except cook. Like, next week? Cook. Next month? Cook. Next year? Cook, for sure. Five years down the road? Still cooking. Ten? Better be dead by then, I guess.

Ten was the point I thought the hole was going to come. Like, I'd arrive at the rim, at some point, since it was the only thing I could see up ahead. So I knew it was there. Just... didn't want to believe it.

Could it be that even with all the forces of the world, of the defying of gravity that each other's seesawing responsibilities may have done onto the other, that despite it all—they were not meant to be?

Given a choice, I'd take the three rooms. Bed, dogs—and it's either a gym or a library because he wasn't gonna let the entire living look like his greatest nightmare, and I'd say no to more than three full shelves, so. Then he'd probably say something about needing a kitchen for practicality, though he clearly can't cook for nuts, so I'd say we'd probably settle for one stove. And a microwave. No oven. No dishwasher.

I could be alone. As in, I'm okay with that.

Given a choice, I would have liked to go on with the crunch of red leaves underneath our feet, listening to the sound of company and the never-ending up and down that was the very reason for a dream that could have been more. Much more.

Given a choice though,
I'd rather spend the rest of my life taking flak
for liking the taste of vanilla.

Given a choice, I'd very much rather spend the rest of my life
listening to that creak;
arguing about the taste of vanilla.

XIX

⟨❦⟩

ON SACRIFICE

a short essay by V. J. White

It is my humble and perhaps ill-informed opinion that the universal favorite theme of sacrifice in love, often glorified in fiction and reality alike, necessitates some suspension of disbelief; vital in momentarily immersing the audience in a world beyond their own that may or may not resemble the ideal that is Eros, Philia and Agape. This essay proposes that the brief suspension not only mitigates the issues any logical, rational being should face in considering the prospect of losing something for nothing in return but creates an odd but necessary disjunct in the heart and the mind.

Speaking from the standpoint of a logician, sacrifice is never an option for the genius or the intelligent. There is nothing risky about placing twenty grand in an investment scheme you know will not produce any form of return; that is not a risk, it is a *mistake*. Regardless of the logical system or reasoning that one subscribes to (inductive, deductive, abductive, etc.), it is necessarily the case that losing something for nothing in return should never be the case.

Yet, why do the eyes sting and our throats constrict and our chests ache at the monstrosity of a lover presenting their heart to their blind, dying beloved who, say, will never know the identity of their donor; of a king abandoning all power and status to be with their beloved in a rival kingdom?

Indeed, these works of fiction, things far beyond our immediate experience are stories of greatness.

I am of the opinion that while greatness can be sacrifice, not all sacrifices are done in greatness. It is the undeniable truth that the majority of the world will never experience or understand the weight of sacrificing one's life to save another, let alone a kingdom for one sole, seemingly insignificant commoner. The great art of sacrifice in fiction cannot be understood in the context of the common-day, rational reader. That is what I had come to believe after all these years of reading and rationalizing; that fiction of such magnitude cannot truly capture what it means to lose something, irrationally and defying all sense of logic, knowing that one will receive less or perhaps even nothing in return—an act belonging only to the fictional fools written in ink, moving across a set, a stage, in movies or a play, selfless fools who think with their heart.

No rational being would ever think sacrifice a plausible solution, unless they should be caught in some moral dilemma where they are required to choose between sacrificing themselves for five others strapped to a railway with a runaway trolley hurtling down their path or leaving them to the reaper. Subscribing to the utilitarian school of thought would necessarily allow the rational being justification in choosing to sacrifice themselves, but swap the self with a loved one and the entire dilemma pales in comparison.

I struggle to term choosing between one's beloved and five strangers a *dilemma*. In the event that a husband encounters his wife and a stranger about to drown in a pool, it is, without a doubt, that he would jump into a pool to save his drowning wife without deliberation, as Harry Frankfurt proposes in *Some Mysteries of Love* (2001). Frankfurt refers to this quite literally, in a sense that the husband should not be deliberating between who he should be saving, or even be *thinking* about the situation, if, at all for that would be 'one thought too many'.

Any form or thought of reason, pause of rationality, strictly speaking, would determine the difference between Love and, well... *not* love. To many and perhaps even myself, it seems entirely plausible that the decision-maker would choose to sacrifice their humanity by allowing the five strangers to meet their respective ends, thereby saving that one, non-fungible person of attraction. This sacrifice and this *decision*, even, lacks the logical reasoning that many of us rely upon to live a fulfilling, meaningful life. This had, once, brought me to conclude that the great art of sacrifice in fiction cannot be understood in the context of the common-day, rational reader.

I now realize that I may have been wrong.

Though I continue to be of the opinion that not all sacrifices are done in greatness, the premises to which this conclusion rests upon have been altered to strengthen the validity, cogence and soundness of the claim; that is, the true reason as to why an everyday, common reader can wholly understand and even relate to great sacrifice in epic works of fiction is that sacrifice has and will never be a physical, tangible phenomena. It cannot be valued or understood as a mere manifestation in the superficial, surface world. I propose that sacrifice in love resonates deep within the core of one's humanity and that it may, indeed, be a universal feeling after all, despite the drastic differences between our fictional, dream-worlds and the reality in which we face.

That while greatness can be the foregoing of a crown and a throne, the presenting of one's heart on a pillow, it can also be a single text; the pouring of a glass of water; the presenting of hot cross buns; the planning of a date; the cooking of a meal; the letting go.

It has come to my attention that I am perhaps not at all the rational being I claim to be when it comes to a certain someone. Indeed, it is rare. Intriguing. And perhaps even a little frightening, I daresay. After all, losing one's ability to reason in the presence of another sounds perfectly absurd, shaking the core, uprooting the very people who have once thought themselves cemented into the ground in which they stand upon.

Why is it that when it comes to that one person, mankind develops the sudden ability to serve themselves up on a platter for as many sacrifices as they can remember?

Could this really be the true love that every great work of fiction writes about, or just a mere figment of our imagination—an ideal that was never meant to be achieved?

It is in present time that I understand the weight of unknown forces pulling two apart; that there may be times when, despite the incredible, paradigm-shifting, world-ending extent of love shared between a pair of existences, they are simply not meant to be.

In conclusion, reasons do not explain the unexplainable phenomena that is true love; or so I have come to realize. Whether or not there is truth in my understanding, I do not know.

What I know now is perhaps thoroughly limited, with respect to my current condition of being terribly far from the objectivity that I had, all my life, strived to embody and did, to the best of my efforts, achieve. What now seizes the mind is the heart that is full of him. Of memories that are him. Of vague, unknowing 'knowledge' that is him. Of moments, of words, of feelings that are him.

And should there come a time I have to forego these 'him's for his happiness and well-being... I find it hard to believe that I will ever have anything against such an idea.

*Of Love
and Sacrifice.*

XX

VANILLA

The decision to allow us both some space apart had been mine. I'd perhaps responded to Leroy's baring of his heart in a way I hadn't quite expected myself to be responding. The odd quivering of one's bottom lip and the cold, numbing touch of a winter breeze at the tip of one's fingers were not signs of sadness and fear but reluctance and disbelief—characteristics far beyond my capacity for understanding.

It was after moments of silence in the midst of the soft falling of snow in the night, the brief, fleeting waves of heat from the electric appliance that Leroy came to terms with my lack of words. My inability to fill the air with something coherent in nature was, for all intents and purposes, an unbelievable phenomenon he may have struggled with. I hadn't myself quite been able to express the entirety of what happened then, but it was in the pause that he proposed some distance.

My immediate reaction had been to turn the offer down since we'd nearly always taken to resolving an issue by laying everything out on the table and communicating effectively about them—but I'd stopped myself upon quickly realizing how different the issue was and how it, logically speaking, would've required a different approach.

Leroy had walked me back to the infirmary, where I was able to inform Chen and the rest about having spoken to him but revealed nothing more. Despite the warmth of the room and the cup of tea I was handed by the school nurse before bed, the chill in my fingers and the stiffness of the heart refused to part.

Having noticed my inability to fall asleep, the nurse had been kind enough to allow a single visitor into the room who had apparently rushed over as soon as she'd heard from Chen and Tenner.

"Vanilla? Where were y—oh my god. You look like you're *freezing*." Si Yin had placed both hands on the sides of my cheeks only to realize that her fingers were much colder than the surface of my skin. Physically speaking, I was fine. Not in the greatest condition, with regard to yesterday's terrifying experience in the freezer, but, still. Fine. "Oh. You're okay. But you look... honestly, you look kinda... I don't know. Like."

"Cold?" I finished, not exactly certain if I'd chosen the right word. She nodded anyway, sitting on the edge of the bed and topping up my mug of tea.

"So um... you found your man? He's okay? You know we were all pretty shocked when he started firing back at the Pierre guy and when I say fire I mean like F-I-R-E there was smoke and flames and he burned that guy to bits! Oh and everyone else was just too stunned to say anything 'cuz we were all like, nervous about the judging and stuff since we were all in the middle of it but so when he left the room everyone was like silent for a whole hour or something and then Chen went after him and Tenner went after Chen because ev-er-y thing was just falling apart and then Pierre even said something about 'don't you dare leave the room' or something like 'if you leave now, I'll personally ensure you get fired—I mean, expelled' or something like that. It was huge. Oh yeah, Leroy's chef's whites are always so clean even after making, like so many dishes in panic. I don't understand how that happens.

"So, anyway... Chef Allan was super in panic and he was like having this argument with Pierre but then Pierre got the headmaster involved and they paused the entire thing to deal with the situation but, like. I mean. They can't *expel* a scholarship holder, right? It makes sense to cut Li and Meyers off 'cuz of what they did to you, but I mean. They were stupid, for sure. But it's your man we're talking about and the school sponsored all of his education here and, like, his dad, for sure... I mean. They wouldn't want to offend him and like, if he *does* get expelled, don't scholars have to, like, return whatever funds they technically used? I don't know. Probably just a few couple grand but, I mean..."

She'd turned to me upon finishing her blow-by-blow update and it wasn't going to attribute my disinterest to the content of her speech but the fact that my mind had, quite simply, been unable to dwell on things other than its immediate concerns of, well, him.

And quite honestly, I wasn't even sure how or when I'd began to shed the spare tears I never knew I had.

"Va-Vanilla? Wait. Hold up. What's... why—did something happen between you and Leroy? What's going on? Do you want to lie down? Should I tuck you in bed? Am I just being boring right now?"

I shook my head, patting her shoulder. "Oh no. No it's... I'm not bored. You're most certainly not boring as well. How strange it is to be... crying, for no particular reason at all."

"That's not strange," Si Yin nearly slapped me in the face. Thankfully, I'd placed my glasses aside. "It's called having feelings. And feelings are like, the norm for humans, you know. And I mean, sometimes I feel like you aren't, and sometimes you feel that way too I mean have you heard yourself answer a casual question, but point is—you are! Human. So like. You're allowed to cry for no reason." She then reverted to a state of gentle pity, reaching over to pull

the covers up to my chest. "I'm always open to listening, so. I mean...
if you don't want to tell me stuff, that's fine. I'll just be waiting."

I thanked her, nodding but not quite sure how else to express my
gratitude. "Maybe it's best if I spend some time thinking. I'll be fine."
She'd patted me on the shoulder as I sunk into the bed and, with
gravity's aid, prevented more tears from flowing down my cheeks.
"Thanks for coming... I'm sorry about the competition. You probably would have done so well without all that... the interruption."

"Doesn't matter, really. I mean I've got years to come and Pierre
honestly deserved whatever Leroy said to him. He's too conservative
to be a judge on any tournament and, like, someone *had* to put him
in place, right?"

I sighed. "Oh but at what cost? Good god. Leroy's absolutely
hopeless."

Si Yin had laughed and pulled the rest of the curtain separating
my sick bed from the three others. "Rest well, okay? Violet was out
there for a good minute or two by the way. Which is a lot, you probably know. Chen's still going on about killing Leroy once he's back
for sticking his neck out and uh... some classmate of ours came by
too. I forgot his name but I thiink it starts with an 'A'. Okay, sleep.
Now. Bye!"

I'd waved and let my hand rest limply along the side of the bed,
staring up at the ceiling where the lights were dim. The nurse was
speaking to someone over the phone, voice barely audible behind
the curtain, and I could only hope that she hadn't informed Uncle Al
and Aunt Julie about what happened last night since... well, knowing my uncle, he wasn't exactly the best at resisting panic and one
thought too many.

Next was my attempt to fall asleep.

And as expected, it was no surprise that my mind found itself
dwelling on matters of the heart that was him and the many truths
that a future together seemed to entail. It did not, and does not take

a genius to observe the mental struggle of pain and hardship Leroy was experiencing at present, perhaps somewhere in his room, or in the shower, eyes closed, thoughts dark and his candle—flickering.

It was in the thinking of this that I gradually drifted down a hole that was a dream; the deepest, darkest sort, that rose high above my head and deemed climbing out of it an impossible feat and so down the rabbit hole I went.

There were thoughts within thoughts and words within words but nothing consisted of an image as frightening as talking caterpillars or painting the roses red. It felt, instead, very much like paths being chosen as I wasn't sure if it was me, on the trolley or the train, or walking with my very own feet, but I was choosing between forks and splits and it had almost seemed *never-ending* but then came the very chance of a dead end.

I woke to that.

Not quite remembering the paths or the forks or the splits but just—the end.

One must understand that not all ends necessarily entail some form of grief and tragedy. Sometimes, all roads converge to one; and that one road leads to an end that we will inevitably have to face and though, as probability stands, there may or may not have been multiple different means to arriving at such a conclusion, I had to admit, the decision seemed almost clear as day.

Leroy must leave.

Premise one, subject is not happy. Evidence one; constant turmoil, temper, anger. Justification for E1; can be explained by pressure from his father, financial anxieties, expectations from the school, responsibilities of a partner, the pressure of hiding all things negative from the former. E1 thus necessarily supports P1. Premise two, subject does not like what he is doing, slight overlaps with E1 would be: Evidence two; only willingly cooks for his partner, does not appear to particularly enjoy classes or competitions in the absence of his partner. Justification for E2: over-work, repetitiveness, boredom as implied by his childhood routine, and explicit mentioning of his dislike for cooking. Premise three, subject loves his partner. Evidence three: everything. Unexplainable. Assumptions made: subject only cooks for his partner, or is the only person he enjoys cooking for; subject is not happy despite the presence of his partner.

Conclusion: subject is torn between his love for his partner (P3) and his dislike for what is often associated with his partner (P2) and therefore is unhappy (P1). Solution to conclusive claim: P2 must be dealt with.

Should P2 be dealt with effectively, the truth of P3 faces the likely possibility of standing whilst changing the nature of P1. And because subject's partner is in pursuit of an academic excellence he is fond of, rationally and reasonably speaking, independent of his emotions, he cannot leave. Therefore, subject must. Leave.

He must leave.

He must.

Leave.

Let him go.

"Please allow Leroy to resign as a student without having to bear the financial and contractual obligations and responsibilities."
Let go.

I was standing in the middle of a lavish, carpeted office that was heavy with the scent of birch. There was little feeling in my feet.

"Mr. White," he sighed, adjusting the angle of his office plaque, placed on the side of his desk. "You seem to have... misunderstood. Mr. Cox is facing *expulsion*. Not resignation, or a mere 'quitting of school'. As a scholarship holder, he has violated the... the moral integrity of our contract. We do not tolerate cases of violence *or* humiliation of culinary instructors! He *must* bear the damages."

"Sir, technically, he hasn't broken the scholarship bond as it states here, on section 2.4 of the contract, that—"

"The bond has been severed. We are no longer associated with the boy and that is final. He was unable to complete or serve to the minimal degree, four complete years of education in our academy. I am sorry, but the financial costs must be paid in full. The annual fee for two academic terms amounts to—"

"Allow me to get straight to the point, Mr. Birchwood. Sir. It is not my wish to waste your time delaying any further. I'm here to inform you—yes, inform—that should you turn down what I have proposed, I will personally *ensure* that the current circumstance involving yourself and Chef Pierre, including the entire reputation of the W-interschool, will crumble into bits. And no, I am not to be persuaded. Do not even think about the clinching the champion title, sir, I am keen on nullifying this tournament and every instance of its future glory."

I was breathing hard, waiting for a response in the middle of a deafening silence whilst quelling the dangerous beat of my heart. The adrenaline pulsed in my temples and numbed the very tips of my fingers; rules and their breaking were not something I'd ever think of associating myself with and yet here I was, issuing verbal threats to the headmaster of a culinary school.

The door clicked open and he'd glanced over my shoulder in an instant. I turned to follow his gaze, registering a still and silent Violet Birchwood, allowing the door to close behind her. "What's going on?"

I turned away, unable to provide a concrete answer that wasn't charged with emotion. Headmaster Birchwood himself did not seem very keen on responding to his daughter with a forward statement of truth. Instead, he gestured to the leather couches adjacent to the shelves of culinary books published by various school alumni.

"Sit down, Mr. White," he said.

"No thank you. I am not in the mood for discussion. Sir."

"I merely wish to hear the rest of your proposal."

"It is simple," I stood my ground. "Mr. Cox is allowed to leave without penalty. Miss Layla Tenner will take over his spot in the tournament. And return to school."

"And the scholarship?" We were back to square one. "He hasn't completed his years. Making Mr. Cox an exception would be unfair to the rest of the scholarship holders."

I paused, unsure. "Well, if it's... the number of academic years he has to complete here in school as per the contract, I could... in some senses, be of use to the school without any additional cost. However you wish."

"What contract? Who are you talking about?" Violet had in the midst of our discussion made her way over to her father's desk, arms folded beside me with confusion on her face and bags under her eyes. Up close, I realized she was bare-faced.

"Violet, dear. This doesn't—"

"You're not making stupid decisions again, are you?" I was shocked to hear Violet say, challenging her father like he was her child. "That thing with Pierre, haven't you learnt your lesson? I told you, this isn't the time to be messing around. Vanilla. Tell me what's going on *now* or I'll kick you out of the room."

I'd nearly choked and coughed in her face before recovering in several blinks and proceeding to relay a concise version of my current proposal. I watched her eyes widen until she pulled me aside.

"You're *begging* for Cox to be expelled?"

"Excuse you," I could not resist the urge to correct her. "No begging was involved. And as far as I can tell, I'm the one with the upper hand. Leroy needs to leave the school, and without bearing the cost of his scholarship."

"What?" The word barely made it past her lips. Her frowning was almost contagious. "Am I hearing this right? Did you and Cox argue or something? What, am I missing something? Are you leaving too?"

"No. I'm staying."

It was hard to look her in the eye; fearing the streak of some vulnerable, tell-tale emotion in behind the glasses that had, as always, protected the windows to the inside.

"Then you're okay with... with being apart?" She said after some time and her father, some distance away, stood up to take a call in the corner of his office. I did not respond to her question. "I don't get it. Don't you want him to stay? He's doing great for the school, right?"

"Exactly my point," I managed. Tight-lipped. "Leroy has been excelling as a pawn. I don't quite see how he's happy in all this. Leaving may not be the only solution, but staying is most *definitely* not the answer, especially in an environment so rife with toxicity for someone like himself. Violet—you don't understand," I heard the words crack like ice under pressure. "He doesn't even *like* cooking."

She could not register this. The school's top culinary student, a prodigy, a born natural with access to the best resources and personal training from the tender age of two—simply did not *allow* for dislike of the very thing he excelled at. I let her think, removing myself from her side to resume the prior discussion but again, she held me back.

"You're going to regret this."

In bated breath, I expressed something most dangerously close to a lie. "I've never regretted a single decision made entirely by my independent mind."

"It's going to be your first, then," she snapped, tightening her grip on my arm. "I'm not telling you this because I don't want Cox to leave, or that I'm defending my dad or my ruined reputation because all that doesn't exist anymore, so it's not like I have any reason to be stopping you from whatever plan it is you have.

"So what makes you think he's *not* happy?" She went on, glancing over her shoulder to check on her father speaking into the receiver. "And you really think getting him out of school, scot-free is going to solve everything?"

"Of course not." We were arguing for the first time, rather irrationally at that. After all, our interactions had always been Violet's expression of discontent and my passive assessment and acceptance of her words as part of her personality. "Do you really think I'm that naïve of a person to think so simply about anything at all? The root cause of Leroy's problems *is* cooking. And me. Mostly me. I apparently bring out the worst in him. The very reason he does anything culinary-related is me and I'd rather he have nothing to do with the industry than suffer a life of expectations and pressure and hatred towards the very thing he excels at just to please a single person—"

"But it's the only thing that brings you two together, isn't it?" Violet was wielding her words like a blade. I felt the mental recoil. "It's the only thing he can hold on to. Don't give me that look, I'm just calling you out on your lies and don't bother denying that because Xu tells me stuff, so I know enough to know... some... stuff... but, yeah." She was hesitant all of a sudden. "You hate lying to other people, so why lie to yourself?"

I watched the words crumble into dust before my eyes and sus-

pend in the morning light filtering through the open window behind the headmaster's desk. "I'm not."

"Stop den—"

"I'm not the solution to his problems." *How strange it was to hear
the sound of frozen lake that was breaking apart.* "Sometimes, Violet, no
amount of love and care and affection is enough to resolve an underlying issue and sometimes, even remaining by their side could
complicate matters so no matter how much I wish I *was* the solution
to his problems and how it hurts to admit that I am far from it, I
am going to do so. I am going to accept that, perhaps for now, he
may have a chance at happiness even if it means that we have to... be
apart. From each other."

She was looking at me as though I was mad. The room was silent
and Headmaster Birchwood was waiting at his desk, tapping his pen
against the side of a black leather folder. Violet showed me to the
door, mumbling something about persuading her father on my behalf. My immediate instinct was to decline her offer, but she'd given
me a look that felt oddly... determined.

The phone in my pocket buzzed. It was Leroy.

* * *

When Leroy told me the exact words sent to him by the headmaster's office in a termination of contract email, the candles in his
eyes were lit.

The vigor was heated and very much alive; glowing in the darkness of a hole I'd never really noticed was present in the first place.
We were together in Cayenne, in his room, and I was seated on the
edge of his bed, watching him toss the clothing in his wardrobe into

a large, over-sized suitcase that came up to being less than half-filled even with his riding gear stuffed inside. I'd taken the liberty to, at the very least, roll up his five pairs of socks.

"He's not even angry," said the idiot, packing his cameras into a separate bag. It was Siegfried he was talking about. "They told him I wasn't part of the school anymore but didn't say a thing about compensating the twelve grand or whatever additional costs for my stay on campus. They're letting me go scot-free—it's fucking great."

"Indeed," was all I could manage, observing the spark that was bright and reflective in his eyes, on his lips. "And no more cooking."

"Yeah, I mean," he laughed, glancing at the culinary texts he had stacked in a corner, already messed up from the month earlier I had dropped by and tidied his place. "That's the whole point... having someone else tell him to give up on me becoming a chef is like, a blow in his face, so. He didn't even sound upset on the phone. Like, he's given up or something. Which is good." He sounded relieved.

"But—your mother?"

At this, he faltered. "Therapy. But... I didn't tell him about the taste condition. He thinks we're moving to London for some private training. And Annie's going to be there, so... he's paying. I guess. It'll work out."

I was stunned by his seeming optimism, a trait I'd never before observed in his behavior, let alone speech and general disposition. "Well. I... most certainly hope so. And you seem rather eager, with all this unfolding."

He looked up from his suitcase that was half-empty. And straight into my eyes. "I mean I've been waiting for Siegfried to get off my back about... all this," he made a vague gesture towards the culinary books. "And... the book. Guess they're terminating the contract, so. It's probably not gonna make it to publishing but," he had the gall to wink, "means you have the only copy in the world."

"Leroy," I stopped him short, standing to level our gaze. "I'm not sure if I... well—quite frankly, you're being rather frightening with so much to say and... you seem awfully eager a-and *prepared* to leave that I don't know how I should be reacting to all this."

The flame in his flickered once. Unsure. "What do you mean?"

"I... all this talk about leaving and going somewhere else seems so oddly detailed and, well, I'd assumed you'd be a little more um, how do I put this—unwilling? Uncertain? Not that I regard you in such a manner, but, any other human being would have been at least slightly upset about being expelled no matter the circumstance. I suppose you must really dislike being a part of the school."

He paused to stare. Searching. "Not the school, just. Cooking. Most of the times, unless it's for you..." He leaned in. "You okay?"

The question prompted an odd, sizzling in the chest that tickled the surface of still waters, sending ripples throughout. I averted my gaze after noticing in his eyes, the reflection of an ocean storm. Almost at once, there was a thundering in the distance and the sound of waves, crashing in the midst of a dark, wretched tempest of a mind.

So was the nature of the truth I'd thought I would've been able to escape. Somewhere, swimming in waters deep, was the monster of a frozen lake that refused to admit the yearning for a cunning, selfish desire—the want, the expectation of loss and sadness.

Unconsciously, I had been preparing myself to comfort a lion, torn and distraught over having to choose between his happiness and myself, of preferring to remain by my side despite an equally strong desire to leave the culinary world behind and start anew, afresh. I had hoped, at the very least, that he would've held on a little longer.

Selfish. How selfish and absorbed and insecure and how terribly, awfully human.

"London?"

The candles in his eyes burned brighter at the only word I could manage. He returned to packing. "Yeah. You like it? All the museums you could ever want."

I held his arm. Something was wrong. "Museums? You mean, me? But Leroy, I don't..."

My gaze must have told him in an instant. He straightened up once more.

"You're coming, right?"

I let the words hang. Nothing came to mind. "No... no I'm not. I'm staying. I don't prefer this, for us to be apart, but I have my own reasons to stay and you... you have reasons to leave."

"So we're doing this," his index went back and forth between us, "long-distance? You're okay with that?"

I was in a terrible mood for calm reasoning. The storm approached. "Leroy, I must make this clear: my choosing to stay is a decision independent of our relationship—"

"Why?" He frowned. "Shouldn't it be the first thing you're considering?"

Goodness, Leroy! Of course it was, and do you think I'd actually arrive at this conclusion if I proceeded to allow myself to be blinded by my desire to have you around and tie you to the ground? "You're really not making this any easier."

"What?"

Oh god, that was not what I meant. "That was not... I did not mean to put it in that manner."

He was giving me his full attention now. Waiting.

"This is for the best. And yes, I don't mind us continuing this relationship five-thousand miles apart but at the same time," *as long as I'm around,* "you need to be pursuing your true passion and interests. Your happiness." *You're going to put me first.*

There was a knock on the door that broke the spell and called for an irate clicking of Leroy's tongue. He crossed the room and answered.

"Uh... someone's waiting for you on the por—"

"Tell him to wait longer." He slammed it shut before turning back to me. "Okay. My turn. Seems to me like you've thought this through. You're unfazed, or something. By the fact that I'm leaving. And that we're going to be spending who knows how fucking long apart."

"I'm sorry if I appear unfazed when I'm..." I breathed, "honestly *struggling* to keep it together, Leroy, because if neither one of us is capable of doing so, we'd both be on the same ship on fire in the middle of a raging storm."

He slowed down.

More noises were coming from the hallway just behind the door and they distracted, turning our attention away from the matter at hand. The moment of hesitance soon translated into urgency when his phone, placed over at the bedside table, began to ring.

"I think you should pick it up."

"Can't wait for five fucking minutes huh," he cursed under his breath, not quite bothering with a second glance at the caller ID. He picked up the phone. "I know. No, I'm not going anymore... Annie needs the therapy." Footsteps stopped right outside his room and yet again, knocking on the door. This time, I answered.

"You were *expelled*, Leroy. You don't get a say in staying here and unless you're okay with your mother going through therapy alone in a different country, you could live here on the streets."

Mr. Siegfried Cox did not look like the person on the cover of his culinary books at present. He had an air of jaded confidence and satisfactory exhaustion; like tiredness was a constant in his life that he'd somehow come to accept. He wasn't as tall as I'd imagined him to be, or as he seemed on television and photographs. Leroy's genes were a mystery, but a single glance at their faces was enough for a fool to be convinced of their shared blood. Just not the eyes.

"I'll figure something out," said his son, turning to me with a brief hardening of his gaze. "I'm not going anywhere. For now."

Siegfried shook his head. He appeared resigned. Worlds apart from how Leroy often described him as. "I billed the hospital in full, paid upfront for her physio and bought her the earliest flight after finding her a spot in the best center but you've done nothing but humiliate and disappoint me time and again.

"Do you think I like to hear about my son offending the culinary dean of a renowned school who happens to be the judge of a tournament he was participating in? You think I don't give a fuck about his scholarship contract being terminated and they want him out enough to waive the ten-over grand he was supposed to hand over before he leaves? Come on, Leroy. Realize that being given a second chance at a sister school in London is miracle and get off that high fucking horse. You're leaving."

He'd ignored my presence completely, gaze sweeping over the rest of the room and frowning at the leftovers that remained unpacked. "We don't have that much time. You have to thank your instructors before you leave, too, since you won't exactly be coming back any time soon."

"Ah."

It hit, then. The iceberg. Something was about to sink and all of a sudden, things started to seem a little too real. Far too close to the heart, where the sound of company felt the loudest.

Heads turned before I could realize the urgency of the sound that I'd let slip. Neither of us had moved from our respective corners of the room and watching Siegfried pick up bits and pieces of stray notebooks, stationery and scraps around the room seemed almost surreal.

"Thanks for dropping by to help with the packing," said his father, directing this to no one other than myself. I couldn't find the words to start a conversation or, at the bare minimum, even express what I was feeling. "He's fine on his own now."

"For, for how long, exactly?" I looked up. "You say not any time soon so I'm assuming he's going to be in London for at least a year but... but now that I think of it, if it's just one year—twelve months or so—I'd be willing to accommodate or, um, for the lack of a better term, put him up at my apartment that is really just a five-minute walk from his workplace a-and without rent, of course, and perhaps monthly visits to see his mother or, or... yes, how long, exactly? By 'not any time soon' you mean a maximum of twelve months, I hope? Sorry. I must sound completely absurd, I-I believe there was some form of miscalculation on my part."

Mr. Cox appeared mildly surprised by my outburst of panicked emotions, taken aback by a stranger's involvement in his son's personal life. He glanced at Leroy for an answer. Leroy was looking at me. I couldn't meet them. Those candles. All of a sudden, I realized just how silly, how indecisive and childish I was being, pulling out all stops in a moment of alarm.

There were traces of a smile on his lips. And a brief shaking of his head.

"Dumbass." He hall the gall to kick his suitcase aside, going straight for my head that was, in an instant, cradled in his hands. "Just say you don't want me to leave."

"Oh that is... that is *so* untrue and—oh you know I can't say that," I managed in a whisper, torn. "You... it's only going to make things harder for both of us. And no, those eyes don't work they way they used to, Leroy. I'm not coming with you and you know it. You know why I can't. You know what it means to put someone else before yourself. You know how hard it is to swim against the forceful currents of instinct for the better reason, a greater truth.

"And you know I wouldn't make any decision without purpose. You, of all people, should know best and I don't even have to promise," here it was, "how much I do not intend to waste my remaining years in this school without, at the very least, ensuring that no one else should ever have to experience what you or Layla did here. Because—because... well.

"Even if I were to be eventually regarded as the world's most mundane, plain, boring and uninteresting person to ever exist," I could hear the creaking, "nothing should stand in the way of a mind who just so happens to prefer truth as it is; cold and hard, or in the way of someone who prefers to race on a beach in imaginary karts, picking up mystery boxes and tossing turtle shells at passing opponents."

The sound of company.

Siegfried had left the room, bringing along with him half of Leroy's belongings and we could hear him out in the hallway, going down the stairs. Curious whispers followed in his wake. Leroy's smile was now at the very core of his flame, in his eyes that I could finally meet. They were still; like a candle in the dark.

"Sounds like a snowstorm," he leaned in.

I watched the flame dim as they drew closer; withholding its heat. Careful not to burn. "Maybe one day, you'll know what it means to like a flavor you can find anywhere else. Maybe you'll see what is complex is something that, at first glance, looks simple. And maybe you'll meet a truth... that isn't just cold and hard."

He brushed his lips against mine and the creak was, perhaps, the loudest it had ever been before, then, being, the last it was ever heard. Against the fall, amidst the crunch of crimson leaves and the rustling of trees in an autumn breeze, I felt my end of board sink at the absence of a balance; the pivot, tipping; the permanence of a lowest point.

XXI

@⧦⧦⧦

SENT

To: leroy.j.cox@gmail.com
From: v.j.white@chronicle.edu.com
Subject: Valentine's Day

Dear Leroy,

I recall the two of us coming to a consensus about the unnecessary nature of Valentine's Day some time ago while you were over at
my apartment for dinner on a random evening very much like today. As I write this email, the clock is ticking and with every passing second, edges dangerously close to the fourteenth of February,
which the majority of human beings regard as a day to express one's
romantic or platonic affections. More so the former than the latter.

Si Yin and Ariq (a classmate of mine) have made plans for a Single's afternoon tea tomorrow, and my best friend had the audacity
to refuse me an invitation. Something along the lines of 'people like
you make us feel lonelier than we already are.' It was quite the shock
of my life.

Apart from being excluded from tea parties, I suppose nothing much has occurred over the past couple of weeks. I understand that we haven't been keeping up with the daily video calls, which, given our busy schedules, have been rather idealistic in the first place.

I am writing this email because it has come to my attention that our everyday texts have seemed to lose their authenticity and initial spark over the past month or so. Indeed, we have been confiding in one another about our new experiences—myself, currently in the second semester and somehow given a spot in the top twenty academics, and you in your brand-new restaurant, production-kitchen life. I find it odd how the fireworks of new information can settle and how, after hearing the loudness of a boom, silence can become further quiet in the darkness of the night.

I sent you something. A week ago, perhaps. It should arrive very soon, if not by today. Inside includes a letter. Actually, this *is* the letter. I'd kept a digital copy because, well, why not. And sending it to you here may or may not eternalize it, seeing that I am unsure if you'd somehow misplace my writing and, knowing you, would have liked to have a second read. Not because you like reading, but because you probably would not understand it the first time.

That was a joke, if you could not tell.

Either way, Leroy. I know what we said about Valentine's Day. I know I said, as I'd once believed, that there should be no special occasion for the true expression of love for what is true should, therefore, be practiced in every present moment. I now understand the importance of special occasions; the strange spark of anticipation in waiting, looking forward to something quite out of the ordinary and perhaps finding it a celebratory event that one can somehow experience alongside the rest of the independent world.

Sometimes, things like that are nice.

As such, I would like to wish you a very happy valentine's day.

Yours,
Vanilla

P.S. I do hope you never check your email because now that I've written this, it is terribly embarrassing but I've also already sent out the parcel and good god, how I regret decisions.

* * *

Hey it's a postcard.

You know I don't do leisure. But Annie made me wheel her around some museum with whale bones hanging overhead. It took us four hours to finish two wings. They have six or something. It's really boring. I spent most of the time thinking how you'd react to everything. Basically, I spent four hours fantasizing.

The photo on the front, it's a left-spiral conch. For you, I made the effort to read the first three words of every description label thing. This one caught my eye. You're a nerd, so you probably know why. Left ones are rare. They say if I blow into this, the one you're yearning for the most will answer your call.

You coming yet?

Leroy

* * *

Dear Leroy,

I'm never quite sure if you're suited for writing postcards, if, at all, but I found myself enjoying the one you wrote me. Thank you. I didn't mention it over text or our call last night even though I discovered it in the mailbox after dinner because it seemed oddly sacred. Like this was a private conversation to be continued elsewhere, undisturbed by the convenience of technology and our daily, everyday conversations. They feel special. And, I daresay, oddly romantic.

I have, in turn, decided to write you a card. There is no specific occasion that should warrant the writing of this handcrafted masterpiece, if I do say so myself. Miki was the one who'd suggested *cardstock*, which is the medium weight paper I am using to write this card. The shade of it, I'd picked, and had the specific craftsman ship it over in a perfect padded envelope. The wax seal is my weakness. I've always wanted to send a card or letter with something of such nature.

Finals are in two weeks. I myself am in a decent position to rising up the ranks with yet another flawless report card. Have you heard? Chef Lindy might be officially replacing Headmaster Birchwood as headmistress. Violet has been particularly distraught. I am doing well. Everyone misses you. Layla Tenner is valedictorian, naturally. The graduation ceremony is in a month. Prom is two weeks after that.

Everyone misses you.

Yours,
Vanilla

Missed Call
Sry I was in the kitchen
U ok?

No worries, it slipped my mind for a second
It's your break now isn't it?

Yeah
U wanna call?
Kinda noisy here but

Oh no it's fine
Did you see the image I sent?
The parcels—they've all been returned
That's why you haven't been receiving them
Good god

Wait what
What about the address?

I'll tell you tonight, perhaps
At what time should we call?

I get off at 6.30 my time so

In about four hours then?
But you have an appointment with Doctor Susanne every
Thursday evening.

Shifted it to tomorrow. Siegfried can't make it.
How's everyone?

Is it finally getting a little warmer, by the way?
Yes we're all good
I just have something else to talk to you about

Er
Okay
Is it bad?

Not exactly
Just a little shocking.
Possibly disappointing too
So is it finally getting a little warmer?
Alright I'll see you tonight

Fuck you
Cliffhangers

Leroy!

Kidding
Anyway
Yeah, it's hot as fuck
Can't wait for a snowstorm

Snowstorms don't just *happen* in London, Leroy

They will if u come
;)

* * *

I am so very sorry

The past three days have been terribly busy and I know that isn't much of an excuse, but I am well aware of how understanding you are of my priorities and the importance I place on both my studies and interpersonal relationships with the people who I might be working with in the near future. Opportunities, mainly. You understand what I mean. I have something to tell you that has been eating at my concentration for the past couple of days: it appears that a transfer student has been having an unnaturally intensified interest in myself. She has been following Si Yin and I around and deliberately swapping gardening or production kitchen duties with the rest of our classmates to match my own schedule. It is extremely strange. Quite recently (yesterday evening), she dropped by Cinnamon lodge and personally knocked on my door with bottles of beer and asked if the two of us could spend some time together!

I have been wanting to speak to you about this but, for the abovementioned reasons, I haven't quite been able to. The recent escalations have somehow warranted some form of action, so. She has also openly invited me to stay over at room in Hudson. Yes, I forgot to mention that. Well... I hope you read this soon. Oh I can envision you laughing already.

What are you up to today?

Waiting for you
Let's call?

To: v.j.white@chronicle.edu.com
From: leroy.j.cox@gmail.com
Subject: [Blank]

I attached a pdf of the restaurant's new menu. Tell me what you think. I know you'll find problems with it anyway. You asked if I could accurately make out the ingredients for at least half the menu. I mean, I tried. Susanne keeps me on tabs for this new thing I'm taking. I'm fine. She says it needs a month or so to really work. Siegfried wasn't too happy about that. Probably why he upped the complexity of the menu in the first place.

Not like I was gonna do him any better.

Didn't know how to tell you over the last call we had (a week ago?) but I think Annie's got a girlfriend. Dk why I can't just tell you this over text but we haven't been sharing much lately. Just everyday things. Anyway, the girlfriend. She's the therapist I've been telling you about. She hasn't said a thing but sometimes you just... know? I guess. They've always been close. Like, going out for lunch close. Sometimes, she doesn't even check in on me in the day because there's someone keeping her occupied. Which is good. They had dinners recently. I usually do take-outs and have them in my apartment, so it doesn't make a difference. She's happy. I'm cool with it. That's all.

My birthday's coming up. You finally surprising me with a snowstorm?

* * *

Dear Leroy,

Happy Birthday. I took extra care to arrange for the parcel to arrive on this exact day, and also, that it is sent to the correct address. I hope you are fond of it. Needless to say, it is, as per my every gift, an extremely practical one. It may or may not add to your delight that the sheets are tried and tested—meaning, I have a set of my own and have found them extremely comfortable. Sleep is essential and having the most soothing bedsheet, accompanied by a matching pillowcase and quilt cover can turn any bed into a nest of comfort, I assure you. Well, at the very least, we are in some way connected while being apart. I hope you find them to your liking.

Oh, the other thing. A thermos! Perfect for rainy days and a time when tea comes in handy, especially when you're living in the part of the world that's known for tea. I hope you're keeping warm and healthy.

Yours,
Vanilla

* * *

Hey

I know you're mad, so I wrote a letter.

I'm sorry you had to find out about it that way. You know everything now; I have nothing else to hide. Everything I said over the call, I swear. It's all I have. You know how I am with things like these. I can't bring myself to tell you things I know you will worry about. And I'm okay with it. With being alone most of the time and dealing with things that way. It's not just me—you too. You said it yourself;

that it's not about needing each other. Which makes sense 'cuz the time we spent apart has played a huge part in realizing how important it is that even without you, I have to be whole. Like, I can't be un-whole without you. That just means I have issues with myself. Or that I'm dependent on you. Which I realize isn't actually a good thing to be.

I suck at essays 'cuz they never really know what my point is. Point is, I don't know my point. I just wanted to let you know that I'm starting to become okay with this. With the disappearing taste. With not cooking. With people giving up on me in the industry 'cuz it only means that I can walk on my own. Find my way. *My* way.

I know it's something we'll never get over with. That I hide things.

It's just really hard to change.

Leroy

You still love me though.
Right?

To: leroy.j.cox@gmail.com
From: v.j.white@chronicle.edu.com
Subject: Application
Attachment: exam.pdf

Dear Leroy,

Thank you for the talk this morning. It has been long since our last, despite the heightened need for one in light of our current standing with each other. Attached is the application for the examination you wish to be taking, and the prior steps and requirements that you need to be meeting before the first screening. I've also included a brief instructional manual on where and how you may obtain a first aid certificate.

That aside, I can bravely, and most certainly say that I am both extremely proud and delighted to hear of your new pursuit. You have known for the past year or so, just how little I associate your worth with anything related to the culinary world. That you have decided upon a path of your own and are in the midst of following through is a whole-hearted relief. I wish you the best of luck; only because everything else, you seem to already possess.

You have always been fairly mature in your thought process, despite embodying the audacity of a fool and being the epitome of a shameless criminal. It is one of the reasons why I respect you and think of you as an equal. Not that, well, I don't think of others in the same way. You know what I mean. Bear in mind, this would not be one of the reasons why I love you. That should never be explained.

Now that you are on your way to rooting yourself in fresh, novel soil, I am at ease. You are going to love it, Leroy. You are going to love the you that has always wanted to be you.

Vanilla

P.S. Finals are coming up and I'm partly glad we're on a break because I cannot afford to drop anywhere below my current CGPA. Chef Marseille says that I am to be seventh place by my third year of study. The campaigning for club elections is next week. You know I'd like to be changing things in the Chronicle. This is miles out of my comfort zone but I feel so, so liberated. How strange it is to be fond of power and control.

* * *

Hey, I sent you my new address, right? They have a post office nearby and they sell some weird-ass cards, so I thought, why not send you one. Raul's graduating, right? I don't have anything for him. But I guess you can relay a message? All the best. Something along those lines. The exam was ez. Kidding, I worked my ass off.

Haven't spoken to Siegfried in a while. Thought it would be funny to send you a postcard with a random dude in the front that looks better than him on TV. Annie's been asking about you. Told her you're fine. That you're gonna kick-ass for SOY. I mean, it's your last year.

Leroy

Happy Birthday, dumbass

Right on time!
I am thoroughly surprised.

I factor in the time difference every year
What are u talking abt

Haha
I know
Thank you
How are you up so early?

Don't worry I'm going straight back to bed ;)
Enjoy your day
Sleep soon
Stop studying
Nerd

You are a fool, Leroy Cox
I shouldn't have gotten you those sheets
How worn are the shoes by now?

[Photo]
Lol

In less than two months!

They're great
Wear them everyday
Your gift should be at your doorstep by 6pm or something

Oh!
Oh I wasn't quite
Expecting something from you

What the
It's your birthday
Dumbass

Well
I would have been happy with a mere call

K I'm
Calling you every 10 minutes for the rest of the day

Please don't
You are a disaster

Oh god Leroy

No

No stop

STOP CALLING ME

Merry Christmas, Leroy.

This card was hand-painted by my god aunt, Giselle. You met her over dinner at my place two years ago. Do you remember how upset you were, that evening? I don't think I've ever had to face the severity of such humanly emotions, whether they belong to somebody other than myself. That one could be so afraid of loving someone else more than the latter loves them; it was a question, a dilemma, a fear that I had never thought of entertaining.

It is with the wisdom and power of hindsight that I am able to reflect upon the cold, brittle surface that I was so fond of glazing over, like the surface of a frozen lake.

There is some truth in the novels that write about foolish love. I cannot deny the unexplainable phenomena that allows or perhaps even, to a certain extent, *guarantees* the loss of reason and the giving of way to the beat of the heart. But what I am about to do is offer an alternative explanation—an account, a description, an observation—to the subjects of love.

I do not speak of infatuation or obsession. I have, over the years and much academic research later, come to fathom or conceive the presence of a greater form of love. This Love; it is not foolish. Neither does it steal from our limited sources of reason and rationality. Nor would it command its subjects to make terrifying, unsound decisions arising from invalid conclusions.

Once advanced, this Love is more than wisdom and intelligence combined. It is a worldly view of what it means to be human. That at some point, in which certain, but not all beings or entities, may experience a higher knowledge with Love's aid and that they will drive themselves (not be driven) to greater heights.

Having felt what I felt for you then, I now see how foolish I was. It is in present time, and with distance and a calm, gentle wave, that I see how the surface of a frozen lake would reflect nothing but the perceiver. That is should be foolish to expect anyone looking into it to see *past* it, let alone *understand* it. I did not think you understood me, back then. I do not think you may understand me now. And I most certainly do not think you will understand me in the future—but perhaps that is precisely the crux of the matter.

I was not letting myself be understood.

For that, I am terribly sorry. Sorry that you have had to be facing something akin to your reflection and nothing beyond the cold, harsh surface, in search for someone behind it. I am sorry. I don't apologize enough, unlike you. I am sorry for that too.

The card is a tribute to my god aunt's most famous painting back in her days as an abstract painter. Before she regained her vision. I was lucky enough to witness it once in my lifetime. The real painting.

I must say, those self-righteous interpreters who attributed the blackness of it all to the *blind* characteristic of love should really re-assess their thought processes. It is not so much the lack of color that makes the painting so blind and lacking of vision or clarity but the very purity of it that adds to the painting a focus that paradoxically extends to the edges of the canvas in an all-encompassing whole. It engulfs, overpowers, but most importantly roots the viewer into nothing and everything at the same time.

You're probably confused.

I think all I am trying to say is: thank you. For having loved me. Or if you still do; for loving me. Thank you.

Vanilla

XXII

⚭

DRAFT

Dear Leroy,

There is something odd about the nature of unsent letters, e-mails, texts, and parcels that seem to possess the incredible, inherent ability of being so beautifully broken. I've always thought nothing of the ethical systems beyond utilitarianism, often regarded as the pinnacle of decision-making in every corporate, private world that our minds can hold. It never once crossed my mind how consequences or anything other than physical manifestations of properly produced results could matter as much; how terribly wrong have I been.

Just yesterday, I realized that the parcels I have been sending to the address you'd provided me have been returned to the doorstep of my previously rented apartment—which I no longer occupy, now that I am a second-year student and have a room of my own in Cinnamon lodge—according to the nice landlady. I'm not sure if you'd ever met her before you left.

The feeling, the emotion I felt after realizing you'd never received the things I thought you had was something beyond my capability of describing, let alone terming it, exactly. It was a strange, odd feeling of... of... the closest word I can think of at the moment is an *almost*, which, itself, doesn't quite make any sense.

Regardless of it being grammatically erroneous, using *almost* as a noun, as though it was a phenomena meant to be recorded down in diaries and planned every step of the way, well. To me, it sounded quite ridiculous. That was this afternoon.

Now, as I am writing this letter I most definitely will not be sending (I don't quite know why I am writing it, either. Now you see what I mean by beginning to understand the mattering of the non-physical returns or results, of practicality, per se), I am finding it increasingly sensible and perhaps even *logical* to be conceiving the idea of an *almost* as a proper, legitimate phenomena.

I am constantly thinking of the things we did not get to do, or have, in some way or another, planned for some near future we were, prior to our separation, fairly sure of. Things like the beach, or that New Year's picnic, or our first trip to a museum. Things like that. Things we never really got to do, together. Things we almost did.

The timeliness of the letters and parcels I sent prior to this are, well... they are now irrelevant. I texted you this afternoon about the parcels, that you mentioned, had not arrived, asking yet again for an address and you told me that your father had had you move to another apartment near West End. Admittedly, I was slightly ticked off by this. Quite frankly, *fuming* by the end of our conversation that lasted less than fifteen minutes.

That it lasted for that amount of time was, obviously, not your fault. And that you had to move, yet again, a month into your recent apartment, is not your fault either. In fact, I hadn't a single clue how or why the most unsettling disappointment about the situation we were experiencing and an utter inability to do anything about it!

Either way, you never did receive that handy leather-bound organizer I'd gotten for you as a gift of practicality (since you did mention having a rather packed schedule) and it was only three days ago that you told me someone else had apparently gotten you one, your neighbor, yes? And so the gift turned out perfectly irrelevant. I mean, it would have arrived two weeks earlier but, well, it missed you narrowly and was hence returned. For the lack of a better word, the gift was, for all intents and purposes, an *almost*.

Vanilla
2/9/2021

* * *

I'm not busy I just look like I am because I don't know how else I should be looking like when you're busier and have less time to be thinking about me when I am thinking about you every fucking second of the day, so I look busy so that I don't feel like a loser who's only missing you too much.

You probably don't know this, but there are different ways to be occupied; like I am, when I'm thinking about you. So what I mean when I say that I am, occupied, is that I'm not really sautéing vegetables when I'm sautéing vegetables—I am thinking of you; I'm not plating that filet mignon when I'm plating that filet mignon—I am thinking of you.

I'm doing things, but that doesn't distract me from you. The you that's in my head. Permanently. You never leave. And that makes me *not* busy when it comes to you, because without even having to think, I *know* that I'm thinking about you, that I spend all my time. On you. It drives me crazy.

Yeah, but I can't say that, can I?

Makes me sound like a loser.

I don't think you think about me as much as I think about you.

2/9/2021

To: leroy.j.cox@gmail.com
From: v.j.white@chronicle.edu.com
Subject: [Draft] Longing and Endearment

I miss you incredibly and

Draft saved 1/11/2021 00:13 AM

* * *

I quit the restaurant. One month ago. And I haven't had the gets to tell you, so I've been making things up over FaceTime... don't know if you can tell. You probably can. Even if you can't call me out, you probably know something's up anyway. I keep telling myself to come clean 'cuz I know you hate it when I hide. I keep saying I don't mean it. I don't know if I really mean it when I say I don't. Anyway, I'm sorry.

I'm sorry I still lie.

Nothing's really working out like how I thought it would? I'm saying this like I thought it would work out in the first place, because I did, but only with you around. I'm starting to get what you meant by not needing someone but wanting them to be there. That's nice and all and it's what I'm working on (have to work on) but at this stage, I'm nowhere near. I still need you and I don't know who I am. I know you're trying to help me find my way. I know you want me to stand on my own. I'm still trying. It's hard to keep the mask up in front of you so that you'd think I'm doing okay. Thank fucks our calls are getting shorter. I have nothing good to tell you.

Except Annie. She's doing decent post-recovery, like I said, but I don't think you got what I actually meant over the call. Her therapist's gay. I think. As in, she likes girls. Interested in. Whatever. Don't think Annie knows much but I didn't want to tell you because it feels weird, talking about budding romances when ours just feels like it's... I don't know. Lukewarm.

I said I was thinking about the sister school offer, right? That's a lie. Siegfried met the board and they want me in for the new semester. It's in two months. I'm not enrolling. I just want you to think I am. That I have something under my belt. Like I'm busy. But I'm not. And it sucks.

I don't even see doctors anymore. I think he's given up on sending me anywhere after a couple of months. The meds don't seem to be working 'cuz all ice cream still tastes like nothing. I'm either washing dishes. Or waitering. Two days ago, they wanted some help julienning carrots. I cut myself by accident. It still hurts.

You're a real fool if you actually think I like the weather here by the way.

3/1/2022

* * *

From: v.j.white@chronicle.edu.com
Subject: [Draft] Butterflies are not Fireworks

Dear Leroy,

Si Yin was confessed to, earlier today. I'd heard this from Violet, who'd overheard a male classmate of ours speaking to Si Yin by the fountain over lunchbreak. The latter, naturally, hadn't any plans on telling anyone about this albeit her extremely generous conversational nature and though we'd spent an afternoon in kitchen nine testing out recipes for the Health and Nutrition Menu Design course project, still, not a word about this curious incident! I don't quite know if I am making any sense, or my curiosity is, for the matter.

Violet was particularly shocked into confusion, and seemed mildly disturbed, on her part. Naturally, I hadn't the emotional or intellectual capacity to be asking what she truly thought of this entire situation since, now, all three of us have moved up into the A-Division class, and she has been relatively well-acquainted with both parties (and by this I mean Si Yin and the male classmate who confessed). Nothing in my realm of knowledge appeared sufficiently sensitive to address the matter in tactful words, and so I opted out entirely.

Nevertheless, her opinions had been oddly concentrated on the stiffly-worded confession (which I refrain judgement upon for the sake of respect) which she seemed particularly bent on repeating. Something about the student having a 'crush' on Si Yin. That she was his 'crush'. That he would very much like her to give him a chance.

There is much rephrasing, thanks to my efficient memory that prioritizes the memorization of... important matters (not that this wasn't, um, well, just of perhaps less significance) and Violet's subpar descriptive capabilities. The repeated, undeniable use of the word 'crush', however, had seized my attention for quite some time after the conversation, even after some prolonged thought into the night. Which is why I am writing this an hour past bedtime, with perhaps the worst eyebags I'd ever had the misfortune of acquiring in my fourth and final year of study.

It is for some apparent reason much more imaginable, conceivable, logically fathomable to be hearing the word from a younger, perhaps adolescent being in their teen years than it is from a thirty-something-year-old, or anyone beyond the seemingly unjaded years of paradise which may or may not come in one's twenties, depending on the circumstance.

I have a crush on someone is a statement that sounds objectively youthful, reminiscent of younger, much more innocent days without the seriousness and significance of a complex relationship that is at the risk of tying one down. The internet describes the feeling as something akin to having butterflies in one's stomach (which, by itself, sounds awfully terrifying) and the nervous, exciting disposition of a racing heart.

It is oddly interesting, how one's susceptibility to butterflies experience a reduction with age. But who is to say that the elderly, the old or the aged, the married, the lonely, the lost—who is to say that they will never be greeted by the same, significant, silly fluttering of the heart? And who is to say that the young and foolish are bound to set themselves free, basking in the presence of the fragile little creatures, beautiful and bright?

It should not be that a youth who has not experienced the butterflies or an older being who possesses as youthhood absent of such must necessarily be looked down upon as a heavy-hearted person of misfortune, never having had the beautiful thrill, rush, captivity that the butterflies can be. Perhaps what they felt was different.

Perhaps the butterflies are as they are in nature; fragile and fleeting. Short-lived and easily swept away. Perhaps they remind us of a small, flighty heart. The sentiments of a crush.

I would like to make the argument that true love does not feel like butterflies in the stomach. Well, if they were, then I'd perhaps like you to know that I've never once felt them. The butterflies. Never quite did. Additionally, I would most certainly be sure to avoid such a medical condition, had I known its existence, or find some sort of medicine or cure for the fleeting flutters. After all, butterflies should not like the acidity of a stomach environment, and neither should my stomach be fond of tenants such as butterflies.

It hits harder. Love does.

Much harder than the soft, papery wings of a butterfly tickling the insides of one's digestive system. At times, they feel thunderous. Earth-shaking. Ground-breaking. The tremors, deep in the core of the chest. A very loud, loud waterfall. Fireworks.

That's what they are—fireworks. But then again, I would be able to falsify such a claim by stating that, in times of patience and understanding, as Love can be, it is awfully silent in wait. And the word here, 'wait', perhaps embodies much more of the unexplainable phenomena than we make it out to be. Waiting is, I am inclined to believe, an essential, critical, vital part of Love. It is sometimes a beautiful anticipation. A struggle that combines loss and yearning with need and want; coming to terms with the void is as important as the thrill that is the flower in the sky. The loud, thunderous boom.

The wait is what is between watching that red spark rise, higher, and up into the night sky before disappearing and *then*, watching it bloom before finally feeling the hit, the strike, the tremors in the core of the heart. That is Love. It is sublime. It is the moment. It is soft and it is sometimes a creak, so silent, like the sound of company.

It is the moment before the boom.

*

EPILOGUE

The trembling of a branch, low and shaken by the wind, blossomed delicate pink flowers that were soft and feathery—infusing every passing breeze with notes of fresh sweetness; the scent of melting ice and the coming of spring that cloaked the land in a shade so shy, he could smell the vanilla.

They brushed the tips of his hair, pink petals did, as he passed under a tree in a hurry, making for the auditorium in the great strides he'd gotten used to walking in. Alone. Which he often did, nowadays. Time was a particularly confusing notion for the young man; an odd construct, almost, that seemed to change based on the magnitude of the events that happened in every frame of the ticking clock that the entire human race appeared to share but could strangely never agree upon. Some often said that it went too fast. Others wanted it to go faster.

The senior had cue cards in his hands that were a tad spent by the time he'd rehearsed his speech eleven times in front of the mirror, fixing his tie every second or two precisely because he knew that was the only thing they could see over his graduation gown. Culinary dean Chef Marseille had made it a point to have the entire cohort in the dressing room two hours before the opening ceremony and yet here he was, barely thirty minutes to showtime, brisk-walking past the barn, the race track, the stands, the commons, the plaza, down Roth Hall and past the ranking boards and into the newly-restored right wing.

Guests were only just beginning to filter into the cocktail reception, mingling among themselves whilst occasionally interacting with the student servers who were making their rounds with hors d'oeuvres on circular trays. This crowd, he made a detour just to avoid. Amongst them were several familiar faces he could not afford to greet at present, knowing the ease at which he could be affected by the words of everyone else. For all intents and purposes, the school's star critic and valedictorian of the graduating cohort had never truly overcome the jittery nerves he had at the mere thought of public speaking.

Slipping past the reception and making his way down the hallway out into the garden and *then* into the adjacent building that housed the waiting room full of graduates in the middle of getting appropriately dressed and lined up, he found himself greeted by a flurry of urgent questions. This was mostly routine.

"I know you make a point to be punctual but being right on the dot can be nerve-wracking." "Mr. White, you have twenty minutes to have lunch, change into your academic robes and assist in the operations. Headmistress Lindy will be taking the stage in twenty before we start on the scrolls. Oh and the press has been looking for you." "Here's your gown." "Your complementary lunchbox. Jasmine rice with a side of *pandan* chicken, fried lotus root slices and sauteed spinach." "You join the class roster in the order of class representative to index numbers. Meaning you're first, even if your name starts with a 'W', followed by your substitute. We'll be positioning the rows by the side of the stage so when your name is called, all you have to do is—"

"Walk up the steps, shake hands, receive the scroll, take a picture, bow and walk off. Yes I read the briefing slides." The chill of a frozen lake, reflective and distant in nature, shivered the spine. He accepted the academic dress held out to him and ran a finger along the silver-blue tassel, then reached for the packed lunch placed on the edge of the table they were using to organize names and attendance. "I'll be stepping out for a short meal first. Has anyone seen Gelb? Scott Gelb. He's covering the event from start to end and I'd like to check in on his news angle. Just yesterday, he was having trouble thinking of a title to run with."

His honorary general secretary pointed him in one direction. A member of the administrative staff gestured in another. Chef Marseille could not be bothered with either. "Do not juggle three things at once, Julian. The press is waiting for you in the main lobby of the left wing, past the gardens. I don't know who this Gelb is but someone by the name of Keith Tang—yes, I know—came by. He should be outside on the benches. Some alumni were gathered there with the leftover lunches and he might have joined them. Be back by the half-hour mark, is that clear?"

"Well, I could make it a whole minute before that." His smile was professionally charming. Almost uncharacteristic of the very person he was only two years ago, swimming in the sea of new and novel. "I don't see how it is a problem."

He took his leave after a polite bow of his head, heading out the door and further down the hallway for the benches that lined the floor-to-ceiling windows. Meeting the gaze of several other students clad in their academic gowns, he was, by habit, able to pick out those on deliberate procrastination—wandering outside the waiting room to mingle around despite having had their lunches. A single glance their way was enough to convey a chilling message. Those of the graduating batch made the split-second, clever decision not to linger. The general movement had caused a decent stir amongst the others gathered outside the waiting room; and it was upon the turning of heads that the graduating batch's valedictorian recognized key figures who played significant, if not critical, roles throughout his academic journey.

"Nillie?" The girl three years his senior came towards him with open arms and at an alarming speed. This, he'd had to brace himself for. "Baby, please don't tell me you chose the pair of glasses you're wearing. Oh but whoever did your hair has good taste... maybe En should try that someday."

"It's not gonna suit people like me, Layla," Chen was much taller—shoulders, perhaps even broader—than he last remembered him to be. "And there's nothing wrong with his glasses."

They exchanged a round of greetings before jumping straight to the matter at hand: his much-anticipated valedictorian speech. After all, it was the main reason they'd returned in the first place. Layla Tenner was not the kind of person who had the luxury of time to attend graduation ceremonies every year when she had, upon *her* graduation, been offered a sous chef position at a world-renowned, Japanese-French rooftop dining experience in New York. Chen on the other hand, had been reluctant to settle on a specific plan in mind, which therefore somehow necessitated the many internships he'd completed before finally deciding, instead, to be furthering his patisserie studies back in Shanghai.

"Well, I must... admittedly, I wasn't expecting either of you to be here, let alone the *both* of you. At the same time, I mean. The—so you... there were flights, yes? Well of course there were, no one could possibly walk their way from... from halfway across the planet."

Chen laughed. "You don't seem thrilled. Guess I'm booking the first flight back." At once, the bespectacled bean was scrambling.

"No, no. Of course not. I mean, I *am* thrilled. It has been so long and I... I've heard how well all of you have been doing and... so I assume you're expecting a speech of great standard and I don't quite know what to feel about that, you see." He glanced down at the boxed lunch in his hands and noticed the ticking time. "That's all."

"We aren't here to put pressure on you, Nillie," Layla patted the space next to her and he obliged, snapping the lunchbox open and appreciating whoever designed the menu for it before tasting each component. "The reason why anyone would fly oceans across to see you is because you're *special*. And you so rightfully deserve the achievements you'd worked so hard for in school and today is... is the day we celebrate that! So yes, we're here to um, send you off."

"That sounds both moving and um, not quite as reassuring, that is, about the term 'sending me off' um as though—"

"It kinda *is* a warzone," Chen had, in his years after graduation, developed an odd inclination towards likening his daily life to chaos and bloodshed. "But I'm not gonna be the one planting ideas in your head. You probably hear from Cox how bad it is, anyway."

Vanilla had paused at the name. His gaze slowed to a stop, resting upon a stray grain of cauliflower rice stuck to the back of his spoon. The *pandan* chicken beside it was incredibly fragrant, splendidly seasoned, perfectly cooked. His gaze returned.

"I, um. Yes... I've heard stories. Not necessarily from a specific source, per se. Just, in general. About the culinary world outside of school. I don't foresee things getting any easier but, admittedly, I have somewhat come to terms with that some three, four years ago when I made the decision to, well... pick up the critic's pen."

Layla was the first to notice the ripple in the pond that was otherwise still; she hesitated, nevertheless, on re-directing the conversation elsewhere. She'd always felt strangely responsible for the two beloved juniors who were, in fact, the ones who'd made her graduation possible in the first place.

"And we're wishing you all the best in everything that you do," she turned to Chen for a follow-up. He didn't quite catch on, and had, in fact, blinked in surprise at their dismissal of a certain name

when the three were fortunately interrupted by fellow graduates—all dressed in their gowns with hats twirling around their fingers.

"You're here! Chef Marseille was like, looking all over for..." Si
Yin was having a hard time gathering her thoughts. She attempted
to do so in a well-practiced manner. Having had an orderly conversation partner who tended to organize his speaking points in
a naturally structured manner for the past four years most *certainly* helped. "Wait, your gown's inside and... okay you're having
lunch, so... lunch first and then change into your gown A-SAP and
is that Tenner? And and *Chen?*" She stopped twirling her hat, grabbing it, instead, by the tassel. Beside her, Violet Birchwood very casually removed the item from her grasp.

"So on the last day of school, you finally decide to reveal that
you're human and capable of being late?" Ranked second, the pastry
chef who'd, months before graduation, already secured herself an internship at a patisserie known for its world tours and grand events,
had been vying for the spot of valedictorian as early as the first
semester of her final year. She was also the one who picked out
Vanilla's eyeglasses for the day.

The pair of school alumni exchanged yet another round of greetings in the presence of the girls while valedictorian-deer finished
his packed lunch in silence, mentally reciting the key points of his
speech. Once, he missed a beat and restarted on instinct.

"Did you guys, like, seriously spend hours on a plane just to hear
the nerdiest speech of your lives?" Violet scoffed, producing a pair
of panna cotta shots from the wide sleeves of her academic dress.
Offering one to Vanilla without quite looking him in the eye. She
finished her portion in one go but winced at the glass. He needn't
taste it himself to know it wasn't the best panna cotta around.
"You're *so* going to regret it."

"Yeah but don't you hover outside Nillie's room sometimes hoping to catch him practicing the speech or something so that you—mffmhhgug." Si Yin was very familiar with the holy hand of Violet Birchwood. Saved, however, by yet another timely announcement of the commencement of the headmistress' opening speech, the graduating trio were, at once, scrambling.

"We'll be listening!" Layla called after the bespectacled bean, who turned over his shoulder with a smile that seemed almost blindingly confident. She felt, strangely enough, the urge to send him back in time for one last memory; something reminiscent of the nervous charm and shy intelligence he once possessed. At present, the adjectives seemed no longer applicable.

Hastily donning his graduation gown whilst answering the rapid-fire questions of Scott Gelb from the Chronicle, he made his way to the row of 'W's and 'V's and 'X's. He could observe the top of Si Yin's head several students down, bobbing up every now and then for an occasional tip-toe. Right beside him was another classmate of his—who was, perhaps, the only other male companion of his who hadn't the urge to exit a casual conversation between them and Vanilla—Ariq.

"Remember the kids who got expelled in our first year?" The latter angled his head slightly towards him, but discreetly enough so that the junior writer furiously scribbling pointers behind them couldn't make out the exact words of the exchange. "I saw them at the fountain. Mingling."

"You mean Lee and... hm," the model student stopped a passing student in their tracks to fix their hat. "I've forgotten their names. The ones who had me locked in a freezer?"

"Yeah them." Ariq did not bat an eyelash. "They were doing selfies and shit as if they were the ones... never mind."

Their eyes came upon a group of students standing idly in the row before them, tapping away at their mobile devices before one of them raised hers at an unusually high angle and all of a sudden, all five had the brightest, merriest smiles on their faces. This went on for quite some time, necessitating an innovative burst of consecutive poses that each lasted for about a second or so. The pair simply observed; silently wondering if the girls taking the pictures were aware of their dumbfounded, awkward expressions present in the very corner of the photographs.

"Julian." Chef Marseille called from several feet by the registration table. "A word."

He could hear the muffled echoes of Headmistress Lindy giving her speech in the auditorium as he neared the front of the room, where the one door leading to a waiting area connected to backstage had been left ajar.

"Is this about having technical issues with those out front?" He laid out the first of simulated realities on a list of things he'd mentally drawn up in a matter of seconds. Marseille scoffed at once.

"You always think something's wrong. There is nothing. Nothing is wrong. Do you think so poorly of your culinary dean that she would not wish her model student the best of luck in his future endeavors?"

A blink. Two blinks.

"But of course there is something wrong with that, Chef Marseille," said Vanilla, quite unintentionally sarcastic. "Except that you don't believe in luck."

A wry smile crossed her features. "Always so innocently bold and daring, under the guise of a harmless little fawn. Those glasses of yours throw people off all the time. Here is a little something for you. A parting gift," she handed him a vial that had its cap attached to a key ring.

His eyes lit up at once. "Could this be the amethyst bamboo salt you were... oh." The contents of the vial were white in color. "Not the most expensive salt in the world then. What is this?"

"Drugs, obviously," Marseille rolled her eyes before privately musing at the expression on her student's face. Indeed, the pair had developed quite a peculiar teacher-student companionship throughout his years of study. "The first ever critic-major to top the entire school, ranked above every other culinary, pastry chef, cannot find it in himself to identify *table salt*?"

His senses dulled at her words, tuning out but momentarily sizzling on a phrase that he could just barely hear through the gap between the doors in the voice of Chef Lindy. 'Create something new every day, even if it sucks.'

Those in their graduation gowns huddled in the waiting area cheered at the closest form of cursing they'd ever had the privilege of hearing onstage, loud enough for those seated in the auditorium—parents, alumni, distinguished guests—to acknowledge and laugh.

"A vial of table salt," clarified the valedictorian, nodding for extra measure. "I see now. How extremely appreciated and valued I must be in your eyes to receive this, um, holy gift."

"Everyone needs a little table salt now and then. Even more so as an established critic! I'm sure you'll be tasting some terrible dishes in the years to come," she humored with a wink, adjusting the angle of his hat. They shared some quiet appreciation for the light-hearted talk that had, for all intents and purposes, achieved its intended effect of shedding the nerves. "Now, as for the speech—"

"You want me to do it right after the headmistress' speech, before the certificates, because the organizing team hasn't quite yet had the fake papers rolled up and ribboned," he read and predicted, all from a single glance at the state of chaos that the student union volunteers in the background were in. That had been him, too. Last year. "A vial of salt is an unfortunate trade, Chef Marseille. I demand something minimally decent. Like a conversation about the chemical make-up of amethyst bamboo salt over a nice quiet dinner in your restaurant. The new one. In London."

Marseille was shaking her head, eyes wide in disbelief but smiling all the same. "You've grown to be the most awfully confident scientific mathematician-thing I've ever known to attend culinary school. Of all things. And of course you are welcome to the restaurant, Julian. I'm sure you'll give the staff quite a beating with your ratings."

"I always do," admitted the model student, producing his cards and giving them one final scan. He knew he'd probably end up having to use them onstage anyway. Public-speaking had never been the slightest bit agreeable with his general character. "Shall I stand in position?"

"Lindy has three more minutes, so you're just in time." She pointed to the door at the very back of the room. "Exit through that door and make your way down the hallway so you arrive at the entrance to the auditorium. You'll walk down the aisle and up onto the stage as soon as she gives you the cue. Yes, she will be introducing you as valedictorian."

Then he was off—making his way down the corridor that had, over the years, grown familiar to a lone back that had, many others, following along behind but never again, someone by his side. A member of the student union received him at the double doors and had him stand several feet away so that there was just enough space for a pair of first-year students to, well... open the doors for him and allow a grand, magnificent entrance. The bespectacled bean, as we all know him, was unfortunately not prepared.

"—changing attitudes towards the industry and what it means to have culinary skill. That while cooking with the mind is vital to making good dishes, cooking with the heart is essential to becoming a good chef."

"Oh good god that is so terribly misleading. Please do not introduce me in the next—"

"This, he has done as the representative of the Chronicle and our student body. In the span of three short years, he has cultivated a new culture *for a school that now understands the value of healthy competition or what he calls 'professionalism with a heart', and most importantly, the importance of truth. In the kitchen. In our food."*

"Please welcome—"

His phone. It buzzed. He produced it from under his academic dress and, after glancing at the preview on his lock screen, could not fight the urge to smile.

* * *

His uncle was in tears. That was the only thing he noticed despite the rapid flashes of light and cameras in his face, courtesy of the public media that had, since years ago, took interest in the student who single-handedly wrote the article that turned all eyes onto every culinary school in the world for checks on power and abuse. The aisle was packed on both sides with members of every local press but past the rolling cameras, tripods and microphones were Aunt Julie and Uncle Al in the crowd, clapping and crying as the hall rose for his welcome.

He neared them as he was walking up the side of the stage and his uncle, though thin-lipped and stiff-faced, had sucked in a single breath for a well-presented façade of professional cool. 'Good job,' he'd mouthed.

The headmistress received her favorite student at the podium and, after shaking his hand with an odd, wobbly thing that was her bottom lip, she let him take over. At once, the valedictorian was reaching for his notes with trembling fingers that could thankfully go unseen at a forgiving distance. The very back of the hall was, to him, *ant-sized*. He'd never seen the auditorium this packed.

"Well um," his voice sounded absolutely alien on the mic. The strangeness of it all rendered him momentarily blank. "Before I start, I'd just... I'd like to commend whoever prepared the *pandan* chicken chunks in the lunchboxes." Thank goodness for laughter. "And say that it was a touch of genius to include yuzu pepper in the marinade. But um, on the other hand, whoever made the pana cotta shots... well. Practice makes perfect. Perhaps coconut cream and some lemon zest instead of the usual heavy cream." If it was speaking about food chemistry then, well, he wasn't quite out of his comfort zone at all. This made him relax a little. "Richness doesn't necessitate that flavor be compromised. Yes, so. And so with that out of the way...

"Congratulations." He turned, somewhat, to those watching from backstage. "To all of you here. With the hats on your heads. You have... come thus far. Not that it is a competition. Graduation is simply a means to an end that we must have." He glanced down. The notes helped. "Nothing is to be won; not the GPA on your report card, not the number of culinary competitions you have medaled—as you can see, I have a grand total of zero under my belt, so—and certainly not the number of elite connections you have made in school. And as per this specific line of reasoning, it would therefore mean that nothing is to be lost either. There is no winning. And no losing.

"What is lost is if you have not made the most of your time here. If you made little of your mistakes. If you have learned nothing but ruthless competition or that the happiness of one must necessarily mean the compromise of another because that is not true. What is true of food is that it is, inevitably—shared. From the very conception of a dish to... to the sourcing of its ingredients, to the kitchen, the pan, the plate, the fork and into the very guest whose identity should never, never matter because all guests—kings, queens, beggars alike—all. Guests. *Matter*."

He paused; having run far off his pointers and skipped ahead in the rush of adrenaline. Moments later, he found the card he was looking for.

"It is unfortunate that people think of me, all of a sudden, so highly throughout these years though I have, as you all know, started off as nothing. Quite a plain jane, in fact. Simple. Boring. Quite... unnoticeable. *Barely*, noticeable. Really. And there is much reason in that.

"There were, and are, other people who were as, if not, more talented, more impressive and more achieving than I could ever hope to be. These lot of people, I learned, did not only belong to or excel in the academics of our school but in other fields of knowledge I had previously never even imagined to properly exist.

"Things like working as a team. Or... knowing when to reserving a seat for someone over lunch at a table. *How* to reserve that seat, for the matter. And and and *conversations*. Friendships. Getting into arguments. Yes and getting out of them, of course. But... well... mostly... into. Them. Because I was very apparently frightening at conversations. Ah, that... should not have been written in past tense," he stared down at the grammatically erroneous bullet point on his speech card. There was laughter. "Thankfully, I am much more versed in humor than I was before. Having friends might have helped.

"I am sure that most of us graduating... well, most of us actually do not have a single clue as to what we will be doing next week. Let alone next year. *Two* years. *Five*. Well, the number doesn't really matter. All we know is that there is a semblance of something out there, lying in wait to be discovered and experienced or, perhaps, as Chef—Headmistress Lindy had put earlier, 'created'. Surely, there must be some form of pressure we all understand to be expectations. Expectations to have a goal, a dream in which one can so willingly strive towards, which is why most of you probably think that it is quite impossible to be standing where I am now primarily because I may seem to have a concrete plan of my future, all mapped out for the next twenty years of my life.

"That is nonsense, by the way. I am no creator. I don't run around thinking of fresh ideas all day for menu design or... ways to, well, criticize someone's culinary passion or venture. I don't have a future set in stone. I don't have something like that at all except, well, maybe just for the next week and what I would like to have for dinner tonight. Those, I tend to think of. Unconsciously. Right, I am derailing.

"My point is that I want you to know... my apologies, headmistress, I mean no offense... that even if the thoughts in your head aren't novel and new and fresh—even if there are days you cannot help but *not* create—that there is nothing wrong with being plain or simple or boring.

"Because while it is easy to impress with the new, the novel, the fresh, the modern—it is compelling one to fall in love with a flavor they can find everywhere else that you just *know* you are good," *said someone by the name of Leroy Cox. Under a red tree... in the autumn breeze... on a seesaw... to someone else.*

Someone
by the name of—

ABOUT L. J. COX

Leroy Jeremy Cox was born on the 13th of August, 2004, and, to the horror of Annabelle Cox and delight of her husband, could wield a kitchen knife by the age of two without parental guidance. His childhood years were mostly spent in his father's, Siegfried Cox's, New York apartment learning new recipes every day and refining his knife skills. As a result of Siegfried's skewed approach to homeschool, Leroy could spell and pronounce words like 'sous vide' and 'coq au vin' by the time he was six but could not, for the love of anything, recognize 'favorite' or 'character'.

Fortunately, with the help of his mother and the internet, he was able to develop an interest in things other than food or cooking. Besides an occasional round of video games on a second-hand console that kept him away from knives for at least an hour, Leroy had always found himself drawn to the art of photography. While taking pictures of fancy dishes and desserts were part of his culinary education, wildlife photography topped his list of interests—apart from shef memes and good music.

On long rides home, Leroy enjoys plugging in to a standard playlist of Imagine Dragons, M83 and Billie Eilish, but also makes it a point to start his day with an imperative 'bad guy', just for an extra sprinkle of bad, ever since his childhood friend expressed a fondness for well-written villains. At times however, he finds himself drawn to the occasional 'La Vie En Rose', only because it reminds him of the past and his memory of falling leaves.